SKY CLAD RYDUL

BY
KAREN L. MILSTEIN

Copyright © 2016 by Karen L. Milstein

Published by Geminorum Publishing

West Palm Beach, Florida

ISBN 13: 978-0-9863295-3-1

ISBN10: 0-9863295-3-3

Cover design and art by Magdalena Almero Nocea

"Crufa" created by Magdalena Almero Nocea

For anyone who has looked to the stars and wondered…..

Many thanks to Eric Kyle, Bruce Boragine, and The Society for Creative Anachronism, Shire of Sea March, and especially Tim Opfer, swordsman extraordinaire, for the invaluable help with sword fighting techniques.

To my fans, who inspire me to continue writing.

As always, many thanks to Magdalena Almero Nocea for her creative talents. Ask her and ye shall receive, in spades!

And of course, to my family for their constant faith and help being my sounding board and calling out for dinner when I'm deep in my muse.

Into the night he sings.

As darkness falls, he calls.

Waiting for her reply

Through thick and forested halls.

His heart beats wild in his chest.

He hopes his love is true.

'Till she answers he'll take no rest.

He needs hear from his love anew.

"Where, where, where are you?" he calls.

"Or bower's made ready, all soft and warm.

"Come to me, come to me, come to me, love,

"With me in our bower as we greet the dawn."

"Stay with me, stay with me

"Throughout all time.

"I offer my heart and take yours for mine."

Deep from the hills she answers his cry

As closer she draws, their union is nigh.

"Here I am, here I am, here," she responds,

"Beside you forever, safe in your arms."

-Song of the Awrhim

Sky Clad Rydul

Prologue

Radine strode through the corridors of the palace, his attention buried in a tablet of writing as he walked, automatically and intuitively stepping around people in the halls without looking up, yet never taking his eyes from his reading. Turning around a corner to the right, he glanced up for a heartbeat, checking his whereabouts, never slowing in his stride, then glancing back to his papers. He'd gladly taken on the task of seeking out Prince Jaima if it would get him out of the never ending Council meetings

Prince Jaima, formerly Lord Jaima, had taken to his new position like a fish to water. Of course, having spent the majority of his life in the palace trotting along beside Radine as the other learned statesmanship for the day when he would become king, gave the new prince a distinct advantage in absorbing his new responsibilities. And he handled them with great aplomb and diplomacy, as well liked as a prince as he had been a non-royal lord.

He still trained with the men, and still commanded the Guard and Army, but found new respect from them – as well as a distinct feeling of being allowed to win at their mock sword fights. Jaima, once he realized what was going on, roundly berated each man, put him on extended duty, and jumped back into the fray hell-bent on proving that even though he was now a prince, he was still expecting the best from his men all of the time no matter who the opponent.

Joanna, now a princess, had joined McKenna in her efforts to form a solid clearing house to gather information about other planets and peoples to pass onto Earth, to report on the conditions of women who had migrated and the advantages for the future for women who wanted to see if there were better chances for them somewhere other than Earth. She was happy on Taburon, working with McKenna and Pologa, lending a hand when needed, especially in the nearby town if a family found themselves in need of nursing assistance.

Jasim was growing like the proverbial weed, already walking well and talking, his best friends Rakenn and Alveda with whom he spent a number of hours under the watchful eyes of the royal nursemaids. But every night, when his papa came to fetch him, he gleefully raced to the sweating man to jump into his arms and join him in a bath for an hour or so of water games while they cleaned.

Joanna had been aghast when she discovered that Jaima had started riding with his son, sitting the child in front of him on the impossibly high *crufa*, frightened that the boy would fall to his death if Jaima ever lost his hold. The child, on the other hand, was giggling with delight, egging the animal on with his little body the way he'd seen his father do.

After suffering her berating, he instead put a wooden sword in the child's hands and was teaching him to sword fight, deciding that twenty-one months wasn't too young to start training the son of the greatest swordsman on the planet. In fact, he'd taken some ribbing from his men, wondering when he was going to start training the boy. Upon discovering this new activity Joanna nearly fainted, but finally simply tossed her hands into the air and went in search of some sanity from McKenna. Unfortunately, the queen couldn't offer any reassurance, having gone through the same thing with her own husband and son not that long ago. The two women commiserated together, plotting how they were going to teach their husbands a lesson.

With his abilities as a royal well established, Radine had been concerned that the prince had not signed off on the manifest for the ship that was leaving well before sunset to head to Earth, taking supplies and relief personnel to the embassy in the Capitol. Keeping track of the supplies and personnel had been one of Jaima's new duties, since many of the personnel were chosen from the Guard because of their loyalty, skills at command, and attention to security.

Having had no success in getting the prince to respond to requests for his attention, the captain of the ship had turned to Radine to get his intervention in the matter. Thus the king's journey through the halls of the family wings of the palace to the quarters of the prince in the middle of the day, tablet in hand.

Reaching his destination, nudging through the outer doors, he passed through the sitting area to stop in front of the entrance to the bedrooms. He lifted one hand and rapped on the door. Hearing a muffled voice he believed responding, he pushed the doors open, entering without looking up. "Jaima," he started to say.

A muffled squeal brought his head up sharply in time to see sheets and blankets float up across the bed and settle upon a figure, hiding it from view, blonde hair flying. His intended target, whose buttocks had been prominently raised over his bedded companion, swung around so quickly he nearly fell from the bed, grabbing a pillow as he twisted, plopping it over the exposed male genitals, now covered, an extremely reddened and very peevish look on the owner's face.

Radine spun on his heel to face the door. They were close, and since they'd grown up together from the time they were six and five, respectively, had seen each other naked numerous times, but this went beyond the pale. He hadn't wanted to see Jaima's naked backside any more than he'd wanted to find his mother in bed with the palace physician

9

in the middle of sharing nadryl– both of whom he saw nearly every day and fought hard to keep the memory at bay. He hoped he wasn't scarred for life. "Gods' rods, Jaima!" he exclaimed. "It's the middle of the day!"

"Gods' rods, Radine," the other replied with disgust. "If you remember, it's supposed to be my day off," he added. "Jasim will never get a brother or sister at this rate," he mumbled.

Glancing hesitantly over his shoulder, Radine saw the couple was as decent as they could get, considering the circumstances. He cleared his throat loudly, inclining his head. "Yes, well, I am sorry, Jo. I guess I forgot. If you could but give me a moment, I'll get out of here."

Jaima slid his glance to the side to check with his wife. Radine saw the blankets shift as she nodded. Lifting a finger, the naked man made a spinning motion for the king to turn his back again, adding an accompanying scowl. Suppressing a chuckle, the king spun around.

Rustling bedclothes told him that Jaima had slid from the bed, his feet thumping to the floor confirming it. He made a disgusted sound. Several curse words followed.

"Jaima!" Jo hissed, "Language."

"Where are my pants?" he asked of her, his voice lowered so he thought only she would hear. Radine choked back a laugh.

A feminine giggle was followed by a sigh of defeat that sounded more like another curse and then the sound of heavy footsteps as Jaima walked across the room. The wardrobe opened, a drawer was pulled, then slammed closed. Hushed curses came on the heels of Jaima dressing in a pair of training togs. "All right," he indicated, going closer to the king, stepping within his peripheral vision. The sooner he got this done with, the sooner he could get back to sharing nadryl with Jo, trying for their second child. Jasim was nearly two years old now, and it was time for a sibling. They were giving it their best effort. They were trying to give it their best effort.

At least it was fun trying.

If the king would leave them be for the afternoon.

"I wanted your approval for this schedule," Radine began, showing Jaima the papers he had been holding. He ignored the half-dressed state of his friend and brother, his bare feet stark against the dark tile flooring.

Jaima felt like busting his king in the jaw for this simple matter. "You came here for this?" he asked, his voice rising with surprise. He promised himself that he'd get even – someday - in a big way.

He gotten his revenge on the Queen for her interference in his attempts at finding time alone with Jo between sky clad and their wedding by making sure Prince Rakenn and Princess Avelda received treats and toys every day for a consecutive two weeks, disguising them as gifts from an anonymous loyal subject that she could not refuse, presenting them to the children not only in front of the queen but the court. The children had been delighted with their presents making it difficult for McKenna to scurry them – the toys - away so her children were not spoiled shamelessly. When she'd found out the truth, he'd bowed and grinned with unabashed delight while Radine laughed helplessly and Jo smirked behind her hand.

"The ship is leaving before the sunset, the stores are being packed even as we speak. The captain asked for the final approval several hours ago, but you weren't responding to his requests."

Jaima took the sheaf and studied it closely. "It seems fine to me. Rydul is going?" he questioned with surprise.

Radine nodded. "He asked for the assignment."

"He's my best man. I don't know that I want to let him go for six months."

"I think he's chomping at the bit to test himself outside of your direct influence. He'll be in charge of the security at the embassy. And he wants the chance to explore another world that he didn't get when you were injured. You know he was excited about going to Earth."

"Yes, there was that," Jaima agreed, remembering with little fondness of the days he'd spent, first unconscious in a hospital bed and then confined to a house as they hid out while he recovered and waited for the return of the ship to take them home. He'd been shot by a man dead set against the arrival of the aliens and that one of them had dared to marry an Earth woman. The fanatic's response to rectifying the 'problem,' as he saw it, was to kill the king on his first official visit to Earth. His bullets had been taken, in defense of his king, by Jaima.

Of course, the time spent on Earth had given him his wife and son, for he'd fallen head over heels for the pretty nurse who'd volunteered to care for him in and out of the hospital despite the danger to herself. She'd felt the same. Neither wanted to admit to their true feelings, blaming what they were experiencing on lust and a healthy dose of curiosity. They'd beat around the bush for several days, coming together then pulling apart. Neither had counted on the hatred of one man, his lust for revenge for a slight he'd never been given, who'd invaded the house with ill intent where they'd been staying. Jaima had saved the inhabitants from the evil man, killing him though he'd himself had been drugged and near collapse. It wasn't until after the danger had passed that circumstances brought them into the same room, the same bed, and the same thoughts, falling into each other's arms passionately and completely, spending the night together but getting very little sleep. Jasim had been the result, though Jaima hadn't known about it until the child had been three months old and still on Earth. He hadn't offered any commitment before he'd returned to Taburon, and she, not wanting to force the issue, not wanting a commitment for the wrong reason, hadn't asked for one.

Rydul was a loyal subject, second in charge of the King's Guards and a captain in the Royal Army. A few years younger than the present king, he'd come up through the ranks as many a man did, proving himself over and over instrumental in helping Radine keep his crown when he first came into it and was challenged for the right to rule. The loss of Radine's father had hit the young soldier as hard as it had the king, the elder adored by the young officer and taken under the old king's wing several times during his growing years. He'd been given an estate for his dedicated service though not a title. So he was just a soldier, a high ranking one, yes, but simply a soldier.

He loved his work, he loved his king, and he loved to expand his knowledge as much as possible, taking on challenges that other men found daunting and throwing himself wholeheartedly into the task. During that fateful voyage to Earth, he'd been in charge of the guards so the king and Jamia could concentrate on the meetings that would occur between the royals and the humans. He'd had command for a full half hour before word had come that Jaima had been shot and all soldiers were to return to the ship and remain on board. Then his only job had been to keep peace among the men who'd thought they were going to have some leave on a new world and were now unhappily confined to their ship.

In the year and six months since their return with Jaima and his new-found family, few words had been exchanged between the Taburons and humans while a very small, very well-guarded contingent established an embassy on Earth to improve relations. A location had been searched for, a building secured with defenses the Taburons could control and coordinate with the humans, and furniture had been made special for the large warriors since human furniture was a foot or so too short. They had hired a human as a driver and obtained a vehicle outfitted for their size and protection. It had all taken time, the search, the coordination, and the approvals from all parties. The embassy had been set up now for three months and the guards there were ready to return home as new soldiers were sent out to relieve them. Only the ambassador and his secretary would remain on a permanent basis, guarded by both Taburons and human soldiers provided directly by the President of the United States. Every six months they would rotate personnel until the Taburons could be assured that their people were safe from fanatics and xenophobes bent on chasing them off the planet. And while the personnel weren't officially confined to the embassy, excursions out into the city were not readily encouraged. The Taburons had learned that familiar faces made for more easily remembered targets and thus, the rotation policy.

"Well, I guess I can't deprive him of the chance to explore a little. He knows the dangers and how to conduct himself. He's a good man, intelligent."

"Then sign off on it, and I'll make sure the captain gets it in time." Jaima scrawled his signature across the bottom of the page and gave the papers back to Radine.

"Now, if you don't mind," Jaima hinted.

"I guess you won't be joining McKenna and me for dinner?" Jaima's response was to scowl at his king. "Guess not. Well, then, carry on. Enjoy your evening." He started to leave the room when an unusual dark shape above his head caught his eye, halting him in his tracks, and he glanced up. Jaima's pants hung from the chandelier overhead, swaying gently from a soft breeze coming in through the opened windows.

Radine snickered loudly, his shoulders shaking in repressed laughter, a masculine groan on his heels as his friend realized what had caught the king's attention. Figuring discretion was the better part of valor, and knowing he would certainly be using the discovery as ammunition in the future, Radine left the rooms, pulling the door closed quietly. Through the door he heard pounding footsteps and the lock on the doorknob turned with a resounding click. He grinned at the masculine growl that issued through the wood of the door, followed immediately by feminine giggling and a definite squeal. Muffled laughter echoed through the room and Radine pushed away from the door, suddenly uncomfortable in his trousers. He needed to visit with his own wife. And very soon.

Turning a corner onto the corridor that led back to the main part of the palace, Radine, looking for a private spot, went several feet before ducking through a narrow archway, pulling up short. He'd come face to face with a portrait of a woman that startled him at first, until he remembered the name of the person in the portrait. She had been the first queen of his line, Kadric, his grandmother ten times removed. He had had his family history drilled into him from the day he could understand words and it all came flooding back as he stared at her picture. Helping her husband, his grandfather Madine, secure his throne with a firm, decisive hand had earned her the nickname The Tigra Queen, comparing her to one of the planet's most ferocious predators. Time had softened her reputation to match the sweet features painted on the canvas, though there was still a hint of hardness in her eyes.

Radine grimaced faintly, shifting his hips, then shrugged. Kadric had also been something of a lusty woman, giving her husband nearly ten children, of whom three survived to adulthood. So he was certain she would understand as his hand slipped under the waistband of his trousers to adjust himself more comfortably. His people knew he loved his wife, and loved sharing nadryl with her, but it wouldn't do for him to encounter any of his lords or ladies in a pronounced engorged state, not at this time of day. Taking several deep breaths, he brought his rampant thoughts under control, as well as his like-minded swollen cock and nodded once with reverence to the portrait before turning to leave the niche.

"Rydul," he called, catching sight of the young officer in question as he continued back to the halls of the main palace. The officer was heading in the direction of the throne room,

17

six or seven steps ahead of his king. He stopped immediately and turned, bowing as Radine approached.

"Your Majesty," he greeted.

Radine held out the tablet. "Jaima signed off on your assignment to Earth and the manifest for the supplies. Would you be so kind as to make sure the captain gets this as soon as possible?"

The other took the papers. "Of course, Your Majesty."

"Looking forward to going?"

"Yes, Sire, I am. I didn't get much chance to see it the last time."

"Well, let's hope you do this time, and without the same results." He clapped a hand on the soldier's shoulder. "We will miss you here, especially the ladies. McKenna tells me that since I and Jaima have married, there have been quite a few of them to sets their sights on you."

Rydul had the grace to lower his head slightly to hide the blush that started to creep up his throat. "I could never compare with you or the prince, Sire," he admitted with embarrassment.

Radine grinned unabashedly. Jaima may have been the best swordsman on the planet, but there wasn't anything shoddy about Rydul's skill with a blade or laser weapon. Whenever he contested with the prince, he always gave the man, only a few years older, a decent run for his money. Radine himself often sweated whether or not he would best the officer, not having as much time to practice as he always wanted.

And the ladies, watching from the sidelines and balconies overlooking the practice yard, twittered and giggled and flirted as much with the younger warriors as they had with the two older men. With the king and prince spoken for, it was only natural that they turn their attention to the next in line who had the ear and favor of the king, even if he wasn't a lord. After all, he was still young enough to earn a title if he wanted one. Or had a wife to egg him on.

"Never doubt your own abilities, Rydul, nor your appeal. You wouldn't have gotten as far as you have without it." He thumped the other's shoulder several times. "Take care, Captain, and enjoy your time on Earth, but don't have too good of a time. I'll expect you to keep me up to date with full reports. This embassy is very important to the queen. I'd hate to disappoint her."

"You have my word, Sire. All will be well and I shall keep you informed." His head bowed as the king turned to leave. Holding the tablet close, he went in the other direction to deliver the manifest before finishing his own preparations for his journey, a new confidence in his step.

CHAPTER ONE

Captain Rydul stood in the doorway of the sitting room of the Taburon Embassy on Earth in Washington D. C. He leaned negligently against the frame, one ankle draped over the other, his arms crossed over his waist.

A smile played on the handsome man's mouth, his golden eyes sparkling in carefully controlled humor as he watched the five men on the other side of the room.

Having tossed all discipline out the window, the soldiers were watching the human crowd on the sidewalk outside the Embassy fencing. Their comments ran the gamut of serious to saucy; the former about the human males, the latter concerning the females. Gestures occasionally punctuated their comments – most of them sexual in nature and at times somewhat graphic.

"Oh, sweet thing, you can come home with this alien," Pursel said.

Asure pointed. "That one could put any *skala* to shame. Her breasts are a handful." He held his hands up as though weighing the mounds of flesh, shaking them up and down a few times.

"Look at the legs on that dark haired one," Atiran pointed out.

Another, Chissa, made as though he held a woman in his hands and thrust his hips forward several times in mimic of the sex act. "She can wrap her legs around my waist any day, there's enough there to hold onto as I thrust."

The rest chuckled, slapping the man on the back for his observation, whistling catcalls to accompany their own mimicry of intercourse.

Rydul decided he'd heard enough. Standing tall, he walked into the room, making his footsteps heavy to be deliberately heard. "All right, gentlemen," he murmured, "you've had your fun. Shouldn't you all be at your posts?"

As one, the men turned and stiffened, going to attention, their faces coloring in embarrassment at being caught. The first rule of duty in the Embassy was to respect the humans, no matter what, and if caught showing disrespect, the punishment could be severe, depending on the severity of the offense.

"Yes, Sir," they answered together.

"Then I suggest you get to them," he ordered. "And Kenlyn will be speaking with each of you at a later time," he added as the men rushed by him. "By the way, if any of you see him, please tell him I'd like to see him."

"Yes, Sir," they murmured as they hurriedly filed out.

Rydul let them pass, then sauntered to the window to peer out at the crowd that had caught their attention.

As usual, there were a few dozen or so people walking in a circle in front of the gate, each holding a sign that read, in essence, 'Aliens go home,' or 'We don't need any out-worlders,' and even worse than that. They'd set up shop as soon as the Embassy had been established and showed up nearly every day, rain, shine, heat or cold. A nuisance at best, as long as they maintained their distance and did not interfere with the business and safety of the Embassy, the Taburons did nothing to encourage, nor discourage them from their protests.

Usually it was a motley crew. A haphazard mix of loosely affiliated people and anyone who wished to join in as long as they were willing to carry a sign. On the days someone brought food or drink for the protesters, a couple of homeless people would attach themselves to the group in order to partake of the offerings. They'd march, eat, march a little more, and then scurry away. How they knew there was food to be had was beyond Rydul. He was merely amused that they appeared and seemed to annoy the dedicated protesters, who would have preferred to have participants who truly believed, but grudgingly accepted anyone if only to increase the numbers.

The news stations had covered the protests in the beginning, but when days went by with no confrontations between the humans and aliens, quickly drifted away to other stories for the ratings. The Taburons maintained a laid back attitude and stayed out of the news as much as possible. Let their efforts to establish good relations with the people of Earth be the news, not yelling matches and confrontations on the sidewalks.

He leaned on the window sill, his arm stretched out along the top of the lower window and stared out. Another winter day in the city, the temperatures moderately cold, the sky overcast, the threat of bad weather inclement. There'd been some snow the last weeks, not enough to shut the city down and discourage the people, but enough to make sure everyone realize that winter had set in and was going to stay for a while.

The men had been like children, gathering in the large courtyard in the center of the Embassy and scooping up handfuls of snow – *vernix* on Taburon - to throw at each other until they had nearly cleared the entire area. Jovial and dripping, they'd come in after, tracking wet footprints that the ambassador made them mop up before the cleaning service quit because of the mess. The next time, they dropped their wet garments and shoes in the mud room and traipsed, naked, to their quarters to shower and change. The ambassador shook his head in defeat and thanked the gods that none of them had to go through the Embassy proper to get to their rooms. Needless to say, the men were a boisterous bunch.

They trained with enthusiasm, they guarded the Embassy as if their lives depended upon it, and they easily became bored when confined to the grounds, unable to explore the city and planet they had drawn as an assignment. Unfortunately, when they did venture out, they were a huge attraction, followed like celebrities, phone cameras flashing, videos taping, heckled and applauded equally by the crowds. They had managed to go to the city known as New York for a weekend, as popular there as they were in Washington without the hostilities, since their plans had not been announced prior to the trip. The protesters hadn't had time to rally, make arrangements and follow.

That had been a pleasant trip, taking in the sights, going to a Broadway show, flirting with the women who seemed to fall all over themselves to catch the eyes of the huge warriors. They'd spent the entire trip back laughing and in good spirits.

But it had been three weeks since their last excursion out, and the men were getting restless. Rydul would have to up the training schedule, get them so tired from working out at keeping their skills sharp that they wouldn't have the energy to complain.

Though, were he honest with himself, he was feeling a little confined as well and anxious to get outside the fences of the Embassy. While the contingent's primary responsibility was to protect the Embassy and keep the peace, they also had to escort the ambassador during his occasional forays into the human world when he met with other dignitaries from around the world, a job that only included two or three of the men at a time.

Rydul had asked for the assignment to Earth. He loved to travel and explore, missing the chance nearly two years ago when King Radine had visited with his wife, son, and the now Prince Jaima. Jaima had been shot during an assassination attempt on the Taburons, the accompanying warriors had been confined to the ship and then all returned to Taburon when a message had come through that the king's mother had been injured. Except for the badly injured prince who could not yet travel and the once Earth resident queen who'd remained behind to oversee Jaima's care. Fortunately for the prince, he had survived, found a wife and gotten a son from the incident. And Rydul had lost his chance to show his commanding officer that he could control a contingent of soldiers on leave on a new planet in a strange city. Thus he had jumped at the chance to return for the six month assignment.

Rydul felt a rubbing at his ankles and glanced down. Ronnie, short for Veronica, the embassy cat, twined around his feet, making s-circles as she sought his attention. Bending he picked up the animal, faking a grunt in tease at her weight, placing her on the window sill, his hand absently scratching the back of her neck.

His mind drifted to when he'd first met the animal and a smile graced his lips as he remembered the nerves that had plagued him as the shuttle touched down in the courtyard of the building. Leaving his personal belongings in the hands of his men, he'd gone directly to the ambassador's office to report and introduce himself. He already knew the other's name – Lord Janel, loyal to the king to his core – but had had little chance to interact with the man over the years on their home planet, encountering him briefly during his occasional visits to the court.

Janel was sixty Taburon years of age, his hair more silver than golden. He was a pleasant man, always with a smile and affable attitude, especially when meeting people for the first time.

Once a soldier, he'd done his time in the military before taking over his place in the hierarchy of the Taburon rule, a lord in his own right, married and happy with his lot in life.

Unfortunately, no matter what he and his wife tried, they were never blessed with children, and when she died, he fell into a depression that no amount of cajoling could break.

Until the position of ambassador came up. Gladly, he gave up his title to a nephew to assume the role of go-between for the Taburons and humans, negotiating how the two peoples could benefit each other. It had been his job to get the Embassy set up, finding the right building and making it secure and comfortable for the soldiers and important visitors who would call it home for short periods of time. The king had approved.

He particularly liked this group of soldiers, especially the commanding officer, Rydul. Too serious when he'd arrived, the shenanigans of the group had softened the edges around the officer until he had become a most valued and liked companion. But he hadn't been that way when he'd first arrived.

Invited to share in a cup of tea, he'd relaxed and been comfortably ensconced in a plush chair, the conversation genial, a time to get reacquainted and discuss protocol, his innate sense of danger at an all-time low.

As he'd started to raise his cup to sip, a heavy furred – something – jumped onto his lap. Rydul's reaction had been instantaneous. And unfortunate.

The saucer from one hand went flying. The cup at first tipped, spilling hot liquid over his hand then shirt. The cup then followed the saucer over the warrior's shoulder to the floor, taking with it the remains of the tea. Both pieces of china crashed, smashed, and spilled on the carpet.

Rydul, frightened near out of his wits, started to rise. The creature, in order to keep from falling, unsheathed its claws in all four feet and dug in through his trousers to sink into the flesh of his thighs.

Intuiting that continued hanging on was futile, the creature sunk its nails even deeper to hold on until there was no choice. Bunching its legs, it launched itself upwards with a screeching yowl and a very verbal hiss, catching Rydul on the shoulder, then over to land behind the warrior with a thud, another yowl and hiss on the floor. Arching its back at him for a heartbeat, it issued a final nasty sound of discontent, its tail the size of a man's wrist and raced from the room.

"Gods' rods!" Rydul cried. "What in the name of all that is sacred was that?" He spun to face the ambassador.

Any semblance of fright or terror that had set his heart to racing fled to be replaced by a scowl at the older man. Janel was leaning back in his chair, a hand covering his mouth, trying desperately to cover his laughter. Unable to hold it in any longer, he chortled softly.

"I find little humor in what happened," Rydul chided, checking out his trousers and injured legs. Both sides were rend with small tears or holes. On one side, the tears were edged with blood that slowly oozed down the material. The other side was speckled with dots of blood which were slowly spreading like ripples on water. And his hand stung smartly while his pristine white shirt was spotted with brown stains.

The ambassador collected himself. "I am sorry, Captain. Your reaction was…to say the least…rather remarkable." He took a deep breath. "That was Veronica, or Ronnie, the embassy cat. There's another, Samuel, but he doesn't like to greet people in quite the same manner. He's more subtle."

"What is a cat?"

"They're kind of like our *afilen*, but much smaller."

Rydul deepened his scowl. "Thank the gods for small favors then. Had that been an *afilen*, I'd most likely be shredded by now."

"Yes, well they both showed up here about four months ago and have never ventured farther than the courtyard since. They seem to like us, and the men like them."

"I wish you had told me before she decided to make the acquaintance. This was my best uniform."

"We have a tailor who can replace the uniform for you. We went through quite a few articles of clothing the first months after the cats appeared and one can't exactly go to the local Walmart to replace them."

Rydul dropped heavily back into the chair and sighed notably. This was going to be an unusual six months. "Walmart?"

"A store where these people like to spend their money, like the market at Bedikai City."

Rydul nodded. The market at Bedikai City was a poor man's market, the quality of the goods questionable, as well as the business practices of the merchants. "How long before I may get a new uniform?"

"See Rasil. He can take the measurements and place the order. In the meanwhile, you shouldn't be needing anything more formal than your regular uniform for the next two weeks as you get settled and schedule your routines." He pointed at the bloodied legs. "You might want to have Sistan take a look at that, though. Make sure to clean it out well."

Rydul grimaced. "Wonderful. *Whernin*," he grumbled, scowling at the liquid the physician seemed so fond of for cleaning wounds. It stung like the Fires of Koloda. Janel chuckled again, having been at the receiving end of Sistan's medical care a few times himself. "Welcome to Earth," Rydul murmured as he stood, bowed to the ambassador and turned to leave the room.

He and both of the cats had made friends after that, the animals taking to the large warrior with a passion, traipsing behind him often, sleeping on his bed to the point where there were nights he had to lock them out of his quarters, then listen to their yowls of protest. His wounds had healed readily and Rydul made it a point to insure that their nails were always trimmed. He'd grown used to their presence and would miss them after his tour.

Which was soon coming to an end. After the human's New Year start, the ship from Taburon would be returning to resupply the Embassy and exchange the guards for a new squadron. His six month tour would be over and he would return to Taburon to pick up his duties there after a short leave to check on his estate. Left in the hands of his brother, his only surviving relative, Rydul hoped all had gone well during his absence.

Bringing his mind back from his wayward thoughts, he glanced back out over the crowd outside. It appeared there were more than normal he determined, counting at least thirty people on the sidewalk. Apparently there was a group of humans who favored the Taburons, marching several feet away from the others in the opposite direction, their signs welcoming the visitors from another world and inviting them to leave their self-imposed confinement and mingle. So far it seemed under control, only scowls and loud, offensive words exchanged between the two groups.

And it appeared the pleasant weather had brought out their one silent admirer, a young woman who appeared nearly every work day to sit on the bench under a tree across the street at mid-day and have her high sun meal. For the forty or so minutes that she stayed, she would quietly eat her meal and read a book while sending surreptitious glances towards the Embassy.

Ever since she'd first appeared, they kept an eye on her, not sure at first why she was there or what she was up to. But as time had passed, and it became clear that she wanted to wonder over the Taburons from a distance and was harmless, they were willing to let her indulge her harmless fantasy. Rydul assumed she'd realized she was being as closely watched as she was watching.

Rydul had become fascinated with her. She had the most wondrous golden coppery red hair that she sometimes let drift around her shoulders. It fell as long as her elbows and waved in soft curls. Her skin was lightly tanned, dark enough to give it a soft cream hue. He wasn't sure, but he thought her eyes were a rich green. She had a glorious figure, hidden now under a coat against the cold, but in the late summer, usually clothed in light dresses that molded around her body like a glove especially when the breeze blew. He'd had a few fantasies about her once or twice on his own during the night.

But she kept to herself, rarely talking to anyone, even if someone sat next to her on the bench. The Taburons had discussed whether or not they should have approached her, find out more about what she was up to, but decided against it with the protesters out there, not wanting to make her a target by their interaction. Their other option, to have a human do it for them, was discarded and the final decision was to simply let it be and let her live out whatever dreams she was living with her presence.

Besides, he reasoned, his tour was soon over and nothing could come of meeting the woman anyway. So he allowed himself to enjoy watching her and living out his own fantasies during the night.

"You wished to see me, Captain?" Kenlyn asked, appearing behind Rydul and stopping two feet away. Like all of the guards, this man was built on the muscular side, his shoulders thick, his arms heavy and his legs like tree trunks. But he was somewhat older than most, having been in the guard for nearly fifteen years now and much to Rydul's surprise, content to take a secondary role in his post. He could have been in command, but found he preferred having the freedom of receiving orders as opposed to having to go through the process of examining a situation, consider the possibilities, and give the orders. Not that he wasn't capable, but he merely preferred it that way.

Rydul turned partway, removing his arm from the sill. "The men have been doing a little unauthorized female watching."

"Again?" Kenlyn asked wearily. This wouldn't have been the first time.

Rydul nodded. "I think they might need a little more time spent training, as well as some building chores to remind them of their responsibilities and duties."

"Should I write a report as well?"

"No, not at this time. But if they're caught again before we leave, I would suggest not only a report, but some disciplinary action as well as soon as we return home." He grinned. "After they've had some leave," he hinted. Of all of the things the Embassy received – food, clothing, news of home – the one thing it lacked were females. Six months was a long time to go without sexual release, yet the men were expected to endure as best they could without companionship. Rydul suspected the *skalas* on Taburon would be seeing a lot of these men in a few weeks.

"Any ones in particular?"

"Let's just cover all of our arses and talk with all of them. This way there's no singling out any one."

"Yes, Sir, will do." Kenlyn started to turn to leave, but stayed his step. "She out there?"

Rydul faced the window again. "Yes."

"You should go out and meet her. We don't have much more time here, at least get to know her name."

"We don't have too much time left," Rydul repeated. "No sense in starting something at this point."

"You don't have to start anything, just be friendly. Take her a cup of tea or something."

Rydul glanced over his shoulder at his second in command. "I'll think about it."

"She's quite pretty, beautiful even."

An eyebrow rose. "She is," Rydul agreed, wondering where exactly Kenlyn was going with his statement.

"So, you should go out and meet her," he persisted. "Even a small amount of time is worth it when there's a beautiful woman involved."

"You have some sort of agenda in mind?"

Kenlyn clapped a hand on Rydul's shoulder. "You've been too long without a woman, my friend."

"Unfortunately, there are no *skalas* on Earth."

"They call them hookers here, and there are plenty of them. Though because of the conditions created on Earth after their war, they can be quite expensive."

Now Rydul faced the other with unabashed censure. "And you would know this how?"

Kenlyn flushed and held his hands up as though warding off an attack. "Not through any personal experience. You have my word on that. But we do have that thing they call the internet and there are plenty of videos on it."

"I have seen them," Rydul admitted. "They're entertaining, but not to my liking, not when I can have a real woman in my arms instead."

Kenlyn's head tipped towards the window. "And there she is. You only have to step outside and invite her in."

"It is too dangerous. Can you imagine what would happen to any human female who crossed our threshold in front of those protesters? The minute she exits, she becomes a target for their hate. I couldn't live with that, and would never place any female in that kind of danger." Rydul took a deep breath. "Less than one more Earth month, and we will be leaving this planet for home. I am not so desperate that I cannot wait until then."

"It is your loss, then," the other decided. "I hope you don't regret it in the long run. Who knows, you might have found the one in her."

"Who says I am looking?" Rydul replied with finality. "Go take care of the men."

"As you order, Sir," Kenlyn answered turning on his heel.

A disturbance from outside caught Rydul's attention and he stared outside. He watched as the tension rose among the humans, their voices becoming loud enough to carry through the thick bullet proof glass installed on all of the windows of the Embassy. Rydul felt his heart beat increase as the yelling became more intense, fists were being pumped in anger, the signs were lowering to be used to push at the people on each side as fighters and defenders took a stand. Only a minute or two passed before a real fight had broken out among the protesters, pro and con with even louder yelling and fists flying, signs swinging in wide arcs as they were used to bash at each other. As he watched, the woman he'd been fascinated with glanced up. "Come on," he whispered, fearful for her. "Get out of there."

Realizing her predicament and the fact that she was much too close to the action, fright crossed her delicate features as she hastily rewrapped her meal to stuff it back into the bag she carried. Standing she twisted to go back in the direction from which she always approached her bench, her back to the fight, never seeing the hand sized rock coming her way. With no warning, the missile flew through the air and smacked into her head behind her temple. She dropped instantly to the ground, unconscious, her possessions scattering.

"No!" Rydul shouted. Kenlyn, nearly at the door, stopped.

"Sir?"

"Six guards, now, laser weapons ready!" he ordered. "There's been an altercation and the woman has been injured." As he headed down the corridor to the entrance of the Embassy, Rydul grabbed his coat hanging from a garment tree and slipped his arms through. With a quick check to his own laser weapon, something he never removed while on duty, he reached for the handle to the door. Running footsteps told him that the troops were coming and he opened the door to step out.

Sky Clad Rydul

CHAPTER TWO

Kathryn Tehyr soaked in the sunshine from her seat on the bench under a tree across the street from the Taburon Embassy. A small park of sorts, the grassy area provided a little piece of greenery in an otherwise concreted and paved section of the city. The day was cool but not cold, warmer than normal for a December winter in Washington D. C., but she wasn't complaining. The snow from the last fall had melted away finally, making the streets safer to navigate for both drivers and pedestrians. Which she appreciated, since she was tired of wearing boots to work every day while carrying regular shoes to change into at her desk and having to dodge puddles of water that seemed to gather at every street crossing.

Turning her face to the sky, she breathed in deeply, closing her eyes, taking a moment to refresh and let go of the stress this particular day had given. She would enjoy her lunch in peace – or at best stress free – since the protesters outside of the Embassy were an ever present annoyance.

Kathryn spared them a brief glance. Out in full force today, it appeared they had been joined by another group, people on the side of the Taburons, welcoming them to Earth.

'About time,' Kathryn thought. "'Somebody needed to come out in favor of these people. They've done nothing wrong except to try to make friends across a galaxy.' She shook her head in disgust, reaching for the lunch box she'd carried with her.

Why she was so fascinated with the Taburons she couldn't begin to guess. Ever since their official arrival on Earth, she'd found the tall aliens alluring. The men were, without a doubt, some of the most handsome men she'd ever seen. Tall, broad of shoulder, muscular, they encompassed all of her images of what a Viking warrior might have looked like. Someone a woman could depend on to protect his woman.

They walked with confidence and command. Their faces were never haughty, but spoke of unchallengeable commitment. And from what she'd heard about the two who had come to Earth and found the love of their life, they were loyal to all ends, following one when she was misled and the other nearly giving his life to defend another. A girl could get used to that in a hurry.

Taburons had the most gorgeous eyes – golden in color - and there had been times when the camera focused on their faces that those eyes seemed to sparkle with fire, whether with joy or anger it made no difference. Fascinated by the effect, she often imagined what it would feel like to have those eyes turned her way, especially in adoration.

Kathryn had no one. She lived alone, able to afford her own apartment because of her accounting position with the government. But at thirty, she longed for someone to greet her at night, to curl next to while she slept, to have someone to just talk to when the walls began to close in and her place felt empty. She did have her cat, but the pet was getting on in years and she didn't know how much longer they would be together.

Don't be mistaken – she loved her cat dearly. Puss In Boots – Pib for short – had been a part of her life for two-thirds of her life, never leaving her side except for the short time Kathryn had done a volunteer stint during her college years. They'd been inseparable otherwise and Kathryn knew not having the soft warm fur of the cat next to her through the night would leave a huge hole. But it would have been nice to have another warm body against her as well, a human body, one that fit the entire length of her and held her in a loving embrace. She knew that even at her height of over five and half feet, one of these alien men could fulfill her dream of a living blanket. She sighed wistfully.

She was tired of living alone. Her parents, having raised their children, seeing the youngest finally graduating and gainfully employed, had kissed her goodbye, wished her well, told her to keep in touch and moved south to a warmer climate. She saw them twice a year, though this year, obligations to the job would keep her from visiting during the holidays. She was happy for them, they'd worked hard and diligently to make sure Kathryn could take care of herself, sacrificing much to put their only daughter through one of the best universities in the country.

The brother she'd toddled behind as a youngster then idolized as a young girl was gone, having served a year in the military towards the end of the war, then deserting right before peace was achieved and disappearing. There'd been no word of him for years now. Even the government had given up on finding him. Her parents' hearts had been broken, but time had softened the loss and brought with it acceptance that he was no longer a part of their lives and most likely would never be again.

She had friends, but no one she cared for deeply enough to take to another level in a more intimate relationship. She never wanted for things to do – she lived in Washington D. C. after all – and though it wasn't the glittering city it had once been before the war, it still held great appeal and lots of activities for young people the world over. Group outings were a part of her life, a gathering of people from work who explored, played and took in the culture as a friendly group.

The ratio of men to women was the hardest hurdle. There were just too many women in the world these days and she was determined to not become a statistic – one of the hundreds if not thousands of women who found themselves picked up by a man only to be too easily discarded.

She was attractive. At least that's what she always heard from both her male and female friends. Her long auburn tresses glowed with health and vitality. She had a fit figure, a nipped in waist, rounded hips that weren't too large, long legs and arms, and breasts that she'd seen men ogle when she wore more revealing clothing. She worked hard to keep in shape and was secretly pleased at the looks she garnered. It was her height that put most men off. Being able to stare a man directly in the eyes made them feel as though she was an equal to them so that she had no need for the sense of protection that a man who towered over his woman could provide.

How wrong they'd been. She wanted someone who could provide for her and protect her, though she had no qualms about keeping her job and the pay it brought home. Just because she could see a man on equal terms didn't mean she felt more powerful and would use it. Even a short man could have fulfilled her needs. It wasn't her fault she was tall. A person couldn't help their genetics.

Ever since the war, when the male population had been devastated by the conflict, things that should have been looking up for the women of the world had, for the most part, remained the same or even gotten worse. It was so easy for a man to take up with a woman, then if he tired of her just as easily replace her with another. Men who had survived the war or not fought still held the positions of authority they'd gained before, and kept now with even tighter reins. And while the war had been good for the planet, it had brought little to nothing rewarding for its women.

If only she could get over wondering if there was a man out there who would listen to her, really listen. While her male friends were pleasant enough, she always got the impression that whatever she had to say, whatever her ideas, they were only paid attention to long enough to judge whether or not she was worth the effort to bed. Her senior colleagues at work had no problem letting her know that her education was a waste, since her best use was to reproduce and replace the male population that had been devastated by the war. The men of her generation subtly agreed, though never to her face. She plodded along, doing her job with efficiency and dexterity, moving very slowly up the ladder only due to seniority, secretly hoping to someday have enough pull within the company to improve things for the other women with whom she worked.

So, she indulged her one fantasy by coming to the Taburon Embassy every workday, bringing her lunch and surreptitiously watching, hoping to get a glance of the handsome men who lived there. A few times her efforts had been rewarded, catching a glimpse of one of the men as they patrolled the grounds, but they had cut back on those patrols since the protesters had become more voracious. The few times the ambassador had left, the windows of the car they used were heavily tinted, not permitting any possibility of seeing inside. And she'd found out that if possible, they usually traveled, when needed, at night when the streets were clear and the rabble gone or lessened for the evening. But a girl could hope.

Her sandwich half gone, she was brought from her musing by the increase in volume of the voices on the sidewalk. The protesters were having some sort of altercation, and it was growing in both volume and risk. Both sides were coming to blows with fists and placards and Kathryn realized the danger in which she found herself if she were to remain on her bench, especially when she saw a rock sail through the air. She never would have believed either side would bring 'weapons' to their protests, they had always been extremely vocal but hazard free.

Gathering her lunch to rewrap, she stuffed the remains back into the lunch bag she carried, adding her small bottle of water. Her purse was next to her and she slipped her arm through the handles, pulled her coat closed tightly and rose.

Checking both ways before crossing the street, she hurried across the pavement and stepped onto the sidewalk in front of the Embassy.

She'd only gone four or five steps, her back to the crowd, when she felt the thump of something heavy hit her towards the back of her head. Pain exploded through her with the force of a baseball bat but lasted but a heartbeat as her vision darkened then faded to black. She didn't feel the sidewalk as she crumpled like a popped balloon to the ground, her purse and bag dropping beside her.

CHAPTER THREE

Rydul stopped for a second on the stairs outside the Embassy door, giving his men time to catch up. The protesters had yet to realize there was a downed woman near their altercation, their voices perhaps even louder now that they were in a full blown fight with each other. He did see someone, on which side he had no idea, pull out a phone and he was speaking into the device.

Kenlyn tapped him on the shoulder to let him know he was there. "Have two men guard the door, I want two more at the gates, and the other two will come with me," Rydul ordered. "Their laser weapons should be set to stun, not kill." He began to move forward.

"Yes, Sir," Kenlyn replied and began to pass on the orders.

The Embassy took up the entire city sized block, bought because it had a square shape with an interior courtyard large enough to handle the shuttle the Taburons used to transport from the ship to the surface. From the outside walls, it was bordered by a ten foot wide swath of grass, bushes, trees, and plants, which was encompassed by a ten foot wide paved roadway that allowed vehicles to enter from the front and drive to the rear of the building here there was a car park and second entrance into the Embassy. The windows had been reinforced with bullet proof glass and tinted so that while the people inside could see out, no one could see in. The entire grounds was encased in six foot high iron fencing, and had monitors that kept watch when the guards could not patrol in person.

Outside the fence was the sidewalk where the protesters would gather daily, and across a narrow street was the small grassy area where the woman would sit on a bench normally used as a waiting area for the local buses.

With his hand on his laser weapon, Rydul walked to the gate at the end of the drive and waited for the guard inside to release the lock that kept it closed. There were four warriors behind him, two of whom took up positions on either side of the gate as Rydul pulled one side open. By now, notice had been taken of the men leaving the Embassy and the fighting was beginning to wane as people stopped to watch the small contingent.

With one eye on the group of humans, Rydul turned towards the downed woman, two men at his heels, their hands also on their weapons, their eyes darting around, keeping wary watch. His gaze never leaving her, he made a beeline for her, the protesters finally noticing the woman as well.

The people for the Taburon contingent began to line up to protect the men as they moved forward, blocking the protestors from physically assaulting the warriors. It didn't stop the rhetoric tossed at them, the same old slogans and curses, the anti-Taburon group struggling to interfere with whatever nefarious purpose the aliens had in mind for the woman, no matter whether she was alive or dead.

Rydul fell to his knee next to her, praying she was alive. There was a small pool of blood under her head. His finger shook slightly as he reached out to place them at the pulse point at her throat and he sighed with relief to find her heart beating steadily. Her chest rose and fell with a breath.

With extreme care, he leaned closer to look at her injury. Her scalp had been cut clean, a swatch about the size of two fingers neatly sliced free from which blood flowed freely. Her beautiful hair was getting soaked. Chissa, to his left, passed a cloth to him which he began to wrap around her head over the wound.

"Leave her alone, you pig," he heard yelled. "You'll not take any of more of our women." Several voices rose in support and the crowd pushed harder against the human barrier to get at the Taburons. From behind the crowd, another rock was thrown, nearly missing the three men and unconscious woman, landing nearby on the sidewalk with a heavy thud. It splintered into shards that bounced in all directions, two of them flying up to graze Rydul's cheek with a stinging pain. A second missile flew overhead, followed by a third.

With one hand, he swiped at the smudge of blood that wetted his cheek where the shard struck, staring at the red moisture as he twisted and rose to his full height. The anger on his face was evident, his fury nearly palpable to those closest as he released his laser weapon from its belt and held it tightly, his fist opening and closing over the grip. Chissa grabbed his wrist. "You cannot," he hissed softly.

"I will not," he promised sotto voice, "not at one of them at least. But we can give a warning." Stepping forward he confronted the crowd. "You are the ones responsible for her injury. We will take care of her. Go home."

"Or what?" the leader of the protesters sneered. "You gonna shoot us with your little toy stick?"

Glancing around quickly, Rydul picked a nearby tree that was away from the people and considered for a heartbeat. Lifting the weapon, he took aim and fired at the side of the tree. It exploded into pieces of branch and leaves, shooting out beyond where the people stood, rising into the air and floating down to the ground. A full third of the tree was missing. "So much for little toy sticks," he said loud enough to be heard, reattaching the weapon. He was pleased to see some of those in their favor were smiling and nodding in the affirmative at his response. "You accuse us of nefarious purposes where your woman are concerned," he continued, his voice fraught with anger and passion. "But it was one of you who has done this to her. You have no devotion for your women, no honor for their well-being. But we do, and we will tend to her. Go home," he finished, "go home and treat your females as they should be, for they hold your future in their hands and hearts."

The crowd had gone silent, stunned by his actions and his words, and in that space of time, he gathered the woman into his arms and headed back towards the Embassy. Weapons at the ready, just in case, the others followed, their eyes on the crowd, retreating in the order they had followed when taking position until everyone was inside and the gates were closed and locked and the people back inside the safety of the building.

By now sirens could heard approaching from the distance and the crowd erupted in a cacophony of sound, screams and yells, demanding for the Taburons to return the woman outside. Rydul ignored them all, barking out orders as he entered the Embassy.

"Get Sistan, have him meet us in the infirmary. Someone let one, and only one, of those police officers inside when they arrive. Keep two guards on the doors and for the gods' sakes, keep your tempers." Standing by the elevator, he punched the button for the car to take him to the next floor where there was a small infirmary for the use of the Taburons.

She was as light as a feather in his arms, hardly worth a sweat as he waited for the elevator, looking down into her face. She had small dots across her nose, the color just deep enough that they were visible under the pallor of skin. Her lips were opened the slightest amount, her teeth white in the shadow of her mouth. Her hair flowed over his arm to hang nearly to his knees, it was so long and felt so soft when he'd gently pushed it aside to look at her wound. She was tall for a human female, though his only real experience with any human female was that of which he'd had with the queen and princess, both women admitting they were shorter than many of their kind. She would be tall enough for him to really hold her without overwhelming her with his body, if he were to ever get a chance to do so.

Her breast pressed against his chest, a full and firm globe of flesh that his male instinct wanted to hold, *tritio* that he was. She would be a handful. He wondered about the color of her nipples, were they dark against her flesh or pink and a perfect match? She smelled of flowers and sunshine and he groaned as he held her, a deep rumble deep in his chest.

Kenlyn caught it. "At least you'll get to know who she is," he murmured softly.

"Fendet," Rydul responded. "Are her parcels here?"

Kenlyn held them up. "I have them. Asure gave them to me."

"You might want to see if you can find any information about her, where she lives, if there is anyone we need to inform about what has happened." The elevators doors opened quietly and he stepped in, Kenlyn beside him. The second in command pushed the button for the second floor, the doors closed and the car began its journey upwards. "She may have a husband or lover."

"Doubtful. What male would allow his woman to come to ogle another without putting a stop to it? If she has a lover, he's a poor excuse for a man."

"Nevertheless, found out what you can. She may have this thing they call a license, or some other form of identification. The last thing we need is an interplanetary incident." Exiting the elevator, he strode down the hall to enter a living room sized room, the walls white, several exam type tables lined against one wall. Opposite there were a number of cabinets, glass fronted, each containing medicines and bandaging, things the warriors would need if injured during a practice training. Sistan also treated the men who overindulged in Earth drink and Earth foods almost as soon as they arrived, suffering a bout of illness they had been told was one known as Montezuma's revenge, whoever in all the worlds was Montezuma. It took time to get used to human food, especially the sweet things it seemed all of the warriors enjoyed immensely.

At the nearest table, Rydul set his burden down with the utmost care, smoothing her hair away from her face and loosening her coat. She was so silent and pale. He was frightened for her. "Where is Sistan?" he growled.

"I'm here, Captain. Don't get your britches in a knot." Sistan was fifteen years older than Rydul, a few countable grey hairs at his temple, his golden eyes retaining the spark more common in younger men. As tall as the other Taburons, he also cut a commanding figure among humans even in his green uniform with no medals on his chest or weapons at his hip. Not being a warrior, he was thicker in the waist than the men in the Embassy, but he'd not any real fat on him, just weight added due to natural aging. He did know how to wield a sword and practiced with the men once or twice a week to keep up his skills, but his talents lay in his ability to quickly learn, diagnose and heal.

Though he was the main physician on the king's vessel, the *Veleda*, his experience when Prince Jaima had been shot had convinced him to spend more time studying Earth medicine and human physiology. Temporarily he'd relinquished his assignment on the *Veleda* to remain on Earth for the six month tour to add to his knowledge.

Rydul grimaced at the physician's use of an Earth colloquialism. "You have been too long on Earth," he commented.

"I'm going home soon. What happened?" he asked as he bent over the prone woman.

"Those protesters. Someone threw a rock and it hit her head. She went down and hasn't regained consciousness."

"Is that what all of the commotion is about?" the physician asked as he probed the injury gently. "Thought I heard a laser weapon."

"Mine, a warning shot."

Sistan went to one of the cabinets and opened it, rummaged through it and pulled out a handful of items, bandaging, cloths, and a bottle of a green liquid. "Get a basin and fill it with warm water," he told Rydul. "I'll need to wash away some of this blood before I can get a decent look at the injury. What's her name?"

Kenlyn folded the wallet he had found in the woman's purse, several card sized items in his hand. "Kathryn," he answered, "Kathryn Tehyr. Appears she works about a block from here at a place called the Financial Center of the United States."

Ambassador Janel entered the room, his face a mixture of concern and worry, concern for the young woman, worry for the results that bringing her into the Embassy might incur. "How is she?"

Rydul set the basin of water next to the exam bed and handed several towels to the physician. "Unconscious."

"You fired a laser weapon?" Sistan soaked a towel, wrung it out and began to bathe the injury. The towel quickly became reddened with blood.

"In warning only. The crowd did not appear happy that we were going to handle the woman they had injured."

"You should not have fired the weapon."

Rydul glared at the man. "Would you have preferred hand to hand combat with humans? Let this woman bleed to death on our doorstep while we took care of the crowd? I guarantee you there would have been a lot more injuries had that happened."

Janel sighed heavily. "I've already received a call from the Washington chief of police, he's on his way over. We'll have to sort this out, but if you're sure there was no other way…"

"I am sure," Rydul growled never taking his gaze from the woman.

"Maybe we can finally get some extra police control here now. I've been asking for it for months. These protesters are getting out of hand." He watched as Sistan rinsed out the cloth and continued his task. "Let me know how she is, if she wakes up. You have a name?"

"Kathryn Tehyr." Kenlyn continued flipping through the cards he'd removed from her wallet then set all of her other personal items on a nearby counter.

"I'll tell the chief when he arrives, they can notify who ever needs notification."

"Kenlyn, go with Janel, take the cards for the chief, but bring them back here once he has seen them."

With the two Taburons gone, Rydul waited as Sistan continued to clean the wound, then applied *whemin* to it, first to stop the bleeding and second to prevent infection from setting in. "Well?" he asked as the physician again probed the injury with his fingers.

"She's probably got a concussion, but I don't have the equipment here to make that determination. I think her skull is cracked. She needs to go to one of their hospitals. I can stitch the wound, cover it, but they'd only take the stitches out once she got to the hospital. You should have her taken to a hospital." He dabbed more *whemin* on the injury, making sure it was totally covered in the medicine, covering it with a large gauze pad, then opened a package of bandaging. Holding it against a spot on her head away from the wound, he began to wrap her head.

"I'll have the car brought to the back. I'll take her in."

"Janel won't like it."

"He'll like it less if she dies here." Sistan nodded, continuing in his task.

At the door to the infirmary, a small group of warriors had gathered to watch the proceedings. "Captain?" Asure asked.

"Have the driver bring the car around the back. She needs their medical facilities. I will go with her, but I have to let Janel know I'm going." There would be hell to pay later, and his presence in a human hospital with a human woman would create just the kind of upheaval the Taburons tried to avoid, but he was determined to stay by her side until he was assured that she was on the road to recovery.

"Yes, Sir."

Sistan dropped the soiled materials into a waste basket, then faced the warrior. "You have two cuts on your cheek. While we wait for the vehicle, let me take care of them."

"*Whemin*?" Rydul asked as though facing the worst thing in the world.

"*Whemin* and keep that pretty face or mar it with scars. Take your choice," the physician replied sarcastically, his foot tapping in impatience.

Rydul sighed heavily and sat in a chair nearby, turning his face to the physician with resignation. The green cream stung like a dozen insects, but did wonders for healing without leaving scars. Rydul would tolerate the treatment as long as he had nothing else to do at this time while he waited, never taking his eyes from the still unconscious woman on the exam table nearby.

CHAPTER FOUR

Kathryn struggled to rise above the murky, muddy darkness that surrounded her, weighted down by uncertainty as to where she was and how she got there. She was floating in some sort of realm where there was no up or down, but lots of pain that only increased as she rose closer to the surface and out of this weird place where time seemed suspended.

Soft rumbling shook her body and she felt a tightening around her torso as she wiggled slightly to move against the shaking. "Shh," she heard a distant voice, deep and warm, say, "you need to lay still for a little longer."

Her eyelids fluttered and lips parted as she took a deep breath, which only increased the pain that thundered through her head, flashes of color racing behind her closed lids. "Wha…?" she breathed.

"You've been injured," the voice responded. "We're taking you to the hospital."

Forcing her lids to lift, she stared into the face of a gorgeous man, his concern visible as his brows drew together. His eyes were the deepest gold in color, almost sparking with interest as he gazed down into her face. "Welcome back," he said.

Licking dry lips, her tongue nearly as dry, she found her voice was weak and brittle. "What happened?" One hand rose weakly to touch at her cheek. Something seemed caught there and was pulling at her skin.

He lifted a hand and gently smoothed a stray strand of hair away from that cheek. "You were in the wrong place at the wrong time. Someone threw a rock and it hit you. You were knocked unconscious. You're bleeding and Sistan insisted we take you to one of your hospitals to get a better examination." He grabbed her hand before she could place it where the pain radiated throughout the rest of her head. "He bandaged your head. Best you not touch it right now. I'm sure it hurts enough already."

"Who are you?"

"My name is Rydul. I'm head of security at the embassy."

Her brows lifted as the fog that had enveloped her cleared. The pain kicked up a notch. "Taburon."

"Yes, I am Taburon." His mouth quirked up in a smile. "You've been sitting outside our embassy for a while now. We've watched you."

"I didn't mean any harm."

"We know," he answered with a larger smile. "We looked forward to seeing you, some of the men even took bets on whether or not you would appear in the beginning." He shifted slightly. Kathryn realized with a start that she was laying across his lap, her head resting against his chest, his arms around her holding her close against his body,. His large, warm, and firm body that smelled like warm spices from an open air market on a summer's afternoon. The cloth against her cheek was rough, the muscles beneath hard and honed, his arm over her like a thick beam. The thighs beneath her buttocks and the small of her back felt like two hardened tree trunks that flexed and relaxed as she adjusted her position. "I'm sorry you were injured."

"Like you said, wrong place, wrong time." She winced.

"Head ache?"

"A lot."

"You have a serious wound. Sistan thinks there is a skull fracture as well."

"Sistan?"

"He's our physician, studying Earth medicine. At the embassy we don't have the equipment you might have in your hospitals, so he did a cursory exam and bandaged your head. He's really not qualified to care for humans, at least not on Earth." The vehicle in which they were traveling began to slow and made a sharp turn. He held her tighter to keep her from slipping as he moved with the turn. The sunlight that had been shining into the side of the vehicle was blocked out by an overhang as the car was pulled to a stop. "We're here." His thighs bunched under her lower back and buttocks as he sat her slightly higher in his embrace, glancing out the window of the Humvee to the surroundings. They were parked in front of the emergency entrance to the Medical Center of Washington D. C., where Jaima had been brought the day he'd been shot.

The driver – a human male - shut off the engine and exited the car, going around to the side where Rydul and Kathryn waited. Opening the door, he stepped to the side.

Rydul set Kathryn to the side and climbed out of the vehicle, then reached back in for her, scooping her into his arms as though she weighed little more than a small sack of potatoes, one arm under her legs and the other across her back. She moaned at the movement, her head spinning, darkness threatening, pain thundering between her ears. "Stay with me," he instructed softly as her head began to fall back, her hair trailing down his side.

"Everything's spinning," she murmured, her stomach roiling. She swallowed and took a deep breath to stave off the feeling that any minute she was going to embarrass herself and vomit all over the ground and the man who held her. She would never live it down if she lived to be a thousand years old. Not if she spewed all over one of the men she had so wanted to meet and fantasized about every night.

"Take the car back to the embassy please," he instructed the driver, "and remain available for when we are through."

The driver shut the door and nodded. "Of course, Captain."

Holding her as though she were the most fragile thing in the world, Rydul walked with care to the entrance. The doors to the emergency room slid open as he stepped closer. A blast of warm air hit the two and he stood for a second just inside, ignoring the hiss of the doors as they closed, to look around. At a desk several feet inside the doors, a guard, who'd been looking at papers on his desk glanced up, his jaw falling open at the tall warrior with a woman in his arms. Beyond the desk, the waiting area was filled with people, some ill, some offering support to their companions, going about their business, until one by one they noticed the new additions and stopped to stare, their own troubles forgotten for the moment, some nudging others who had yet to look up.

The guard stood, his hand going to his gun at his side to rest on it gently, warningly, one finger releasing the snap. "Sir?" he questioned.

By now, the crowd had recovered their wits and had begun to pull out and open cell phones, some taking pictures while others started recording the entrance and ensuing encounter with one of the large alien men who carried a prone woman in his arms. Rydul sighed softly, there was nothing he could do about them. His concern was for Kathryn and only for Kathryn. The Embassy and the ambassador would have to deal with the fallout later.

"This woman has been injured and needs the care of your physicians."

"Let me call for a nurse," the guard replied, his expression wary, but he picked up the receiver to the phone, punched in three numbers and spoke into it softly, never taking his hand from his weapon.

Rydul glanced down at Kathryn. She was keeping her eyes closed and breathing steadily but with short shallow breaths, trying to control her queasy stomach. "How are you?" he asked in a voice meant only for her to hear.

"Hanging in there," she replied, not looking to him. Her brows drew together and her breath hitched as another shot of pain raced through her. He could feel her tremble against his chest and he ached for her.

"Soon," he promised.

A nurse approached, her steps hurried as an orderly on her heels followed, pushing a wheelchair. She gave a passing glance to the guard, whose head tilted the smallest amount towards Rydul and Kathryn, as if she could have possibly missed seeing the tall warrior in uniform holding the injured woman. She responded with an equally small nod and walked up to the two. "Sir? May I help you?"

"She has had a head injury. Our physician believed it better she be seen by one of your doctors. Is Dr. Tripp here?"

"He's in the hospital seeing patients, but I'll have him paged. How about we get her into an exam room? Get her vitals and ready for the doctor?" She set a hand on the back of the wheelchair, a not so subtle hint to place his burden there. The orderly had backed up out of the way, not wanting to anger this man in any way, shape, or form.

Rydul shook his head. "I will carry her to your exam room," he decided, his tone firm and unquestionable.

The nurse paused for a moment, debating whether or not to argue with the tall man before nodding her acquiescence. "Follow me then." Spinning on her heel, she strode towards a set of double doors, confident that Rydul would follow. Using her hand to hit at a large round disc in the wall, the doors swung open and she took a position just inside the doors, waiting for Rydul to catch up.

Leading them to an open room, he ignored the stares they garnered, his eyes wary of the large desk in the center of the emergency area, the flow of nurses, orderlies and other staff who stopped whatever they had been doing to follow the progress of the large male, then giving the empty room a quick investigative glance to take note of everything in it. An exam bed was placed in the center of the room, a folded blanket at its foot end and a pillow at the head. There were wall cabinets to the bed's right and behind it tubes and wires lead from various outlets on the wall. A set of monitors hung from poles by the left head side of the bed, unengaged and quiet for the moment. The nurse patted the top of the exam bed. "You may set her down here."

Rydul gently lowered Kathryn to the bed, his heart aching for the soft groan she uttered at the movement. He'd had a knock or two to the head over the course of his service and knew just how painful they could be with even the smallest of jarring. As he put her on the mattress, helping her to sit up, keeping a hand on her shoulder, the nurse bent to a low cabinet and pulled out a folded piece of material. "All right?" Rydul asked.

Kathryn looked to him and barely nodded, her eyes dulled from pain. "I think so," she whispered.

"You'll need to change into the gown," the nurse instructed. "Will you need help?"

"I would appreciate it, yes, please."

"If you could step outside for a few minutes?" the nurse asked of Rydul.

"I'll be near, if you need me," he promised the girl, giving her shoulder a slight squeeze. The look he gave the nurse said distinctly that he was not going far and was ready to respond to any cry Kathryn might utter, so don't hurt her any more than she'd already been injured. Peering at her name tag, he memorized her name in case he needed it – Ms. S. Brenan. Rydul left the room and took up position just outside the door, his back to the room, his arms crossed over his chest, staring down any person who gazed at him too long, his ear tuned to the conversation behind him. As Kathryn changed clothes, the nurse asked her what had happened as well as other vital information. Only a few minutes passed before the nurse was at the door, inviting Rydul to come back inside.

Kathryn was stretched out on the bed, a light blanket over her. He couldn't believe that her face had appeared to have paled even more, her skin nearly as white as the blanket over her. Next to the bed, on one of the chairs provided, her clothes were neatly folded and waiting. Taking her hand, he held tightly. "Kathryn?" S. Brennan left the room to retrieve a new patient chart and other equipment she needed to get the exam started for the doctor.

"The light is too bright," she complained. Finding the light control, he dimmed the room until she sighed and finally opened her eyes to gaze at him with gratitude. "You don't have to stay if you need to go back."

"I wish to stay," he corrected.

Her lips curved in a small smile. "Thank you." She glanced around the room. "Which hospital is this?"

"Medical Center of Washington. Prince Jaima was brought here when he was shot. We have come to trust this Dr. Tripp to care for our people if necessary."

"I remember when that happened. The whole city was on edge, and then the man who was shot disappeared."

"He was taken to a secure location when the crowds became too large and unpredictable here."

"Protesters," she mumbled with disgust. "I wish they'd leave you alone."

"As do we."

"I know he recovered and went back to Taburon. Is he okay?"

"He is quite content. He married the woman who had been caring for him and they have a son."

"Just like the king after he married that woman."

"Queen McKenna is well liked on Taburon. She has given the king a son and daughter."

Returning with equipment, the nurse took a position next to the bed. As she set her tools both on the mattress by Kathryn and the counter behind her, she separated out the items as she would need them in order. "I spoke with Dr. Tripp, he's on his way down, especially after finding out who was here. I need to get your vitals first, and then he asked that the bandage be removed." She wrapped a blood pressure cuff around Kathryn's upper arm and set the measuring machine to start. The cuff tightened, nearly unbearably so before loosening. While Kathryn's blood pressure was being taken, the nurse took her pulse and counted her breathing, then stuck a thermometer in her mouth, writing her readings down on a chart while she awaited the temperature reading. That number was added to the chart.

Putting the previous equipment aside, Nurse Brennan donned a pair of gloves and grabbed a pair of scissors from her pocket. Gently lifting an edge of the bandaging that wrapped around Kathryn's head, she snipped through it and pulled it free, placing a hand over the gauze padding Sistan had placed directly over the wound.

As the pad fell free, there was a soft rap at the doorway and Dr. Martin Tripp entered the room, his hands in his physician's coat pockets until he saw the large warrior who had been carefully watching the nurse. His hand extended in greeting.

Rydul gave the human a once over glance. He wore a suit of dark blue over which he'd draped his white physician's coat, a stethoscope hanging around his neck. One hand was shoved into one of the deep pockets of the coat, the other one the one he held out, tapered into long, well-trimmed fingers. Rydul had known the man had shown genuine care for his people a year ago, placing their safety over the concerns of the authorities when Jaima had insisted on making sure that queen was safe and unharmed, especially since she had been carrying the next royal child. He trusted this tall human who eyes seemed lively and all encompassing, but there was a not quite hidden sadness there. If he had grown up on Taburon, he would have fit into their society with ease despite the short, dark thatch on his head and the thin line of hair that covered his chin and upper lip. His smile seemed pleasant enough, and he had an air of authority about him, the nurse moving to the side almost as soon as he'd entered the room.

"Martin Tripp," the human doctor introduced.

Rydul took the other's hand, having been informed upon his arrival on Earth that shaking hands was a common way for people to greet each other. "Captain Rydul, in charge of security at the Taburon Embassy."

"Nice to meet you, Captain. I hear there was been a bit of a to-do there this afternoon."

"There was a fight," Rydul corrected, "and Ms. Tehyr was unfortunate to suffer for it. She was struck by a rock and knocked unconscious."

"How long was she out?"

"Perhaps fifteen, twenty minutes. She came to in the car on the way here."

The nurse, having removed all of the bandaging, tossed everything into a nearby biohazard waste can, removed her gloves and handed the chart to the doctor. He perused the information for a moment, then set it aside on the counter. "Let's have a look then, shall we?" he mused, leaning over Kathryn's head to peer closely. Hand extended, Ms. Brennan placed a pair of disposable gloves in it, which he drew on without looking.

"I'll try not to hurt you anymore than you must be feeling," he promised as he reached to part her hair further. "Did your Sistan dress this?"

"Yes. We took her inside as soon as we could."

"And this green coloring here? This is your *whemin*?"

"Yes. After he cleaned the wound as best he could he determined that we could not tend to her properly, but applied the *whemin* as a preventative."

Tripp grabbed the overhead lamp and flipped the switch to turn it on, making Kathryn flinch at the sudden bright light. After donning sterile gloves, he probed the wound with delicate fingers, pushing into the injury, feeling the edges, blood rising fresh from his manipulations. "Gauze, please, nurse," he requested. Applying the material, he pressed gently to stem the flow of blood. "How's your head feel?"

"Pounding, worse than I've ever had in my life."

"Any dizziness? Nausea?"

"Yes. Double vision. The light bothers me."

Tripp straightened. "I think we'll run a CAT scan anyway, just to play safe, take an x-ray as well. You'll need some stitches to close your scalp. But I believe Sistan was right, best you came in. You probably have a mild fracture and a concussion." Stripping off the gloves, he retrieved the chart and began writing with a pen he grabbed from his shirt pocket. "Schedule the tests asap," he instructed, "and order 4 milligrams of dilaudid to be given I.M. before she goes for those tests. That should help her headache." He finished writing on the chart and signed his name with a flourish before handing it back to the nurse. "Let me know when she returns and we'll get that wound stitched properly. Cover it for the time being though."

"Yes Doctor."

Tripp patted Kathryn's leg. "I'll be back shortly. Try to relax." He smiled reassuringly. "I don't think it's fatal, but you're going to have a whopping headache for a few days."

Kathryn grimaced. "Thanks for the head's up," she mumbled, "pun intended." Tripp chuckled softly as he left the room.

The nurse finished putting the equipment away. "I need to get that medicine and a wheelchair, and we'll get you up to x-ray as soon as possible. Be back soon."

Rydul reached up to turn off the lamp Tripp had left on, watching as the tension on Kathryn's face eased at the dimming of the light. "You will most probably be light sensitive for a while. It should ease as you heal."

"I just wish the pain would stop."

"I am sorry, Kathryn. Hopefully, the ambassador will be able to convince the police to keep the protesters under better control."

"Why do you put up with it?" she asked. "Have them arrested for trespassing or something."

"We had been instructed that as long as they do not cause any physical damage to the grounds or our people and do not interfere in our duties, they are to be left alone." He shrugged slightly. "Until today they have been a mere nuisance. Today they have proven to be more dangerous than believed. Janel will be asking for more protection from your police officers because of what happened."

Kathryn hesitantly reached up to touch her injury with delicate fingers. "I could wish he had done that sooner," she murmured without accusation.

"As could I, though I never would have had a chance to meet you had he done so."

"I don't think this is the standard way to say hello," she quipped, delighting, despite her pain, in his responding chuckle. "Why didn't you just come out and ask if you wanted to meet me?"

"I did not want to take the chance of you becoming a target for those protestors. Those few humans who work for us live at the embassy most of the time. Otherwise, they could be followed, their families threatened. We could not have that on our conscience were any one of them to be hurt."

Kathryn uttered a very unlady-like snort. "People suck," she decided with disgust.

"I believe many do. But we have also found many who are more reasonable and pleasant to work with." He reached over to take her hand. "Still, I am glad now to have met you." He gave her a squeeze. "And you could have always knocked on our door to say hello," he pointed out.

"Oh no," she protested. "I would have been afraid I would have embarrassed myself by saying something stupid when the door was opened. Or I might have tripped over my own feet if I'd been invited in." She shook her head and instantly regretted it, taking several deep breaths before gaining some control over the pain. "I couldn't have."

His smile spread completely to his eyes. "I promise had you said something embarrassing, I would not have noticed. And if you'd tripped, I would have caught you."

"Wow," she breathed. "A warrior and a gentleman, all in one. Who'd've thought?"

"You shall have to explain that," he demanded.

She swallowed defensively. "Well, you all look so fierce, and you're so tall, and... everything. Never considered you have a soft side."

Rydul laughed, then made a fierce face for her. "We kill our dinner with our bare hands and eat raw meat only twice a week, I assure you," he teased. Once she'd realized he was teasing, he gently smoothed a hand down her cheek. "Do we really look that intimidating?"

"Most of the time, yes. Whenever you're on the news, you have this 'don't mess with me" expression on your faces. It can be quite off putting."

His eyes lifted as he pondered her words. They did their best to discourage people – humans – from getting too close, from interfering in their times when they were outside the embassy, from even thinking about causing trouble. Maybe they were too intimidating, too fierce looking, as she said, too unfriendly and brought some of their problems on themselves. He would have to discuss this with the ambassador when he got back to the embassy. "I shall consider what you have said," he told her.

She plucked at the blanket. "I'm sorry to have to say this, but my head is pounding and I can't remember your name."

"Rydul."

"Rydul what?"

"Just Rydul. We do not have last names as you humans do. Sometimes we give our house name as well, but as I have none, it is simply Rydul."

"Why don't you have a house name?"

"My family was of no consequence and had none."

"That doesn't seem fair."

"It is how it is."

"Have you been on Earth the entire time? Since the embassy was set up?"

"Only for the last five of your months. I came with the first official contingent, but once Prince Jaima was injured, we were confined to the ship. The king did not wish to chance any violence."

"Would you have – committed violence?"

"The thought crossed our minds. Our king had been shot at, Jaima was injured and we did not know if he would live or die. It was satisfying to know that the man who shot him was killed."

"I'm sorry it happened."

"As were we. That is why we are trying to become allies with your planet, but there are those who will never accept our friendship."

"I'm afraid it's a fatal flaw with some of us."

"And they are the loudest of all of you as well."

The two shared a moment of silence. Kathryn's forehead furrowed as she glanced around the room, looking to her clothes. "My purse. Is it here?"

"It is at the embassy and safe. Was there something you needed?"

"My insurance information for the bill. I have coverage."

"Do not worry about the bill. We are taking care of the costs."

"I can't let you do that."

"You can and you will. It is because of us that you were injured. The least you can do is let us take care of the expense."

She thought for a moment, her face conveying her concerns of having her bills paid for by the Taburons as she considered the implications, then nodded. "All right. What about my job?" she asked. "Has anyone let them know what happened?"

From a back pocket, Rydul revealed a cell phone. Opening the device, he keyed in the code then passed it to her. "I do not know if anyone has been informed of your injury."

Kathryn dialed and spoke briefly with her boss, explaining the situation and that she had no idea when she'd be able to come back to work. She found out that what had happened had already been on the news and her boss was surprised that she was the victim mentioned, since the Ambassador had not revealed that information. He assured her that she could take what time she needed and asked if she would need any help. Kathryn assured him that she was being taken care of and thanked him for his concern. She would call in the morning after she got home and had a chance to get some rest.

"You do not like your employer?" Rydul asked.

"I'm uncomfortable with his attitude towards women. He believes women should be more concerned with repopulating the males lost in the war instead of working to support themselves." She scowled. "I want to be more than a baby making machine."

Sympathy filled his expression. Joanna's husband had divorced her when she was unable to provide him with children after years of trying. His suggestion that she have sex with a slew of his friends and her subsequent refusal had been the straw that had broken their marriage. Yet she had had a child with Jaima and they were hoping to have more –

at least the rumor was that they were trying when he left Taburon.

Women were more than their ability to have children. They were artists, statesmen, merchants and so many other things on Taburon, encouraged to seek out their interests and dreams. McKenna could have merely sat back and been a beautiful addition to the court. Yet she worked hard to support her husband and rule equally by his side, even taking over if Radine had to leave temporarily. She was loved by the people and she loved them back equally.

Of course, having a warm body to greet a man when he completed his work day was desirable - to lay next to at night, to ease the tension of day to day living and to share life and nadryl. What a great possibility. However, there were still things he wanted to do before he could consider taking a wife, mostly making sure his goals for his property were being fulfilled. Whatever his wife did for herself, and he fully agreed that she should do what she desired, he wanted to make sure neither of them would ever have to worry about a future for either themselves or their children. Getting his *crufa* breeding program well established, making a name for himself as the premier breeder of the best *crufas* on Taburon – then would he consider himself successful and begin looking around for a wife. There were plenty of eligible females back home.

Though right now, he was regretting not having introduced himself to Kathryn sooner. About to reply to her comment, he closed his mouth as the nurse returned with a needle in hand, the painkiller the doctor ordered. Taking a packet from her pocket, she ripped the top from it and pulled out the alcohol wipe. Indicating for Kathryn to roll slightly to the side, she exposed a spot on the young woman's hip, wiped it and gave her the injection. She rubbed at the site a moment, recovered the exposed area and after informing Kathryn that she would be going to x-ray in the next few moments, left the room.

"Would you mind if I make a second call?" she asked, her voice softened from the stress of her injury as it finally started catching up with her. With a nod from him towards the instrument she held, she dialed again. When there was no answer, she left a message before ending the call and returning the phone to him. He took the phone to replace in his pocket as she rolled slightly onto her side, closing her eyes.

Rydul pushed the only chair in the room closer to the bed and sat, waiting while the medicine took over and Kathryn began to nod off as the pain eased. With her hand in his, he let her drift, a silent watcher.

Sky Clad Rydul

CHAPTER FIVE

Despite Dr. Tripp's protests, Kathryn insisted on going home after her treatment at the hospital, her head wrapped in a turban of gauze bandaging and with the promise that she would not be alone for the next twenty-four hours. With instructions on what to keep a watch for, a small number of pain pills and a prescription for more if needed, he reluctantly let her leave with the Taburon, whom he trusted implicitly. Rydul allowed her to be taken to the car in a wheelchair but picked her up to place her inside, climbing in beside her before they could be swarmed by the reporters who had tracked them to the hospital and were anxious for any kind of story.

He settled her against his side, covering her with a blanket. She was still groggy from the medication given to her for the pain and that which was used to deaden the feeling of having her scalp stitched. The anti-nausea injection added to her general lethargy and she was more than willing to let someone else help her, even if it meant no being at her best in front of a man she so desperately wished to impress. If only he could have seen her dressed to the nines and looking her prettiest, she would at least feel more likeable. How could he come to like her when she was an unkempt bloody mess with bedraggled hair and wrinkled clothes? She didn't even know where her underwear was at the moment, and really didn't care. All she wanted to do was crawl under the covers and sleep for the rest of her life.

At least she hadn't thrown up.

She was aware but didn't acknowledge that the car had pulled up in front of her apartment building. Her protests at being manhandled out of the vehicle went unheeded as he lifted her once again in his arms to carry her inside and into the elevator. She snuggled closer to his chest as they rode the elevator up to the third floor and he carried her to the door of her apartment where he stopped.

"Kathryn," he called softly, giving her a little shake. "Kathryn, I need the code to open the door." Her door, instead of relying on an actual key or card, had a pad into which a code had to be entered to be unlocked.

"Um?" she asked, mostly asleep in the comfort of his arms.

"The code. What is it to open the door?"

"Um," she replied again with contentment. "It's eight, one, zero, three, star."

Shifting her slightly in order to free one hand, Rydul punched in the code and heard a click as the door's lock sprung and it swung open enough for him to give it a slight nudge with his foot, opening it further.

His opinion of her elevated immediately upon entering the apartment. She'd decorated with tasteful furniture that matched, the chairs and sofa plush and inviting. The color scheme was subtle; tans, pastel blues and greens, inviting inhabitants to sit and relax and let the worries of the day float away. Her apartment was a corner unit, with windows on two sides that let in the light. The entrance lead into an overlarge living room that had a dining nook to the side. The kitchen was actually closed off from the rest of the living room. He would find she had two bedrooms, one of which she'd turned into a small library/office where she could either relax and read or work on those days when she had to remain at home. He approved of her living quarters. It was neat and clean, which spoke well of the woman who lived within.

Only the tree in the corner to his right puzzled him. It stood on a table about three feet above the floor and was decorated with lights and sparkling ornaments in varying shapes and sizes. The whole effect was festive without being gaudy, but its presence was out of place with the rest of the décor.

"Where is your bedroom?" he asked her, pushing the door closed behind him with the same foot he'd used to open it.

Her free arm rose limply, pointing half-heartedly. "That way," she murmured.

Dropping the bag of her personal items from the hospital on a chair as he passed, he followed her direction to find her bedroom as comforting and lush as the woman herself, the king-sized bed covered with a thick comforter in pale colors of red, green, blue and yellow, a pile of pillows at the headboard. She had a dresser to one side and a clothes tree next to it from which hung a pressed jacket. The floor had a thick carpet under the bed. There was a pair of slippers waiting patiently for the owner into which to slip tired feet.

His footsteps were muffled by the thick carpet as he strode across the room to lay her gently on the bed. Kathryn sank into the comforter with a sigh. "You should change for bed," he suggested. "Or do you sleep in nothing?" He knew what answer he wanted to hear, but he was trying to be a gentleman here.

With effort, she struggled to rise, leaning back on her elbows. "I have night clothes in my dresser," she answered, pointing to the furniture against one wall. "Second drawer on the left."

He went to the dresser to open the indicated drawer. "Which ones?"

"Any ones will do." The idea that a man was going through her night clothes flitted through her mind and she felt her skin warm with a flush, but was just as quickly forgotten. Her head hurt and her thoughts were muddled from the medications.

His eyes sparkled as he brought over a light blue set of pajamas. "Will you need help?" he asked innocently. At least he hoped he sounded innocent enough.

She read his expression correctly, befuddlement aside. Reaching out she took the clothing, grinning mischievously. "I'm sure you'd love to help," she accused half-heartedly. Slowly she rose further, swinging her legs over the edge of the bed and rising into a sitting position. Lifting a finger, she made a spinning motion. "You may turn around, if you please, sir."

He smiled at her and turned, clasping his hands behind his back. Listening as she changed, imagining all sorts of things in his head, he waited until she reseated herself, the bed making soft noises as she settled in with a sigh.

"Okay, I'm decent."

She had stretched out on one side of the bed, tossing the comforter back and loosening the sheet, piling the pillows to one side against which she rested. Her feet were ensconced just under the edge of the sheets. The glimpse he caught of her toes before they disappeared showed they were painted a delicate shade of pink.

He lowered himself next to her, perching on the edge of the mattress. "Are you all right now?" he asked.

"Yes. Finally feel like I can relax now "

He smoothed down her hair. "How does your head feel?"

"It hurts."

"You should eat something. We were a long time at the hospital, and you didn't get much of your high sun meal eaten before you were injured."

"High sun?"

"You call it lunch. We say high sun. If there is food in your kitchen, I will make something easy for you to eat."

The look of surprise that crossed her face was expected. "You cook?"

"I have been taking care of myself since I was sixteen years of age. While I cannot make anything complex, I can make a decent enough meal that will not make you regret that I made it."

She giggled softly, waving a negligent hand to the outside portion of the apartment. "Have at it then. The kitchen should be will be stocked since I shopped two days ago." He stood as she snuggled deeper into the bed. "I'll just take a short nap while you slave over a hot stove."

Leaning over her, his hands braced on either side of her hips, he brought himself to eye level. "I should not be long," he whispered then surprised her completely by kissing her. A quick buss, but on the lips, a taste he'd been dreaming about for a long time. And it was as sweet as he'd imagined, even though she smelled and tasted of hospital. Her lips were pliant under his, but he didn't prolong the kiss, waiting for when she might feel better before taking the time to explore and enjoy as much as he could from a kiss. When he pulled away, there was a look of wonder on her face, of surprise, and of bafflement. She had not expected the gesture, though she had enjoyed the kiss more than she'd expected. And she was willing to give it another try.

He smiled, satisfied that he had made an impression on her, pleased that she had responded to it, and promising himself that he would be coming back for more. Straightening, Rydul left the room to seek out her kitchen.

He removed his jacket and sword belt as he walked back to the front of the apartment, placing them both on the same chair as her bag of clothes. He wouldn't need the articles through the night, and he still wore his laser weapon tied to his trouser belt. He took a moment to ponder the tree in the living room, deciding he would ask her about it later as they ate evening meal. With a quick glance, he located the kitchen off to the left of the living room.

Like everything else in her place, her kitchen was neat, clean and well organized. Finding foodstuffs and equipment to prepare it had been easy. Soon he had a pot of a chicken stew simmering on the stove, placing the lid over the pot after the contents had come to a gentle simmer, reaching into his pocket to remove his phone. A quick call to the embassy and conversation with the ambassador relayed an update about the woman and the fact that he planned on remaining until at least the morning to keep an eye on her. Kenlyn, who then got on the line, on the other hand, chortled with delight, that his prediction of Rydul having more than a passing interest in the woman was coming to fruition, making the other hang up mid-chortle so as to not listen to any more of the other's teasing comments.

He'd been about to check on the patient when the entrance of a cat into the kitchen stayed him and he sank to his haunches to come closer to its viewpoint as he reached out tentative fingers. "Hello, kitty," he greeted. "Are you friendly?"

The animal, walking directly to him, arched its back and rubbed one cheek against his hand, uttering a soft 'meow.' The creature had long hair in a multitude of colors – brown, black, white, orange and gray, and its tail was held straight up from its base. Its paws were white, as though it wore shoes or stockings on each one.

After one pass against his hand in one direction, the cat circled around to rub the other side, going for a full body swipe as it passed. Rydul chuckled and sat completely on the floor to get even more on its level and allow the animal to engage further in its displays of neediness. He casually scratched behind its ears, which set the cat to purring loudly as it continued in its rub, circle, rub, circuit.

Rydul genuinely liked cats. He would miss the embassy ones when he returned to Taburon and was seriously considering getting one of the *afilens* to keep in his quarters as a pet. It would be an adjustment, for he'd never had a pet before, not even as a child, but he would make the effort if it meant having a warm fuzzy body next to him at night.

Of course, his first task was to find a wife, and the woman napping in the bedroom was becoming more and more the object of his desire. But they were too new to each other, too much strangers to make any kind of decision right now. And she was too wrapped up in her injury to think clearly, which he completely understood and accepted.

The cat rubbed against his thigh then gave him a light nip. Scooping the animal up, he settled it in his lap, continuing to pet it as he considered his life. He didn't get very far as the pot on the stove began to boil over, the lid bubbling up and the contents dribbling over. Scurrying to his feet, he lowered the temperature and removed the lid.

In the bedroom, Kathryn nestled deeper into the bed, pulling the blankets up to her chest. Closing her eyes, she fought to ease the ache in her head as well as the tingle in her scalp from the stitching where it pulled on her hair. She'd whined slightly when the scissors had been brought out to clip around the wound, cutting her hair away in thin hanks to be dropped to the floor. Her hair was her best, favorite attribute. She knew it was beautiful, shiny and colorful with reds, auburns, browns, and golds highlighting throughout. She hadn't cut it in years and kept it clean and well brushed, spending more time than usual on her tresses. It was her one vanity.

She was content, aside from the pain and general discomfort from being beaned on the noggin. There was a very handsome man in her kitchen making her something that smelled heavenly. He hadn't abandoned her at the hospital, standing by her side or nearby every minute she was in the emergency room, overseeing Dr. Tripp as he stitched her scalp, hanging diligently on every word the physician uttered as to her continued care. He didn't side with the doctor when he wanted her to remain through the night, instead stepping up to offer his babysitting services so she could go home. Tripp had given him a deep going over, considering the person that he knew the tall warrior to be, then nodded his approval before signing the release papers.

Rydul had carried her from the wheelchair to the car, sat her in his lap and held on as they were driven back to her apartment, then insisted on carrying her to the actual door and through it, never letting her go until he'd settled her on her bed.

She'd at first thought she'd be embarrassed by having him going through her dresser drawer in search of nightclothes for her, but just as quickly dismissed it when he carried out the task without comment or pause. He'd turned his back as she'd changed, though she could see that he would have preferred watching, if not helping her to change, giving him a chance to get his hands on her. She could tell from the look on his face as he turned that he have liked to help for more than altruistic reasons. She wasn't stupid, nor that naive that she couldn't read desire in a man's eyes. And he had it in spades.

Which wasn't all that bad, since she was feeling it as well. He was a handsome man, there was no question there. He was built like a god - tall, muscular, strong and well groomed. He smelled like heaven, even through all of the scents that had assailed them at the hospital. Burying her nose in his chest had been more than seeking solace, it had been to gather as much of his scent as possible to keep in her memory before he left her on her own. Her emotions and her heart had done a little happy dance when he had announced that he was intending to remain for the night to care for her. They had practically done cartwheels at his offer to make her food.

No man had gone to such lengths to take care of her, especially one she hardly knew. She found herself thinking about what she could do once she was feeling more herself in order to get to know him better. He'd already confessed that he didn't want to endanger anyone by having them seen with the Taburon contingent, but there had to be some way for the two of them to spend time together without having to worry about her safety. Maybe once things settled down from this recent incident, with the police establishing more visible protection, the protestors would back off and allow the visitors some freedom, especially from harassment by the masses. She was sure they only wanted to go about their business normally without having to face the gauntlet of protestors and curiosity seekers.

But for now, she had to concentrate on getting better. If there was to be a relationship between them, it would happen. They would find a way to make it happen, and she would take whatever he was willing to share with her, including his bed if he wanted.

Sex was a mystery to her. She had never gone all the way with any man – heavy petting was her furthest experience. She knew what a man looked like without his clothes, she knew how all the parts worked and how they went together. She'd just never given in to the chance to put part A into slot B. Her heart had never been involved deep enough to do the construction.

But with Rydul, something was different. He touched her on a visceral level. His kiss earlier had rocked her world right off its axis, going straight to her heart and igniting a tingling want sensation between her thighs that she had never felt before. Had he asked then and there, she would have done anything he demanded of her in order to have him in her bed and between her legs to teach her the secrets of making love. And she believed intuitively that he would be a great lover. Any man as virile as he, yet gentle and considerate, had to know how to please a woman in bed and take her to the ultimate pinnacle. That part of him that was the proof of his virility hadn't been dormant when he held her. She'd felt something long and steel hard against her lower back while they traveled to her apartment. So he was obviously interested in her beyond a mere feeling of responsibility for her injury.

What to do, she wondered, what to do? It was too hard to think with her head pounding with every heartbeat. If she rested, tried to get some sleep, maybe things would be clearer when she woke and then she could give better thought as to how to keep him in her life. Or even just in her bed. But like the famous line in the story, tomorrow was another day and she would give things their due in the morning.

Sky Clad Rydul

CHAPTER SIX

Rydul sat gingerly on the edge of the mattress, reaching out with his hand to awaken Kathryn, but then pulling it back to simply sit and stare at her. The cat twisted and curled around his feet.

She looked so peaceful, turned slightly on her side away from her injury, her one hand under her cheek. Her eyes were closed, thick lashes a crescent against the soft skin of her upper cheek. Her lips were slightly parted, the very edges of her teeth showing through the blushed pink coloring.

She breathed at a steady pace, her chest rising. The blanket had fallen to her waist and the top of her pajamas was pulled tight, outlining her generous breasts. Full globes that he wished he could get in his hands, knowing they would be a handful, even for his big palms and long fingers. He would admit to it – he loved a woman's breasts, he loved playing with them, molding them in his hands and plucking at the delicate nipples until they hardened into fine hard points, suckling at them like a starving child, whatever else he could do to sharpen the pleasure for her as he explored her flesh. After her face, a woman's breasts were the next thing a man noticed – how big they were, how they moved beneath her clothing, were her nipples peaked and where did they point when hardened? Other than a flush to her skin, a woman's attraction to him and his subtle hints at a sexual rendezvous showed in her breasts, their reaction always told him whether or not she might be receptive to his advances.

But now, in sleep, Kathryn's breasts were soft and uncontained and somnolent, only the entirety of the mounds was visible below the material, the nipples softened and only outlined by their color. Her breasts shuddered slightly as she breathed and he took a deep breath to bring his own rampant emotions – and swelling cock – under control. No sense in rousing the girl to a man who would rather join her in that bed, strip her of those clothes and explore every part of her body until he knew it as well as his own and give her pleasure after pleasure than continue caring for her like a gentleman would.

He took her shoulder in hand and squeezed. "Kathryn," he called, "time to wake up. I have something for you to eat." He gave her a little shake. "Kathryn."

She stirred, stretching, undulating under the sheet and his traitorous cock swelled again at the luscious movement as she roused, turning her head towards the sound of his voice. Blinking, her eyes finally opened and she gazed up at him, frowning until he finally came into focus. She answered his smile with one of her own. "Hi." Her voice was soft from sleep. It would be glorious to hear her sound like that because he had loved her completely and thoroughly, to have her greet him with that husky warmth every morning.

"You had a good sleep for over an hour."

"I feel relaxed." The hand that she had rested by her cheek swept up to comb through her hair on the side of her head not covered in bandaging. "I must look a mess."

"You look beautiful," he complimented. "How do you feel?"

"My head hurts, but I can deal with it."

He perused her closely, checking her eyes for any sign of evasion, searching to see if she was withholding the truth, nodding slightly when he decided that he believed her. Twisting to his left, he bent to the floor, reaching for something, rising with the cat in his hands. "I think this is yours," he murmured.

Kathryn reached for the animal, a smile on her face. Bringing it closer to her, she rubbed her cheek against its fur, then hugged it against her chest. "Oh, Pib, I bet you missed me," she cooed, placing a kiss on its head. "I missed you. And I'm sorry I'm late with your dinner. But I'll make it up to you with an extra portion, I promise."

Rydul watched with fascination as she cuddled the cat, petting it and planting kisses over its head as the animal purred loudly and snuggled into her bosom. He envied the cat, wishing it was his head buried between her breasts, his head she was petting so lovingly, his lips she was kissing with enthusiasm. He was such a tritio. However….

One eyebrow quirked. "Pib?" he asked.

Kathryn stopped showering affection on the animal and lifted one of its feet. "She has white boots on all four of her feet, so I named her Puss in Boots, Pib for short. She's been with me for nearly twenty years."

"Is that long?"

"For a cat, yes. I can't stand the thought of when the day comes that I don't have her…" Her voice hitched, her eyes teared slightly and she took a deep breath, fighting the emotion of a bleak future without her beloved cat. "But she's doing well for now. She's been with me through a lot of good times and bad."

Rydul added his hand to Kathryn's, scratching near the cat's ears. "We have two cats at the embassy. The creatures seem to like the warriors, and the warriors like them."

"They know good people when they see them," Kathryn answered with assurance. "A cat's sense of trust is very strong." She shot him a sly glance. "Any one a cat likes can't be all bad," she teased.

He didn't even pretend to misunderstand her. "That depends on your definition of bad," he rejoined, rising. His hand extended to her. "Come, dinner waits and it's getting cold."

Setting the cat aside, she slid her hand into his and let him help her from the bed, wrapping his arm around her waist to steady her. "I…um…need to use the bathroom," she said softly, indicating where it was with a tilt to her head. Steering her in that direction, he waited while she took care of her needs, his back turned to the mostly closed door, facing her immediately as she reappeared to sweep her into his arms.

She squealed softly. "Rydul, I can walk, honestly," she protested. "I must weigh a ton."

"You feel as light as a feather. Besides, I enjoy holding you. Now, be quiet," he ordered as he carried her to the table which he'd already set. She humphed on the way but obeyed. A moment after leaving her to settle in her seat, unfolding a napkin, he returned, carrying two large bowls of steaming food.

Rydul sat opposite her at his own place, putting a napkin next to his utensils, picking up his spoon. He watched with hooded eyes as she tasted the stew, taking a delicate bite before scooping a full spoonful up to eat.

"This is wonderful!" she complimented.

He gave her an 'I told you so' smirk and spooned a mouthful up. "It was easy once I found everything."

"I should keep you to cook for me every day," she mused with a glint.

"I'm open to negotiations," he offered. Kathryn giggled and blushed, hanging her head slightly, concentrating on her meal. Rydul continued to eat but kept slipping glances her way, waiting to see if she was going to speak or linger in strying to hide from embarrassment. When the silence began to drag out, he wiped at his mouth, taking a drink from his water glass. "I am curious about the tree over there."

Following his gaze, she looked over to the decorated tree in the corner. "It's a Christmas tree," she explained as though that was enough.

One Taburon eyebrow rose. "You follow a pagan tradition to celebrate a Christian holiday that has been designated for the wrong time of year?" he asked.

"What…what do you mean?" she responded, surprise in her voice.

"When your television began broadcasting images for this holiday, I researched it. Decorating a tree was a pagan ritual to please their pagan gods and assure a bountiful planting and harvest. They honored the evergreen tree because it never appeared to die and survived through the harsh winters. If you combine all of the data available through astrological charts and historical records, the child for whom you celebrate this holiday was most likely born in the late spring or summer. The correct name for this celebration at this time of year is Yule, which is why you wish your friends yuletide cheer."

She refused to bristle or take offense. He was new to Earth and did not understand how humans did some of the things that they did. Or why. "While all of what you said is true, we have been celebrating Christmas for hundreds of years in this fashion. It's become a tradition, so I guess we humans stick to it because it's familiar. Don't you have any holidays you celebrate that seem outdated or unnecessarily traditional today?"

He was silent as he thought. There was one tradition Taburons observed, yearly in fact, that had no significance whatsoever in their modern lives, yet the people found it a pleasant celebration, especially since it involved nudity and sex. Lots of sex if the participants were of a mind. Sky Clad was an ancient tradition, but only a tradition now. Yet every year, thousands of Taburons participated around the planet. There were a high number of births just over nine months after every Sky Clad celebration.

He nodded. "There are a few. Please understand, I meant no disrespect. I am just trying to understand your reasoning. These things are new to us, and confusing."

"Why confusing?"

"Your people fight readily, as proven by your history, for what at times seems over a petty disagreement. Yet you daily profess to admire and even advocate peace and harmony, tolerance and understanding."

"You have no war on your planet?"

"Our last conflict was when Radine became king. There were factions interested in taking the crown from him. They were quickly defeated and put down."

"They were killed?"

"We have a small planet two days journey from Taburon we call Taburon Prime. It is primitive – no modern conveniences, no communications, nor space flight. Those who would oppose Radine to the point of war are exiled there for the rest of their lives. Executions are reserved only for the most heinous of offenses, and there has only been the possibility of one of those in the last handful of years."

"What happened?"

"A woman who kidnapped the queen and was intent on torturing and killing her was killed. But not by the king. The queen killed her during a fight for her life. But Radine would have had her executed for her offense."

"That's horrible," she whispered, horrified. That someone would torture and attempt to kill someone was beyond her. She would never have it in her to do such a thing, no matter the circumstances. But she would defend herself and anyone she loved to the end if it came down to it. She acknowledged that the queen had been justified in her actions.

"King Radine loves Queen McKenna very much. He would move the very heavens if he had to in order to keep her by his side and safe." His expression was meaningful. "As would any of us," he added.

She heard his words and kept them close to her heart, his way of saying that if they became further involved, he would do whatever it took to protect her and keep her safe. As he was doing now by being here and taking care of her though he had no obligation where she was concerned. Everything about him said he would be a conscientious boyfriend and lover, and most likely an even better husband. If she would give him a chance.

Disturbed by the feeling racing through her, Kathryn rose from the table to go to the tree, leaning over carefully, her arm outstretched. Fumbling for something, she grabbed whatever it was and pushed it against the wall. Suddenly the tree lit up, lights woven throughout the branches in colors of white and blue, small sparkles that after a moment began to blink. Rydul rose as well, dropping the napkin to the table and went to stand beside her, watching with fascination.

"I do not wish to fight with you," he said softly in apology.

"Nor I with you," she agreed, reaching over to take his hand for a heartbeat and squeeze. He was pleased by her gesture, returning her show of affection with one of his own as he kept his eyes forward.

Getting a closer look than he had earlier, he discovered the hanging ornaments were a variety of shapes, colors, and textures, many of them reflecting the lights in bits of star-like shimmers. "It's quite pretty," he commented.

Her touch on one of the ornaments was delicate. "This was one my parents got when I was first born." She turned it around and on the opposite side was written 'Baby's First Christmas – Kathryn – 12/2046.' Letting it fall freely, she twisted another, the writing the same, only the name was for a male Christopher, and a date four years earlier. "This was for my brother. Mom couldn't take seeing it anymore, so she gave it to me."

"Your brother is dead?" he asked with a soft voice.

Kathryn sighed, letting the ornament swung free. "We don't know. He went to war and when he came home, he was different. He disappeared a year or so later, and no one knows where he is. Mom and Dad have pretty much given up hope of ever seeing him again. But I have to believe he's out there somewhere and will come home someday."

Rydul drew her back against his body at the sorrow in her voice. "I am sorry, Kathryn, for your loss."

She rested her head on his chest, taking his arms in her hands. "I've learned to live with it. At least I still have my parents."

"Where are they?"

"They moved to Florida when the weather here became too much for them, especially in the winter. They're content."

"Do you see them often?"

"I try to get down there once a year. Depends on my schedule and what's happening here." She took a deep breath. "What about you? Any family back on Taburon?"

"I have a brother. He lives on my estate and takes care of it when I cannot be there because of my duties."

"No mother or father?"

"They were killed when I was sixteen, along with our baby sister."

Twisting in his embrace, she gazed up to his eyes, sympathy in her expression for the terrible loss he suffered while still nearly a child himself. Cupping his cheek, she softened in his arms. "I'm sorry," she said. "That's why you've been taking care of yourself for so long."

"I joined the army to support both of us. Khail was only eight and we had no one else to take over the responsibility."

"It's still tough for a young man who still has so much growing yet to do for himself to suddenly become the parent."

Rydul shrugged. "I believe that I am better for it." Loosening his grip, he let her slide from his embrace, Kathryn suspecting that he was uncomfortable talking about his hardships and wanting to keep it private for the time being. If they were going to have a relationship, sooner or later they would have a lot of discussions about their lives and what happened to them to bring them to this point. As he started to gather their empty dishes and utensils, the phone in her purse began to chime. He stopped, waiting to see if she needed any help from him. With a shake of her head, she rummaged through the purse to dig out her phone.

Kathryn looked at the caller id before opening the device, going to the sofa to sit as she talked to the caller, assuring the other that she was fine and not alone for now, but it would be a big help if her friend could come over in the morning to stay with her when her current 'nurse' returned to his own job. When the caller obviously inquired about the 'he' in her statement, Kathryn quickly brushed the request off and hung up with a good bye and promise to explain at a later date.

Rydul had caught the end of her conversation, standing in the doorway to the kitchen. That she had a friend who would be available to keep watch over her for the rest of the time the doctor had requested reminded him that he had to return to the embassy because the longer he was outside its confines the greater the chances that he would be found out and the more perilous his life would become. As well as hers.

And as much as he wanted to stay, he would not, not even for all of the *vireck* stones on Taburon, if it would put her in danger.

Kathryn caught him as he watched her, snapping the phone device closed and putting it on the end table nearby. "That was my friend, Rosalind. I called her from the hospital earlier to see if she could come stay with me tonight. I didn't know she was out of town and not getting back until the middle of the night." She gathered the remaining items from dinner.

"It is no difficulty for me to remain until you have someone else here, Kathryn," he assured as she passed by him to deposit her handful in the sink.

"I don't want to trouble you," she started to say.

Rydul took her arm gently, turning her to face him. "I wish to stay," he said softly. "Not because you are my responsibility, but because *I* wish it."

"But won't it be dangerous, if you're found here? The protestors..."

"I am but a phone call away from rescue," he promised. "And who would challenge me?" he asked, standing slightly away and spreading his arms wide. He was big, muscular, so very much a warrior, and so very handsome. She wasn't sure if the protestors would be what he might need to defend himself from. Her gaze rose from perusing his body to his eyes where she found gentle amusement and genuine attraction. Once he was sure she'd had her fill of looking at him, he pulled her into an embrace. "I am attracted to you, if you have not figured that out already. I want to get to know you better. I promise, I will be behave myself, but give us this small amount of time tonight before the world comes crashing in on us again. And it will come crashing in, I can promise you that," he added ruefully.

Standing on tiptoe, she brushed her lips across his. "Wash or dry?" she asked.

He'd been ready to settle her body tighter against his, relishing that she was agreeable to his desires. Her question threw him. "What?"

"Do you want to wash the dishes or dry them?"

With a chuckle, he released her, moving to the sink to turn on the faucet. Tossing the towel there over his shoulder to her, he rolled up his sleeves. "I hate drying," he mumbled, grabbing the detergent and squeezing a hefty dollop onto a washcloth.

She'd tired fairly quickly after they'd finished the kitchen duties and put away any leftovers, feeding the cat and settling on the couch in her living room. Turning on the console, Kathryn had been surprised that he had a favorite show and that it came on that night, but as it drew to a close, she couldn't help the yawn that occurred. He insisted that she go to bed, picking her up and carrying her once more – something she could easily get used to - insuring that if she needed anything first that she had it before tucking her in and placing a light kiss on her brow.

A little disappointed that he had not tried to sneak into her bed, or outright asked for she would have easily accepted, she found herself drifting off in peace, knowing there was a handsome guardian nearby should she need him.

And as much as he ached to join her, he waited until her eyes closed and her breathing evened out before retiring back to the living room, switching through the networks until he stopped, watching with distaste the report that he - or one of the Taburons since he was not specifically identified – had taken a young woman, the one injured earlier in the day, to the hospital and remained with her, then carried her out to the Taburon limousine, gotten in with her and been driven away. The station was still in the process of trying to locate the couple's identities, since the embassy was being very uncooperative.

Rydul would have to discuss with Janel what they could do to protect her, if it became necessary, for once her name was known she would find herself in the center of whomever wanted more information from her, about her, about the Taburons and her relationship to them. And as much as he wanted to pursue a relationship with Kathryn, with his limited time, it would probably become impossible without putting her in danger. He swiped his hands down his face and sighed, sinking deeper into the couch. He would have to give this a lot of thought.

CHAPTER SEVEN

It had been decided and negotiated that if enough people showed interest, Taburon would welcome humans to come to their planet for an extended visit with the understanding that they were allowed to stay permanently. Such arrangements provided several perks for both peoples: the humans could see a new planet and establish a new life there with new goals as long as they kept the peace. The Taburons would get a chance to show humans that they weren't the evil aliens they were being depicted by those whose only goal was to discredit them every chance they got. For the women on other planets, if they decided to return home, Taburon would be a stopping off point in their travels and to find people of their own kind in residence would assure them before continuing on to Earth. Should they wish, they could remain on Taburon and then would have compatriots on a different and more friendly new world.

The newcomers would have six months to make up their minds whether to stay or return to Earth. By the end of that time period, if they decided to return to Earth, they would go on the next ship back. There would be an exchange of newcomers every six months until the Taburons decided there were enough humans on their planet. Those who chose to stay would be welcomed in an elaborate ceremony and expected to swear allegiance to Taburon and her king. Any person committing a crime against the king, the people or the planet after that would be dealt with according to Taburon law.

They were allowed to bring a large trunk and suitcase with them, the hope being that over time they would begin to adapt to wearing Taburon styles. And while each person was encouraged to seek some sort of occupation there, the Taburons would provide for them for the first month and if they wished, they could bring money, in the form of gold which could be converted to Taburon coin.

A dormitory was being built to house the newcomers. Each single person would get a room much like a hotel room with a sleeping area and a separate bathing area. Each couple would be allotted a small suite. There would be a common room for meetings with information about Taburon history and society and a common kitchen. Human food would be brought from Earth, but just as with the dress, the Taburons hoped that the humans would soon adapt to their new home diet. They did let the newcomers know that with a human as queen, there had been some additions to the Taburon menu, like pizza and chocolate, so it wouldn't be that difficult.

Each person was expected to undergo vetting, including their health and mental state. Anyone showing any illness would not be permitted to board the shuttle when it arrived, and any person with a lingering animosity towards the Taburons would be dismissed from the group.

Each person had to take a 'class' on Taburon life, what the planet was like, the philosophy of the people and what was expected of them. Should alliances be made between a Taburon and a human, there would be no hindrance to it, at least not from the Taburon side. But it was pointed out that Taburons, while more open about sexual matters than humans, were not promiscuous in the least. They did not have any sexually transmitted diseases, and did not expect any human to bring them to Taburon. Birth control was available, but not in the same way as on Earth. While it appeared very medieval, birth control was in the hands of the females of the planet. Women used a tea to control conception, though in time, that could change as more humans migrated.

Questions were welcomed, readily and honestly answered, and the ambassador often sat in on these sessions so the humans would become acquainted with having a number of these tall, warrior like people in their midst. They were not told about the *vireck* stones, that wouldn't come until after they'd fulfilled their time on the planet and made their pledge. There was no sense in giving the humans any reason to want to appropriate the energy source or seek to make deals with other alien races that already knew about the stones.

Once all of the requirements had been filled and each person had been vetted, the manifest was drawn up and those chosen to go were informed of the decision. Total, there were thirty humans planning on leaving Earth; four couples, twelve women and ten men. To say excitement was high the night before they boarded would have been a vast understatement. It was noted that not a one of them got much sleep the night before.

Sky Clad Rydul

CHAPTER EIGHT

The sun was bright, the temperatures cool and comfortable for being the middle of the day as Rydul steered his crufa carefully through the crowd of Taburons that had gathered to watch the debarkation of the first Earthlings to relocate to Taburon. For the shuttle (the one built for the king after his first born had arrived) to land, a large, grassy area the size of several freema fields outside of the city proper had been chosen and cleared once the vehicle had been constructed. It was roped off to keep spectators from getting too close, interfering with the loading and unloading and possibly being injured.

To the side of the landing area, five crufa drawn carriages waited to take the humans to the dormitory. Behind them were ten wagons, readying to haul the luggage and supplies brought from Earth. The animals snorted and stirred restlessly, disturbed by the large vehicle, bored with waiting for their chance to do their jobs.

The people parted as his crufa snorted loudly, irritated at the sheer number of people that hampered the animal's progress when all it really wanted to do was canter forward without hesitation. Rydul held the reins tightly and squeezed slightly with his knees to remind the animal who was in control and watch its step. He chuckled softly as the crufa tossed its head and snorted more loudly, sassing him. "Enough, *adelu*," he scolded, pinching the animal just under the saddle, "or no extra treats for you tonight."

Scanning over the heads of the gathered crowd, he spotted his target, a Taburon in the uniform of the regular army, his head bent over a tablet, busily scribbling. Steering his crufa in the other's direction, Rydul called out. "Kendrin."

Kendrin finished whatever it was he was writing before glancing up towards the source of the voice. His face broke into a huge smile at seeing Rydul and he started towards the mounted warrior. "Capt. Rydul, what brings you out here in this mob?" With the crufa stopped, Kendrin grabbed the animal's reins to keep it still.

"Wanted to see the newcomers."

"They're still on the ship at the moment. Think there's a problem with getting the quarter assignments straight. They should off load in a moment or so."

"You have the manifest?"

Kendrin indicated the tablet he held. "Yes, came through about an hour ago." He handed the papers up to the warrior. "Some crowd," he commented as Rydul flipped through the pages looking for the list of passengers.

Rydul spared a short glance. "Like when we first arrived on Earth," he recalled, going back to the list. "People are people across the galaxies," he observed then suddenly straightened, his breath hitching in his chest, his heart beginning to beat a furious pace. Forcing himself to control, to take a deep breath and relax back into his saddle, he calmed his reaction before speaking. "Is this correct?" he asked.

Kendrin frowned. "Sent by the captain directly. Why?"

Rydul gave the list back. "Someone I know is on it," he murmured, turning his attention skyward.

Kathryn was coming to Taburon. He remembered their last few weeks together. After leaving her at her apartment, a friend promising to come over to continue watching over her until her twenty four hours was over, he'd returned to the embassy feeling empty inside. He wanted to see her again and often, to develop a relationship and see where it might lead, hoping to take them to a lifelong commitment. For he'd decided in that short space of time that she was the one person with whom he would willingly spend the rest of his life, take care of her and help her to realize her dreams and hopefully someday have his children.

He and the ambassador spoke at length about how he might go about getting her to the embassy so they could spend time together, sneaking her in but never able to go out in public. He would protect her at all costs, despite the fact that their picture had made the news from him taking her to then from the hospital. The ambassador had had to give a statement because of that picture as to the facts of the incident and then hope it blew over. It didn't.

Once her identity had been revealed, Kathryn had been harassed daily for the next week, at home, at work, on the way to and from her job. Her daily sojourn to the park bench ended and she was afforded a police escort for several days in order for her to simply get around her regular life. Eventually, as it became clear that she had no inside information about the aliens, interest began to drop off, including that from the protestors, who'd also gathered to accost her simply because one of 'those creatures' had tended to her. She had been alternately dismayed and disgusted by the attention.

But it hadn't stopped Rydul from doing what he could to see her again.

The first time she'd been brought to the embassy under cover had been arranged by the ambassador himself. Rydul had been in the courtyard training, giving the men probably the hardest time he'd ever given, working out his frustrations. She had stood at one of the windows inside, watching him as he wielded his sword, his shirt gone since he'd worked up a sweat even in the winter cold, his muscles bunching and flexing as he swung the heavy but non-lethal weapon around. Even from inside, she could hear the clash of the steel, the grunts and groans of the men and the challenges he issued as one by one, each man dropped out of the fray. Finally, with no opponent, Rydul had bent over, his hands on his knees taking heaving breaths and for some reason, glanced up. Seeing her in the window, he wasted no time in grabbing his shirt, tossing the practice sword to someone and racing inside.

The hug he gave her was crushing, lasting a long time before he released her, taking her face between his hands and planting a kiss on her lips. Janel grinned, watching the whole time, remembering when he was young and in love, giving a nod, signaling his approval. Rydul thanked him with a return nod. Grabbing her hand, he raced her through the embassy to his quarters where he made her wait as he showered and dressed. The evening had been filled with quiet time for the two of them as he first gave her the tour and they then ate dinner alone.

It wasn't the first time they managed to arrange a visit with each other. Each time they got together they found something to do within the embassy – watching a movie, having a quiet meal alone, or joining the men in the general dining hall to share meals and time listening to them jostle and tease each other in heartfelt camaraderie, including the man sitting by her side, much to her blushing sensibility.

Their one and only public time together had been when Janel had attended a Christmas party given by the Vice President. Rydul had gone as security for the ambassador, dressed to the nines in his best uniform, his chest filled with medals. Already a handsome pair, the formal attire of the Taburons only served to attract the eye of every women in the room, but Rydul only had eyes for the young redhead that appeared as part of her office's contingent, her hair softly draped down her shoulders, her dress daring to fall from her body if given the right opportunity. She was gorgeous, confident and more than pleased to find him there as well. Had she truly been his, and he free to express his feelings, he would have gone up to her and kissed her so thoroughly as to leave no doubt in her mind, nor in the minds of those watching that he had laid a claim to this woman. Instead, when he approached her to ask for a dance, all polite and aboveboard, she readily agreed, moving into his arms as though she'd been there forever. That he knew how to dance surprised her, having not known that learning some basic dance was part of his duty as an escort to the ambassador, but they moved together with ease as if they'd danced a hundred times before.

He couldn't help his reaction. Each time they'd gotten together his emotions had ravished his body with need until he felt he'd explode by the time she'd left at the end of the evening. Rydul didn't know how much longer he'd be able to hold out before turning this fire loose and burning them both with it. He only had another ten days, yet he wasn't sure he could keep a gentleman for much longer.

He had her in his arms, clasped against his body, swaying to the music in a polite imitation of sex, twirling and twisting against each other. His cock swelled, a visible length down the side of his thigh, hard and full, pressing against her insistently. She'd stalled a step in the middle of their dance when she felt him and finally realized what was pressing into the soft roundness of her belly and blushed furiously, darkening even further at his soft chuckle. Bending he whispered in her ear, making her shudder at the naughty words he uttered.

At the end of the dance, holding her just so to hide his reaction from the casual onlooker, he'd escorted her outside to escape embarrassment and stave off a scandal. It was then he knew from her reaction that she was a virgin, and any thought of the two of them sharing nadryl in the time he had left flew out the window with the knowledge. And he had been hoping to share nadryl with her before he'd left for home, his body screaming out to bury itself inside her and see if she truly was the one person in all of the galaxy to complete him in every way. But he did not want to chance that she would become pregnant, as had happened to the king and prince. He did not want to force her into making a decision because of circumstances. Though had that happened, he would not have left her, nor his unborn child alone on Earth. So, prior to the evening, he'd done some research and had sent the limo driver out to purchase what the humans called condoms, two of which were buried deep in a pocket even as they'd danced. He had hoped after all.

As his body cooled, he finally told her that he was returning to Taburon in little over a week. She'd stiffened at the news, turning despairing and disbelieving eyes his way. He could see the sense of betrayal she was feeling, that he had courted her, getting close and developing a relationship while knowing he was leaving and having led her on.

He'd wished he could have made it easier for her, but there was no help for either of them. The decision had been made that for the time being, until things quieted with the protestors, Earthbound tours were limited to six months, and he deeply regretted not having made her acquaintance so much earlier. And while it wouldn't make up for what he'd just done, he withdrew from his coat pocket a small box to present to her.

Blinking back tears, she opened the box to find an exquisite necklace with the bluest of jewel pendants at its heart. He explained it was a *vireck* crystal and he wanted her to have it as a gift and a remembrance from him. Taking the necklace from its bed of satin, he lifted it over her head and clasped it around her neck, turning her to gaze at the pendant as it nestled in the cleavage of her bosom. He gave her a wane smile and kissed her lips lightly, a sad sort of kiss, an apologetic sort of kiss that she didn't refuse, drinking it in hungrily, then letting him go readily. Once she'd gotten her emotions under control, he escorted her back inside, and they spent the rest of the evening in a bittersweet time together.

They met one final time, the day the ship arrived to exchange the personnel, replenish supplies and take the present unit home. Meeting in the afternoon, his bags packed, as they walked around the embassy, he asked her to go with him.

Kathryn had so wanted to, but as she explained, she had a bigger obligation to fulfill. Pib was not in the best of health and she was afraid that if she took her beloved pet on an intergalactic trip, it would kill the animal. Yet she didn't have the heart to leave her behind, not after all of the years they had spent together and all that the cat had given to her. She also couldn't just take off without first talking to her parents, not after the way her brother had disappeared. They wouldn't be able to handle her loss on top of his desertion.

Rydul was disappointed, there was no question about that, but he also understood. Loyalty was a key requisite for the King's Army, and especially within the King's Guard. If a man couldn't depend on his fellow warriors, then how was he expected to function in battle? So he knew what she was doing and why, though he wished things could have been different for both their sakes. She'd accompanied him to the landing at the military base, riding in the official embassy vehicle, her body tense, vibrating with sorrow. He'd held her hand tightly, looking forward, not daring to broach the subject again, fighting his own emotions, questioning whether or not bringing her had been the best idea.

But as he stood outside the car, holding her one last time just prior to boarding, he knew he could have never denied himself this last chance. To hold her, to kiss her, to feel her in his arms, and promise himself that he would return as soon as he could and do whatever he had to do in order to have her and keep her in his life. With reluctance, he turned away and boarded the shuttle.

Normally, he had no qualms with sharing quarters with the men, but this time, after transferring to the big ship, he bedded down in quarters alone, his heart heavy, not wanting to join in the merriment the others were feeling and celebrating at going home. He decided that as soon as they landed, he would put his name in for the first chance he could return to Earth, where he'd left his heart and soul.

But now it appeared she'd beaten him to it and was here on Taburon. His heart was racing, finding himself uncharacteristically anxious for the shuttle to lower its hatch to let the newcomers disembark. There was so much he would show her, take her to his estate, and show off his crufas and the fields of quality *freema* flowers that grew in abundance on his estate, providing a substantial income, which he reinvested in this crufa breeding program. Carefully, he urged his crufa closer to watch for her when she descended, ignoring the growls of the people on foot who also crowded closer to get a better view.

Finally the hatch of the shuttle opened and fell to the ground. First to walk off, the returning guardsmen, who marched smartly down the platform, their gear over their shoulders. From the crowd, several women raced forward to greet their men whom they'd not seen for six months, jumping into their waiting arms with enthusiastic hugs and almost embarrassing displays of affection. The men made their way further on, passing into the crowd to scatter.

As a group, the thirty humans began to descend, staring wide-eyed as they exited, looking in every possible direction to take it all in with wonder and surprise. Whatever they had expected on Taburon, this was as good as they had been told or better. A general cheer went up from the natives, a welcome for these intrepid adventurers who braved journeying to another world to make a new life and new friends.

Rydul rose in his stirrups, searching every head for the auburn haired beauty he'd missed terribly these last months, letting out a soft sigh as he saw her finally appear, looking as anxious and awestruck as the rest of her fellow passengers. She was dressed in what the humans had called jeans with a shirt that buttoned up the front tucked in the waist. Over that she'd put on a light sweater, having been informed that it was a cool day on Taburon. In one smooth move, Rydul dismounted and pushed through the crowd.

She didn't see him at first, not knowing where to look first at this new planet she was hoping to call home, until he stood nearly in front of her. "Kathryn," he greeted, his voice warm, husky.

Kathryn turned. He was here, much to her surprise. He stood tall and handsome, his uniform pressed and sharply creased, an unbuttoned jacket over his shoulders against the chill. There was his ever present sword at his side and he'd pinned several medals to the shirt inside the jacket. His hair had grown out some, now long enough to tie the ends in a short ponytail with a leather thong. But the expression in his eyes was the same – filled with that hint of laughter that she had come to love and sparkling with joy. Catching his gaze, she looked up to him, smiling warmly in return. He was pleased to see that she had worn the *vireck* necklace he'd given her on Earth. It hung snugly in the cleavage between her breasts, her skin taking on the cool color from the jewel.

Trying very hard to control himself, to keep from sweeping her up into his arms, Rydul simply took her hand. "Welcome to Taburon. I was not expecting you."

"I wanted to surprise you," she murmured.

"Oh, *Alana*, you have done that and more," he replied. And then gave in to his first desire. Scooping her up, he gave her a full body hug as he pressed his lips against hers in a kiss to beat all kisses from all time. Her feet left the ground as he straightened, holding her tightly to him, swiping her lips with his until he'd told her with only his mouth how much he had missed her and how glad he was that she was here.

She gave as good as she got, returning kiss for kiss, flattening her body as tight to him as she could until there was no distance between them, no force in the universe was capable of coming between them. They ignored the chuckles and laughter around them as they greeted each other in an endless kiss, but finally a bump from one of the other passengers broke them apart and he gently set her on the ground, though he kept his hold on her.

"I have so missed you," he said once they found a spot just beyond the end and to the side of the platform. "Did you bring Pib?" he asked, searching around for a carrier with the cat. Kathryn's eyes teared, the corners filling with drops of moisture that he saw as soon as he faced her. He cupped her cheeks with his hands. "Oh, Kathryn, I'm so sorry."

A tear fell onto her cheek. "I lost her two months ago," she managed to say with a wavering voice before more tears fell, readily and unchecked. When her pet had died, it had been Rydul she had wanted to run to to hold her through her sorrow. That he had not been there had made the loss more bitter and more profound. But now that he was here…Gathering her close again, he embraced her with sympathy, rubbing along her back, letting her get it out of her system.

"Captain, can you move on, please?" he was asked by a crewman. Rydul glanced around and realized that they were hindering the rest of the debarkation by standing so close to the platform. Wagons had begun to arrive to carry the belongings the newcomers had brought, as well as the cargo that had been shipped from Earth. Pushing her back, he slid his arm around her waist and led her away from the lines of crewmen who were beginning to unload the shuttle. The visitors, directed to the waiting carriages, would be taken to the dormitory that had been built for them until they adjusted to their new home and could find their own lodgings. Their luggage would be delivered.

Going to his crufa, Rydul swept her up onto the saddle and swung up behind her, taking the reins back in hand from a young man who had gathered them to hold for the anxious soldier once he seen the other's intent. Rydul offered his thanks with a nod, starting to urge the animal forward.

Kathryn tensed. "Is this a crufa?" she asked with wariness. He'd spoken often of the animals he wanted to breed once he left the military. And while they looked like a horse, they looked unlike any horse she could have ever imagined. The beast was broad and thick bodied as well as tall, a foot or more higher at the withers than her head. It had shaggy feet with long featherlike tufts growing from just above the hooves. From its chin there was a matching tuft of fur. The tail reached almost to the ground and was wrapped with leather thongs. It sported a heavy mane of curly fur. The head was heavy with a round muzzle. But the most unusual feature was the rounded, ram like horns that grew from either side of the top of its head, curling into a full circle that turned back on itself. She was reminded of a sheep because of the horns, and knew instinctively that were she ever butted with them, she would be seriously injured.

This particular creature was decked out in a saddle of hard leather that had been polished to a golden sheen. Under the saddle was a blanket that reached as far back as the hind end to the tip of the tail and split to join under the tail, the sides tied together, its edges braided with what appeared to be satin ribbon. Across its chest was a leather plate and over its face it wore a matching leather cover that was cinched beneath its chin.

"My favorite," he answered with pride.

"It's big," she decided.

Rydul chuckled softly. "He is as gentle as a newborn babe. You are completely safe, *Alana*." He eased the creature through the crowd with expertise. "Relax, or he will feel your fright."

"You promise he's safe?"

"Totally. His name is Ferrin. If you scratch behind his ears, he will forever fawn at your feet. How is it you say – he's a sucker for an ear scratch."

Leaning forward as much as Rydul would allow her, she dipped her fingers around the horns of the animal and through the mane to rub gently against the fur there at the base of its ears, crooning to the animal softly. Ferrin tossed his head and grumbled softly, his ears twitching, but kept a steady pace. Rydul gave the reins a slight tug to keep the animal's mind on track, but was pleased that Ferrin showed such a positive response to the strange person who'd been dumped on his back. After several moments, Kathryn straightened and sighed, letting her body flow with the rhythm of the crufa. Ferrin might have been huge, but this one was a huge pussycat underneath.

"Captain?" Kendrin interrupted his thoughts, standing in front of the crufa, forcing it to stop or run the man over. "The orders were that the humans should be kept together."

"I'll take this woman to the dormitory myself," he countermanded. "She is a personal friend."

The other scoffed, his glance shifting from one to the other, then grinned, stepping to the side. "I'd say more than friend, if that greeting were any indication."

"And you'd be right," Rydul confirmed with a wink, turning his crufa toward the city proper and the dormitory as the rest of the humans were directed into carriages.

Kathryn kept her eyes on their surroundings as he steered the crufa, meeting the stares turned her way by those attending the landing look for look, smiling pleasantly at everyone who met her eyes. Some returned her smile, some turned away from her as they passed, the distrust evident in their expressions, things little different than it had been on Earth in reverse.

Quite frankly, she was more worried about the crufa on which she sat, even with his arm encircling her waist. The animal, Ferrin, had seemed so big and frightening at first, but she was willing to give it the benefit of the doubt the longer she sat on it, especially with Rydul behind her keeping it under control. She refused to consider how well she would fare if she fell.

The landing area had been well out of the city boundaries, but close enough to see the buildings growing in the distance, light in color, clean and brightened by the sun. Unlike many Earth cities, there were plenty of trees in amongst the buildings, giving the whole area the feel of a forested village, only much bigger. The sky was turquoise clear, white clouds drifting across the horizon, the temperature pleasantly cool. She couldn't see enough of it.

"How is your head?"

"All healed." Reaching back, she released the ponytail she'd gathered her hair into, letting the strands fall about her shoulders. Parting her hair at the spot where she'd been injured, she showed him that the wound had healed completely and the hair was grown out, the strands only an inch or so shorter than the rest and easily blended into the fall of her hair. Unable to resist, he placed a light kiss over the spot before allowing her to drop the tresses. She quickly gathered them back into a loose ponytail. He vowed she would rarely do that, loving the thought of having her hair fall freely and flowing over his body as they shared nadryl.

He forced himself to change the direction of his thoughts. "Your parents, they know you came?" he asked.

"I waited until after I passed the vetting, though I was sure that I wouldn't not pass, so I saw them two weeks ago, explained that we had started something and I wanted…needed to find out if there truly was a chance for us." She rested her hand on the arm he had wrapped around her waist. "They gave me their blessing."

"Never fear, there is something between us, and I intend to show you just how strong it is," he promised. "I would you could stay with me, but I only have a room in the barracks. I will search for a place for us to stay near the palace where we can be together and alone when I am not on duty. For now, you will have to stay in the dormitory that was built for all of you, though you will have your own room there."

"We were given a schedule of sorts before we transferred to the shuttle. I am so looking forward to the tours of your planet."

"You will get to see Taburon, but your tour will be personal, I promise. I will show you everything and more. I can't wait to take you to my estate. It is as peaceful as it is beautiful, and we will be able to be completely alone. I have leave coming to me. I will tell Prince Jaima that I wish to take it as soon as possible."

"I don't want you to get into trouble."

"The prince will understand," Rydul assured her. And he knew he spoke the truth. Once he'd stowed his gear after arriving home, he'd reported to the prince, mainly to put his name in for the first opportunity to return to Earth. Hearing the anxiety in the captain's voice, Jaima had made him explain his request, and the two men had had a long talk then. Having gone through the same thing several years prior when Jaima had fallen in love with the woman who would become his wife. Having left her behind on Earth, then himself dropping into a sort of manic melancholy which was only relieved when the two had reunited, Jaima was totally in agreement with the younger's request, assuring him that he if ever needed to talk, the prince was available.

Now that she had changed the plans, he was certain that he could get the time he needed to establish and cement his love for her. Her presence assured him that she wanted to be with him, so he had no doubts about her feelings. If things went as he was now imagining, they would be married and he would finally have everything he wanted. And he was not willing to take his time about it either.

"In the meantime, you must get settled. There are some events you should attend before we can get away – there is a welcoming mid-morning meal planned for all of you for two days from now where you will be officially greeted by the king."

"And the queen?"

"I do not know if she will attend. She is expecting and heavy with child, she tires easily. As does the princess, who is further along than the queen. You will be given today to settle in, have a light sunset meal and a long rest. Tomorrow is the demonstration tournament."

There was a dreamy quality to her voice. "That sounded so exciting when we were told about it. Knights in shining armor and all that, like in medieval times."

He chuckled, knowing what she was talking about, having looked it up while on Earth after she'd mentioned the warriors of old when she'd first caught him training. She'd said the swords reminded her of tales of days when chivalry was the code of men and they rode off into battle on white horses wearing suits of metal armor. "We do not ride white horses or wear shining armor," he corrected with laughter. "Your small animals could never hold us, and we wear leather instead." He pulled the crufa to a stop, easing the tension on the reins. "Have you brought a scarf with you? Or a handkerchief?"

Leaning back, she twisted to gaze up at him and his strange request. "No, I don't think so. Why?"

"I will be competing in the tournament and would like to wear your colors." With his knees, he urged the animal to move. "I will find something to give to you that you can then return to me. Wear blue. I have a blue sash that will suffice."

"I would be honored," she answered.

"The honor is mine, *Alana,* believe me." He placed a kiss on her forehead, then slipped his mouth down to cover hers with a second kiss. "It is mine," he breathed against her mouth. "You are mine."

Sky Clad Rydul

CHAPTER EIGHT

Rydul pulled Ferrin to stop, twisting in his saddle to make sure Kathryn had no trouble stopping her beast. While she still pulled on the reins a little too hard, the animal recognized the inexperience of its rider and came to a standstill, snuffling loudly as it stomped one hoof on the ground. Kathryn's look of relief was obvious and heartfelt. With a smile, Rydul stood in his saddle.

"We'll spend the night here," he stated, swinging a leg over the pommel and sliding down the animal's side to drop to the ground. Tugging the reins over the animal's head, he let them fall to the ground. Should the crufa take more than a few steps forward, it would step on its own reins and stop itself. The crufa bent its head to the nearest source of foliage and began to nibble.

At Kathryn's side, he put his hands to her waist. "Ready?" he asked. She nodded as she straightened and leaned back slightly. Holding her firmly to keep her from falling, she also swung her leg over her saddle and let her body drop, Rydul directing her the entire way, sneaking in a full body rub as she slipped down, grinning the entire time, a growl deep in his throat as he realized his own folly in igniting fires he couldn't put out quite yet. Kathryn sighed. He'd been teasing her like this ever since she'd arrived - subtle and not so subtle touches that let her know he wasn't going to wait much longer for them to make love. Her time as a virgin was growing very short.

He kept his grip on her until she stood steady on her own. As she stretched her back, he grabbed the reins of her crufa and then those of his and led the beasts to another bush where he tied them off, twining the leather around the branches. Kathryn took a look around.

A hot spring about ten feet across rippled gently fifteen feet away. Surrounded by large flat boulders and thick brush, it presented as a perfect oasis, private and inviting. A large cleared area, grassy and blue-green, made for an ideal spot to lay out the bedrolls.

Beyond the spring the landscape stretched miles without a man-made structure in sight – just tress, bushes, open flatland, all bordered in the far distance by the mountain range, the peaks topped with white.

Above the spring, the steam that rose from it stirred and swirled with a light breeze. The water would be invigorating, the air temperatures on their skin once exiting the water brisk.

Rydul began to unlace the packs from the crufas, bringing one over to set closest to Kathryn. "If you'll unpack the cookware, I'll get the rest of the camp set up." He went back.

"Of course." She bent to the task, opening the pack.

"What'll be?" he asked, dragging a heavy bundle from the back of her ride. "Bedrolls or tents?"

Kathryn paused from stacking the cookware to glance skyward. "I assume there's no rain or other bad weather coming?"

"Not a drop."

"Then bedrolls," she chose.

"I was hoping you'd say that. I prefer not using a tent."

She resumed setting things aside, organizing them neatly. "My family camped out once when we were children. My mother decided that she didn't care for it. Her idea of roughing it meant a decent hotel with a connecting restaurant. We never went again."

Rydul dropped to his haunches, setting the bundles on the ground. "One of the first things we learn in basic training," he said, "how to set up a camp, take care of ourselves, cook our own meals." Unlacing the combination bedrolls and tent, separating the two items and placing the tent to the right side near where he stooped, Rydul pulled a folded shovel from between the tent folds, extended and locked the handle, rose then started peering intently at the ground nearby. He turned in a circle as he searched for something.

"What are you looking for?"

"Where the last person to spend the night here built their fire, if they did. I'd rather not dig a new hole." He stepped three feet to his right. "See here?" he asked. "The grass is slightly different, as though it has been disturbed." He pushed the shovel into the ground, shoving it deeper with the edge of his booted foot.

Removing a three inch deep, one and a half foot wide piece of ground, he set it aside, roots down so as to not lose moisture, then began to dig deeper, making a pile of the dirt. Once he was satisfied with the hole, he gathered a dozen or so rocks to line the bottom. He set four hand sized rocks in a square pattern around the outside rim.

"Give me that grate," he asked, pointing to the piece of metal. He placed it on the four rocks to create a platform for the cookware. "When we're ready, I'll add wood and start the fire. If you will gather sticks and make a pile over here, I'll finish setting up camp."

Tending to their chores, within a half hour the camp was completed, bedrolls laid out and waiting, dinner set aside for preparation. He'd shown her where and what to do if she had to relieve herself, then turned his back, bedding down the crufas for the night as she made use of the 'facilities.' Rydul stretched, arching his back.

"I don't know about you, but that *lavella* looks very inviting."

Kathryn looked beyond Rydul to the hot spring he indicated, steam rising visibly. She agreed, it looked very inviting and she was beginning to feel the effects of riding on the crufa for the near long day. They'd left just after sunrise and while she'd ridden horses before, they were small compared to the large beast he'd tied off in front of the dormitory. Her back, thigh and crotch ached, and her butt felt bruised, though she knew the saddle had been comfortable and the ride steady without bouncing. But her muscles were protesting, both physically and vehemently, and a good long soak would be immensely welcomed and ease the discomfort. There was only one problem.

"I didn't bring a bathing suit," she informed him.

He was already shedding his shirt. "Why would you need a bathing suit?"

There was surprise and wariness in her voice. "Go naked?"

His smile was as sexy as it was mischievous. "We are both adults. I trust you will not accost me?" His shirt fell to the bedroll.

He didn't know how tempted she'd been to do exactly that in her apartment that night after her injury, with or without a skull fracture. He was so handsome, a protector, and warrior. But oh, did he have the most gorgeous body, a chest that was sculpted and hard, his pectorals outlined through the material of his shirt, the male nipples hard buds. She later discovered that he had washboard abs that disappeared into the low waistband of his trousers. His smile was devastating when he turned it on full force and he had those eyes sparkled with delight as easily as they did with danger.

His manhood had been clearly outlined, long and thick, down the side of his right thigh. An impressive piece of flesh, she had been both fascinated and frightened by it the first time it had come to her attention; wanting to rid herself of that pesky virginity but unsure if this man was the right choice to accomplish the task without shredding her body. She may have been innocent, but she wasn't naïve, and the internet was full of information that she looked up. The horror stories she'd heard and read from other women of men who showed no concern or their partners she could not allow to color her ideal of her first time.

He'd shown restraint that initial night at her apartment, proving himself considerate, taking care of her without making inappropriate overtures, treating her as a gentleman should. Even that night at the party, when they'd danced, their bodies so close she couldn't help but feel his cock pressed into her, he'd kept control, taking them outside so he could cool off and not prove an embarrassment to either of them. Though his cheeks had been colored nearly as much as her own when she'd glanced up at him.

Surely he would show the same restraint if – when - she gave herself to him. While he was big, and most likely would grow larger before initiating actual intercourse, her body should be able to handle his size with minimum problems. After all, a baby's head passed through where he would join their flesh. And the two human women married to Taburon men didn't seem to have any reservations about their husbands, not suffering in their physical relationship and if rumors were true, relishing it fully.

By the time she came out of her musings, focusing on Rydul, he had begun to toe off his boots, quirking an eyebrow in question at her as he placed them next to the bedroll. Rather than respond vocally, Kathryn reached up to begin unbuttoning her shirt.

Rydul withheld his sigh of relief. He'd started to doubt she would allow herself the freedom to abandon her modesty and enjoy herself in some innocent nudity. Not that he wasn't dying to see her naked.

The few brief glimpses he'd had of her in clothes, such as her summer tops while she sat outside the embassy, the night of the party in that dress that threatened to fall from her breasts at any moment, the feel of her body tight against his as they danced had sent all of his blood racing to his man parts with a vengeance and intense desire. He wanted her, pure and simple. He wanted to sink himself in her body, to taste her essence, to be joined with her as they both flew apart in the ultimate ecstasy then floated back to reality and the real world. He wanted to cuddle with her afterwards, a sweet denouement to a satisfying union and slide into somnolence.

Rydul knew he could spend the rest of his life with her, that he was in love with this human woman, and it had happened as easily as taking a breath. The days after he'd returned to Taburon had been just days spent going about his duties with little excitement or color, plodding from one assignment and training to the next. Only after finding her name on the manifest had he felt his heart begin to beat again, to race and his blood pound, more grounded and complete than ever before. He knew then why the one time he'd sought out a *skala* to relieve some of his pent up tension had ended in failure. No one came close to Kathryn. He'd been waiting only for Kathryn.

While he kept his eyes glued to her face as she disrobed, his peripheral vision did not miss the splendor she revealed as her clothes hit the ground piece by piece.

Her breasts fell free of the binding garment she wore – a bra he recalled – as full and firm as he'd imagined, wine colored nipples peaked to hardness and upthrust. She would fill his hands and overflow. Her skin was flushed – he hoped from arousal but conceded more likely from embarrassment.

He could span her waist with his hands. There was the smallest of indentations in the center of her belly. The curls that covered her mound perfectly matched the waves of hair that fell from her head – a dark auburn. He thought he detected a hint of moisture clinging to the ends of the curls.

Her hips, thighs and calves were trim, leading to narrow ankles and tapered feet. She'd colored the nails of her toes the same shade of soft pink as that on her fingernails.

Catching him watching her surreptitiously, she began to lift her hands to cover her breasts and mound, then let them hang at her sides with an audacious expression, daring and cheeky.

Boldly he let his gaze travel down her body, taking in every dip and curve, then slid it back up to her face and smiled. "You are absolutely beautiful," he breathed.

Her expression softened at the compliment, her flush darkening. "And I'm the only one completely naked," she challenged.

His smile widened into a grin as he unfastened his trousers and peeled them down his legs. When he straightened, topping the small pile of his clothes with the trousers, his cock stood straight out from his groin, pointing right at her.

What she hadn't seen while still on Earth was revealed to her now. He had no hair on his body, just a small u-shaped patch growing right over his manhood. His hips were lean, his thighs thick and muscled. His feet were long making her wonder about that saying she'd heard about men's feet in relation to the length of their cock. Obviously, whomever had made the observation hadn't met Taburons.

He chuckled at her wide eyed look. He'd gotten the impression that McKenna and Joanna had had the same reaction upon first seeing their Taburcn men in all their naked glory. It hadn't kept them from sharing nadryl and enjoying it, if rumors were true. The women were enthusiastic lovers, their husbands well satisfied. Kathryn would learn and adjust.

Rydul held his hand out in invitation. "Ignore him," he explained. "He's just happy right now."

She slid her hand into his as she laughed. "I'd say a little more than happy," she pointed out.

"He'll behave himself, I promise." Dragging her closer, he turned her around, itching to take her heart-shaped arse cheeks in hand and touch to his heart's content. Instead, he began to pull the pins and combs she used in her hair to tie it back and off her neck, dropping the articles to the bedroll at his feet. He turned her around. With all of the restraints out, he finger combed through her tresses until they fell softly around her shoulders and across her chest, hiding those luscious breasts from view, especially those delightful nipples. "There," he decided, "like the *riscuas* from the stories my mother used to tell me as a child."

"Riscuas?" she asked as she turned back to face him.

"Mythical women who live in the forests, speaking to and attending the creatures there. You can never see her, for she can turn into a mist in less than a heartbeat. But she will play with children in her own way and delights in leaving small gifts for the good ones."

Kathryn's head slanted. "And the bad ones?" He could tell from the tease in her voice that she knew he'd not always been a 'good' child. No child was ever always a good child.

"I was never a bad child," he answered indignantly, leading her to the spring.

"I doubt that," she corrected.

"I swear that I had nothing to do with the *rigi* my mother had made that morning disappearing later that day. Just because I broke out in a rash that night…"

"Riscua's revenge?" she asked insightfully.

"Allergies," he responded. "At least that's what we found out later. Never got to eat *rigi* again, unfortunately. They're very good. Careful, the water can be hot."

Kathryn tested with her foot, dipping her toes into the top of the water. "It's warm, but tolerable."

Rydul stepped into the pool, the water covering him to his hips. "There is a ledge here. Be careful," he warned, though he kept her hand in his.

Once she joined him, he turned and sat on the ledge, placing her in front of him between his legs. The water came up to his chest while it covered, to his dismay, her gorgeous breasts.

Kathryn leaned back, her head resting on his shoulder. She could feel his cock, still hard, possibly even harder, digging into her spine. Rydul kneaded her neck. "You're tight."

"Sore from riding so long."

He continued to knead until he felt her relax further, her muscles going lax, her body melting into him. Only she tensed when his hands then moved from her neck down her waist to smooth along her thighs and grab her knees. As he started to part her legs, she resisted, snapping them closed, her hands taking hold of his arms.

He chuckled, pushing against her resistance. "The warmth will soothe those aching muscles," he chided, "but only of you allow it to go where it needs to go."

After a moment, he felt her relax her legs and he parted them, rubbing her knees and keeping his hands well away from the part of her that ached the most. Instantly the warmth spread along the inside of her thighs and between her legs, soothing her pussy and the area of her buttocks that had thumped repeatedly against the saddle.

Rydul rubbed along her thighs, keeping clear of the place he most wanted to touch and explore, but wouldn't without some sort of signal of acquiescence from her. She sighed softly, her body easing even more, leaning into the vee of his thighs and the hollow of his shoulder. "Better?" he asked after a moment.

"Heaven," she whispered, not wanting to disturb the tranquility.

"Couple of weeks riding and you'll get used to it."

"Weeks?" she asked, alarmed.

"Yes. It's ride or walk. It took me a few days to regain my seat after being on Earth for so long. I wish I'd ridden some of your horses while at the embassy."

"I think I'll stick to walking," she decided. "Crufas scare me."

"They're as gentle as a newborn babe," he refuted with a mild affront.

"They look as big as a house," she rebutted. "I'm afraid I'll break every bone in my body if I fall."

His voice was filled with humor. "Then I shall have to teach you the proper way to fall."

"Oh, goody," she retorted.

He chuckled, his hands moving to her spine to rub along the vertebra. She began to melt as he ministered to her. "You must do this often," she murmured after a while. "You know just where it hurts the most."

"You are the first woman I have done this for. Most people learn how to ride while they are young so they grow up without suffering sore muscles from prolonged rides."

"Lucky them."

He leaned closer to whisper in her ear, nuzzling with his lips. "I could take your mind off of your sore muscles," he offered. With his lips, he pulled at the soft skin just under her ear, then licked it with just the tip of his tongue.

Her breath hitched. "Rydul," she whispered huskily, caught up in the desires he was creating with his mouth and hands. First he pulled her even tighter against his body, his erection prodding into her spine. He then moved those strong, capable hands to her waist, inches from her breasts. All he had to do was turn them over and he could fill them with her flesh.

"Um?" he asked, concentrating on the area just under her ear where her neck met her throat, his mouth exploring along her hairline until it settled at the back of her neck. The skin there was soft and warmed. He nuzzled under the line of her hair.

Kathryn knew she had to confess. They were naked in a hot spring. He was obviously very aroused though he'd made a promise to behave. And if she were honest with herself, she was so aroused as well, her blood racing through her body, sending tingles down to her fingers and toes, her breasts felt fuller and her nipples were so tight and brick-hard that they almost hurt all by themselves. There was a discomfort between her legs, a desperate longing and want that she needed to find an answer to, to complete, to fill an emptiness that was threatening to overwhelm her.

She'd come to Taburon to see what a new life could offer. She'd come because he called to her across the heavens, to explore the possibilities she'd thought had been created while he'd been on Earth. Her attraction to him had only grown once he'd left. The only thing that had held her back was her devotion to Pib and the promise she'd made to the animal as a kitten to never abandon her or do her harm. Kathryn had truly feared for the effects traveling across the galaxy might have had on her pet had she made the trip with Pib. She'd held her obligation to her pet with extreme high regard.

Nor could she simply fly off to a new world without the approval of her parents, never knowing when she might see them again, if ever. The loss of her brother had been hurtful enough for the two people. She had to know they would be okay without her, knowing she was happy with her decision, knowing she was going to find the man who moved her heart and filled her soul.

But while she and Rydul had discussed so many things during the beginning of their relationship, hope and love budding but still so very new, she'd never told him her deepest secret. She had assumed he was an experienced man, he appeared to know his way around a woman as easily as he did a stove and she did a set of numbers. But she had read that there were many men who had no interest in virgins, preferring an experienced woman they didn't have to teach the ins and outs – no pun – of sex. The thought had crossed her mind to seek out a one night stand, to give her at least the first encounter to correct her 'flaw,' but the thought became more and more abhorrent the longer she thought about it. So she kept her virginity and hoped he wouldn't mind. She didn't want to lose him.

"Rydul," she repeated, "I've never…never…" It was hard to think while he nibbled at her neck. She took a deep breath, shifting her body, restless with nervous energy. "I've never made love."

"I know," he answered, lifting his head from his nuzzling as she twisted to face him. "Any man who uses his head with the actual brain in it can recognize the signs."

"What signs?"

He caressed her cheek. "You flush easily, your pupils dilate. There's a want in your expression that you're not sure about that you hide by crossing your arms over your stomach. You shift nervously when aroused. Shall I go on?"

"I didn't realize I was so obvious."

"I wasn't completely sure until the time we danced and I held you close. When I became aroused, you seemed surprised by the feel of my cock against your body. I could tell part of you wanted to continue rubbing against me, yet part of you was confused by your reaction. I found it charming."

She snorted softly. "I'd have been embarrassed if I'd known."

"You were. I think you were embarrassed enough feeling my wayward cock prodding you. You cannot hide the redness of your blush, like now. You look lovely with pink in your cheeks." He dropped a kiss on her nose. "But I gave my word. You are safe from me – unless you change your mind," he added seductively. "Then all promises are off."

Sky Clad Rydul

CHAPTER NINE

Kathryn turned to study his face, the honesty in his eyes not really tempering the desire. Smoothing her hands down his arms she recalled the strength in them, the ease with which he held her and power with which he'd wielded his sword. He was a warrior, but he was a protector, a man vowed to give his all if called upon to right wrongs and defend the honor of those around him. She sincerely believed with every fiber of her being he could be trusted, with her life, with her secrets, with her body, and with her heart.

She turned, straddling his lap, her legs wrapping around his waist as he scooted forward on the ledge to give her feet room behind his back. Cupping his cheeks in her palms, she gazed into his eyes. The lighthearted expression gave way to seriousness as he sensed the change in her mood. As she traced along his jaw, she watched the fingers of her hand, her lips pursed slightly, hazel eyes dilated until the pupils were round, a window into her thoughts. "I'm going to tell you something I've never told another man. If you don't feel the same, I'll understand. And I don't expect anything in return…"

"I love you," he interrupted. Kathryn stopped mid-sentence, her jaw hanging open in surprise until he closed it with a single fingertip to her chin. "Was that what you were going to say?"

Her gaze lowered to his throat where she stared as if looking for an answer. She counted the pulse beats for a half minute before nodding. Wow. Today was going to be the day for confessions on both their parts. Though she was glad that he had beat her to the punch, for gearing up to say the words had taken a great deal of courage on her part. She had thought it was going to be much more difficult. Turned out that all she had to do was say the words. "I think I fell in love with you before you left Earth. I missed you so much. My dreams were filled with your face and I only thought about you maybe twenty times a day. I couldn't get you out of my head and after a while, I discovered I didn't want to"

"And I was sure the moment I saw you again as you stepped off that ship. So what do you want to do about it?"

Kathryn's response was to undulate her hips along his thighs causing his cock to jerk, bouncing up against her feminine folds. Her pussy pulsed as it was kissed by his manhood, swelling and heating beyond the surrounding heat of the *lavella*.

Rydul cupped her buttocks, willing to accept her invitation. "Are you sure, Kathryn?"

Clasping her hands around his neck, Kathryn's breasts flattened to his chest. "When I boarded that ship to come here, I was terrified. I didn't know if you'd even remember me, let alone want to spend time with me. That you love me makes the whole thing – leaving my job, my family, my planet – worth all the chances in the world." She moved her hips again more insistently. "I have never been more sure about anything than I am right now."

Bending, he took her mouth with his, plundering her lips, taking her breath into his mouth before returning it to her. He swiped along her lips, the soft, warm flesh swelling as he slid back and forth, the tip of his tongue breaching his lips to taste her, tease her, coax her to open and let him in.

He felt her stiffen at first, then relax as he found purchase and entrance into the warm cavern of her mouth, and he held her until he felt her allow herself to fall into his kiss and experience it fully. With a tentative touch, she used the tip of her tongue to touch his, giving in to a dance between the two of them as he explored and let her explore his mouth. She was naïve, inexperienced, and he was going to delight in being her teacher.

His eyes were lit with a light, a sparkle that gleamed from within as they parted and he caressed her face along her cheek. Both were breathing heavily. "I am going to enjoy teaching you about sharing nadryl," he murmured. "But you must promise me one thing. If you ever feel uncomfortable, or hurt, if I do anything you do not like, you must tell me. You are a virgin and I am a large man, even more so than other Taburon males. I know you will feel some discomfort in the beginning, but your body will adjust in time. I will try to be as gentle as I can."

She nodded, finding his chest fascinating, her thoughts on what he had said, what was coming. And she was a little frightened, as she was sure many were at the idea of the first time they were to have sex. Losing one's virginity, she had read, could be painful.

"Kathryn, you can change your mind," he granted. "I will not be offended, though a little disappointed. I so want to share nadryl with you."

"Share nadryl?"

"It is what we call making love. I know your people say they fuck, but that sounds so mechanical and unloving, an act of need instead of passion. We have always said share nadryl."

"I like it," she determined, "and you're right. The other term does sound like something a person does without emotion or connection for their partner. And no, I don't want to change my mind. I want you to teach me, I want to know what makes you feel wonderful."

"You do, Kathryn. Being here with me feels wonderful. Knowing we have something to give each other feels wonderful. Knowing there's a future with you in it with me feels wonderful. You are so beautiful, Kathryn. I am a very fortunate man." This time his kiss was more loving, more gentle, a vow he was making with his mouth, a promise for now, for the future, forever. "Touch me," he murmured against her lips. "Take my cock in your hands. If I come now, I won't be so anxious later. I want to be inside you so much, I couldn't promise to not be hard on you if I try it now."

"I don't know what to do," she confessed.

Placing his hands behind him on the edges of the spring, with a heave, Rydul lifted himself from the water to set his arse on the edge. He spread his legs, his cock fully extended and heavy, his balls hanging down between his thighs, two large eggs that swung freely. A crescent moon swath of sodden curls hovered over the base of his cock.

That particular piece of man flesh was tumescent, engorged, the head dark purplish in color, with thick veins running along its length. The crown was split with a deep slit from which dangled a whitish pearl drop, precariously holding on until it lengthened and finally fell into the water between them.

Kathryn had stared at the drop of pre-cum as it formed then fell, her first close up look at the organ that was going to finally make her fully fledged woman. His confident expression when she looked to him encouraged her and she lifted slightly to rest her arms on his thighs and her knees on the ledge in the spring.

He smiled as he ran a hand through her hair. "It won't bite," he promised, "though he might enjoy a little nibble or two from you." Rydul chuckled as her eyes widened. "Just wrap your fingers around him and rub up and down. Not too hard, but firmly. You can play with my balls, roll them around in your hands and squeeze them lightly. Lean closer so I can play with your breasts and your gorgeous nipples."

Tentatively, her hands encircled his cock. "It's so soft, yet so hard," she whispered. "And so big."

Bending, he tipped her chin up and placed a kiss on her lips. "It'll fit when the time comes." Keeping his back bent, he reached under her to cup her breasts, one in each hand.

Turning her attention to his cock, Kathryn started a gentle smoothing motion along his shaft, feeling every dent and indentation, following each vein individually, patently ignoring the tugging he was giving to her nipples, rolling the hardened nubs between his fingers. When she checked his face, his eyes were closed, but he kept moving his fingers and hands on her breasts.

He couldn't help but stiffen slightly when she found that one spot just under the helmet of his cock where he was he most sensitive, his breath hitching. Seeing his reaction, she lightly scratched under there again with just the tip of her fingernail, causing him to react the same again. Seeing she was determined to tickle there again, he stayed her with one hand.

"Sensitive?"

"Very. Too much."

Deviously, she did it again, pleased with his soft hiss. With her thumb, she swiped at the second burgeoning drop of pre-cum that gathered at the tip, keeping it on her thumb.

The fluid had a musky but not unpleasant scent, an exotic aroma that brought to mind desert sands and tropical climes. Remembering what he'd said about nibbling, she tasted the drop with the tip of her tongue, then licked the rest of it completely off her digit. The slight salty taste was not off-putting and she sucked her entire thumb into her mouth, looking up at him with a sultry expression.

"Gods' rods!" he breathed, "That's beautiful, watching you taste me." If Rydul had thought his heart stopped at her innocently decadent gesture, he was positive his body was entirely paralyzed when she cupped his balls in one hand, encircled his shaft with the other and licked the end of his cock with her tongue. A long, deep, slow lick that started at the base of his cock with the back of her tongue to the underside of his cock and swept to the tip of her tongue at the tip of his organ, pointed and dipping into the slit there to gather more moisture.

"Again," he rasped. If she did this naturally, she would kill him once she perfected her technique. He'd die a happy man.

Kathryn hadn't been sure of what to do, but with everything she tried, his reaction indicated that he liked her attempts. She remembered watching videos of women giving head as they called it, hoping that men were the same here as on Earth. Oh she knew the men in the videos were actors and could get a hard-on and come at the drop of a hat, but there were times when it seemed as though they really enjoyed what the girls did to them, and in all honesty, she didn't think a man couldn't easily fake an orgasm. So she tried to remember what she'd seen and put it into practice now.

He bodily shuddered as she licked his entire length once more, finally taking the end into her mouth. She had to open wide to accommodate his girth, but the head fit in with a gentle suck as her tongue danced around the mushroom shaped cap.

With her cheeks sunken, she sucked more of his cock inside her mouth, placing the organ on her tongue, increasing the pressure as she slid back and forth along his length, holding the base with her free hand, the other cupping his balls. He sank further inside the warm cavern of her mouth until near half of his cock was engulfed inside. As tempted as he was to pump his cock, to start a steady thrusting motion, he held himself in check, not wanting to frighten or discourage her. They had a lifetime together to learn and experiment, the day would come when she might be able to take his entire shaft in her mouth and down her throat. This was the time to let her experiment on her own, to learn her own limits and test her own resolve. He reminded himself to pinch her nipples but not too harshly. He didn't want to hurt her before he got to the good parts.

Kathryn determined to make the experience as pleasant as possible for Rydul, and swallowed more of his cock until it touched on the very entrance to her throat. When she felt as though she was going to choke and her breath was blocked, she retreated, never releasing the organ in its entirety, swirling her tongue around the head as she pulled away. He continued to leak pre-cum which she licked greedily, finding she liked the flavor and the heat of his fluids. She tightened her grip at the base of his cock, rubbing up and down the parts that weren't engulfed in her mouth, his balls starting to pull up into his body in preparation for his orgasm.

Increasing the pressure of her sucking, she pulled on his cock harder, the suction intense, her tongue teasing around the head and delving into the slit to lick out the musky fluids. Rydul knew he was close – it had been so long since he'd had nadryl – small spurts of cum spitting out in signal to his impending orgasm.

"I'm going to come," he ground out. "Release me unless you want a mouthful," he warned.

Kathryn leaned back, not sure that she wanted to experience the shooting of cum into her mouth and down her throat to settle in her stomach. Not on her first try at least. With her fingers still wrapped around the base of his cock, she pumped his shaft with the other. His balls drew up even tighter until they seemed to disappear and his body tightened. With a resonant groan from Rydul that came from deep in his chest, a stream of milky white fluid shot out from the end of his cock with a sharp blast.

The dip in her throat took the first shot, coated with viscous fluid. Rising higher, she aimed the next blast to her breasts, the spurt hitting her directly on her left nipple, then the right one as he erupted again immediately. His hips jerked and he grunted with the final spurt of seed. Whatever remained dripped readily from the tip of his cock until he was emptied and Rydul collapsed to the ground, sighing. His cock started to deflate, its relaxed size still larger than most human males even when erect. Kathryn smoothed the crème into her skin, watching as he took deep breaths.

"Gods' rods, woman, if that's what you do when you have no experience, I dread when you've gained more knowledge." He took a deep breath. "You'll be the death of me."

She scooted forward and rose enough to lay her torso across his groin, his cock nestled in the cleavage of her breasts. "I hope not."

He suddenly sat up. "I am so going to love teaching you and being your willing victim." He slipped into the water, taking her into his arms while she still faced him. "Come, wash up. I have plans for you."

Sky Clad Rydul

CHAPTER TEN

Rydul added more wood to the fire he'd started in the pit
he'd dug earlier, stirring the ashes so that those hottest below
were brought to the top to ignite the new wood. They'd
exited the *lavella*, running to their bedrolls to grab blankets
and wrap them around their bodies. Digging through her
pack, Kathryn took out a brush, dropped to her bedroll and
began to brush the knots out of her hair.

After he'd gotten their dinner cooking, Rydul, having
seen what she was doing, stepped over the sleeping beds and
knelt behind her, taking the brush from her hands. He
continued to brush out the long strands and once the knots
were out and her hair drier, he separated the strands into
three parts to braid. He'd surprised her yet again with his

ability, never expecting a man to know how to do this seemingly feminine and simple act. She was wowed, he cooked, cleaned, read a girl's thoughts and braided hair. Definitely a keeper.

He explained that often they braided the tails of the *crufas* before going into tournaments and during times of fighting. It also gave him another chance to get his hands on her since he coupled taking care of her hair with caresses and touches. He milked it for all he could as long as he could, only stopping when the scent of dinner began to fill the camp area and he needed to tend to it.

Dressing in a pair of loose training togs, he tossed her one of his shirts to don while he stirred their meal, a stew, and began to spoon it into bowls for them. Handing one to Kathryn, they sat side by side on their bedrolls and ate in pleasant companionship, talking low and of non-important things. After they'd eaten, he took her bowl and his own to clean, telling her to pull the bedrolls together next to each other then take off the shirt since he intended to follow through on the plans he'd promised to her earlier. A moment later he changed his mind and asked her to keep the shirt on, that she would be a delightful gift to unwrap. Kathryn had no objections – the downy shirt, softened from wear, smelled like him, exotic, spicy, and warm, and she wanted to keep it with her as long as possible.

She watched from the combined bedding as he straightened the camp, packing away the utensils and making sure the food was secured for the night. Slipping out of his togs, he grabbed a carafe of wine and two glasses to bring to where she waited, the blanket wrapped around her barely clothed body. The slowly setting sun had brought with it a chill to the air which gave her goosebumps and tightened her nipples. It seemed to have had no effect on his body though, his shaft long and heavily engorged.

He poured a glass for her, then one for himself, setting the carafe aside as he lowered himself next to her. "Open," he ordered, indicating the blanket. She drew one side out and he scooted inside, snuggling up to her from behind, his own glass in hand.

"This is delicious," she said after tasting her wine.

"It's *Bakkan*, the best on the planet. Never find any better."

"I'm honored that you believe me worthy of it."

"Of this and more, *Olana*. Always." He lessen the space between them, his crotch touching her bottom, his legs wrapping around her hips to hold her in place. He would find out that he wouldn't need much to get her engine revved for the rest of the night. Once he'd lost his togs, and started walking around the camp site in the nude, her heart had sped up every time she'd dared to glance up and watch. Kneeling, walking, bending, his cock had become engorged again, bouncing and swaying with his movements, a constant reminder of what she'd already done with him and what was to come. He was all man, an Adonis in the flesh, comfortable within his own skin, more than she'd ever expected for herself, and right now, this night, he was all hers. With one arm around her waist, he shelved her left breast and cupped the right one, gently taking the nipple under the material in hand, strumming casually over the bud with his thumb. With the blanket hiding his actions from any strangers, she was already hot and heating further with his ministrations. Kathryn felt herself sway.

"What does it mean?" she asked dreamily.

"What does what mean?" he replied, his lips never ceasing.

"Olana. You called me *alana* earlier, but just now you said *olana*."

He gave her neck one long swipe with his tongue before lifting his head, his mouth close to her ear. "Alana means dear one, a term of affection. Olana means beloved, what you are to me."

"Is there a version for a man?"

"They are one and the same."

"So, if I called you *olana*, it would mean beloved?"

His voice was husky. "It would mean the world to me." A light kiss to the side of her neck, a swift nibble, a cool lick to soothe, and she moaned in rising want. He was playing a high stakes game here, the prize a lifetime of happiness. And Rydul had no intention of losing.

"How are you doing?" he asked giving her nipple a pinch that made her catch her breath. The pain softened to a kind of energy that traveled without hesitation directly to her pussy and settled there, thrumming with need. His hand followed unerringly.

She shuddered. "The wine is going to my head," she replied.

"Among other places," he discovered, finding a place in the nest of hair that covered her pussy and delving through the curls. She was so wet already, so hot, swollen, and soft. "Spread your legs for me," he asked. Obeying, his fingers went deeper, taking up her moisture and spreading it over her feminine lips. Parting those petals with his questing fingers, he unerringly found her clit, pulsing and engorged with blood, begging for attention. "You're soaking wet," he murmured close to her ear, "and engorged here," he added, coating her clit with her fluids.

Kathryn squirmed as he toyed with her, tapping the little bundle of nerves, rubbing along either side of it, the saddle area, where a goodly number of nerves resided and he'd once discovered could bring a woman to orgasm just by rubbing there. Her head dropped against his shoulder and she opened her mouth to breathe, a soft moan issuing unbidden.

Her skin flushed and she heated even more, especially her pussy, but he wasn't ready to let her come quite yet. Withdrawing his fingers, he brought them to his mouth and inserted the ones glistening with her juices, sucking them in with relish. "Sweet," he commented, "the sweetest nectar ever, and all woman. I can't wait to taste it from the source."

"You're killing me," she groaned.

"Gods' rods, I hope not," he argued. "At least, not for a while yet. I've heard said that when some women orgasm, they seem to die a little death, the emotion is so strong." He placed a kiss on her ear. "Maybe you'll be one of those women," he suggested.

"I suspect if there is anyone who can bring that out in me, it's you."

"Ah, a compliment I shall try my best to live up to." Kathryn giggled softly, drinking the last of her wine. Rydul finished his, taking both of their glasses to set them by the sleeping bags but out of the way, in case they got a little energetic. When he tossed the edges of the blanket aside, she knew the time had come.

Her stomach fluttered, her body trembled slightly. She wasn't naïve, just inexperienced, and this man was about to take her through the first steps of becoming a woman. She hoped she didn't disappoint him with her lack of knowledge. That he wouldn't find her unacceptable after. She realized that there was so much more to a relationship; looks were one part and emotions were another. But a good physical relationship was the last ingredient, and if a man wasn't satisfied, the rest could hold very little weight in keeping a relationship going. At least, that's how things had become on her planet the last dozen years or so.

Her fantasies had her being swept off her feet by a man, a faceless being, who would take her to place where no one ever intruded on their time together. Where he put her needs on an equal par with his own and not see her as just some place to satisfy his cock and maybe get a child or two out of her, or tire of her if she didn't measure up to his ideals and discard her. She dreamed of a life –long love, a relationship built on caring, trust, and respect.

Then the Taburons arrived and her fantasy man suddenly had a face, a voice, a body and her dreams not only took on a sense of reality, but a sense of futility – for she would never have a chance to meet any of the tall warriors. And why would she – a simple CPA with no ties that would get her through their doors, no way to find herself in their company.

Then fate – or fortune – had stepped in and given her fondest desire life, even if for a short period of time. And her fantasy man had eyes that seemed to always spark with humor, a smile that stretched readily across his face, and a personality that said honor, bravery, loyalty, and mostly, respect for her as a person and a woman.

And while she never would have wished ill to her beloved Pib, when the cat had succumbed to fate, a great weight had been lifted off her shoulders to allow her to feel real hope. Contacting the ambassador to see if she could go to Taburon to find him landed her on the first ship of settlers with ease. And Rydul still wanted her, remembered her and loved her. There were no obligations here except to each other, right now, to explore deeper about each other, to cement what had started on Earth.

She appreciated that he had given her the chance to experiment with him, patient with her at her first blow job, considerate that this would be her first time when she'd only expected to be laid on her back, her legs spread and he would thrust himself into her body. She trusted that he would conscientiously make the experience loving and joyful, his concern not for getting his satisfaction, but her pleasure. Her confidence in herself for the next hours soared.

His hand delved between her thighs again, running through the curls until he parted her folds, finding her wetness, coating his fingers with her moisture before searching out the opening to her body. "Are you still intact?"

"Intact?"

"Your maidenhood," he explained. "Some women's maidenhoods are broken before they actually engage in nadryl." He circled her opening, spreading the moisture before pressing forward slightly. He felt her tense. "Have you never had anything inside you besides a cock? A dildo, or your fingers?"

She arched slightly as he probed further inside, her breathing hitching, her face coloring. "A dildo," she confessed finally. "I had a dildo for a while."

"Why did you stop using it?" he asked as he slipped further inside, smoothing his finger along her passage. Her blood rushed through her body, the want settling between her legs with a desire that pulsed and swelled her feminine tissues, making them weep more.

"I didn't find it satisfying."

"I'm pleased to hear that. There is nothing like the real thing."

Despite having his finger delving through her folds, she still managed to laugh once. "You had a woman on-call for when you got lonely?"

He responded with a chuckle of his own. "There was no need. What kind of man would I be if I could not control my lusts? Believe me Olana, you tried my patience mightily before I left Earth. I was going slowly mad with lust. But when it comes right down to it, hands work quite well when things became overwhelming." He nuzzled at her neck. "I will be honest with you, I have had women, a few, in my life when I was younger and didn't know better. Since I met you, however, I have not spent a single moment of time with a *skala*. They no longer hold any appeal."

"What's a *skala*?"

"You call them prostitutes on your planet. It is only natural to want to relieve one's natural urges, all living creatures have them, and we are no different on Taburon. A man has to learn somehow, as does a woman. If we were all virgins until we married, there would be a lot fewer people in the world."

Buried inside her almost to the knuckle, he withdrew slightly, feeling her warm interior cling to his digit with a vice like grip as though it didn't want to release him. She was going to be tight around his cock, binding him to her until her body became used to him. But that wasn't necessarily a bad thing. He would have to go slow and easy, gently introducing her to nadryl with a Taburon male. He would love every minute. He pushed deeper until he was buried to the hilt.

Kathryn took a sharp breath. "You are flushing," he pointed out, a smile in his voice. "Your body temperature just rose and the skin on your chest has reddened." Swirling his finger around, he started to explore. "Relax," he whispered against her temple.

"I'm trying," she breathed, squirming in his arms.

He knew he would have to loosen her up more if he ever expected to penetrate her body. Her maidenhead had been broken, only the tightness of her passage indicated she'd never indulged in nadryl. The walls of her vagina were soft and swollen, weeping profusely onto his palm as he twisted the finger around.

Once he felt her relax, he pulled free of her body only to add a second finger to his efforts, spreading her open more. "You're very tight," he murmured.

Her voice vibrated with growing lust. "And you're very big," she reminded.

His chuckle was louder. "Yes, I am," he agreed. "Don't worry, I'll try to loosen you up a little. If this hurts too much, tell me. It might be uncomfortable, but if I don't do this, you won't want to share nadryl with me ever again."

Her voice was saucy. "Is that a touch of over confidence on your part?"

"It is truth, Olana. Pain here," he explained, giving her insides a slight jolt, "can translate to pain here," he continued, tapping at her temple with his free hand, "and you might never enjoy the act again." Pumping two fingers, he worked her body until she relaxed even more. Inserting three fingers served to open her passage further as he spread his fingers widely apart, continuing with the in and out motion.

He didn't ignore the rest of her either, nibbling at her throat, breathing soft breaths against her ear, his other hand returning to play with her breast and rolling the nipple around. "Your body is so responsive," he murmured, "your nipple has tightened until it is rock hard and your pussy is weeping like a fountain. You were made to share nadryl. Once I am inside you, I will be able to take you so high you will never want to come down."

Kathryn shuddered, his words and actions painting pictures in her head, stoking the fires higher, taking the simmer she'd started the evening with and bringing it to a fierce boil. She arched her back, pushing her breasts out further for him, the momentary pain of the pinch quickly morphing into an electrifying connection that went directly to her pussy. How it came from a short nip of pain she didn't understand – she'd never felt this way before, this restlessness and this need, but her body yearned for more. Rydul was proving that understood her body better than she did, and she was giving it over to him freely. Her legs spread further apart in open invitation.

"Like that did you?" he asked. "You are so wet you could compete with the *lavella*." With a soft sucking sound, he pulled his fingers free of her body, shifting her to the side. "I need to taste you," he continued. "Here, lay on your back." He scooted to the side as she settled back against the bedrolls, the uncertainty, yet the desire to please him in her eyes that she kept on his face.

She was so beautiful, laid out before him like a sumptuous feast. Her hair lay over one shoulder. He should have unbraided it so it could spread out below her, so he could comb his fingers through the silken strands as he made love to her. But the braid also provided possibilities – he could hold it and direct her if he mounted her from behind, keep her body lifted so he could reach her breasts and nipples.

He pupils were wide with hesitancy, not knowing exactly what was going to happen, but there was also unfaltering trust in him in her gaze. Her heartbeat pulsed on the sides of her throat. Beneath the shirt, her breasts rose and fell with shallow pants, the full mounds, topped by pointed nipples, shivered with each breath. "Gods' rods, you are so beautiful," he declared, kneeling between her thighs, taking a moment to just drink her in. In her shimmying to get settled, the shirt had ridden up to expose her pussy, wet and partially opened to his perusal. The hair there was a novelty – once they returned to the city, he would give her the option to keep it or remove it permanently.

Her hips would cushion him as he made love to her and were wide enough to allow safe passage for his child when she gave birth. Her belly was flat under the shirt, but would, he hoped, someday swell once his seed took root.

Kathryn had her fill of looking at him as well, on his knees between her thighs, hunger in his eyes raging beneath a show of pleasure as he perused her body. All hard planes and sculpted muscle, he was a girl's wet dream. The hard points of his masculine nipples were finger-tip sized discs on his chest. Six pack abs flexed as he moved.

And his cock, rising forward, pulsing with his every heartbeat, was a formidable weapon that stood testament above two large testicles in their hairless ball sac. She was one lucky girl.

Reaching out, he slipped one button free. It would be tortuous, for both of them, but he would take his time, prolong the mystery, heighten the anticipation, and insure that she was beyond ready for him, for he knew that once he got inside her, he would have to fight hard to last any amount of time so she could find her pleasure.

One by one he unbuttoned the shirt, not spreading the sides apart until he had the entire garment unbuttoned. Lowering himself to his elbows, planted on either side of her body, he hovered over her and slowly drew the right side of the shirt to the side.

The rosy-violet flesh of her nipple instantly pebbled. They looked so tempting, the roundness of her full breast topped with a sweet berry, like a bowl of *haspen* fruit. And he loved *haspen* fruit. Bending, he swiped the nubbin with a single lick of his tongue then blew on it softly, watching as it hardened even more. With his lips, he pulled her nipple into his mouth, grabbing it gently with his teeth and set to sucking on it like he could draw the most delicious wine from it.

The material covering her other breast fell to the side, her nipple drawing in on itself as his hand covered the flesh, palpating the mound that was the right size for his grip. Her back arched as she sought more, more of his touch, more of his lips, more of his attention to the fire rising inside her body as he swiped his lips over and around her nipple, his other hand plucking at the twin beaded nub topping her breast.

Satisfied after several moments that he'd paid enough homage to her right breast, he raised his head to grin at her in mischief, delighting in her expression of unfulfilled desire and desperation before tilting it down to repeat the entire process to her left breast.

Kathryn moaned as he serviced her flesh, wiggling under his body, seeking a release that he was keeping from her, villain that he was. With his body, he kept her pinned to the bedroll, her shifting body only heightening his own passions, his cock aching to find her warmth and expend itself inside her. But she wasn't there yet, not deep enough lost in want for him to breach her and together reach ecstasy.

Tracing a wet path between her breasts, he meandered down her body to her navel, where he dipped the tip of his tongue inside and swirled it around until he tasted every bit inside then kept on his original course until he came to the curls that topped her mound.

Hands at her knees, her spread her open further and looked down. The hair covering her between her legs was the same color as that on her head, only darker to due rarely ever seeing the sunlight. Combing through the curls, Rydul was amazed at how soft they felt, twisting around each other as they spread from the top of her mound to deep below over the lips of her pussy. Taburon women had no pussy hair, making use of a permanent depilatory as young girls almost as soon as growth began to appear. Perhaps someday she would agree to making use of the cream, but if not he was fine with it.

But for now, the novelty was exciting. A new way to explore a woman's charms, to part not only her folds to find her treasures, but to sift through soft curls to get there.

His grin was positively lascivious. "I've never shared nadryl with a woman with hair here," he said, palming her mound. The confidence she'd been feeling faded – he was disappointed in her body, in the hair she sported as a normal, human, woman. She started to cover herself. Immediately he grabbed her hands and held them to the sides. "Don't hide from me. Your curls are fascinating and intriguing, and part of what makes you beautiful."

Kathryn gave him a wane smile and let her hands go limp in his grip. Releasing them, she dropped them to her side, nodding once. The grin he returned was deadly, a snake seeing its prey and licking it lips at the feast it anticipated.

Stretching out onto his belly, he rested his head on top of her mound, his hands holding her thighs open so he could fit his broad shoulders between them. "I assume no man has done this for you?" he asked. She replied with a jerky shake of her head. "Then relax and enjoy. Let what might happen, happen," he instructed before his mouth disappeared into her feminine secrets.

Using both thumbs and forefingers, Rydul spread her outer lips wide. She was pink, swollen and wet, coated with her dew, the moisture running between her buttocks. If she continued to ooze as much as she was, the bedrolls would be spotted with it. He vowed he'd never wash them in order to keep her scent for whenever he wanted to remember.

At the top of her slit, her clitoris peeked out from under its fleshy hood, hardening in response to the spark in his eyes that flared, the golden color deepening. Kathryn's breath stopped in her chest, never having ever been so exposed to a man before, embarrassed at his scrutiny even as she watched his expression become more aroused.

Her cry echoed through the clearing when his tongue swiped up her slit, licking her from bottom to top, circling around her clit to head back along the path he'd taken. Her flesh was heated and warmed more, his tongue swirling around her pussy, learning every dip and fold, scooping up the juice that dripped profusely. Her hands clenched on the bedroll, her back arched, he had to keep her legs opened as she tried to bring them together.

"Open," he murmured, holding her thighs firmly, his face buried in her pussy. His tongue traced up and down, through and around, until he'd tasted every part of her and drank of her emission. With his fingertips, he spread her more, revealing the opening to her body to his gaze, its color a deep red and shadowed.

She flushed. "Rydul," she pleaded, undulating. "Please," she begged.

Two fingers slipped in easily. "What, Olana?"

"I need you."

"Not yet," he refuted, "but soon," he promised. "You are so tight, like a soft glove. My cock is going to be in *ceileo* inside you." Pumping several times, he withdrew the two fingers, only to return with three. At the same time, he slid slightly forward to cover her clit with his mouth.

With the tip of his tongue, he flicked her clit back and forth like a living vibrator. Her back bowed, her breasts reached for the sky and she cried out. A gentle nip and he grabbed her clit with his teeth, holding it as he applied a suction so strong she thought he was trying to suck her clit from her body.

Below, he continued to pump his fingers in and out of her hole, spreading them to expand her insides, diving as deep as he could to test her passage so he'd know how far he could thrust when he took her at last.

He felt her sheath begin to pulse, to tighten on his fingers and he knew she was close. Increasing his efforts, he pulled harder on her clit and thrust his fingers faster into her, her hips thrashing. Nerve endings sparked, blood flowed, electricity zinged across her body and she screamed with the hardest orgasm she'd ever felt in her entire life. Her entire torso lifted from the bedroll, her arms and legs went rigid, her head was thrown back, her throat tight. Her scream reverberated through the bushes, the crufas danced, startled at the sudden sound. He drank of her orgasm until she stopped vibrating, stopped flowing, finally managing to take a shuddering breath, her breasts trembling.

Rydul was so pleased. She was very responsive, easily reaching orgasm. They would have a satisfying sex life, he bringing her to her pleasure and she learning with him the willing subject of her experimentation.

Rummaging through the nearby saddle bag, he grabbed a small square package from inside it, held it to his mouth and tore a corner from it. Taking out the condom, he rolled it over his steel hardened cock. The king and prince had gotten their women pregnant almost immediately. Rydul wanted that to happen when Kathryn and he decided, not nature, so he wrapped himself in latex and hoped it worked as described.

Rising, he pulled her thighs over his own, bringing her pussy closer to his cock. Coating the head of his cock with her moisture, he rubbed it up and down her slit until it glistened. "Deep breath," he told her. "Relax." With little effort he fit the head of his cock just inside her pussy and waited.

Kathryn's eyes widened at the intrusion but she drew in a deep breath, then another, spreading her legs more in invitation.

Rydul pulled back, stretching her opening, then pushed forward, sheathing a little more of his cock inside. Inch by inch, he retreated then returned, each time pushing more of his cock into her body, gauging her reaction with each inward foray, slowing down if he felt her tighten, venturing further as she relaxed and her sheath expanded to accommodate his size and length. Human women had not adapted to Taburon men through thousands of years of evolution, but they could learn over time to take their cocks into their body with care and consideration until their body adjusted. Queen McKenna certainly had no problems sharing nadryl with the king, nor did Princess Joanna with her husband the prince. Eventually, Kathryn's body would learn to take him, crave him, to relax around him when he speared into her in lust.

But for now, he was teaching her flesh to yield to the invader of his cock, to let him conquer her body with love, passion, and his flesh. Inch by inch, he filled her until he buried himself as deep as her body would allow, the head of his cock flush against her cervix. The breath he'd been holding rushed out in a sigh.

"Okay?" he asked, having kept his eyes on her face as he filled her.

She opened her own eyes, searching him out. There was undisguised need in her expression, a look of raw passion that said get on with it and end this feeling of want. He'd started a fire within her and he had to either end it one way or another, even if they both went up in flames. Especially if they went up in flames together. Nodding, she lifted her hips, sinking his cock that little bit more until he believed that eventually, once he was buried deep inside her, he would be able to touch her very soul.

Wrapping his arms around her thighs, he lifted them up and over his shoulders, closing her pussy tightly around his cock. He wouldn't be able to thrust too hard nor too deep in this position, as long as he didn't push her knees back towards her head or separate her legs. Anchoring her legs to his chest, he pulled his cock back, then thrust forward.

Rydul started with a slow steady pace of forward thrusts and backward withdrawals, penetrating her sheath little by little, separating the tight walls until they relaxed enough to accept his shaft, keenly keeping an eye on her face to judge, increasing the momentum as she fell into the rhythm, lifting her hips to meet him thrust for thrust. It had hurt at first, not a painful hurt, but uncomfortable, when he'd buried himself inside completely, but as he controlled his movements, the tension gave way to a gentle clutching, a fluttering inside, an increase, a sweltering, an abundance of fluid flowing.

As much as his body said pound into this warm tight place, he held himself in check, in-out, in-out, time and time again until she clenched around him like a vise, her sheath a continuous wave of tightening pulses that crawled up and down his shaft. His balls pulled up, an electrical shock ripped up his spine and he fought to hold on until she crested. Reaching between them, he found her clit and began to strum it with his thumb, tilting his hips to rub the crest of his cock along that sweet spot inside her to bring her to climax.

Her keen started softly and rose in volume as she peaked, his name on her lips as she reached the precipice and hovered, then like a balloon popping, she exploded, her body held rigid, her sheath clamping down on his cock.

His orgasm followed, his back arching as he thrust as deep as possible to empty himself, his spine tingling and lungs heaving, his cock throbbing as it pulsed, spraying cum that would have filled her passage save for the condom. Rydul breathed deeply, shaking from the explosiveness of the orgasm, something that had never happened to him before with any *skala*. His sharing nadryl with them had been pleasant, a way to ease tension and relieve a basic need, but never had he felt this deeply, nor come this strongly with any of them.

His hairline was wet, sweat dripping from his forehead. Sliding his gaze to her, he found her eyes closed, her mouth slightly open. Her chest rose and fell with panting breaths, moisture clung to the space between her breasts and puddled in the valley of her stomach. Keeping the connection, he released her legs, letting them fall gently to his sides, the motion burying him that last inch inside her body, a mini orgasm ripping through her as the head of his cock kissed her cervix. She squealed and reached to place a hand on his abdomen, a gesture to tell him to not move, she was still coming down from her first orgasm. But he ignored her, leaning over her, covering her body with his, his hands sliding under her shoulders to hold himself high enough without losing body contact so as to not crush her. He placed kisses along her jaw, working his way to her mouth. Plundering her lips, he took a kiss, then another, combing one hand through her hair.

His voice was soft, intimate. "Are you all right?"

Her eyes were still slightly glazed, but she recognized him, nodding. "You?"

"Perfect."

She cupped his cheeks. "I never knew."

"Never knew what, Olana?"

Her chest rose with a deep breath. "That was amazing. I've never felt such a strong orgasm."

He chuckled softly. "Because you've never shared nadryl with the right man." He placed a kiss on the tip of her nose. "We are not done," he promised. "There is so much more. And just so you know, it's never been that strong for me either."

Her responding grin was sassy. "Just needed the right woman," she shot back.

He pinched the closest nipple until she squealed. "*Adelu*," he growled playfully.

"Now what does that mean?"

"It is a naughty child," he explained disengaging his cock from her. He sat back on his heels, reaching out to help her rise to a sitting position. Surprise crossed her face as she saw him remove the condom.

"You used a condom?" she asked. "We were told during one of our briefings that Taburons don't have any sexually transmitted diseases. If we decided to have sex with one of them," she added.

He set the used condom to the side to dispose of later. There were plenty more in his saddle bag. He had been optimistic when packing. "We have had two women share nadryl with two of our men and they became pregnant almost immediately. While I would love to see your belly swell with my child, it is not my decision to make alone. Until we are ready to have children, I will use condoms so that you do not become pregnant." He stretched out beside her, turning her on her side so he could pull her into his embrace. "There is a tea that you may drink to prevent conception, our women have used it for generations. I do not know if the queen and the princess use it, so I am unsure if it is effective for humans."

"We can have children," she said with a hint of wistfulness. "I've always wanted children."

"So have I. But I would rather have a wife first." He hinted, his look undisguised desire.

"Married?"

"If you will have me, yes."

"But we hardly know each other."

"We know enough to share nadryl. I love you." He rose to an elbow to look down at her. "I still have some time on my enlistment, but we can find a place close to the palace to live until then. After, that estate will provide enough income to support both us and a family."

"I'll be able work, won't I?"

"I want you to do what you want, Kathryn. If that means finding something to do to make you happy, then I will support you in your efforts."

"I've supported myself for a long time. I don't want you to feel as though you have to take care of me, Rydul."

"I don't *feel* as if I have to. If I do, it is because I want to." Sitting up, he reached for the shirt and handed it back to her. As she pulled it over her shoulders, he shoved his feet into the togs and stood. With the condom in one hand and shovel in the other, Rydul disappeared behind a bush, dug a hole and buried the piece of latex deep, patting down the dirt.

He banked the fire so it would last through the night and be easier to restoke come morning, making sure with a final glance that everything was put away, safe from attracting any unwanted guests while they slept. Kathryn watched as he moved about the campsite, the slight ache he'd created at penetration easing minute by minute, the rapture of an orgasm more exalting than she'd ever felt settling down into a pleasant feeling of contentment and relaxation drifting over her as sleep called. When he rejoined her on the bedrolls, he shook out the blanket first before stretching out along the thick material, drawing her down beside him, tossing the blanket over their forms. The chill in the nighttime air called for snuggling, and snuggling he was all for.

He'd slept with women before, exhaustion taking over after a vigorous few hours with a *skala*, but that had only been fulfilling a basic need – scratching an itch as the humans said. The last time had been before his six month tour at the embassy on Earth, a year ago. There'd had been a lot of pent-up sexual energy that self-satisfaction hadn't been able to relieve. Until tonight. His mind and his hormones had been focused on one woman. The one he held now, her back to his chest, his upper leg pinning her.

And while his cock thought otherwise, Rydul knew she needed time to recover from her first nadryl and grow used to him. His male part, having a mind of its own, lengthening and hardening, tucked against her arse – her delightful, shapely, enticing arse – needed to learn patience. He had control. Rydul eased away from that handful of female flesh, shifting his hips back.

Kathryn wiggled, seeking out the contact with his body he was now denying.

He gripped her a little tighter. "Don't," he whispered hoarsely. "Stay still, for both our sakes."

Her eyes opened to stare across the campsite. "What? Have I done something wrong?"

"I want you again, too much. You need to recover from your first time."

"Oh," she breathed softly. "I'm sorry."

"Don't be, Olana. You are so tempting, all soft and warm and I am a miserable *tritio* for wanting you so fiercely."

He could feel her shoulders start to shake, his brow furrowing in fear that he had frightened her. Rising to his elbow, puzzled and concerned, he peered into her face to find her giggling, trying hard to hold it in and not let him see. "Why do you laugh?"

She burst into laughter, turning slightly to gaze up at him. Cupping his cheek, she let her joy shine through to ease his fears. "I've never had such a back-handed compliment before," she replied softly. "Of course, I have no idea what a *tritio* is, but I might hazard a guess." She lifted her head up enough to kiss him. "I love you."

"And I you," came his reply before he returned the kiss. "*Tritio* means arse, ass as you say."

She loved the smoothness of his skin, no five o'clock shadow and raspy beard, as she slid fingers along his jaw. "When I can share nadryl again with you, there will be no place you can hide to escape me," she warned.

"You will not have to go far to find me," he promised. Reclining, he pulled her back to settle against him again, this time keeping her arse well away from his wayward shaft. "Sleep," he murmured, "We have a long way to go yet and we start out at first light"

"So early?"

"I would like to get home before high sun meal."

"So far then?"

"Nearly a day and a half, even with our stop here."

Her sigh was resigned. "Another crufa ride."

He chuckled softly, lifting her hand to place a kiss on her palm. "Yes, Olana, another crufa ride." A deep breath of contentment and he settled down for a peaceful night.

He was in that state where a body drifts between sound sleep and sleepy awareness, when a person is not sure what is real and what is a dream, when Kathryn jolted awake, sitting up, startled, her breathing harsh, startling him awake.

"What was that?" she whispered into the darkness.

Rydul sat up to peer into the dark, searching, alerted, his heart starting to race, adrenaline flowing. If there was danger, he would defend her to the death. His sword was laying next to the bedroll, his laser weapon was above the tent roll they were using for pillows. "What?" he asked, his voice lowered.

"I heard something."

"What?"

"I'm not sure. Sounded like a whistle"

Rydul knew there were several creatures on Taburon that could make a whistling noise, and some of them were not very friendly. Slipping his hand under the pillow, he pulled his laser weapon free, flipping on the switch in the process.

In the distance, a mournful sound echoed through the night, a whistle low in pitch and dreary, as though something were saddened to its very soul. It repeated rhythmically several times before ending on a note drawn out for several heartbeats. Rydul relaxed, thumbing off the weapon. "It is an *awrhim*," he said softly.

"A what?"

"*Awrhim*, a bird. If you listen, you may hear a reply."

The first call repeated as they waited silently. Within a few seconds, after yet another whistle from the first, from even further away came a response. A whistle, higher pitched, less mournful, a trilling answer, echoed back.

For several minutes the birds called to each other, speaking in a language only they understood. Rydul returned the weapon to its hiding place and resettled with Kathryn.

"The first was the male, calling to his mate: 'Where, where, where are you, he calls. Our bower's made ready, all soft and warm. Come to me, come to me, come to me, love, With me in our bower, As we greet the dawn.'" He tightened his arms around her.

"If she is near and willing, she answers: 'Here I am, here I am, here, she responds, Beside you forever, safe in your arms.'"

Kathryn, having held her breath as she listened to him, his voice low and sexy, sighed. "That's so beautiful," she whispered with awe.

"The *awrhim* mate for life, but only come together to nest and raise their young. Every year, after he has built the nest, he must call to her until she responds."

"What if she doesn't? If something happened to her?"

"Then there is no nesting, no young. If he cannot find a new mate, he will eventually die alone."

"That's so sad."

"It is how it has been for a thousand years or more." He placed a kiss against her hair, burying his nose in the subtle fragrance of her shampoo, takin a deep sniff. It wasn't *freemas,* but the hint of a flowery scent under the odor of the lavella water, light and pleasant, one he remembered from their time on Earth. "When you find that one person who fills your heart," he offered. "Sleep, Olana."

CHAPTER ELEVEN

Rydul pulled his crufa to a stop and surveyed the landscape before him. Kathryn, having gained more confidence in handling her animal, maneuvered her crufa to a standstill next to his, resting the reins along the pommel of the saddle.

He swept his hand out in a semi-circle. "This is all my land," he said with pride, "from the mountains to west to the lake in the east, over ten thousand of what you call acres. Two thirds are planted in *freemas*, half of what is left is planted with feed, and the rest is for the crufas."

"I'm impressed," Kathryn complimented. She squinted to the distance. "Is that the house?" she asked, indicating a structure that appeared to be two story, white in color.

"Yes. It was in disrepair when I received it, but over the last years, I have been able to make repairs and improvements, modernize it and replace the old furniture." He glanced her way and looked closely. Her brow was furrowed and there was an expression of wariness in her eyes. "What?" he asked.

"What, what?" she replied, shaking off the expression and turning curious eyes his way.

"You have something on your mind. What is it, Olana?"

"Nothing important."

"If it bothers you, then it is important," he insisted.

She flushed and looked away, stray strands of her hair hiding her face, though she had braided most of off of her face. A slight breeze ruffled the material of her blouse and she slouched slightly in the saddle. "I was just wondering about something, but I decided it wasn't important. Not even my business."

He watched her as she fidgeted and tried to do anything and look anywhere but at him, pretending that what she had wondered about was truly unimportant. Rydul shifted in his saddle, the well-kept leather creaking softly.

The night before had been one of the best he'd ever spent in his life. Sleeping next to her had been contentment personified, the best he'd ever slept in years. Waking up with her soft and warm and pliant next to him was what he'd been searching for for a long time. And he knew he wanted it more than he wanted his next breath, more than he needed his next heartbeat, more than anything in the universe. With a certainty he'd never felt about anything before now, he knew he wanted Kathryn for his wife, for the mother of his children, for his lifetime.

They'd slept for several hours after making love. Sometime in the middle of the night, he'd become aware of her lying next to him, awake, staring up at the night sky. After being assured that she was well, just unused to sleeping outside and fascinated by the abundance of stars showing in a lightless sky, he'd leaned over her and kissed her senseless, revving her up again for another session of love making as long as she wasn't too sore for it. She gave as good as she got, never too tired to share her body with him. They'd gone back to sleep afterwards, still intimately connected.

In the morning, he'd risen before her, stoking the fire and setting a kettle to boil for tea. She'd snuggled into the blankets, strands of her hair falling from the braid in curly tendrils, her head resting on her hands under her cheek. He'd not denied himself the pleasure of watching her sleep for several minutes before gently rousing her to start the day. A quick breakfast followed by an even quicker wash in the lavella where she playfully fended off his lascivious looks and touches, dressing and climbing back onto the crufas (which had her moaning in despair) and they were on their way.

The landscape fascinated her. Rydul pointed out things as they rode, spying animals in the trees or the distance, naming the plants and whether or not they had any kind of use other than being just plain pretty. Kathryn told him more about her life growing up as a child, the happy times they had doing family things, the sadness when her brother went to war and then missing. She talked about her dreams as a young girl, looking for a boyfriend like every other girl and how things were for women on Earth since the war. She wanted what he did, a home and family and someone to love for the rest of her life, but was hesitant to push him into something he may not have wanted to give. Life on Earth had taught most women well.

So when he saw the look in her eyes as they approached the estate house and the sudden retreat of the joy she'd been showing the whole time they'd been riding as they neared his property, he took a leap.

And he thought he knew what was bothering her. "Of course, the finishing touches on the decorating will be left up to my wife," he added softly, shooting her a meaningful look, "since it has not had the fortune of a woman's touch."

She visibly relaxed in the saddle and he knew he'd guessed right – she'd been wondering of he'd brought other women to house estate. The thought had never occurred to him in the past, this was something he'd always wanted to share with that one special woman who would take part in his life and have his devotion. That she was jealous of a female he'd never had filled him with a sense of gladness. Kathryn was completely engaged with him. He could count on her to make him her priority for the future.

Rydul wanted to yell out how happy he was, how contented Kathryn was making him feel. He slid a sideways glance to her. His first inclination had been to ask her if she wanted to race the rest of the way, to feel the exhilaration of the wind blowing through her hair and the crufa beneath her as it flew across the grounds. But she was unused to riding as yet, the idea wasn't the best one right now.

Instead he inched his animal as close to hers as possible and leaned over to plant a stunning kiss on her mouth, holding her head steady against his onslaught as he swiped his lips back and forth over her lips. The look she gave him when he released her was puzzling, but she licked the moisture he'd left behind in a gesture that had his cock raging in his trousers, anxious to be released. "I love you," he breathed.

Her return look was brilliant, relaxed, and loving. "I know. I love you, too."

"Come on. Hopefully, Khail has some high sun meal waiting for us. I know I could use a cold drink right about now."

Her glance fell to his thigh and his obvious need. "Or a cold shower," she teased.

"More like a warm bed and hot woman," he corrected with a devilish grin.

"Promises, promises," she rejoined, egging her crufa to a start. With a shake of his head, he followed.

He had been content as they rode along, yet as they neared even closer, his brows wrinkled in a frown as he scanned the landscape. Fields that should have been white with blossoming freemas were dark instead. The air that should have been redolent with the sweet pungency of flowers was clean, but not filled with the scent he expected. The house appeared too quiet, the one paddock easily seen upon approach deserted.

There had been two large beds of freemas in front of the house, both now empty, the blossoms gone, the ground bare of flower stalks. Rydul wondered if the flowers had bloomed early and been harvested already. That might have been unusual, but growing seasons at time varied and perhaps the blossoms had come into full flower earlier this season.

He was puzzled, but led Kathryn around the house to the stables behind. No crufas greeted him as they approached, but all of the animals could have been let out to high pasture. Dismounting, he tied the reins of his crufa to a post and walked around to help Kathryn from her beast.

Together they pulled the crufas into the stable, where Rydul directed her on how to unsaddle the animal and where to place both saddle and blanket. He would come out later and brush the animals down, but for now, he made sure they each had several scoops of grain and fresh water. The emptiness of the remaining stalls pricked at the back of his mind, but he was willing to assume the crufas normally there were most likely out to pasture. The day was glorious, a good day for the animals to be outside. Picking up the packs, he took Kathryn's hand and steered her to the back entrance of the house.

They came in through a mud room and continued in beyond a kitchen to a hallway where it led to a long corridor, doors on both sides. "Khail," Rydul called as he pulled her along the hallway.

Passing several rooms with closed doors, he told her what each one was, inviting her to spend as much time in the library as she might want while at the estate. The dining room had an open arch, a table built for six dead center and a sideboard lining one entire wall. There was a large door she assumed led to the kitchen on the back wall.

Near the front entrance, a large arched wall opened into a living room area. Windows graced the wall facing the front of the house, the curtains drawn back to allow the sunlight in. In the center was a collection of chairs and small settees arranged around a large rug. A fireplace filled almost half of one wall. Decorations were few, a painting here and a flowerless vase there. Table lamps bordered three of the couches and stood guard over one of the heavy chairs, obviously a spot for the 'lord' of the house to sit and be comfortable during an evening of relaxation and reading.

A man rose as they entered the room, his hair disheveled, a glass of some sort of drink in hand. Kathryn knew, if this was Khail that he was younger then Rydul, but the lines in his face and bleary redness of his eyes showed instead that he was bothered by some problem of great importance. He looked as though he had aged several years more than he was in reality.

Dropping Kathryn's hand, Rydul engulfed Khail in an embrace. While Khail's arms lifted, he didn't really embrace Rydul in return. The look in his eyes was more distant than welcoming, until he settled his gaze on the human woman watching the brothers with interest.

"You look terrible," Rydul said as he released his grip.

"Lots on my mind," the other replied absently, stepping out of his brother's personal space and lifting the glass to take a drink. "Who's the woman?" he asked, pointing the glass her way.

Rydul couldn't contain his smile as he stepped to Kathryn's side, sliding a hand around her waist. "This is Kathryn Tehyr. She's from Earth."

"Human?"

Rydul stiffened defensively for a moment. "Yes, and to be my wife as well as your sister."

Khail saluted her with his glass. "Welcome to the family," he greeted half-heartedly, his eyes hooded.

Rydul frowned and spun with Kathryn, leading her out of the room and down the hall to a closed door that he had pointed out as leading to the library. Opening the door, he allowed her to enter first, following on her heels. "I'm sorry my brother is behaving so poorly. Give me few minutes, let me see if I can find out what's wrong with him and I'll come back. Then we can have something to eat." He indicated for her to take a seat in one of the comfortable chairs that occupied the room. "There are plenty of books if you want to find something to read for a short time."

"I'll be fine," she assured. "I hope your brother is okay."

Leaning down, he bussed her mouth tightly, then liking it so much, did it again for good measure. "Be back soon," he promised. He left the door open behind him.

Khail hadn't left the room when Rydul returned, his glass refilled, standing by the window, gazing out. "What was that about?" Rydul asked, annoyance in his voice.

"What was what about?"

"Your sarcasm in greeting Kathryn. She's going to be my wife and deserves your respect."

"Fine, she has it. What else?"

Rydul perused his brother for a moment. He looked haggard, as though he wasn't sleeping, or at least not well. He'd said he had a lot on his mind. Maybe if he talked it out it would help to ease the burden. "Want to talk about what's bothering you?"

"No. Everything is fine."

So be it. Khail would talk when he was ready. Meanwhile, Rydul had some questions of his own. "I noticed there were no crufas in the pasture. Have you moved them to the high ground? And the freema fields are harvested."

"Sold."

"The flowers bloomed early?"

"Close enough."

"I calculated at least another week before they'd be ready. Was there some sort of early conditions that brought them out sooner?"

Khail turned towards the interior of the room, walked over to a chair and sat. "Something like that," he hedged.

"You got a fair market price for them, I assume."

"Close enough," he repeated.

Rydul's look was confused, his brows furrowing, eyes narrowed as he tried to sort out why his brother had used the same expression twice now and wouldn't answer directly any questions. He was starting to become annoyed. "What does 'close enough' mean?" he asked. "What did you get for the freemas?"

Khail sighed. "Ten percent under market value," he finally, reluctantly, admitted.

"Ten…?" Rydul breathed. "That's well below market value for the quality freemas I grow, even when harvested early. What were you thinking?"

Khail's sigh was even deeper. "I needed the money."

There was dead silence in the room for several heartbeats as that information sank in. "For what?"

"I owed some people."

"How much?"

"Enough."

"All of the freemas?"

"Among other things."

"At least there should be some left over to pay for the new stable."

"Not necessarily," Khail said, "and not needed now."

Rydul sat heavily in the chair, suddenly aware of why he hadn't seen any grazing crufas, why the animals were missing. Not missing. Gone. "The crufas?"

"Them, too."

He was almost afraid to ask, but he needed to know. "When?"

"Last week."

"And how much did you get for them?" His voice had softened, wearied.

"Lots."

"Khail, what have you done?" he whispered softly, disbelief in his voice. He cleared his throat. "Why? You knew I planned on breeding those animals and the freemas were paying for them until I could get the program going. Why would you need so much money that you would destroy my dream?"

Khail seemed unusually calm, very controlled, and resigned. "I got in with a bad group of people last year and I couldn't get out from under them. Selling the crufas and the freemas was the only way for the most part."

There was a dangerous quality growing in Rydul's mood as he perused his brother with a new perspective. He'd thought Khail fairly stable, uninvolved in unsavory pursuits. With the running of the estate, he shouldn't have had time to get in with a bad group of people for any reason. But Khail had had a penchant for wanting what he wanted when he wanted it, and a sense of entitlement, having been deprived of his parents, had driven Rydul to indulge the boy, since he'd been so young when things had gone so horribly wrong for him. Now he was seeing that he had been so misguided.

"The most part? What else aren't you telling me?" he asked. "Do I still own the estate?"

Khail's shrug was nonchalant. "Yes. For a while there you didn't, but I remembered that they're here, and I couldn't sell them out. I convinced the men I owed that I could pay the balance with cash."

"From where?"

"Your accounts. I discovered the passwords and took that as well. But it's all settled and I'm done with them."

Rydul was silent, crushed, his heart broken, his chest feeling as though he'd been kicked straight through a wall and then stomped on.

Everything was gone – the freemas, the crufas, the accounts. His dreams, his goals, his future. All gone.

He was betrayed. By the one person he thought he could trust with his life until he'd met Kathryn. He'd worked, he'd sacrificed, he'd put everything he held dear on hold to take care of his brother. And this was how he was to be repaid.

His gaze rose to the walls around him, seeing the paintings that surrounded him, the tapestry that hanged over the fireplace. The ceiling was painted with a pastoral scene that he'd had restored with pride when he'd inherited the estate. There was still so much more that needed to be done to make the house a home for him, his wife and future children. The crufas were going to provide all of that for them and more. He was going to be able to give up the Guard, allay the chances that someday, somewhere, he would be called upon to make a sacrifice that could claim him, for even though he had his own dreams and goals, his loyalty was thorough. That had come first in his life, until he'd met Kathryn. That day, everything had changed, fulfilling the dream a priority with her in mind. He had known within days of meeting her that he would finish his duty to his king, but after that, on the day he was free, everything he did from then on would be for her and the life they would share together.

And now it was gone. He'd lived day to day with as little as he could, depending upon the magnanimity of the Guard to provide the basics so he could sink everything he could into the estate and providing for his future, his brother given a place in his life until he could make one of his own.

He had nothing to offer Kathryn now.

He realized she was no child, that she had supported herself on Earth, but he wanted to be able to give her the opportunity to do what she wanted in order to be happy, not what she had to do in order to survive. And certainly what had to be done to keep the estate going, rebuild the crufa stock, replant the fields, continue upgrading the estate....

It would take years to get back to where he thought he'd been when he'd arrived here today, so proud of his accomplishments, so content with where his life was going. He could do without for himself. He couldn't ask that of

Kathryn, not when things were so new to her and she would be feeling her own way in this new life she had innocently chosen. The burden was his and his alone.

Khail dropping his now empty glass onto a table top brought Rydul from his musings as a sudden, fierce anger flooded through him. As if pulled by strings, he rose from his chair and stepped up to his brother, grabbing him by the front of his shirt and lifting him nearly off of his feet. His free hand, fisted, drew back as far as he could pull it, readying to attack.

But the look of absolute defeat on Khail's face stayed him. The younger man knew what he had done, knew that it had all but destroyed his brother, knew that this would be the result of his perfidy and was willing to take everything the Rydul wanted to dish out. And more. His body unresisting, he waited for the damage that was sure to come.

Rydul let the man drop. Khail, the release of his body taking him by surprise, fell in a heap to the floor as Rydul turned away from him. "You're a Gods be damned *veniasa*. Get out," Rydul ordered harshly, every ounce of control he had leashed, his fury harnessed but vibrating through in the harshness of his voice. Khail flinched at the harsh epithet. "I want to kill you for this, but I can live with never seeing you again. Get out, take only your clothes. You're on your own from now on." Rydul forced himself to turn, to look one last time, bereft now of all family, knowing the pain would come once the anger had a chance to dissipate, but he couldn't trust himself to not injure Khail any time in the near future. And Khail knew he had escaped serious harm, for the look in his brother's eyes was nothing short of deadly. The training of the soldier would have been enough to put Khail in dire straits for many months, if he even survived the beating he so justly deserved. Rydul had been nothing but the best he could have been, considering all he had done to keep his younger brother happy. For the first time, Khail felt an enormous guilt settle on his shoulders, wishing he could go back in time to erase the damage he had caused. He would give Rydul time and space. Someday, he hoped, his brother would find it in himself to forgive him. Someday.

"I'm taking a walk. I don't want Kathryn to see me like this. But you had better be gone by the time I return." With that, Rydul spun and stomped from the room and down the hall, the door slamming with finality. Khail picked himself up, swiping his mouth with the back of his hand.

CHAPTER TWELVE

McKenna loved the morning. The light filtering through the windows and open balcony doors was a gentle way to awaken, her consciousness rising as the light increased with the rising of the sun.

She especially enjoyed this time of year, when the temperatures fell and the nights were crisp and clear. It was this kind of weather when she would toss another layer of blankets on the bed then snuggle next to her living bed warmer – her husband - and curl into his embrace for the night.

And since she as expecting again, and her body temperature was naturally higher, cool temperatures were welcomed to help her through the days until she gave birth. Radine complained sometimes, not particularly fond of cold night and a cold bed, but if he got a chance to snuggle with his wife, all of his complaints became unimportant.

As the light penetrated her closed eyes, she rolled onto her back and stretched, her arms rising to the head board of the bed and her toes reaching for the end of the bed, pulling back as soon as she touched those of her still sleeping husband. She rubbed at her expanded tummy, the little one asleep inside – finally.

"Thank you, sweetness," she murmured. Last night had been the first time in nearly two weeks that her unborn had given her the chance to sleep through the night, not waking her to run to the bathroom or give her a unrelenting case of heartburn. She was truly grateful for the reprieve.

Once this child arrived, she would have three children five or younger. Add to that the two from Prince Jaima and Joanna – once their second child was born – and the nursery would be full to the top with little ones. The nannies would have their hands full with children of royal blood.

Not that the total care of the children was left in the hands of the nannies. Both Radine and Jaima were hands-on fathers, very hands-on in fact. Each man spent a considerable amount of time with their children. The two older boys were constantly at their sides when the men went to the lists, watching from the sidelines as the elders practiced. And the two men had put wooden swords in the hands of their boys, teaching them rudimentary moves and countermoves. They would have their sons learn how to fight with swords, especially since the one father was the best swordsman on the planet. It wouldn't do to have his son ignorant to the ways of the blade.

And Radine had been teaching Rakenn how to ride. McKenna and he had already had this conversation soon after she'd discovered that he'd been putting the boy on a crufa. Realizing there would be no stopping them, she only warned them that if either one was injured, even the slightest scratch, both would be banned from the royal bed chamber until the injury was healed. And they would still be in what the humans called the doghouse – whatever that meant - until she forgave them. And when Joanna had seen Jaima put Jasim on a horse, she'd appealed to McKenna, to no avail, leaving her to throw her hands up in disgust issuing the same threat.

Being pregnant had given both women an unexpected advantage – neither one had to attend any function they deemed useless or boring by simply claiming they weren't feeling up to it due to their pregnancy. It got them out of a lot of things.

Such as the mid-morning meet and greet meal that had been held yesterday. According to Radine, it had gone very well. A relaxing brunch of Taburon food had put everyone in the right mood, especially after the show of force that had been the demonstration of might on the tournament field the day before. Seeing a dozen or so men, dressed in leather armor, wielding swords that most human men couldn't even lift, swinging those weapons around like so much fluff, had certainly shown the humans just what these people could do with little effort.

Especially effective had been when Rydul, second in command of the King's Guard and one of the best swordsmen on the planet, had ridden his crufa towards the crowd at the end of his contest, lowered his sword and indicated for the red-headed woman to take the scarf he'd placed on the end of his blade. After sliding it from the sword, she placed it around her throat, but Rydul had not then ridden off as he might have any other time after a lady received his favor.

Instead he pushed his crufa closer to the audience, scattering some of the humans scared of the large animal, reached down and took the woman's forearm in his as she clasped his in return, lifting her easily onto the saddle and riding away with her to the cheers and applause of the Taburon people. She'd gone willingly, a smile on her face and delight in her eyes. A warrior had just claimed his woman, leaving no doubt in the minds of the people watching. McKenna had been especially pleased with the man's action. She'd been told by Radine and Jaima that the warrior had a deep interest in the woman that had started on Earth. He intended to pursue it now that she was on Taburon. McKenna wished him the best and would certainly do whatever she could to aid Rydul, as soon as she got a hold of the woman and put her through a thorough grilling. Unfortunately, the woman had not been at the luncheon that McKenna had avoided. They would have to connect another time as soon as possible. She would order it. After all she was the queen.

So, as she continued to commune with her child and remember the past few days, she sighed with contentment. Excitement was a mild word to use with the arrival of the humans from Earth. It had been momentous for the people of Taburon, to take this first step in sealing the friendship of the two worlds.

The light continued to brighten further as the sun rose higher outside. The birds that had made their nests in the trees in the garden below were waking and starting their day, soft noises filtering up through the open balcony doors. She come to love the wildlife on Taburon, especially that which inhabited the gardens around the palace. She'd even, on occasion, managed to coax some of those little gems of bright colors onto her hand when she brought food outside to feed them. Alveda enjoyed being with her mother then and showed a real affinity for creatures. Sometimes Joanna would join the two to enjoy the peace of the garden.

Soon Purnia and Annatt would enter the room to get the couple up and start the day. At times it was annoying to have someone who knew their schedule better than they did themselves, both servants pulling out the proper clothing and getting the two into a bath if needed. Of course, if the servants turned their back, leaving the couple in the bathing room alone, bathing wasn't the only thing that got done then. The servants had learned to keep a close eye on the royal couple to keep them on schedule.

But McKenna loved Radine with all her heart. After the problems they'd faced before they'd wed, that he'd come to her on Earth to return a picture she'd left when Lord Quorol had convinced her that Radine truly wasn't interested in her for a wife, but only a plaything – a chance to see how humans rated in sharing nadryl – her love for him had done nothing but grow with every passing day. And she knew he loved her beyond all reason. He could be ruthless when he had to, but underneath was a heart as golden as the hair on his head.

And she knew Joanna and Jaima shared the same kind of feelings for each other. They were truly fortunate women.

Grabbing the headboard to help, since rolling had become such a chore, McKenna twisted awkwardly towards her husband. Hopefully, there would be some time for cuddling before they had to start the day. Lifting her head and bracing her cheek on one palm, she placed the other on his chest, his shirt discarded before he'd gotten into bed.

Five years and she'd never tired of watching him sleep. His face was relaxed, the lines of rule and worry softened, his long eyelashes resting gently on his upper cheeks. His lips were slightly parted, a hint of white teeth showing. He'd let his hair go the last few months and it needed a trim, unless he intended to put it in a queue like so many of the Taburon men. She'd start bugging him one way or the other in about a week. Let the newness of the human arrivals die down. But she did love to run her fingers through it.

This was her man. A man who rarely did anything less than fully. Whether it was ruling his people with fairness and compassion; playing with his children; training with his men or making love to her. He brought out the best in everyone and she would love him forever.

With the very tip of her finger, she traced along his bottom lip. "Hey, sleepy head. Time to get up." With her nail, she tickled his lip. "Radine, I'll bring Rakenn in any minute now," she threatened. The child delighted in bouncing on his father. Alveda on the other hand, was a snuggler, crawling into her father's embrace and burying herself deep into his side.

When the threat didn't move him – and Radine usually wasn't this hard to wake, coming fully aware at the drop of a hat – McKenna rose up higher to look down into his face. "Radine," she called, shaking him.

He felt warm to her. Naturally, he always felt warmer, Taburons having a slightly higher body temperature than humans. She'd grown used to it over the years – her living bed warmer she would tease him - but now it seemed as though he felt warmer than normal, and he wouldn't wake as he usually did.

McKenna shook him harder. "Radine!" she called. "Radine!" Frightened now, her voice tinged with hysteria, she violently shook him a final time. "Radine!" she nearly screamed. Sitting higher on the bed, she turned towards where the two servants usually entered the room. "Purnia!"

The servant entered at her scream, obviously not completely ready for his day, his shirt untucked and half buttoned, feet shoeless. "Madam?" he asked.

"I can't wake Radine," she said, her voice wavering, tears forming in her eyes. "Get Pologa, and hurry please."

Sending but one glance at the sleeping king, the servant bowed and hurried from the room, not bothering to worry about completing his wardrobe. Annatt came in, having heard the commotion and went immediately to her mistress, taking her by the arms and making her sit on the mattress, holding her in a comforting embrace as McKenna's eyes never strayed from her husband, her shoulders shaking in fear.

She watched as the royal physician Pologa bent over Radine, examining the still unconscious man, his assistant handing him instruments as he called for them. She'd not stopped shaking the entire time despite the warm robe that Annatt had forced her into and the hot tea she'd downed as they waited for Pologa to appear and examine the king. She chewed on her fingernail as she stood at the foot end of the bed, Inoa's arms around her shoulders. The queen mother had appeared as soon as she'd heard that something was wrong with the king, her only child and son, her dress in disarray since she'd also not had time to dress.

Finally, the physician straightened, handing the instrument he held to his assistant. He faced the small waiting group – Inoa, McKenna, Annart, and Purnia. "I do not know what is wrong with the king," he admitted. "He is running a fever, and seems to have some trouble breathing at the moment, but why is beyond me." He sighed slightly. "I can try to treat the symptoms, but unless we can identify the underlying cause, he will not improve."

"I think it's the flu," they heard from behind them as Joanna stepped up to the worried group, her voice despondent, having entered without anyone taking notice. She still wore her own bedclothes, her hair was in disarray. She looked worried, more worried than she'd ever been in several years.

"Flu?" McKenna asked, her brow furrowed deeply.

"What is flu?" Pologa queried.

"It is a virus, influenza, usually not deadly except in rare cases, and not curable. You treat the symptoms, make the patient comfortable, but their body has to fight the disease itself. Common enough among humans, but here...." She shrugged. "I came looking for Pologa. Jaima is sick, too."

"How contagious is this flu?" Pologa asked, his physician interest taking over.

"In a population with no immunity? Very," Joanna confirmed.

"Dear God," McKenna murmured.

"We need to isolate the sick," Pologa decided. "I was told that there have been several people found ill since last night, but no one told me how serious they were." He faced Joanna. "Have Prince Jaima brought here, find out how many others are ill. Is this confined to the palace, or has it moved beyond the walls? You say this is a human disease?"

"Yes."

"Then we have to quarantine the humans in the dormitory, restrict them there until we find out who brought this here."

"There'll be other symptoms," Joanna added, "vomiting, diarrhea, they won't be able to keep food or liquids down if it's really serious. The sick will dehydrate quickly."

"Do we have enough of those intravenous kits you brought from Earth to handle that?"

"It would depend on how many become ill and how quickly it's caught. If I recall correctly, there are about three hundred." When Joanna had come to Taburon, she'd brought medical devices that she'd been given to understand they did not have on the planet. Between the hospital where Jaima had been treated and the United States government, she'd made off with several cargo-sized carriers of merchandise. She had been spending time teaching healers and others how to utilize the equipment she'd brought. Since the two peoples were genetically close, it was assumed that many human treatments would work for Taburons, and now couldn't be a better time to institute that belief.

"The first step," she continued, "as you pointed out is to find those who might be sick and or might have been exposed to the virus and isolate them to contain the spread. Treat them aggressively, especially the young, the elderly, and anyone with an underlying condition that makes them more vulnerable. Should keep the death rate low."

"Death rate?" Inoa repeated with horror.

Joanna reluctantly sighed. "In the early twentieth century on Earth, nearly fifty million people died from the flu, about thirty per cent of the global population." She reached out helplessly. "I'm sorry, but you need to treat this as the biggest threat your people have ever faced." She waved a hand to encompass everyone. "You should send a ship to Earth to get medicine. There are anti-virals that may help. Unfortunately, they need to be administered within two days of falling ill, too late for Radine and Jaima."

"The *Veleda* is still in port. I can have it sent out within a few hours," Inoa supplied.

"What drugs?" McKenna asked.

"I can give Sistan a list. If he goes to Dr. Tripp, together they'll get the right medications."

"Even if the ship leaves today, it won't get back until six days from now."

"Identify and isolate," Pologa repeated. "The only way we'll get this under some kind of control. And pray."

McKenna's eyes widened as a new thought crossed her mind. "The children," she whispered with horror, her hands covering the baby in her belly. Tears started to form in her eyes, threatening to spill over.

"Get them away from everyone," Pologa said, "isolate them from anyone showing any signs of sickness, as well as yourself, Your Majesty." He slid his glance to Joanna. "Your Highness," he added.

"But Radine…"

"Will have round the clock care, I assure you."

"And when the ship returns, we can give the children a prophylactic dose of medicine to protect them. Mostly, keeping them away from the illness will keep them safe," Joanna provided.

"You need to care for your unborn child, Your Majesty," Pologa insisted. "If, Gods forbid, something should happen to the king, your son becomes king. We cannot take any chances and risk them both. And should

Prince Rakenn fall to this illness, that leaves the child you carry, another son, king when he is born."

"McKenna," Inoa said pleadingly when the younger woman remained immobile, her eyes on her husband, "you need to go. The children, think of the children. I'll stay with Radine."

"Someone needs to be here to take charge of the Guard," McKenna murmured. "Isn't Rydul second in command?"

"Yes, Your Majesty," Purnia replied. "But I understand he is on leave and went to his estate, near two days from here."

"No matter, send for him. He needs to take command of the army as well as the Guard. Send a vehicle."

"Immediately, Madam," Purnia promised, bowing and taking his leave. It was the only time he would leave the room, returning within minutes to help take care of the king.

"McKenna," Inoa reminded.

With helplessness in her eyes, McKenna nodded, crying silently as Inoa steered her towards the silent Annatt. The servant led her from the room. "You too, Joanna," Inoa reminded the other woman.

"I know," Joanna agreed. "Promise to keep us informed?" she asked. Both Inoa and Pologa nodded. "Be careful yourself, wear protective clothing, wash often, especially your hands."

"We will. I'll send someone to get Prince Jaima as soon as you've gone."

Purnia walked around the king's bedroom, turning on lights and closing windows that had remained partially open during the day. The king remained on the bed where he'd been when McKenna had tried to wake him that previous morning. He had yet to awaken, though his breathing stayed steady, shallow breaths that came on a regular basis. His brow was dotted with sweat, his hair matted to his head, his skin color pale with illness.

Purnia bathed his body hourly, wiping it free of sweat, cooling his fever but a little. Once he finished caring for the king, he moved to the other side of the bed and repeated the process with the ill prince, who lay on what was normally McKenna's side of the bed. Though conscious when brought into the room, he had since then spent most of his time sleeping.

Both men had been connected to intravenous fluids, glass containers hanging from above the head end of the bed, tubing disappearing under the blankets that directed the fluid to catheters inserted into the backs of one of each man's hand. Jaima had tried to drink earlier, but couldn't keep even fluids down, vomiting his intake within minutes. He refused food.

Each caregiver wore protective clothing and masks which were discarded every time they left the room, which wasn't often, spending most of their resting time sleeping on cots nearby. Food was left for them at the entrance to the sleeping area, used dishes placed in the same spot after. Supplies were replenished as needed.

Within the palace, a dozen more people had fallen ill. Among the guard, ten were sick, confined to the barracks. Outside the palace, in the city, sixty had caught the disease and one person had already died. He was an elderly man, his health in decline without the onslaught of the virus devastating his body further. The disease had pushed him over the edge within twelve hours.

Pologa had traced the outbreak to a single woman who had attended the mid-morning welcoming meal the day before. As the people had mingled throughout the meal, both humans and Taburons, the woman had spread her illness among everyone. Not knowing they'd been infected, those people then spread the disease further to those they came into contact with, who then spread it even more. The ripples had no end, and the queen had resorted to closing off the city, forbidding any travel outside for the inhabitants and anyone from entering unless they had a very just reason.

The woman had been put under quarantine, confined to her room in the dormitory, a guard outside her room, though many of the humans had volunteered to help. They were angry that someone had plotted to jeopardize their chances of establishing a new life and were willing to prove how much they wanted to be considered useful members of their new society. Even Kathryn had volunteered to stand guard over the woman, anything to make Rydul's job easier.

Purnia twisted to rinse out the cloth he had been using to wipe the forehead of the king, surprise crossing his face as he found the ill man staring at him, confusion in his expression, his brows drawn together. "Purnia?" he questioned, his voice raspy.

The attendant nodded. "Yes, my Lord." He set a gentle hand on the king's shoulder. "Lay still, Sire," he instructed. "Pologa," he called.

The physician, dozing nearby in a chair, woke instantly, leaning forward. Seeing the king awake, he stood and stepped to the side of the bed. "Your Majesty," he breathed, "thank the gods you've awakened." Purnia moved to the side so the physician could sit on the edge of the mattress, a hand coming to rest on the king's forehead. "Still feverish, but not deathly so. You're not out of danger yet though."

Radine swallowed, closing his eyes momentarily, his throat dry, his mouth feeling like it was full of cloth and swollen. His chest hurt every time he took a breath. "What?" he whispered.

"You are ill, Sire, very ill, and nowhere near well."

"How?"

"One of the humans brought a disease to Taburon, Princess Joanna called it influenza."

"McKenna? The children?"

"They are well, Sire, moved to the other side of the palace and isolated. Do not fear for them. You must fight to get well yourself."

Radine shifted under the covers. His body was sluggish, heavy feeling. His clothing, what little he wore, felt moist and mushy. His back hurt, his buttocks were numb from laying in one position for a long time. Pain in his limbs convinced him to settle quickly, a soft groan he couldn't control escaping. "I hurt, all over," he said.

"I know," Purnia confirmed. "Joanna said that the illness can cause body aches and pain," he continued as he leaned towards the table beside the bed. Opening a small bottle there, he poured a few drops of blue liquid into a glass, added water and swirled the contents until they were mixed. Slipping his hand beneath the king's head, he lifted the ill man enough to allow him to drink from the glass. "This should help the pain, Sire." The king drank more than half of the medicine before refusing more and the physician waited to see if it would stay down before replacing the glass on the table.

"Who else is sick?" the king asked.

"Prince Jaima, next to you there," he answered, pointing. Radine turned his head to find his best friend and brother sleeping next to him, covers pulled as high as his throat, his breathing deep but congested. "There are others in the city, but we should have the spread under control," the physician hedged, not wanting to upset the king anymore.

Radine's heart sank. If he had to be ill, he knew he could rely on Jaima to take over for him. But with Jaima ill as well, he wondered who was running the kingdom, hoping it wasn't the Council. Nothing would get done if so. McKenna was capable, but even though she'd lived on Taburon for five years now, she was still new to the position and he was afraid the Council could easily overwhelm her. Hopefully Inoa was lending a hand, unless she was also ill.

"My mother?"

"I have asked her to stay in isolation for a few days. She attended the meal as well, but as of now, is not showing any signs of illness." Pologa pulled the covers straight over Radine. "If she goes the rest of today and tomorrow and there is no sign of her becoming ill, I will allow her to aid the queen in the affairs of the kingdom. Feel better now?" he asked knowingly.

"Yes, thank you. How long have I been ill?"

"This is the middle of the second day. As soon as we found you ill, and discovered there were more people down with it, the queen ordered the *Veleda* to go to Earth with a list of medicines the princess requested be brought back to help combat this. It should be back in four and a half days."

"You're sure McKenna is all right?"

Pologa smiled indulgently. "Yes, Sire. She is quite angry about the disease being brought here, and taking 'no prisoners,' as she likes to say, when dealing with the Council. I have heard they have already tried to take over, saying a pregnant woman whose concern is her sick husband, is in no condition to rule with a sound mind. She roundly put them in their place, banishing the whole lot for their own good, as she said."

Radine chuckled hoarsely. Leave it to his McKenna to take charge with a vengeance. After what the Council had put them through before they were married, she held no love for many of its members. They knew it, and she knew they knew it. "Gods' rods, how I love that woman," he breathed as his lids fell, sending him back into much needed sleep.

Pologa patted his shoulder. "As do we all, Sire," he agreed, rising.

CHAPTER THIRTEEN

The moon's light filtered through the bedroom window, falling across the bed in splotches of wavering light. Kathryn lay on one side of the bed, face down, the blankets bunched around her waist. Her back rose and fell steadily while she slept though once or twice she stirred restlessly, her hand reaching out to the other side of the bed in search of Rydul.

She'd picked this room even before Khail directed her to it and being told it was Rydul's. Though sparse in furnishings it was, for the most part, clean, only a thin visible layer of dust on the dresser as if it hadn't been wiped in weeks. The bed had been made, only the top coverlet slightly dusty. The only other bedroom that had been worth looking at had been Khail's and he had left it in a chaotic state as though a violent storm had passed through.

She'd carried her pack into this room setting it at the foot end of the bed and went in search of something to eat.

Surprisingly, for all of the austerity in the rest of the house – which she understood since Rydul didn't live here full time yet – the pantry and the cooling unit were well-stocked. What everything was she hadn't a clue, but she rooted through the provisions, pulling out what she believed she'd recognized, making a light meal.

Sitting at the table she ate in silence, feeling lost. Kathryn had never seen anyone as angry as Rydul, especially after he'd discovered Khail had raided and emptied his accounts. She'd genuinely feared that the fight that had ensued would be brutal. Later, she'd been grateful it had been less violent.

And she had known who would win. Though Khail had two inches and maybe two dozen pounds on Rydul, his indulgent lifestyle had left him out of shape and untrained when pitted against his warrior brother. Perhaps realizing that he had little chance of winning an extended fight, after the initial knocked on his ass blows, Khail had admitted defeat and took the safer road. Within an hour after Rydul had stomped out, the younger man had packed three bags, loaded a crufa and ridden away.

Of course the scowl he'd tossed her way as he passed through the kitchen to the stables did little to assure her that things would improve between the two brothers any time in the near future. Having lived with the uncertainty of the whereabouts of her own brother after all of these years, her heart bled for Rydul and the estrangement.

She would support him even if she thought he'd been rash. She understood. His dreams had hinged on those animals and the freema fields. To have it all taken away in the span of a few minutes was devastating, but he had to do what he thought was best. She only wished he'd stayed in or at least near the house where she could offer comfort.

And so she wouldn't be all alone in a strange place.

Feeling the bed dip brought her instantly and totally awake. Silhouetted by the light from the window, the shadowed outline of a man seated on the edge of the bed blocked out much of her view of the portal itself. Once her heart had stopped pounding, she realized Rydul had returned. Whether or not he had recognized that she had stretched out on his bed remained unanswered.

As she watched, waiting, he lifted an ornate, glass carafe and took a deep pull of the liquid within. She could hear as he swallowed several times before lowering the carafe. His shoulders rose then fell with a deep breath.

"Rydul?"

His back stiffened and his head turned slightly at her softly spoken question and he took another breath as he relaxed. "Um?"

"Are you all right?"

In response, he lifted the carafe to drink again. "No," he finally answered.

"Are you drunk?"

"Probably. I hope so."

Kathryn scooted across the bed, closing the small distance between them until she could place a hand on his right shoulder blade. "What can I do for you?"

For a moment she didn't think he was going to answer. But when he did, his voice soft with despondency, his shoulders sagging. "There is nothing," he sighed.

She moved closer until she could press her body against his back, her lips closer to his ear. "I am sorry."

He took a deep swig. "I guess I should be happy I at least have the house and land yet." Placing the carafe between his knees, he scrubbed at his face with both hands. "Who knows? If I'd waited another month that might have gone as well."

"Can you not start over?"

Tilting the carafe, he finished the drink it held then set the empty bottle on the night table with a heavy thud. Standing abruptly, his back still to her, he swayed before steadying, his hands grabbing at the material of his shirt at his waist.

With a grunt he pulled the garment free and over his head, letting it slide from his arms to drop to the floor.

He swayed again before falling onto the mattress, crossing one ankle over the opposite knee tugging at his boot. It fell with a clunk followed closely by the second boot.

Kathryn moved back as he swung his legs up and lay back, but he grabbed her arm and pulled her close, tucking her against his body. With a hand resting on his chest above his heart, she snuggled into his embrace. He smelled of sweat, alcohol, anger and that unique manly scent she'd come to associate as his alone.

"You are dressed," he mumbled into the dark. His fingers plucked at the sleeve of the oversized t-shirt she wore.

"I didn't know what to do, where you'd gone or when you might return."

"I'm sorry I walked out. I shouldn't have left you unprotected."

"I was a little frightened," she admitted, "but mostly it was for you."

"I was too angry to be around anyone," he answered, resting his head on his free arm. "Still, if you had been injured in any way…"

"But I wasn't," she assured. "He's gone, you know."

"I know. I watched him ride off." He lay still, his breathing even. For a moment, she thought he might have gone to sleep.

His voice when he finally spoke was low as if he didn't want to disturb the night.

"We had such a happy family. I was the oldest, Khail was the second son and Myrysca our baby sister. We weren't rich, but not poor, yet there wasn't anything we needed we couldn't have.

"I was going to learn everything there was about crufas and breeding them. I had always wanted to work around the animals.

"Myrysca was a beauty even as a child. She was destined to make some man happy as a wife and partner, having grown up around the example of the love between our parents.

"Khail had no goals, but he was young yet. He had time to grow up before he had to give up the things one enjoys as a child.

"Our parents were killed with our baby sister when I was sixteen. Khail was eight and badly injured in that accident, but he was given great care. We had no money for the house we grew up in, no family to take over, it was just Khail and me. The house was sold to pay his bills for his care, the medicine, the nursing. He was months in recovery.

"I had one option, to bring in an income, to find a way to keep a roof over our heads, food on the table. I joined the army. Everything I earned went to his bills, then to keeping us housed and fed, to educate Khail. I practically raised him, both brother and father, and now I see that I failed at that.

"When he turned sixteen, I asked him to join the army with me. He asked for two more years, he wanted to give himself more time. He'd missed out on so much because of the accident.

"Since I'd finally begun to be able to save some of my income, I agreed. After all we had lost, what was two more years before he had to become a man?"

Kathryn remained silent. Rydul had given up the rest of his youth to become a man for his brother, time he should have had to finish his own education, to meet a girl, fall in love...He'd sacrificed it all to give his brother everything. And been betrayed. She ached for him to her very soul.

Unaware of the silent struggle she was going through on his behalf, he kept talking. "Because of my proven skills and dedication, I was able to join the Guard only four years after I'd enlisted. That's an accomplishment unheard of. Most men wait ten, fifteen, twenty years before the offer is made. But I had a strong incentive – my brother.

"I was given the estate a year later when I'd done something for the king above and beyond the call of duty. I knew it would take a great deal of work. The house had been run-down, neglected. But I was determined.

"I had a dream. I didn't want to be a soldier all of my life. I wanted to be the best crufa breeder on Taburon, provide a home for myself and brother and someday, for our families. I wanted to retire while still young enough to enjoy what I'd worked for."

Lifting his head, he covered his eyes with his arm. "So close," he murmured. "I estimated perhaps another five years and I would have reached my goal." His arm tightened around her. "Now it's all for nothing," he finished with a heavy sigh.

"There's absolutely no chance you can start again? Rebuild with what little is left?"

"No. What stock I had was carefully selected. Pedigreed and expensive. No one is going to sell them back to me, even if I had the money. What savings I had was slated for the last three mares and to build a proper stable. I may have to sell the estate just to pay the bills."

Rydul fell silent. The pain in his chest was beyond anything he'd ever felt before, even at the death of his parents.

What he hadn't told her was that as he'd wandered the property, his heart heavy, he'd found himself standing, staring down, at the graves of his mother, father and little sister. Once he'd been assured that the land was his, he'd had their graves moved so they would be near where he could tend to them and remember.

Falling to his knees, he'd begged their forgiveness for his failure with Khail. And then he'd wept, like he'd never wept before, the tears pouring from his eyes like a flood, a dam broken in his soul that could only be relieved with a bevy of tears. He'd dropped to his side, clutching at his stomach, pain rendering him in half, and he'd lain there for several hours until he could rise to stagger back to the house where he'd found a carafe of wine untouched by Khail.

Kathryn waited, her hand sliding up and down his chest. Finally he turned his head to look at her. "Know that I love you, with everything I hold true. But love won't put a roof over our heads or food on the table. It won't support children. And the life of a soldier is no life for a family."

She didn't believe a word of it, shaking her head in denial. She'd worked all of her adult life and there was no reason why if she could find work here on Taburon that she couldn't work to help the man she loved. "If we work together, we can make it happen," she suggested.

"Perhaps. But I want surety. I don't want to wake up some distant morning to find I'm too old to enjoy everything we've worked for. Or that I missed my children's growing because I was too busy working.

"I would never begrudge you the right to work, if that is what you wish to do. But I want us to be able to enjoy our life together and not spend it apart because we spent too much time working to replenish what has been lost."

Her voice wavered. Tears began to pool in her eyes. "Are we over then?" She couldn't stand the thought, her heart would break and never mend if true.

"No," he answered firmly. "Gods be damned I hope not. I need to think, but my mind is all muddled now."

"Please don't give up just yet. There has to be a way, we just have to find it." Raising to an elbow, she gazed into his shadowed eyes. "Don't do anything rash. We'll talk about it together."

The light cast her skin in a soft glow, the moisture of tears glistening on her cheeks. A glittering tear hovered on the edge of each eye.

Rydul felt every bit of the anger he'd held onto so tightly wash away as he gently tucked a loosened strand of hair behind her ear. She was so sweet. People had believed in him in the past – Kings Tylene and Radine, the men in his unit – but no one had ever cried for him. Yet she wept, she comforted, she gave him hope that no matter what the future held for him, he could face it and she would be right by his side. It was where he wanted her, where he needed her.

His hand dropped to her shoulder, fingering the material of the shirt. "Are you naked under this?"

Her head bobbed, her hair swayed. "Yes."

"Take it off. I need to hold you, skin to skin." He swallowed deeply. "I'm too drunk to share nadryl. Just let me hold you."

In response, she sat up enough to shrug out of the shirt as he reached for the placket of his trousers. H stopped to watch her, her beautiful breasts jiggling as she moved, his alcohol soaked emotions as appreciative of her body as his sober ones might have been, though his cock lay dormant along his material covered thigh.

He then shucked his trousers and stretched out again, hand extended in invitation. Kathryn readily settled next to him, head pillowed on his shoulder, breasts pressed into his side, a sigh escaping. "I'm sorry," he murmured against her head. "I wanted to show you my home with pleasure and pride."

Kathryn smoothed a hand across his chest. "You have nothing to apologize for. You put your trust in someone who betrayed you. Even a brother can do that. I'm sorry for him. And you have a beautiful home, no matter what happened." His slight tightening of his hand around her body was his only response to her comforting words. Her wonderful acceptance.

She'd been right, whatever the future might bring, if they faced it together, the road might be smoother, not necessarily easier, but smoother. Tomorrow they'd begin to look at the possibilities.

Tonight he would willingly accept her comfort, let someone else take on the burdens and be the protector, to chase away the bad monsters. Tonight, he would let love rule.

A pounding headache woke Rydul nine hours later, the day brightening outside as he stared at the window. Kathryn still cuddled next to him, her body soft and warm, her breasts hugging his side tightly, holding his body in a somnolent embrace.

His sleep had been dreamless and alcohol deep. He'd hardly moved through the night, but when he did, Kathryn never strayed from his side, rearranging her body around his, a hand always touching him, soothingly moving across his chest or waist.

So while his troubles had left him alone for the night, they'd returned full force with the dawn, bringing a headache to beat all headaches to pound at him with every heartbeat, drumming his troubles deep into his brain and ripping at his very soul.

The dream he'd created of raising crufas was over. It would take years to build up the funds to replace the animals his brother had sold. Then he would need more funds to build the proper housing for breeding mares. And while the cost was much less by comparison to refurbish the freema fields, the choice was whether to do flowers first or the animals. Of course, once the flowers were bringing in an income that could be put towards the crufas, things would be easier to assess. But he had to first determine how badly the fields had been neglected and stripped. How long it would take for them to again be profitable.

That still didn't leave much for supporting a wife, family and estate. Until his obligations to the Guard ended, he'd have to hire a manager or two, one for the crufas and one for the plants. More funds he would need to procure. There would be no end to where he would need to spread his funds, and not much in the way of those to spread around.

It would be difficult to accept, but his plans had to change. How – he did not know. To what he did not know.

All he knew was he wanted this woman with him, at his side, sharing their love and bodies, facing the future together. He had intended to propose to her, to ask her to become his wife. But until he knew which path they would forge from the ruins his brother had created, he would delay making the offer. And insure that if they shared nadryl – when they shared nadryl – no child would be the result of their joining.

Sounds from beyond the closed bedroom door roused him from his musings. Someone was in the house, several someones if he heard correctly, and they were heading in his direction.

Ignoring the pounding in his head, he rolled over to give Kathryn a shake. "Kathryn, wake up," he said softly, not wanting to alert the intruders that he'd heard them or alarm the girl. "Come, Olana, wake up." She stirred, then jerked, her eyes opening wide as she searched for her lover. The surprise she'd shown upon waking disappeared as soon as she recognized him, then turned alarmed at his next words. "Someone is in the house. Get dressed."

Twisting, he swung his legs over the edge of the bed and started to rise into a sitting position, clutching at his head as the room spun and the throb increased two fold. Behind his back he heard the bed clothes rustle as she began to move.

With a deep breath, he bent to grab his trousers, righting the garment and shoving both feet in at the same time, standing, yanking the pants passed his hips.

He'd just fastened the front when the footsteps stopped and a heavy knock sounded at the bedroom door.

"Captain Rydul."

His heart returning to its normal pace as he recognized Kenlyn's voice, Rydul took a step towards the door, shooting a quick glance to Kathryn to make sure she'd covered enough that he could open the door. The shirt she'd worn to bed drifted over her hips, covering just enough to get by.

Kenlyn and Chissa waited outside, their uniforms crisp, short swords at their hips, hands on their laser weapons. Kenlyn snapped to attention at the sight of Rydul.

"What is it?"

"Sir, by command of the queen, you are ordered to return to the palace immediately."

"I am on leave."

"It has been cancelled, sir."

"What has happened?" he asked, moving back into the room. Bending, and instantly regretting it, though he ignored the pain, he retrieved his shirt, turning it right side out.

Kenlyn and Chissa followed on his heels. Stopping upon seeing Kathryn on the other side of the bed. She flushed when they both perused her, recognizing the state of her undress, the shirt covering her nudity but not hiding the fact that her breasts hung unrestrained underneath. Her hair was tousled, draping her shoulders freely. While they'd not shared nadryl during the night, she looked, save for the confusion in her eyes, thoroughly satisfied. The men could guess what her presence meant. Both men's expressions became amused and curious at the same time.

The lack of response and silence caught Rydul's attention and he scowled as he saw the direction of their gaze, the expressions on their faces and recognized the path their thoughts had taken. "Gentlemen," he reprimanded sharply.

Kenlyn cleared his throat, facing his commanding officer. "There has been an outbreak of an illness in Duguid. Both the king and prince have been stricken and are severely ill.

Pologa is cautious with his prognosis. It has been traced back to the humans. You are needed to take over."

His mood deflated and sobered, Rydul dropped onto the bed. The king – and prince – ill? Possibly deathly ill? The regime could easily fall with a child king on the throne should Radine die. While McKenna was well–loved, she did not have the lifetime of being a Taburon to fend off any coup attempt. The queen mother Inoa, while a formidable woman of and by herself, would be too grief filled at the loss of her only son and adopted son to exert her power and take control.

Prince Jaima was more than qualified to both support the young heir and rule in his stead. But if he was also ill and died, that responsibility would fall in Rydul's shoulders. He hoped the situation was not as dire as it felt at the moment. The road would be difficult, rounding up those loyal to the crown and restating their oaths to a child king, then keeping them in line until Rakenn came of age. Controlling the Council would be one of his most difficult tasks. They would either side with Rakenn, or make a concerted effort to take control. At least until the prince/king reached his majority. Though there was no telling what kind of damage a power possessed Council would do until that time.

So much for needing to give thought for his own future. The king must survive, or Prince Rakenn given all the aid his loyal subjects could provide to see him reach adulthood and rule. Not to mention taking charge of both the guard and the army.

"The crufas we came on are stabled," he started to say to indicate that they had to be saddled and repacked to return to the city.

"We have a vehicle, sir," Kenlyn interrupted, then cleared his throat, uncomfortable with his next words. "The Council has ordered all humans, except for the queen and princess, confined to the dormitory. That would include her, Captain," he finished, his head inclined towards Kathryn.

Rydul's jaw dropped, stunned as Kathryn turned, wide-eyed, to Rydul. Swiftly he went to her side, taking her arms. "Just a precaution, Olana. You will not be harmed, by anyone," he added with emphasis for the benefit of the soldiers. "Just until this passes."

Pressing her head to his chest, she nodded, forcing herself to calm. She would trust this man, trust in his love for her and trust in his honor. He'd not lied to her once. Rydul had proven that he would care both for and about her even before himself.

Cupping her face, he tilted her head, meeting her lips with his own, not caring what the two men who'd ended their interlude would make of the gesture.

"Kenlyn," he finally said, "there was an unpleasant incident here yesterday which I am not ashamed to admit I tried to drown with drink. I stink of it. Since you brought a vehicle there is time for me to shower. I will explain what happened on the way back. Give us some privacy to dress, will you? And I hope you've got someone else with you to bring our crufas back?"

"Laeve waits outside."

"Then join him," he ordered. "Oh, and by the way," he added as they spun on their heels to exit, "you are to never enter my house unannounced again."

Both men saluted. "Yes, sir," they answered in harmony then hastened out, pulling the door closed.

"Do you want to shower?" he asked Kathryn.

"Can they really think one of us is responsible for this illness?"

"Pologa is quite thorough when it comes to the health of the royals. Yes, I am sure they know exactly where it came from. But you are not ill, so I cannot see them laying the blame at your feet, Olana. Confining your people is just a precaution to keep it from spreading."

"I hope the king is all right."

"As do I. There will be a terrible price to pay if he does not survive. Both on Taburon and Earth."

"That scares me." There was a sadness in her voice, a remoteness in her body language that Rydul could feel as he embraced her.

"Kathryn, I love you. Never doubt that. We'll take each day as it comes until this situation is settled and the king well again." She answered with a smile, rising on tiptoe to offer her lips for a kiss. He obliged, taking his time to explore, savoring the kiss until he reluctantly realized that their time right now was limited – and passing quickly. "Are you sure you don't want to shower with me?"

She offered him a smile. "No, I'm fine. You go ahead and I'll meet you in the outer room."

"Under different circumstances, I would take you back to that bed and keep you there for an entire day. Or two," he added with a grin. She giggled softly. "While I shower, would you get me a drink? There should be a container of a green juice in the cooling unit. And make sure you're completely dressed. Don't give those two *tritios* out there any more ideas." He dropped a peck of a kiss on the tip of her nose. "You're mine."

CHAPTER FOURTEEN

Rydul waited patiently as Queen McKenna finished reading a petition and signed off on it. Glancing up as she handed the paper back to a courtier, she smiled upon seeing him as he nodded briefly, keeping to the rear of the room until she could get away from the number of people filling the throne room. Of course, most were there to hear any news about the king and prince, disguising their curiosity in petitions and warrants.

She waved off every other person surrounding her – sycophants, courtiers, lords and ladies – pasting a wider smile on her face as she went to greet the captain.

Except the smile faded as soon as her back was turned to everyone but Rydul. Worry lines etched her face, pulling down her mouth and shadowing her eyes. Her shoulders sagged, her steps seemed heavy.

The rounded tummy of her seven, nearly eight month's pregnancy preceded her but a few inches as she reached out to touch his arm. Rydul bowed.

"Your Majesty."

"Come with me," she ordered, leaving the throne room. Following on her heels, she led him to a small sitting room, closing the door after him.

Racing in front of her, he held a chair out in invitation. "You look tired, Madam."

With a deep sigh, McKenna lowered herself into the chair. "Exhausted is more like it."

His voice was anxious. "The king? Prince Jaima?"

"I honestly don't know. They have a high fever that doesn't want to break, both hurt all over and they're having trouble breathing. They're so very ill."

"With what? Kenlyn said the illness was from the humans."

"We call it influenza. Normally it's an illness that makes you feel miserable for a week or so, but it isn't deadly unless there are other complications."

"Such as?"

"The very young, the very old, people with other illnesses. If you're otherwise healthy, you get sick, you get better. The problem is your people have no inherent immunity to it. And it can spread like wildfire if not caught soon enough, especially among people with no past exposure."

"How did it get here? I thought all of the humans were screened."

She heaved a deep sigh. "Not well enough obviously. It appears one woman went through the screening process in place of the ill one. She stayed isolated as much as possible, claiming nerves at the journey, but came to the welcoming gathering."

"How many are ill?"

"Five hundred so far. Thirty have died. We hope we've isolated it, and when a day or two goes by without a new case, we might assume it has been contained. So far that hasn't happened. We weren't aware of the infection until after everyone who'd attended the breakfast had already gone their separate ways, meeting with others outside, who met with others, and the ripple effect goes on and on."

"Princess Joanna, is she well? The children?"

"Yes, thank the gods. We've moved to the other side of the palace until..." McKenna's voice choked. She paused as she fought to bring her emotions under control. "I haven't seen Radine in four days. If I weren't pregnant, I'd be taking care of him, but neither he nor Pologa will let me near."

Rydul filled with sympathy. "Tell me what you need for me to help."

"Keep the peace, keep control. Squash any rumors that Radine is dying and keep an ear out for any murmurings of a take-over."

Rydul frowned at this news. Radine was a well-loved and gracious king. To jump on his illness now, to begin making plans was little short of treason. After the betrayal he'd just experienced, Rydul had no tolerance for a betrayal to his king.

There had been resistance when Radine had first taken the throne and an outright attempt to control him when he'd planned to marry McKenna. But it had been five years since any overt attack on his rule had surfaced.

"And who would be speaking of treason against the king at this time?" he asked, making his distaste obvious.

She waved a hand. "Same old group. Quorol may have been gotten rid of, but not the sentiment. I can't handle anymore with having to deal with Radine being sick and trying to keep things running smoothly with the court."

"Where's Inoa?"

"She wanted to tend to Radine, but he wouldn't hear of it. Instead, he's had her isolated, just in case, since she also attended the breakfast. She'll be a force to contend with if Rakenn inherits the throne now, but her grief will be very deep. She's angry at the thought, but concedes the logic in not taking chances with her own life."

Rydul shot a pointed look to McKenna's expanded waistline. "Nor should you," he added, "not with a babe on the way."

"I've spoken with Joanna. She feels that our natural immunity – or at least our human ancestry – will provide enough of a shield to protect our babies from the virus. She's helping Pologa when she can – from a distance – and agreed to his request to send for medicines from Earth. The ship left three days ago. But it'll be at least another three days or so until it returns." Her voice was but a whisper. "I hope it's not too late."

Rydul paced a moment, his thoughts churning and his emotions on high. "Where is this woman who brought this?"

"Locked in and under guard in her room at the dormitory. There were several people who volunteered to make sure she stays put, including some from Earth. They're just as concerned, and angry, as the rest of us since they want to make a life here and this woman is undermining all that we are trying to do. They had such high hopes and wanted to be a part of our world. Someone has to go and ruin it."

Rydul bowed. "You know the Guard is loyal to Radine, and by extension, you. I will do everything in my power to keep the king and his family safe." His hand settled on his laser weapon, secured firmly at his hip. "And in power," he added meaningfully.

McKenna couldn't help the tears that suddenly made her vision bleary and she blinked rapidly. "Thank you, Rydul. I'm sorry we cut your leave short, but I needed someone I knew I could trust."

He bowed again. "With my life, Your Majesty," he pledged. And realized that whatever he had going with Kathryn, whatever plans he'd made or wanted to make were insignificant for the moment. His loyalties required he remain focused here until the crisis passed. He hoped Kathryn would understand.

"I will pass word around to a select few of the Guard. They will keep close watch on the court and listen. With your permission, I would like to visit the king briefly first, then question this woman."

McKenna nodded. "Of course. Just, please, be careful. If you get ill, I have no one to turn to."

"I shall be very careful," he promised. He had more than just his concern for the queen to insure that he stayed safe, but now was not the time to divulge that information. He offered his arm. "If you will allow me, I will escort you back to the court." McKenna sniffled but gave him a wane smile as she slid her hand across his arm.

CHAPTER FIFTEEN

Rydul felt as though it hadn't been that long since he'd waited at the landing area for the shuttle to allow its passengers to disembark. Of course, the last time, he had found Kathryn in the group of newcomers to the planet, the love of his life taking things into her own hands and following him to his home.

Now though the circumstances were much more dire as he stood next to the carriage in which Princes Joanna sat, fidgeting, waiting for the hatch to lower. She was adamant that she would check the medicines Sistan was supposed to have obtained from Earth to help in the epidemic that was running ramped through Duguid. Nearly a thousand people had been infected, already a couple dozen had died. They were running out of the equipment and intravenous set-ups Joanna had brought with her and everyone was worried. She fretted as they watched, her hand constantly smoothing over the bulge of her unborn child. At least, she thought, there were no further worries there. Both she and McKenna had shown no signs of illness, and the other children were as healthy as ever. But she looked tired, exhausted from helping to direct treatment from a distance, emotionally lost since she'd not seen her husband in nearly six days though the reports were he had not gotten any worse. He just wasn't improving as fast as he should.

McKenna was in the same 'boat,' not having seen Radine in as many days, his reports being that the king had been having ups and downs with the infection. He would seem to rally, then fall back, also not improving, but not worsening. Just not healing. The reasons were puzzling, something that would be examined and discussed at a later date when everyone was doing better and there wasn't this overwhelming sense of urgency hanging over the city.

Plus, McKenna had the kingdom to consider. And while Inoa helped, the people looked to their queen for guidance through this crisis. What she felt they felt and visa-versa. They suffered together, those that suffered, and those that didn't prayed for their king, their prince and their planet.

The hatch started its downward journey, Rydul lending a hand to Joanna as she awkwardly climbed from the carriage, anxious to get to the supplies. They barely waited until it had touched the ground and settled before stepping on the platform, heading into the vehicle.

And pulling up short at the tall human man that greeted them at the end of the hatch. Joanna's face broke into the first smile she'd smiled in nearly a week and she hurried the last two steps to throw her arms around the neck of the man. "Dr. Tripp, what are you doing here?"

"Heard you have a little virus problem," he quipped back, giving her as tight a hug as he dared. "I came to help." He pushed her back to hold her at the shoulders, looking her over. "Look at you," he declared. "You look wonderful."

She snorted in response, her arms dropping to her sides. "Hah, I'm as big as a house."

"You're beautiful. I hear things worked out quite well for you and Jaima after all."

She shot him a coy look. "Not every day a girl starts out a lowly nurse and ends up a princess."

He grinned. "Should I bow, or is there some other protocol I should know?"

"I heard the touching of your forehead to my feet was discontinued a handful of years ago, but we could always revive it," she hinted with a chuckle. "Just be yourself, as I remember, at least in private." Her face lost all joy and turned serious. "I hope you were able to bring the items I requested?"

"Everything you asked for and more. I was surprised to hear of the outbreak, sorry too." Together they walked into the shuttle, Rydul following, keeping guard over the princess. "How has it been going?"

"Nearly a thousand infected, about three dozen lost, six of those were children. McKenna is furious, the woman who brought it is confined and guarded and we're at our wit's end here. Radine and Jaima don't seem to be improving, but they're not on death's door at least. The entire planet will revolt if either one of them dies."

"Radine is the king?" Tripp asked, not having had much contact with the man when he cared for Jaima after the prince had been shot. They followed the corridors through the shuttle to where a large storage room held the needed supplies.

"His Majesty is beloved by the people." Rydul explained. Tripp eyed him, trying to remember where he'd seen this person in the past, his name suddenly coming to the forefront in his brain. He spoke as one with authority though Tripp remembered him as a captain. "If he dies, his son will become king, but he is too young to hold the throne without the backing of the army and the Guard. Prince Jaima, who controls both, would make an excellent advisor, but not if he also perishes." The soldier bowed his head in Joanna's direction. "With all due respect, Your Highness."

"I'm sorry, Rydul. Dr. Martin Tripp, this is Captain Rydul. While Radine and Jaima are ill, the unfortunate task of being in charge of both the army and the Guard has fallen to him. You two never met back when Jaima had been shot."

"No, but we did meet, back when the Captain was assigned to Earth last year." Tripp stopped in front of the cargo room doors, extending his hand before they entered. "Sorry to be meeting again under these circumstances," he said as the two shook. "Most everything is in here. There are more supplies on the big ship that didn't come down this time. I think Sistan is here as well, checking them for the twentieth time."

"The healer is nothing if not thorough," Joanna complimented, passing through the doors as they opened.

"Your healers are familiar with how to work this equipment?"

"I've had two years to train them, yes. They're very adept, very quick students, and have been taking care of the sick outside of the palace. We set up a triage and a hospital of sorts where people can go to keep them separated from the healthy. It wasn't easy, but these people jump to work when they need to and it was up and running within six hours."

"Impressive," Tripp complimented. "Let's get this stuff where it will do the most good then, shall we?" Together the group turned their attention to the supplies and began directing what to take off first and where to take it.

Sky Clad Rydul

CHAPTER SIXTEEN

Pacing in front of the entrance doors to the dormitory, Kathryn waited impatiently for Rydul to arrive. She wrung her hands together, then let them drop, suddenly aware that she seemed too anxious for the arrival of the warrior to anyone watching, and she was being watched. There was an older couple seated in the lounge just off the entrance, married for forty years and in search of a new life, peeking over the books they were reading and smiling indulgently at the young woman. They'd been young once, too, and remembered how the soldier had swept the girl up onto his saddle at the tournament demonstration. It had been one of the most romantic things the woman had ever seen – right out of the knights on white horses stories.

The pacing woman took a deep breath and leaned against the table by the door, her gaze outside. He'd promised to come by, had let her know he was on his way, but it had seemed like such a long time since his message. She wondered what was keeping him.

After returning to Duguid, Rydul had walked with her, hand in hand to her small apartment in the dormitory, standing for a good five minutes, holding her, reassurance for her and himself. He'd kissed her, long and deep, taking her tongue into his mouth to remember her flavor, making sure she didn't forget him either. Promising to keep her up to date as much as possible, he reluctantly took his leave of her.

He spoke with her daily, a quick conversation to see how she was doing and let her know that with both the Guard and the Army in his hands, he was constantly doing something. The queen was running the planet and he was her back-up in case anyone had any ideas about who really was in charge. He would stand with Queen McKenna when need be if she needed. He assured her that if he had any free time, he would try to get out to see her.

Straightening abruptly, her expression broke into a smile as he pulled Ferrin to a halt right outside, the guard there taking the reins as Rydul slipped from the saddle to land lightly on the ground. Fishing something from a pocket, he held the tidbit under the animal's nose. Ferrin snuffled at it then delicately grabbed it with his lips, chewing contentedly. Rydul spoke briefly to the soldier, pulling his gloves from his hands and fixing his sword belt at his hips. The soldier nodded and Rydul stepped around him.

Kathryn didn't wait for him to reach for the handle to the door, pulling it open when he was just one step beyond it. He wore his full uniform: black boots that reached to his knees, black trousers, a blue coat over a white shirt, a few of his medals pinned to the left breast side. There were epaulets at his shoulders, the sword belt was knotted around his waist, the sword dangling easily within reach. He cut a handsome figure, as she always thought he did, the air of command and seriousness in his expression letting the casual observer know this was a man in charge and one with lots on his mind.

The determined look in his eyes turned to delight though as he saw her waiting, a spark appearing, lips turned up in a smile, the lines of duty across his brow softening. The tenseness in his shoulders relaxed.

She returned his smile, though there was a touch of worry in her eyes that couldn't be hidden in the smile.

Rydul enfolded her in a tight embrace. He'd been so consumed with his duties that he'd not been able to see her in several days. And he missed her sorely.

As luck would have it, when she'd contacted him and asked to see him, he'd finally had a brief reprieve – an hour

– he could give before he had to return. Not enough to share nadryl, but he could stoke the fires quite well to keep them burning.

"I've missed you," he murmured before taking her mouth in a kiss.

"As have I," she replied as soon as he came up for air.

"Are you all right? Not feeling too confined are you?"

"I'm all right." She smoothed her hand down his chest. Under the material of his coat she could feel his muscles bunch as he rubbed along her spine, keeping her tight against his body. "How is the king? Is he any better?"

With a sigh, Rydul released her and stepped back slightly, his face crestfallen. "He's no better, but no worse. Same for Prince Jaima. But it has only been one day since the medicines arrived. Dr. Tripp says it could take several days before they show signs of improvement. And with them both down that leaves me in charge, which also leaves me with very little free time for anything, even decent rest."

"You do look tired. I'm sorry."

"It is not your fault, Olana."

She took his hand, holding it gently, her expression wistful. "Can we go to my room?" she asked lowering her voice. "I'd like some privacy, if you know what I mean."

That spark returned and brightened as he slipped a hand behind her knees and lifted. She squealed softly, still convinced that she weighed too much, but he merely hefted her into a better grip and started walking. Passing the lounge, he heard a soft chuckle. Glancing into the room, he saw the older couple watching, their books forgotten. Rydul responded with a lascivious grin and continued on past the room.

Once inside her room, he set her on her feet and turned the lock on the door to her room. Facing her, he wrapped his arms around her, pulling her even tighter against his body than he'd done in the entry way. "Now for a proper hello," he declared, bending his head.

His kiss was sweet and tender, full of longing, rife with promises. Ashe plundered her mouth, he pulled her so tight against his body, spreading his legs slightly as he tucked her into the cradle of his hips. His reaction pressed, full and firm into her belly.

There was deep regret in his voice. "I wish I had more time. I'd make love to you for hours." He backed away, sighing, not bothering to hide his erection. "When this is over, we will go back to my estate, such as it is, and not leave the bedroom for days."

"It sounds wonderful, and I can't wait to join you." Her brow furrowed in concern and worry, her hands clasped together. "But I have something to tell you. I don't know if it means anything, but you should know."

He took her arm, the romantic mood shattered, his own face etched with worry. "What?" he asked. "Kathryn, what's wrong?"

"I heard something yesterday. I'm hoping it was just talk…."

"What? Tell me, Olana."

"I heard two people, one of them I'm sure was that woman who brought the infection. I don't know who the other person was. They were saying that 'he' wasn't dying fast enough, that they had to take more drastic measures to end this alien intrusion. He said he'd brought the material with him, and the palace wouldn't be much more than a pile of rubble. Rydul, I think they're planning on blowing up the palace to kill the king."

His response was incredulity, staring at Kathryn as though she'd suddenly grown a second head or sprouted wings as the enormity of what she'd said started to sink in.

"By all the gods!" he breathed. "Are you sure?"

She shrugged. "As best I can be."

Sinking down onto the mattress of her bed, Rydul looked lost for a moment. If true, these humans were a far worse lot than anyone had ever conceived. To blow up the palace, to destroy the symbol of Taburon rule and kill the king…..The people of Taburon would surely declare war on Earth and its inhabitants, destroying every living being on that planet.

And the revenge wouldn't be confined to Earth. Every human on Taburon would suffer as well, confined or even exiled, including the queen and princess. And the woman he loved. Their presence would not be tolerated no matter how loyal they appeared.

The queen's efforts to inquire after humans on other planets would come to an end. She'd already located several dozen. Most were content with their lives. But a handful wanted – needed – to be rescued and either settle on Taburon or be returned to Earth. Endeavors to create plans were proving more difficult than expected, yet still being explored.

And if the king were killed, the Council would take over, the child prince way too young to rule. There were still lingering feeling about the king taking a human for a wife. The Council would do everything in their power to shut McKenna out I order to mold the child to their way of thinking and things would not be pleasant for humans on Taburon of that happened.

With an outcry against humans, Rydul's own future hung in the balance. If Kathryn were even permitted to remain, making her his wife was now uncertain, let alone having children. As a high ranking officer in the Guard, taking a non-Taburon as a wife could call into question his loyalties and cost him his position and home. Of course, he would give it all up for her, but he would always feel unjustly accused.

His glance rose to Kathryn, the fear and worry in her expression taking precedence over even his own thoughts. With a tug, he settled her on his lap, pressing a kiss to her temple. "It's all right," he soothed, "it's all right." He felt her nod against his shoulder, her chest rising with a deep breath. "Now tell me everything," he instructed tenderly.

"I was going to the kitchen to find something to eat. I had to go passed that woman's room to get there. I know which one is hers, I volunteered to keep watch a day ago. The door was open, which it shouldn't have been, and there were voices. I stopped when I heard the king's name mentioned. The man said he was angry that the king hadn't died yet, that there were rumors that medicine was coming from Earth and if they wanted to accomplish their goal they had to move on to a new plan. Do something more drastic, more immediate. He said he had all of the materials and had assembled them. His contact in the palace would get him inside...."

"What?" Rydul interrupted. "Someone in the palace is helping?"

She nodded. "That's what I heard."

"Did he say who? When? When he planned this attack?"

"No, he didn't use a name, didn't say when, just that it was going to be soon."

"Did you see this man? Know who he is?"

"No. When it seemed they were finished, I raced back towards my room, making it look like I had just exited the room. He was walking away from me. I only saw his back. He wore a jacket with the hood pulled up, I didn't even see what color his hair was."

"Anything else? Did you hear him say anything else about his palace contact?"

She shook her head. "No. I wish I had heard more," she confessed. Her eyes brightened slightly and she bent to reach for something under the bed. "I have a gift for you," she said as she pulled out a long flat box. Standing tall, she passed it to him, setting it on his lap.

He queried with a look, then set to opening the box, splitting the tape that held it closed along its length and at the ends. When he lifted the lid, he found a layer of what the humans called styrofoam covering the entire length of the box. She nodded at his expression, giving him the go-ahead and he peeled off the white covering.

Hi eyes widened at her gift, his hand carefully lifting the sword from its bed of white, the leather sheath a stark brown contrast to the interior. "A sword?"

"It's supposed to be made of the finest steel on Earth, called Damascus steel. It's so sharp it can cut a piece of cloth dropped on it from above without having to do anything more than drop it."

Putting the box on the floor, Rydul hefted the sword and slipped it from its case. The metal gleamed in the light, bright as a star, the pommel wrapped in fine, tooled leather. He stood, holding the sword to check its balance, pleased to find it perfectly balanced. Within the blade, he could see a pattern of waves, as though the metal were alive, reminding him of the action of a small whirlpool of water.

It was a superior sword, better, he believed, than even the king's sword. He would have to guard it carefully from the royal whom he knew would want to try it out for himself then demand one as well if it turned out to be as fabulous as he believed.

Moving away from Kathryn, he swung the sword in several arcs, a smile on his face. The blade whistled as it pierced the air, a good solid sound. Looking it over again, he found the swordsmith's mark along the end of the pommel, a scrollwork of ornate symbols he could not understand. "It is wonderful, Olana, thank you." He returned the steel to its sheath. "Why?"

"You mean a lot to me and did so much for me when I was hurt. I wanted to give you something you could use, even if you only use it when you dress up."

"You did not have to gift me, Kathryn, but I will treasure this." H leaned close to place a kiss on her cheek, frowning when he saw the look of worry on her face. "What?"

"Rydul, I'm scared."

He pulled her close, making her stand in the space between his spread legs. "Don't be. You've told me about the threat, now it's up to me." He leaned down enough to give her another kiss. When he lifted his head, he took a good look at her hair. Running his fingers through her tresses, he loosened many of the strands and fluffed her hair slightly, enough to make it look like she'd been tousled.

She raised a hand to her head as his fell to the top buttons of her blouse. "What?" she asked, confused, watching as he slipped a button through the button hole.

His grin was downright bawdy. "Can't have anyone who sees us thinking we were only talking," he explained as he opened a second button, spreading the sides of her shirt apart. "A little messy with a loosened button or two will speak volumes." Kathryn flushed a deep red from her hairline to the exposed skin under her shirt. "Just one more thing," Rydul decided, standing just before he took her mouth.

Wasting no time, he plundered her lips, rubbing across them with his own, opening her to his exploration, making sure there'd be no question as to what they'd been doing in even with a short space of time. And he needed to kiss her, wanted to taste her again, needed to have her warmth and deliciousness with him when he returned to the palace and tackled this newest threat to the kingdom. With everything he believed, he wished he was still on Earth and spending a quiet evening with her at the embassy, watching television then heading to his room for a long session of sharing nadryl. For if he had still been on Earth after all of this time, he wouldn't have hesitated to get her in his bed and his randy cock inside her body.

When he lifted his head, he was quite pleased to see her lips looked thoroughly ravished, red and swollen. With the tip of one finger, he traced her lower lip.

"You look so beautiful. Wanton right now, thoroughly kissed and loved." Unbuckling his sword belt, he grabbed the sheathed weapon and leather strap as it fell from his hips, holding it in one hand. "Come, walk with me to the front door." He held both swords in one hand, taking one of her hands in the other.

"You'll keep me informed?" she asked, sotto voice as they walked hand in hand.

"When I can. I have both the army and the Guard to oversee and now the palace to be concerned about." He glanced down at her as they walked together, her seriousness and faraway look giving him pause. "What?"

She shook her head. "I don't know. It's as though there's something I'm missing, something that's passing through my brain, but I can't catch hold of it." She shrugged. "I guess it's not important."

"If you think of it, will you let me know?"

Kathryn nodded. "If it matters."

"Even if you think it doesn't at the time. You never know, it might be relevant to the situation." They halted in front of the door, he passed her the gift sword and buckled his sword belt around his waist, settling it comfortably, making a show of it for the audience still in the lounge room, now totaling six. He grinned when her sideways glance revealed their watchers, her blush returning with a vengeance. Bending, he kissed her, sliding the gift sword from her hand.

"When this is over," he promised.

"Please, be careful," she asked, her hand on his chest. "I don't want to lose you."

"Never happen, Olana." With reluctance, he pulled on the door, never taking his eyes from her until he'd completely stepped through, the sunlight casting his hair in brilliant gold. The guards outside straightened as he turned around, one of them grabbing Ferrin's reins and handing them off. For a moment he spoke with the guards, particularly one of them, gesturing at the dormitory as he spoke. Taking a small device from a pocket the guard gave it a quick glance then responded to a question Rydul must have asked. Nodding his head, Rydul gave Kathryn one last glance, a smile of reassurance in his eyes. With a hand on the horn of the saddle, he swung up onto the back of his crufa with practiced ease, turned it and set off in a gentle canter away from the building.

Hugging herself, Kathryn, worried for his safety and fearful for everyone involved, spun away from the door, pulling up short upon seeing the older couple standing in the entrance to the lounge. The man had his arm around the shoulders of the woman, she with a smile on her lips.

Blushing at what they might have been thinking, that she'd been spending the better part of the last half hour or so indulging in a booty call of shameless wanton behavior, Kathryn gave them both a wane smile and headed back to her room.

Sky Clad Rydul

CHAPTER SEVENTEEN

After leaving Kathryn, Rydul rode through the streets, his attention not on where he was going, his thoughts swirling. A bomb placed perfectly in the palace could bring a good portion of it down. And since both the king and prince resided in the family wing, he decided that would be the bomber's target. Were he determined to destroy the family quarters, Rydul had a fairly good idea where he would plant a bomb.

The basement was filled with storage areas under the family wing. There were columns there that were the base supports for the entire wing. Bring down the central support and the rest would follow readily.

However, a person required some sort of clearance in order to get into the basement. He dismissed the possibility of it being one of the servants. Most of them had no access to the cellars, only those in charge of their particular department could get downstairs and he knew each one personally. Each one had been a trusted employee for well over twenty years.

That someone – a trusted Guardsman – was helping disturbed Rydul more than anything else. Every man took a loyalty oath, and no one had broken that oath in over fifty years. That had been a few years after Tylene had come to the throne. A conspiracy between several lords, enlisting the aid of three Guardsmen, had attempted to take over the palace. Only the loyalty of the rest of the troop and the cunning of the king had cut the traitors down before too much damage had been done.

His biggest concern had been how to discern who had turned without showing that he knew. He needed help. He couldn't search the entire basement and insure that the king, prince, their families, and the rest of the staff were moved somewhere safe until the danger passed or, if he were unsuccessful, he failed and the bomb went off. He was absolutely sure he would need several helpers.

Arriving at the barracks, he dismounted Ferrin, tying the reins to a post, giving a quick scratch to the creature's nose before mounting the steps into the building.

Heading to his room, he kept his steps hurried but his attitude casual in case he passed anyone. Closing the door, he first went to his dresser and placed the gift sword on top of it, spending a second to once more admire the gift, hoping he would someday have a chance to wear it. As special as it was, he would save it for ceremonial dress.

At the foot of his bunk, he opened the trunk there as he undid the belt of his sword around his hips, laying the belt and weapon on his bunk.

Taking out leather greaves, he placed them around his legs, then added leather arm braces. Pulling out his leather cuirass, he belted it around his chest, then put the sword belt back on over the cuirass, tightening the belt and looping the end over the buckle. Kicking the lid of the trunk closed with a foot, he turned and left the room, making sure the door was shut firmly. Not that he didn't trust anyone, but it would be nice to know that his new gift would still be there when this was finished.

Rydul was fortunate that no one questioned him as he left the barracks to take the short walk to the palace. Seeing him in armor would have certainly raised a few eyebrows and invited a couple of queries. He went unaccosted as he entered the palace through a side door casually used by Guardsmen, soldiers and servants alike. A single servant polishing a table eyed him for a brief second before returning to her task. Down a short hallway to his right he saw Kenlyn, the soldier's back turned towards Rydul as he read something he held in his hands.

Carefully, soundlessly, Rydul withdrew his dagger from its sheath, gripping the handle tightly. The servant stopped working, an eyebrow rising this time in fear. Rydul made a quiet motion, signaling the servant away. The woman wasted no time in scurrying out as Rydul moved forward.

Throwing his left arm around Kenlyn's shoulders, Rydul pressed the edge of his blade against the other's throat before he had a chance to react.

At first, the soldier tensed, his hand falling to his laser weapon, whatever he had been reading falling to the floor. Then realizing he was in a no-win bind, that the knife could slice him before he could defend himself, Kenlyn allowed his body to relax, his hand falling to his side away from his weapon.

His voice was calm. "If you slit my throat, I might still be able to scream. However, if you push the tip of the blade into the back of my neck, you can kill me instantly."

Rydul pressed the blade deeper, but not enough to cut. "Gods, king and Taburon..." he quoted.

"I pledge my life before my surrender," Kenlyn finished. "Rydul? Care to explain?" he asked as Rydul released him and sheathed his dagger. Kenlyn turned slowly, not wanting to alarm his attacker.

"I've gotten information that there is a plan to bomb the palace."

Kenlyn stared at his friend a moment before he shook off the shock. "You're kidding."

"No. My source is reliable, too. Sorry about the dagger. There's also information that there is inside help."

Now he wouldn't contain his shock. "Gods' rods!" he breathed.

"Indeed," Rydul agreed. "My source didn't hear a name, doesn't know who the man is set on bombing the palace, but I'm assuming the accomplice is in the Guard or army, since they're the only ones who have clearance. I just don't know who."

"What do you want me to do?"

"I'm going to search for the bomb. I would like you to get the palace evacuated, everyone out, especially the royals."

"Radine and Jaima are still very ill."

"Better ill and alive then dead," Rydul replied. "Get Purnia and Pologa to evacuate the king and prince. Hemac can do the kitchen staff, Annatt can handle the queen, princess, and get the children moved. Send everyone to the front garden. I think this bomber will try to take down the family wing, opposite the garden. Try to keep it as quiet as possible."

"Should I try that little dagger trick you pulled on me?"

Rydul shook his head. "Again, I'm sorry about that. You're my best friend, but when it comes to the royals…"

Kenlyn's hand landed on Rydul's shoulder. "I understand. I would have done the same thing in your place."

Rydul was taken aback. "Really?"

Kenlyn grinned. "Tritio," he murmured, giving the shoulder a shove.

"Is everyone at their posts?"

"As far as I know, yes. I didn't see Cithan when I did a walk through ten minutes ago, but he must have taken a piss break."

"I'll swing by his post and check it out." He pulled his sword free. "Get on that evacuation. I don't know when this is supposed to happen, but better safe than sorry. Keep the king safe," he ordered, "at all costs."

"Yes, sir," Kenlyn answered. "Keep yourself safe as well."

"From your mouth to the ears of the gods," Rydul murmured as they separated.

Without hesitation, Rydul headed directly to Cithan's post, ordering servants to go to the front gardens and wait as he passed them, hoping to find the man where he was supposed to be. If Cithan couldn't do in ten minutes what needed to be done, he was either in dire straits and needed help, or, Gods' forbid, up to no good. Rydul would know which it was in about ten seconds.

Today was to be one of disappointments, for Cithan was still not at his post. Swearing softly under his breath, Rydul reached for the handle of the door that opened into the stairs to the cellars, turning it as carefully as possible and opening the door quietly and only enough to allow him to slip through. He locked the door behind him to slow any one attempting to flee.

There were only twenty steps between the floors, Rydul took each one as though they were each trapped, his eyes sharp. The lights were on in the cellars, casting deep shadows around the items stored there. The basement area under the family wing was through several rooms he would have to traverse first, a good opportunity for an ambush.

His steps were as silent a he could make them upon entering the first room. To the sides, crates and furniture were stacked against the walls as high as a man, aisles created between them to allow passage for someone to light the wall sconces that threw shadows over everything in front of them and split the floor into narrow shafts of light.

Exiting through an archway, he left the first room and entered the second without incident. He was halfway through this room when a light stirring of the air and dust caught his attention and he halted, his sword held at the ready.

Cithan appeared out from among the crates, his face almost inscrutable, maybe even slightly curious as though he wondered at Rydul's presence. He strolled with nonchalance as he approached, taking in the leather armor his commanding officer wore. "Rydul?" he questioned. "What's going on?"

"Why aren't you at your post?"

"I came down to check out the basement. Thought I heard something."

"What?" Rydul asked. There was dust on the other's shoes and the knees of his trousers were coated in dust. A cobweb in his hair blew in the slight breeze.

"I'm not sure, a noise." His head tilted. "So, what's going on?" he asked again.

"There's been a rumor of an intruder in the palace," Rydul hedged. "With the king and prince out of commission, it seemed better to search the entire palace to make sure it's just a rumor."

Cithan gave a quick glance over his shoulder. "Well, everything is fine back there," he said.

Rydul frowned slightly. "You don't mind if I take a look, do you? Just to ease my own mind?"

Cithan's gaze hardened, his shoulders visibly tightened and his hand lifted to rest on his sword without drawing the weapon. "I'm afraid I can't allow that, sir," he said calmly.

Rydul's heart sank, his voice barely more than a whisper. "Oh, Cithan, why?"

The other shrugged as he pulled his weapon free and held it up. "Maybe because it's not right, that the king has a woman who is not Taburon, that his son and heir isn't Taburon. Their loyalties will be divided if they ever have to choose. I stand for Taburon, only Taburon." He pointed his sword towards Rydul. "You should, too. Stand up for your people, find a woman from your own people instead of that human you are so enamored with. You pledged your loyalty to Taburon…"

"And to my king," Rydul interrupted, "and his laws. He works for the good of the people. Who knows what these humans may give us, bring to us, if we don't give them a chance to show us, teach us? If nothing else, tolerance for those different from us. We've been to enough other planets to know there is good in all peoples, why not humans, too?"

"We haven't bred with any of those others," Cithan answered hotly. "We've kept our blood pure, at least the blood of the royal family. Mating with a human, an inferior race, will only pollute us, make us weak, and what will we do then when some of those other people arrive to take over? Flee to Earth? Leave our world to those who would destroy it and exploit it until there is nothing left? We have the most powerful source of energy in this part of the galaxy. Don't be fooled that there are none out there who would rather they have it than us."

"They wouldn't dare," Rydul argued.

"They might, if they see a king half human on the throne."

"Can you not see that being raised by our king would make Rakenn as strong a king as his father?"

"No. He still has ties to Earth, he could be swayed if Earth is threatened."

"There are no ties to Earth for him. His mother is an orphan, she has no family there."

"But she may still have feelings for her fellow humans. They sent to Earth for medicine. Don't you see this?"

"I see asking humans for help for a disease brought here by humans. I see humans giving their help readily without condition. I see a future where we sit at the same table in fellowship and not over drawn swords." Rydul shook himself. "When?" he asked. "When did you turn against us?"

"I decided to fight for right while we were on Earth."

"And how did the human contact you here?"

"I helped set them up in the dormitory," he explained. "Enough talk. Turn around and sheath your sword, Rydul, I'll tie you up and take you out of here before it blows up. I don't want to have to kill you."

Rydul tightened his grip on his own sword then relaxed it, prepared to do whatever necessary and took a defensive stance. "I can't let you do that, Cithan, you know that. You will have to kill me, or I you. Only one of us will be walking out of here today."

He'd barely uttered the last word when Cithan attacked, rushing Rydul, his sword raised as though he meant to strike Rydul at the shoulder in order to cleave him in half. With a quick flip of his own blade, Rydul redirected the swing and stepped back out of the range of Cithan's reach. Let him come at him. Rydul would take a defensive posture, parrying blow after blow until the other tired. He was surprised by the younger soldier, and disappointed as well. Rydul had thought him better trained than he was showing.

The room rang out as the swords clashed, metal against metal, the two men dancing around each other. Sparks flew and Rydul worried but briefly that one of them would set the room on fire, retreating and circling as he tried to keep the fight away from the packages and furniture and in the more open area.

Rydul's forearm burst with biting pain as Cithan's sword connected with one of his braces, leaving a deep gash in the leather, but not penetrating. A second blow would cut through and cause a serious wound to his arm if he allowed it. In retaliation, he aimed for Cithan's leg, swiping the tip of his sword against the other's thigh, leaving a shallow cut from one side to the other. Cithan cried out in pain, momentarily distracted, taking a step back to gather his courage, his hand covering the wound, dismiss the pain and take a deeply needed breath. The look he shot at Rydul was filled with both disbelief – that the officer would really injure him – and hatred, that the officer would really injure him. Rydul returned a look of confidence and command, a distinct expression of his intent to follow through on his claim that only one of them would be walking out of the basement.

Cithan's brow was dotted with sweat, his chest heaving with breath, he grunted with every attack, yet Rydul was but mildly tired. The younger man now realized that he would have to truly kill his commanding officer if he wished to survive this day. His threat earlier had been mostly for show, an attempt to avoid he engagement in what he now found himself. Knowing there was more danger if he let this continue, that there was someone still in the basement area with a bomb, seeing the realization that Cithan had finally come to, Rydul decided to put an end to this. "Stop now, Cithan, I really don't want to have to kill you," he offered.

"And end up how?"

"You'll be alive," Rydul reminded.

"For going against the king, I might end up executed."

"There's that possibility," Rydul concurred. "But I can speak for you, your record up to now has been exemplary. You might end up exiled to Taburon Prime."

"Might as well be dead," Cithan murmured, readying his stance with a mid-guard position, his body turned sideways towards Rydul, his sword held point up from his waist. Rydul took a mirrored stance, waiting, his posture relaxed but on guard, waiting.

With a flip, Cithan's sword arced downward and came around, an effort to bring the point up and cut Rydul across the waist. Rydul circled his sword in the opposite direction, pushing Cithan's blade out of the way. Taking a step forward, as his blade ended its circle, Rydul immediately brought it up and pushed it forward, burying the point in Cithan's torso just under the ribs.

The younger man stopped as he tried to recover to continue his own attack, shock on his face, disbelief in his eyes. The world came to a screeching halt for an instant, breaths held, then Cithan's gaze fell to the blade that had penetrated his body in a most violent and deadly way. His own sword, falling with a loud clang to the floor and forgotten, the soldier started to reach for the metal thrust through him but the life was draining from him quickly and his hand barely raised, only the fingertips touching the edge of the blade.

Resignation filled his eyes as he lifted them to Rydul and he nodded once. He had gone into it knowing there had been a chance he would not survive and now realized he should have accepted Rydul's offer of salvation, no matter how unpleasant it may have seemed at the time.

The blood seeping out of his wound was hot as it spread across his shirt and soaked into the waistband of his trousers. His heart pumped furiously, but to no avail. He was doomed; the wound had hit a vital organ and only the placement of the sword still held inside him was keeping him from instant death.

"Sorry," he whispered to Rydul. With a final surge of strength, Cithan pulled himself free of the blade. Blood spewed from the now opened wound, pulsing free with every dying heartbeat. With a sigh, the soldier sank to the ground and fell to his side, his eyes closing gently against his quickly whitening skin.

Rydul fell to one knee next to the body, immobile, watching as the flow slowed, then stopped altogether, red dripping from the tip of his sword to leave little puddles of Cithan's life force on the floor at his feet. He'd not wanted to kill, he'd hated to kill, but there were more important things to do and so very little time in which to get them done. There was still the possibility that he wouldn't succeed, but he had to give it the best try he could and to spend more time fighting had been eating up precious seconds. He had to get moving.

Wiping his sword across Cithan's black trousers to clean the blood, Rydul kicked the dead man's blade across the room, over several storage boxes and behind them. He grabbed the dirk the man carried on his belt, carefully sheathing it through the waistband of his trousers.

He stood, his glance falling to the man he'd thought his companion and friend and his heart turned over as he fell to one knee. This should have never happened, his loyalties should have remained with Taburon and the king. Rydul would never understand how the man could have believed siding with the humans a logical choice – the species was still childlike and dangerous. But what was one was done, there was no going back now.

He gently laid his hand on the man's chest. "I am sorry, my friend," he murmured, bowing his head. As much as he wanted to take the time and allow the sorrow to run its course, to mourn for this lost man, he had other immediate concerns which took precedent right now Somewhere down here in the cellar a man was planning on blowing up the palace and kill the king.

Stepping over the body, Rydul headed deeper into the cellar. He knew that anyone determined enough to blow up the palace, especially the family quarters, would know to plant that bomb in the grand storage room two floors below the family quarters. There was a main supporting column there – take it down and the whole section would readily collapse.

Quietly, he stalked the corridors until he stood outside the archway to the grand storage room. The entire room was lighted with scones mounted every ten feet along the walls. There were shelves of packages, piles of boxes stacked on the floor, and unused furniture gathering dust here and there.

Rydul skirted around several crates, the column in question straight ahead and easily coming in sight, his sword held at the ready. He'd considered using his laser weapon but realized that if he hit the bomb, it would set off the very explosion he was trying to prevent.

Clearing the obstacles, Rydul spotted his target, hunched over, squatting on his heels at the base of the column. An empty pack lay on the floor at his side, the man's attention drawn to what he was doing in front of him. Rydul halted, his hand tightening on the pommel of his sword.

Drawing in a deep breath, quietly stepping up behind the man, prodding the back of the man's shoulder with his sword, he made his presence known. "In the name of the king, stop what you are doing and show your hands."

The man started and began to straighten, rethinking the move when the tip of the sword pressed deeper into his skin. His left hand rose.

Rydul pushed the sword closer. "The other hand now, please," he ordered.

Before the warrior could respond, the man twisted to his left and lifted his right hand, a weapon held there that he pointed in the direction of the Taburon.

The sound it made when the trigger was pulled was deafening in the room as a searing pain hit Rydul on the outside of his right thigh. His leg buckled and he collapsed to the floor, his sword clattering away.

The intruder jumped on the wounded warrior, throwing himself bodily onto the Taburon, wrapping his arm around his throat to squeeze tightly.

Momentarily blindsided by the pain of the injury, realizing this was going to be another life or death fight kicked Rydul's instincts and years of training into gear. He knew he had more weight than the intruder. He only hoped his training was more advanced than the human's.

"You think you can stop us?" the human snarled viciously, tightening his hold. "You won't, you never will." The depth of his commitment coupled with his sense of righteousness gave the human untoward strength. Rydul grabbed the arm that was cutting off his breath with fanatical determination. "We don't want your kind, we don't need your kind. Ever," he growled.

Rydul knew that it was going to be futile to try to pry the arm from around his neck. As his vision began to blur, the vise tightening even more around his neck, he gritted his teeth and twisted his body in half, ignoring the pain that shot through his leg as he wrapped and locked his ankles around the human's shoulders and over his chest. He heaved with every ounce of strength he could muster and pulled the intruder to the side of his own body to land heavily to the right with a thump, loosening the death grip the man had had on his throat.

Rydul gasped for breath, twisting to push himself up, his leg singing in agony, yet he found himself scrabbling for the sword that lay not too distant to his side.

The human plowed into his side with a thud, rolling both men into a stack of boxes. The stack fell over, burying them, one corner of one box falling onto Rydul's injury. He cried out, nearly screamed, and shoved the box away angrily, righting himself, lifting to his feet. There was no time for giving in to the pain that agonized through his body. Nearby, the human was also righting himself, shaking his head to get rid of the daze.

"You'll never win," Rydul croaked, reaching into his waist to grab the knife he'd tucked there earlier. Bending into a crouch, the warrior waited, watching.

In a move that surprised the Taburon, the human began to laugh, producing the gun that he'd not lost in the scuffle and pointing it directly at Rydul. "Oh, I think I will," he chuckled, a mad light shining from his eyes.

Without hesitation, Rydul dove to the side and threw the dagger. With the precision honed out of years of training and practice, the hilt slammed into the human's wrist, knocking the gun free as it discharged, the bullet going wild.

Before he could recover, and knowing that his leg was going to give out soon, Rydul dove at the man and wrestled him to the ground, wrapping his legs around his torso and bending one arm behind his back as he reached for the dagger with this other hand, bringing it to rest against the man's throat.

"I would disagree," he refuted. "How do I stop the bomb?"

"Go to hell," the man growled.

"Not before you." Laying the sharpened edge next to the man's skin, he pressed it in. "Tell me."

"Fuck you."

"You'll die."

"As will you," the other answered, "and your king and his little whore."

Rydul pressed in with the knife's edge. The sting of the cut and the warmth of the blood that appeared should have convinced the intruder that Rydul meant business. "The king is safe as is his family." At least Rydul hoped everyone had gotten out of danger if he couldn't stop the bomb.

"And what about your little whore?"

Rydul's heart nearly stopped. Kathryn was in danger? How? Had she somehow been kidnapped? Were there more than just the two humans and the one traitor involved in this scheme? And if so, who else had slipped through, aware of his feelings for the woman so that they could hold her captive and threaten her life? Force him to yield to their goals to spare her? How far did this conspiracy go?

For a heartbeat, Rydul's grip on the dagger loosened, but then it tightened even more-so. He had to believe that she was safe, that she wasn't in danger, and that whatever this human said could not affect him now. Not without proof.

The palace, the king, they had to be his priority. He had to save them, even if it meant he sacrificed his own life in the process.

"I have no whore," he ground out truthfully. Kathryn was pure and innocent, the woman he loved, inexperienced in the ways of nadryl, but not a whore by any definition. They would be married, husband and wife, if he survived this. "The bomb," he insisted. "How do I stop it?"

"She'll die. If I don't get back, get word to my companion, she will die."

"The bomb," Rydul persisted. "Tell me."

"Fuck off."

He'd had enough. Giving the dagger a slight but careful and well-rehearsed flip, he grabbed it by the blade and slammed the thickened end into the human's head. The man bodily heaved once. Rydul hit him again with a forceful, heavy thud. The man's body went limp.

Tossing the human to the side, Rydul took a few deep breaths before rising to limp towards the column, tucking the dagger back into the waistband of his trousers. His thigh screamed with pain, blood soaking the material of his pants and sluicing down his leg. He covered the wound with one hand, gasping when he touched it, but grinding his teeth against the agony. There was a job he had to do. His sword he picked up on the way, the blade slid back into the sheath.

Knowing if he went down to his knees he might never rise because of his injury, Rydul bent over to examine the device. It did not appear to be tied down, making it easier for him to pick up. The bomb appeared to be a simple black box, he assumed that the explosive material was inside. There was a clock of some kind flush with the top of the box, a digital readout counting down. He had just over two minutes to get the device out of the cellar and away from the palace where it would cause damage.

Rydul hugged the device to his chest as he quickly scanned the room. In front of him and to the right was a doorway installed for the purpose of bringing goods directly to the cellar for storage. Rydul searched his mind for the layout of the grounds outside of that door, focusing on the Queen's Garden about one hundred feet beyond the door. He headed in that direction, limping, but forcing himself to jog as best he could.

His heart raced and his lungs began to burn as he made for the door, praying it wasn't locked and slamming his shoulder into it to shove it open, allowing him to leave the cellar and race along the path. Frantic, he tried to remember the walkways of the garden, which direction would take him the fastest and furthest from the building. His brain wasn't functioning as it should, the pain from his wound clouding his thought processes and memory. Where was the information he needed when he needed it the most?

Sixty seconds.

A spark of inspiration hit him as he raced along as fast as his injury would allow. There was a deep pond on the far side of the garden, the bomb might be contained if he could reach it in time and drop it into the water. And if it sank far enough. He turned a corner and the entrance to the garden was in front of him. The walls surrounding the garden stood six feet tall, but were narrow, not meant to stop an explosion but to contain the foliage inside. If the bomb went off now, it could cause considerable damage to the palace.

Ducking through the entrance, Rydul headed for the paths that would take him to the pond. He turned to the left.

He realized he might not make it. Rydul was prepared to take the brunt of the force of the bomb with his body if necessary. But he would, with his last thought, regret it, thinking of Kathryn and all that would be lost. He loved her.

Nothing like eminent death to clarify life, what meant the most and reset one's priorities. Breeding crufas meant little if he couldn't have Kathryn by his side. If she was lost to him, if there was any truth to what the human had said about her being in danger, then his choice to save the monarchy had sealed her death. There was no time to send someone to check on her, no one who knew the struggle he now faced and what it would mean to him.

If he survived, he would live the rest of his life in mourning, dealing every day with regrets and guilt. Life was nothing without his Kathryn by his side – whatever life handed him he would be able to face to it with Kathryn. Whether a prince or a pauper, he would find contentment if he could only have her. He prayed with everything he knew that the man had lied, that she was safe, even if it was his fate to die.

Twenty seconds.

Any second his leg was going to give out. Rydul took a deep breath, finding reserves from deep inside and bringing them forward. Turning another corner, the pond was directly in sight. The garden was blooming with fragrant flowers, colorful and beautiful. The trees were dressed in green skirts of leaves, shading the garden in selected spots where a couple could sneak a kiss out of sight. A peaceful place to die. Somewhere off to his left a bird chirruped happily in a nearby tree, completely oblivious to what was about to happen. Not an unpleasant sound if it was to be his last.

Ten seconds.

At the edge of the pond, he glanced over the four foot high rock retaining wall. *Nekon,* Taburon's version of goldfish, drifted lazily just under the top of the water, their fins rippling gently. They looked up to him, believing he had food, as the queen often came to feed the fish when she strolled through her garden.

"Sorry," Rydul murmured to the watery creatures, lifting the bomb over the water. He let it drop and spun away.

Two steps away, his leg buckled and he went down to his hands and knees with a groan. Hanging his head, Rydul growled in frustration and pushed against the ground, dragging his good leg under his body and heaving himself upright. Grabbing his thigh in a deathly grip, calling on his last reserves of strength, he rose unsteadily and started forward again, limping heavily, praying with all he believed and held dear to be able to get just that much further away.

The blast hit him with all the force of a full-on crufa kick and then some. He felt himself lifted from the ground as debris from the destroyed pond and surrounding foliage slammed into him from behind. Any birdsong he may have heard was drowned out by the deafening roar of the blast and he regretted that he wouldn't have that as his last sound.

His eyes shuttered closed – let fate take what it would – as he sailed through the air carried along by the concussion.

Stone and gravel scraped his skin raw as he landed hard on the path. It seemed that fate was going to beat the life from him rather than impale him on a tree branch and end it quickly. Landing on his legs, he screamed in agony.

His head exploded in torture, his chest broke, his cheek left several layers of skin behind as he slid to a standstill, face down on the path. He tried to rise, he thought seriously about trying, but his body was saying no way, refusing to answer to his mental commands. Leaves, flowers, twigs and rocks rained down on him as he lay there, forcing his lungs to take breaths despite the incredible hurt and fighting to remain conscious. Water doused his back.

But it was too much. For his body, for his mind. Blackness swirled around the edges of his consciousness, calling for him to give himself over, to end the pain and this horror forever.

His thoughts were for one thing and one thing only, the prayer in his head short, a few words spoken to gods he'd never paid much attention to in the past, asking to keep her safe, for her to know that he had loved her with all his heart. His voice was little more than a whisper.

"Kathryn."

Rydul gave over to the darkness.

CHAPTER EIGHTEEN

Kathryn rose from the chair that she was now believing was becoming a part of her body and stretched her back. She'd been sitting now for near six hours straight, keeping watch over the unconscious man on the bed before her, praying, hoping, wishing that he would soon awaken. But he slept on, oblivious to her vigil.

And she was fine with that, as long as his chest rose and fell with steady breaths, as long as his heart continued to beat, as long as blood pumped through his broken body. He had a chance, the doctor had said, as long as he held on for the next twenty four hours.

Kenlyn had been the first to find him, bloody, bruised, and unconscious on one of the paths in the Queen's Garden after the blast, his body covered in debris from the destroyed foliage and retaining wall of the pond. The soldier had sunk to his knees and screamed in despair for his friend, thinking him dead. But a single breath and barely audible moan had him yelling for help at the top of his lungs. He'd dared to not move the injured man by himself, not knowing the extent of his injuries or whether or not he would cause more harm than good.

It had only taken a moment for others to come running, alerted by the sound of the blast. Together, they rigged a makeshift travois for the injured man and without bending his neck or back, settled him on it. Entering the palace, the hue and cry for medical help had rung through the halls.

Dr. Tripp had been the first to attend to Rydul, Joanna, a trained nurse on his heels. Placing the man on a bed, making a quick assessment, Tripp had ordered an iv inserted immediately, water for cleaning his injuries be brought, and a laser suture to suture his numerous cuts and bandages be set near so he could work.

Two hours later, the physician heaved a tired sigh and stepped away from Rydul, finished with what he could. His leg had been set and was being casted in Taburon's version of a cast – a metallic tube that closed over the injured limb and was locked into place. The gunshot wound was cleaned, the bullet removed, and dressed. His ribs had been taped. The numerous cuts and scrapes had been cleaned, doused with *whemin* and bandaged. Tripp suspected there was a concussion as well, judging by the amount of blood cleaned from his hair. Kenlyn sent two guardsmen to fetch the woman with whom Rydul was forging a relationship.

Joanna checked the intravenous drip and readjusted it, giving her own sigh. Her back hurt near constantly from her pregnancy, but she'd ignored it until just now, finally glad that she could at least help out here. Both Tripp and Pologa had forbidden her from tending to her husband, the king, nor any of the other sick patients in the palace.

Tripp knew he would live or die now, depending upon the extensiveness of his head injury, whether or not he avoided any infection. Without that knowledge, he was guessing about it since the Taburons had yet to get any kind of x-ray equipment. He would make sure that changed as soon as possible. With Rydul, it boiled down to a matter of waiting and praying.

Which Kathryn had been doing a lot of since she'd been told. Still waiting at the dormitory for any news, the whole building had heard the explosion. Her heart had choked in her throat with worry.

When the Guardsmen had appeared to request her presence, and not said why, she braced herself the entire ride back to the palace to face the worst. Rydul had died and they didn't want to tell her except in person.

But she kicked herself soon after that thought passed through her mind. He had to be alive, she told herself, she couldn't accept anything else.

But her legs had nearly given out when she saw him, laying silent, unconscious, and bloody, deathly still on the bed, his tattered clothes in a heap on the floor. The physician was working on an injury to his leg, the Princess Joanna was washing blood from his face and shoulders.

Girding herself, Kathryn bravely walked up to the princess and took the washcloth from her, indicating for her to tend to more important injuries or help the doctor. She would handle the simple things like washing him. Joanna gladly let her take over.

Then began the wait. Kathryn sat next to the bed for hours before someone, she couldn't remember now who, had insisted that she rest herself. Refusing on the belief that he might wake, Kathryn resisted leaving his bedside, until it was pointed out to her that a cot had been set up in the room so she could still be near. Even so, she only slept for two hours before she was back in the chair by the bed.

So those who kept a watch on the watcher made sure she had food and drink available and spelled her every so often so she could care for her own needs and not look like something from a horror movie when her lover finally did awaken.

And lover he was, for even though he'd spoken about getting married, he hadn't actually gotten around to asking her directly. The people around her knew she loved him and that was good enough for her for the time being. Those closest to Rydul understood he had a deep affection for the human woman. Kenlyn suspected marriage had been on his mind even before they had left Earth.

Sixteen hours had passed since he'd been found. Sixteen hours of hoping and praying. Servants had brought her food, one of his fellow soldiers had brought a suitcase of clothes for her to change into, the doctor and Princess Joanna had stopped by every hour on a rotating schedule to check on the patient and a guard was stationed outside the bedroom door in case she needed medical help sooner.

The sun outside was rising, a new day starting. Outside the balcony doors of the room, she could hear the sounds of men starting the clean-up of the garden, collecting debris and tossing it into barrels they would haul away. Someone had said the king wanted the garden rebuilt as soon as possible. Birds were singing in the trees, a merry denouement to the destruction wrought by the bomb.

A discreet knock at the bedroom door had her turning from the balcony doors as it opened. Dr. Tripp peeked around the edge of the door then pushed it open to enter the room fully. He shoved his hands through his haggard looking hair, as though he'd also not slept in several days. Circles surrounded his eyes and there were lines at the edges of his mouth that pulled an otherwise pair of adorable lips down in the corners. He wore a white physician's coat over gray trousers, a light blue shirt and brown suede shoes.

"Morning," he murmured as he sauntered closer. "How's our patient?" There was a night table next to the bed and he went directly to it to pick up a stethoscope.

"He stirred a little about an hour ago, but didn't wake."

Tripp folded the covers over Rydul's body back and placed the earpieces in his ears. Bending over he listened to the man's heart and lungs for several minutes. Having seen this several times already, Kathryn turned to the food tray to check the tea pot there for any dregs. Even cold, it would have given her just that little bit more energy she needed to continue for another few hours.

"Miss Tehyr," the doctor called softly.

Dropping the lid back onto the pot, Kathryn turned, curious at what the doctor needed, then hurried to the bedside. With a slight inclination of his head, her gaze turned to the unconscious man.

Rydul's fingers on his right hand were moving, flexing. His chest rose in a deep breath, which brought a muffled groan from his lips. Beneath his closed lids, his eyes moved.

As Tripp moved out of the way, Kathryn took the chair and gripped Rydul's hand, carefully, considering the bandaging. "Rydul," she said softly, "time to wake up, Olana. Come back to me now."

His lips parted. The hand being held by two others gripped tightly, squeezing. His breathing increased, a soft pant as pain began to make its presence known.

"Kathryn," he whispered.

"I'm here, love, right beside you." Her palm was cool against his cheek as she caressed.

Rydul turned towards the feminine voice, his brow furrowing. It couldn't be Kathryn. She'd been killed, slain because he'd chosen to save the king and the palace, taking up the bomb and racing from the cellar. He'd knocked the human man unconscious, sealing her fate.

And as he'd soared through the air, the force of the blast carrying him, his last thoughts had been of the woman he loved, how he'd betrayed her, how he hoped he would be fortunate enough to join her in forever.

But the voice that now penetrated the haze sounded so familiar and so real that he believed it had to be a trick his brain was playing on him.

Or he had truly died and she was there to welcome him into eternity at her side. He would be content to spend eternity on the other side of life, as long as she was with him.

Yet, as he took another deep breath and pain wracked his chest, reality hit with a thud, reminding him that he was facing a future alone and broke. He was going to miss her so much.

Cool lips pressed against his temple in a kiss. "Rydul."

The first thing he saw when he opened his eyes was the ceiling of a room which he did not recognize. He was not in the barracks where he had a private room because of his rank. The picture painted on the plaster ceiling above was pastoral and calming, like many of those in the palace guestrooms.

A feminine sigh drew his eyes to his right where he found dreams were still possible. Kathryn smiled, her eyes tearing. "Hi."

He blinked, his brow furrowing. "Kathryn?"

She nodded and leaned down, burying her face into his shoulder. When he'd opened his eyes, it was the most brilliant thing she'd ever seen – those golden colors, though subdued in pain and confusion, but alive and aware. She couldn't help her reaction, hiding her head to hide her tears of joy.

Rydul placed a hand on the back of her head. "He lied," he said. "Thank the gods he lied," he whispered tilting his face into her hair. He couldn't stop the moisture that gathered in the corner of his eyes and pooled there, threatening to spill over.

"Who? Who lied?"

"The man - the human – who set the bomb – told me you would be killed. He lied."

"I was never in danger."

"He made me choose. Forgive me, Clana."

She lifted her head, her eyes filled with unshed tears. With her thumbs, she swiped the tears that ran down his temples. Faced with a terrible choice, he'd made the only decision he knew had the most definite outcome – to save the royals and the palace. She couldn't fault him for that, but she could see that guilt in his eyes – that he hadn't chosen her and she would hate him.

Palming his uninjured cheek, she let her love shine through. "I love you, more than I ever thought I could love anyone, and that just got bigger." A single tear fell. "I'd thought I'd lost you. Life isn't worth living without you."

The lips she touched against his were gentle in consideration for his facial injuries, but had she not pressed her lips to his, he would have pulled her to him to share a kiss, pain be damned. "You couldn't have known I wasn't in danger, but you chose correctly. I might have done the same thing, given the same circumstances. Besides," she continued, "had the king died, it might have meant war. I love Taburon, I look forward to spending the rest of my life here with you. But I love Earth as well. My parents and some of my friends live there. I don't want them to suffer."

"I promise it will never happen again, Kathryn. You will always be my first choice."

She shook her head, a fingertip to his lips to silence him. "Don't make promises you might not be able to and I wouldn't expect you to keep. You are a soldier and loyal, it's your duty, and I would be upset if you let anything happen to the royals if you could prevent it."

He lay silent, thinking, wonder filling him. This was love, self-sacrificing and total. Now he understood what Radine and Jaima had come to know. Both men would go through the Pits of Koloda for their women. As would he.

"I am probably the most fortunate man on Taburon right now."

She sighed and gave her head another shake. "No, I am the luckiest woman in the galaxy. You found me." She placed a kiss on his mouth.

Tripp, having given them a few moments to get the mushy stuff done, cleared his throat. Kathryn giggled, breaking the kiss, her hand sliding along his cheek in a caress as she straightened. "If I may?" the physician asked, indicating for her to switch places with him.

"Captain," he greeted, "welcome back. You had us worried there for a while. Can you tell me how you're feeling?"

Rydul took a moment to make a mental assessment. He hurt everywhere, there were tight feelings around his right leg, his hands, his chest. His cheek on the left burned. "I hurt," he replied, "all over. How bad am I?"

"Bad enough. Short and sweet –you were nearly blown up. We figured you didn't get far when that bomb exploded."

"My leg gave out. The human shot me."

"Yeah, we found that and wondered how that happened. You have a half dozen or so scrapes – your hands and face – from when you hit the ground. Pologa showed me how to repair the cuts with the laser suture, but they're still healing. You broke your right leg when you landed and cracked a few ribs. The bullet wound was a simple thigh shot where the bullet lodged, but it did enough damage and you lost some blood. I suspect you also have a mild concussion?" Rydul answered with a nod which he instantly regretted. His head was throbbing. "Thought so. You'll be laid up for several weeks."

Rydul lay silent, processing the information, shooting a look at Kathryn. She nodded, her lips drawn up in a smile, wanting him to accept the limitations since they would only be temporary. He acquiesced. "Very well," he agreed. Tripp perched on the edge of the mattress and leaned close enough to listen to the injured man's heart and breathing again, now that he was awake, putting the earpieces of the stethoscope in place. "Are you in a lot of pain? Your heart is beating awfully fast."

"I hurt, yes."

Hanging the stethoscope around his neck, Tripp pulled a black physician bag close and rummaged through it. Removing a bottle of clear liquid and a syringe, he pulled a measured amount of the liquid from the bottle then injected it into one of the iv lines that had been inserted when Rydul had first come in. He dropped the used syringe back into the bag.

"Give that five to ten minutes. It should take the edge off." He placed the stethoscope back on the night table for the next person to use. "You should have something to eat.

I'll get the kitchen to send up a light meal for you. I want you to stay completely in bed except to use the bathroom for at least one more day. Ask for help to get up – don't do it on your own, not for a while at least. Don't take a chance on further injuring those ribs." Tripp gave Rydul his best 'and I mean business' look until the Taburon capitulated. "Good man," he complimented. "I'll leave you alone for now. Let me know if that medicine doesn't help." Standing, he stepped away from the bed, placing a hand on Kathryn's shoulder as he passed her on his way out of the room. He intended to seek out a bed and get some much needed sleep now that his primary patient appeared to be on the road to recovery. "Call me if you need," he whispered to her as he passed.

Kathryn retook her place at the bedside, her hand covering his. "I was so frightened. We heard that explosion at the dormitory."

"I dropped it into the pond in the Queen's Garden. I assume there's a lot of damage."

"Everything within a sixty foot diameter. The queen's not that upset about it though. Your warning came in time to get everyone out of the palace. You were the only one injured."

Not the only one, he thought. Unless he'd been found, there was one dead man in the cellar, killed by his own hand. If she wasn't mentioning Cithan, then she probably didn't know about him yet, hadn't been told, or he hadn't been found. "The king? Is he well?"

"Getting there. Both he and the prince are recovering from the flu, but still under close watch. As you will be for the next day or so."

Rydul glanced around again. "I'm in the palace?"

"When the king heard you'd been injured, he insisted you be brought here to be cared for."

"The man, the human, has he been caught? Where is he?"

"In the dungeon, as is the woman who brought the virus with her."

Rydul saw his leg was higher than his head, raised on a pillow. "My leg?"

"Dr. Tripp said it needed to be higher than your heart to prevent blood clots. Both bones in your lower leg were broken, and it's been casted, which you'll have to wear for six to eight weeks." He didn't look happy at the news, but resigned to tolerate it. "It'll be over before you know it," she promised.

He shifted restlessly, the pain eased but not gone. "I am not a man who takes to lying about easily."

"I know, love, but try to be patient. I'll do anything I can to keep you occupied, and your friends have said the same thing."

A devilish look entered his eyes. "Anything?" he asked.

Kathryn giggled, reading his look completely. "You, Captain Rydul, are not ready for that," she scolded with amusement, "yet," she added with promise.

She smiled at his responding chuckle as he pulled her down for a kiss to seal that promise, his hand buried in her hair to hold her close. "Two days," he warned her.

"Four," she countered hovering over his mouth.

He growled softly. "Two," he reiterated firmly, "no more," and he closed his mouth over hers again. Another throat being cleared kept him from continuing the kiss. "Gods be damned," he swore as she looked behind her.

Kenlyn waited, somewhat sheepishly for the couple to separate, stepping forward as Kathryn straightened. "The physician said you were awake." He colored slightly. "I can come back."

"No, it's all right," Rydul grumbled affectionately for his friend, but his eyes, darting to rest on her face, held the promise that, even injured he wasn't done with her just yet.

Kathryn gathered fresh clothing from her suitcase, stopping next to Kenlyn on her way past him to the bathroom. The two men needed some time alone and she needed to not only shower but to release some of the pent – up emotions she'd been keeping in check. "He needs his rest," she said softly.

"I'll not stay long," Kenlyn promised, watching her as she disappeared into the bathing room, his grin obvious as he seated himself where she had been but a moment before.

"Back off," Rydul warned with a growl, recognizing the other's wayward thoughts.

"Can't admire a beautiful woman?"

"Not that one. She's mine."

He crossed one ankle over the other. "If I recall correctly, about seven months ago, I suggested that to you. You were too obstinate to accept it."

"I have now. She is going to be my wife as soon as possible."

"I would venture to say yesterday were it not for an unfortunate encounter with a bomb."

"It would have been within an hour after she'd stepped off the shuttle if it wouldn't have scared her to death."

"Humans are a strange lot," Kenlyn observed, "with some exceptions. You have my congratulations and my envy. So how are you doing?"

"For a man nearly blown up, I'll live."

"Your injuries are not that serious then?"

"Serious enough to keep me idle or weeks," Rydul grumbled. "Tell me what happened after the explosion."

"Once the palace stopped shaking, we went looking for you. I found you in the garden, yelled for help and several of us dragged you inside where Dr. Tripp and Princess Joanna tended to you. We caught the human trying to leave the grounds. He's in the dungeon and not saying a word. According to the manifest, his name is John Taker.

"The woman, on the other hand, is the complete opposite. She never shuts her mouth when one of us is anywhere in sight." Kenlyn rolled his eyes. "A lady shouldn't use that kind of language."

"Then she's no lady," Rydul pointed out.

Kenlyn nodded in agreement. "The gardens are being cleared and readied for replanting. The king wants them as finished as possible before the new child arrives."

"Ambitious."

"Determined," Kenlyn corrected. "He loves his wife. Anyway, we've posted guards throughout the palace and increased them at the dormitory. There have been rumors of retaliation on the humans.

"The Council is conducting an investigation, though we already know how that will end. But they want everything open and aboveboard. Don't want the humans taking action against the embassy and our people on Earth."

"You're in command now?"

"Only temporarily. As soon as you're able, I'm handing it back to you. Or Prince Jaima, if he'll take it."

"Tritio," Rydul mumbled affectionately.

Kenlyn chuckled, then sobered. "About Cithan. We found his body. What happened?"

"He turned. Claimed to agree with the humans, that we should have never gotten involved. He tried to stop me, keep me from getting to the bomb. I had no choice. I had to kill him or be killed by him."

His chest expanding with a deep breath, Kenlyn nodded. Like Rydul, he'd thought the man a friend. Never would he have believed that he'd harbored doubts about Taburon's relationship with humans. "Very well. Only you and I know this."

"You should tell Prince Jaima. You need to root out any other men who share those feelings, decide what to do with them. As for Cithan, he only had an elderly mother, no sense in destroying her affection for her only son. Bury him honorably, but no more than that."

"I'll see to it. Anything else?"

"Did that *afilen* give birth yet? The one in the stable?"

"Two days ago, a litter of six."

"I would like to have one for Kathryn. She lost her cat recently."

"She ready for another pet?"

"I won't know until she sees them. You know they're too adorable, or so the ladies say, to resist when they're babies."

"I can bring the litter here when they're older if you wish."

"Or take Kathryn to see them. I would like to be there, but if not, then that's what it has to be."

"I'll pass the word you want first pick."

"Thanks."

"What about what happened with Khail?"

"I'm not sure yet. I may end up having to sell the estate, move closer to the palace so I can re-enlist when the time comes."

"You'll give up breeding crufas?" Kenlyn asked with surprise. It was all Rydul had planned on and talked about for the last several years.

"There are no funds to replace the ones Khail sold. He raided and emptied my savings. I can't support a wife and family and save for buying animals, no less feeding them, at the same time. If I have to choose, I choose Kathryn."

Kenlyn was silent, his thoughts far away. A man should not have to give up his dreams because of another man's selfish actions. Rydul had risked his life to save the royal families. He deserved better.

He stated to speak, but Rydul held his hand up, silencing him, the injured man's head turning towards the bathing room.

"What?" Kenlyn whispered, rising, his hand falling to his laser weapon.

"Kathryn. Something is wrong." With the flick of his wrist, Rydul indicated for Kenlyn to check it out.

The soldier stepped closer carefully, listening all the while, stopping two feet from the door to the bathing room.

His hand relaxed on his weapon as he listened to the sound of bitter weeping, barely disguised by the running water.

"She is crying," he told Rydul going back to the bed. "Can I do anything? Send for someone?"

"No. She has had a tough time the last few days. Let her get it out of her system. I will talk to her Later."

"I can understand it though," Kenlyn said looking back to the bathing room once.

One of Rydul's eyebrows quirked. "How so?"

"To borrow a human phrase, you look like shit. The right side of your face is all bruised and swollen, you have bruises all over your chest, and if you haven't already noticed, the skin under the bandages on your hands is scraped and bruised as well. Quite a sight for someone who hovered over you for the last day and a half, not knowing if you were going to wake up or not."

Rydul frowned. "That bad?"

"You'd scare a child to death if he saw you as you are now."

"Yes, well, there's not much I can do about it now can I? All part of nearly being blown to death." He shuffled under the covers. "I'll heal soon enough."

"And be your pretty self again," Kenlyn added with a grin. "So, I'll leave you to it. Anything else you need?"

"Some clothes. It would appear I am naked under the bedclothes."

Kenlyn chuckled loudly. "Were it not for your injuries, I would ignore that request with good reason and a lot of envy. But I'll bring some things by for you later."

"Thank you."

Kenlyn waved a salute. "Get better."

CHAPTER NINETEEN

It hadn't taken much for King Radine to learn his lesson as he tapped lightly at the door to Rydul's bedroom. Walking in on his mother once in the act of sharing nadryl then later interrupting Prince Jaima with Joanna had cured him. So he waited a moment, then knocked again a little harder, turning the knob and pushing the door open enough to peek around it.

The room was lighted by the soft glow of the morning sunshine streaming through the curtained windows and opened balcony door. On the bed, the figure was silent, still enthralled with sleep. He was sitting up, braced by a half dozen or so pillows. His right leg was resting on a pillow, one arm was stretched out by his side, the other draped over his waist. He was shirtless, but his chest was still wrapped in heavy bandaging. He wore only a pair of loose training togs, the material of one leg split to accommodate the cast.

Radine stood at the foot end of the bed, watching the sleeping figure. His body was bruised in more than a dozen places, and scraped raw in a few more and the cuts that had been healed with the laser suture still showed the white lines of healing. They would fade over time. He didn't fail to notice that the opposite side of the bed looked well used, the sheets scattered, the pillow indented where a head had recently rested. His guardsman was obviously not sleeping alone.

This man had saved Radine, Jaima, their families, and his throne. The king would be forever grateful. And he knew exactly how to thank him for it.

Radine was just over a week from being declared no longer contagious, though he still felt weak and completely uninterested in returning to work. Besides, McKenna and Inoa were doing a fine job filling in, coming to him for advice if necessary. Jaima had gone back to his own quarters just two days ago and for Radine that meant having his wife back in their bed again. He was carefully ecstatic. No sense in going overboard – McKenna would have him bedridden at the slightest sign of relapse. Pologa, the traitor, would concur gleefully.

But his talk with Kenlyn several days ago had been preying on his mind. So, despite his somewhat tiredness, he'd dragged himself out of bed - actually snuck out - slipped on a robe and trotted down the hallways, surprising the guards who'd not expected to see the king up so early. And all without disturbing McKenna, who would thrash him soundly once she discovered him gone and caught up with him.

A sound to his right had him tensing for a heartbeat. Had someone somehow managed to get passed the guards and enter the palace?

He knew better with the next heartbeat. What was the saying the humans had? You couldn't swing a dead cat anywhere in the palace without hitting a guard right now. No one would have gotten through their security in place today. There was no danger.

Several steps to his right brought him closer to what was the bathing room in these quarters as a woman exited, her body encased in a thick towel, a second towel being used to squeeze the moisture from her freshly washed hair.

Though married, and quite happily at that, Radine could still appreciate a beautiful woman, and this one rated right up there with the rest of them. She was quite a lovely female with hair the color of a late sunset. She had breasts that would fill a man's hands, hips he could hold onto during nadryl, and legs to wrap around a man's body to pull him tightly into the cradle of her thighs. Her hands tapered into long fingers that would hold a man's cock firmly.

Her skin glistened from her shower. There was a contented expression on her face. This was the woman the palace was buzzing about, the one who had captured Rydul's heart and had stayed by his side as he recovered from his injuries. The king was happy for his officer.

Radine cleared his throat.

Kathryn stumbled as she stopped, glancing up, momentary fright crossing her face, then warming to pleasant surprise. Remembering, she touched at the towel at her bosom, making sure it was still in place, making her color in embarrassment at the action. The man's knowing gaze and smile told her he knew why she seemed so contented, but she wasn't about to confirm the suspicion. Her gaze darted to the sleeping man on the bed. Radine's eyes followed her look.

"Ah, so that's the way of it," he murmured, keeping his voice low.

"Your Majesty," she greeted. She'd seen his picture often enough to know what he looked like. To have him show up here unannounced, surprising her right out of the shower - that was unsettling. Flustered, she held the hair towel to her front.

"So, you know who I am. We have never formally met, but I have heard the rumors. Your name is Kathryn."

"Tehyr, Sire, Kathryn Tehyr. What rumors?"

"That Captain Rydul had taken a lover. Why did we not meet formally? Were you not at the mid-day breakfast?"

"I wasn't there. Rydul…that is Captain Rydul and I had left that morning to go to his estate." She tilted her head. "There are other rumors?"

"You will find, Miss Tehyr, that the palace is full of gossip. Not much gets by my servant Purnia, and he doesn't keep much of it from me, not when it involves one of the King's Guard. So he took you to his estate? I hadn't heard that he'd ever done that before with a woman."

Kathryn flushed even darker red. "No, Sire."

Radine looked thoughtful. "I see. And how is your patient?"

There was pride and relief in her voice. "He's doing better every day. Stubborn, incorrigible, impatient, but better."

"That is good to hear. I like this man, a lot." Glancing around, Radine spied a desk against one wall. Moving with purpose, he went to it and pulled out the chair, opened a drawer and rummaged through it until he found paper and a pen. Seating himself, he thought for a second. "I would like to speak with Rydul in private, with your permission of course, if you feel he is well enough."

Kathryn's head tilted slightly as if judging how stubborn this man might be if she refused. "Would my telling you no stop you, Your Majesty?"

Having started writing, Radine stopped to slide her a glance. This one was feisty and protective. "Most likely not, madam," he replied and went back to his writing. "You should dress. When you have I will send you to my wife. She would like to meet another of her compatriots." He chuckled. "And while she interrogates you, it will give me some time to talk to Capt. Rydul before she sets the whole palace in an uproar looking for me." He waved a hand. "Go on then and come back here when you're dressed."

Kathryn stared at him a moment, confused. He'd appeared out of nowhere and was not what she'd expected. Though her heart belonged to Rydul she could see the king was a handsome man, built tall and muscular, carrying himself like he owned the world. Dressed in bedclothes with but a robe over them and minus a crown, he seemed genuinely normal, like any man. But he was definitely a man with a lot of power.

And he held a great deal of loyalty given to him from his people. But he returned it equally, taking care of them with compassion and selflessness. She would be forever grateful that he had afforded – no, insisted on - giving Rydul the best care.

Grabbing a bunch of clothing from a drawer that Rydul had insisted on her taking and not living from a suitcase, Kathryn held it close to her chest, perusing the man seated at the desk, a thoughtful expression in his faraway look. With a shake of her head – who would ever understand the minds of men - she disappeared into the bathing room as the king continued to write.

Once dressed, she went back to where the king was seated, pulling her hair into what was called a ponytail. The king was folding two pieces of paper.

He passed the first one to her. "Give this to the guards. It will allow you to pass through the palace." Before giving her the second, he placed his initials on the outside. "Give this one to my wife. Try to keep her occupied as long as you can. She's too protective," he complained though he was smiling. "Ask the guards, they'll direct you."

She pocketed the second paper. "Is there anything else I can do for you, Sire?"

Radine rose, turning to look to his injured soldier. "Be good to him," he murmured. "He's a good man."

She flushed but her smile was loving. "Oh, I know that already," she confirmed. He could see the love in her eyes, the desire and the utter contentment in the softening of her body language. With a tilt of his head, she, not having more to say, nodded and left.

Radine followed a moment later, going as far as the door to the bedroom to ask one of the guards to have Purnia join him. Back in the bedroom, he moved a comfortable chair closer to the side of the bed and sank into it with a sigh, closing his eyes.

He'd only been out of bed a limited number of times and for a limited amount of time. He was exhausted more often than not. Playing with his children – five year old Rakenn and almost three year old Avelda wore him out easily. He was anxious to get back to normal, including training with the men.

Radine wasn't sure how long he'd sat there, but he had started to doze off when a hand on his shoulder roused him.

"My Lord?" Purnia inquired. When the guardsman had told him that the king wanted him in the injured man's room, his concern for his sovereign had shot up. The king was supposed to be resting in his family quarters, not traipsing about the palace unsupervised and unguarded as well. Purnia knew the man well, and didn't trust that he wouldn't relapse if they didn't keep a closer eye on him and he pushed too hard. "You need help?"

"You could say that," he replied sitting straighter. "I am hungry."

"Had you stayed in your room, Sire, I was bringing breakfast," he scolded mildly.

Radine ignored the whole rebuke, used to it after so many years. "I want to speak with Rydul, something that's been bothering me. May I have that meal here?"

"Of course, Sire." Purnia bowed.

"Also, would you see if there is someone available to help Captain Rydul as a valet? While I'm sure he's happy with things as they are, stronger arms may become necessary as he starts wanting to get around more."

Purnia ran all of the possibilities through his head. "There is one man, Sire. I will see if he is available today."

"Good. Bring enough for two of that breakfast."

"Of course, Sire." The man servant bowed again and left the room.

Breakfast had always been one of Rydul's favorite meals. To greet the morning with a cup of tea, watching the sun rise, then go inside and mix a phantasm of colors and tastes to

awaken his palette and digestion and prepare for the day –
his favorite two hours.

The scent of cooked food, sweet pastries and hot drink
roused him, the clink of silverware in dishes bringing him
fully awake.

"Kathryn?" he called, feeling for her in the space where
she'd slept and finding it empty.

"I sent her to McKenna," Radine answered.

Head swiveling, Rydul found the king, napkin in hand,
wiping at his mouth between bites. There was a dish of food
set on a small table next to the chair in which the king was
seated. Already in a seated position, Rydul placed a hand
across his ribs and straightened more. "Your Majesty."

"Can you get out of bed? Join me?"

"With help, Sire, yes."

Radine pushed the table aside and rose, offering a hand.
Rydul glanced down then to his king's face. "With all due
respect, Sire, you don't look all that well yourself."

He offered his hand again. "Just take it."

With a few grunts peppered with a groan or two, plus the
king's help, Rydul managed to stand. The king pulled
another chair close enough for the warrior to sit by the table.

From a large service tray, Radine put together a plate of food, added utensils and a napkin, and brought it all to Rydul. "How are you feeling?" the king asked, settling back in his own chair.

"Improving. There is still some pain, but that is to be expected yet." Rydul hesitated. He'd never eaten with the king one on one and he wasn't sure what to do. The royal, seeing the man's predicament, nodded to the plate as he resumed digging into his own meal. Following suit, Rydul cut off a forkful.

"What has Pologa said?"

"Six to eight weeks in the cast, then more time exercising, strengthening, until I am back to normal."

"I am sorry to hear that."

"As am I, Sire." He took a bite, chewed. "It is good to see you out and about."

"Only as long as McKenna doesn't know about it, yes. She would keep me in a bubble right now."

"She loves you." The officer understood. Kathryn had been rumbling something familiar the last days and to give her her due, he knew it was fear that motivated her emotion. He admitted he'd feel the same had their roles been reversed.

Radine's face took on a contented look. Having someone to care about him as McKenna did was wonderful – most times. There were times when she read him better than he knew himself, giving him what he needed before he knew he needed it. He loved her all the more for her insight, and the fact that she acted on it more times than he did in reverse for her. He shook off the indulgence and general languorous feeling they provoked then. "Yes, well, we men cannot live like that all of the time, now can we?"

"No, Sire, and not do our jobs effectively."

Radine agreed with a nod as Purnia returned to the bedroom carrying a tray with a carafe of hot tea, cups, sweetener, and cream. He fixed a cup or the king. "Sir," he asked Rydul, "how do you take your tea?"

"Plain, please." The servant poured, placed a cup in front of the warrior.

"Is there anything else you need, Sire?"

"I think we're fine here, Purnia, thank you." He concentrated on his meal as the servant left the two men alone. "I met your lady a short time ago."

"Kathryn?"

"You have another?" The king's head reared back in mock surprise. "Really, Captain, how many human woman do you have here?"

"There is just the one, Sire."

"She's quite lovely."

There was pride in his voice. "She is."

"Tell me about her." He spread fruit pomade on a piece of toasted bread.

Rydul's chest expanded in a deep breath, unsure how much he wanted to disclose about his relationship with Kathryn, even to his king. But this was his king asking. He set his fork down, picked up the cup of tea and leaned further back into the chair.

"We had noticed a woman sitting outside the embassy every day during high sun meal. As long as we determined she was non-threatening, we let her be, keeping an eye on her.

"She intrigued me. She was beautiful, unassuming, watchful, but discreet. At least she believed she was discreet. But just her appearance said she was fascinated with us.

"It crossed my mind several times to go out, meet her, invite into the embassy. But, as you know, there are protestors outside the building. Bringing her inside, just seen speaking with her would have made her a target of their animosity. I could not do that.

"One afternoon there was a fight outside the embassy, Kathryn was hit by a rock, knocked unconscious. We took charge of the situation and her, and I realized that my feelings were more than a passing interest.

"We began to spend time together, the ambassador arranging for her to be brought to the embassy under stealth. I knew I had little time left on my tour and asked her to return with me. But she had other obligations she could not ignore and remained behind.

"I was surprised to find her among the first group of colonists. Surprised and overjoyed. I love her and she loves me."

"I am happy for you. Will you be marrying her?"

"That had been my intent. I am not so sure now."

"Explain that," the king demanded. "We cannot have men enticing human females to Taburon to strand them here."

"No, Your Majesty, that is not the case. It is just that I cannot support a wife now nor offer her anything a wife might expect from her husband."

"You are a high-ranking officer in the Guard…" the king started to protest.

"I am penniless," Rydul interrupted.

"How?"

Rydul fidgeted. This was personal. Radine waited a moment then arched an eyebrow in expectation. "Anything that affects the efficiency of my guardsmen is no longer personal, Rydul. You know this."

"I do, Sire," he reluctantly admitted.

"And I also already know some of what happened. I want to hear it from you."

"Kenlyn?"

The king nodded. "He spoke with Jaima and me several days ago."

Rydul nodded. While it hadn't been for Kenlyn to speak about, having the situation out in the open – in a limited way of course – might ease the burden. "It would appear my brother got himself into a financial situation which he solved by selling the pure-bred crufas I owned, stripping my *freema* fields of flowers and decimating my savings. All I have left is the estate which will require whatever I earn from now on just to maintain it. I am considering selling."

"You have my sincere regrets," the king offered.

Rydul acknowledged with a bowing of his head. "Thank you, Your Majesty."

"If there was a way to recoup what you have lost, would you take it?"

"I would be a fool otherwise if I did not even consider it."

Reaching for a pastry, Radine placed it on Rydul's plate, pushing it closer. The officer glanced at the sweet, catching the eye of the king as he placed one on his own plate.

"Jaima and I had a long talk after Kenlyn's visit and we both agree. I know when my father gave you that estate it was in disrepair. You've revitalized it admirably. Your *freemas* are the highest quality. McKenna only uses products made from your plants.

"Without your warning, my family, Jaima's, and many others might have died when that bomb exploded. I've seen the damage to the garden, the impact unimaginable. You saved us, the palace, my throne. I can never thank you enough.

"That being said, I have asked my stable master to send out word that I want a half dozen of the highest quality crufas, four mares and two studs, sent to your estate for your approval." He raised his hand when Rydul started to protest. "Not a word, Captain Rydul. You might even get back one or two of the ones your brother sold. I've also asked for a team of gardeners to examine your fields and replenish the plants. You should be ready for the next harvest if all works out well. Is this all right with you?"

"Sire," he started, shocked, "I don't know....It's too much."

"It's not near enough," Radine refuted. "If any of my children had been injured...." He paused, the horror of losing his son or daughter heart rending. He remembered the terror he'd gone through and the relief upon seeing his family safe as the palace was being evacuated. "Accept it with grace, my friend. Grow the best *freemas*, breed the finest crufas Taburon has ever seen. I'll be the first in line for one of the foals. Rakenn will need one of his own soon. Marry Kathryn, have lots of children. Be happy. I highly recommend it."

Radine was pleased as he watched the future cross through Rydul's mind, the planning he was already doing, the resurrection of his dreams, the next few years laid out before him and fulfilled. He was glad that he could be part of that, it always made him happy when one of his guardsmen and a personal acquaintance could do well with their life.

"Sire, thank you. I promise I will do well by what you have done for me."

"I will hold you to your word. Now, finish your breakfast."

The two men pretty much decimated the rest of the meal, leaving little on the plates that had been filled to the top. The conversation was subdued, general stuff, Rydul still in shock over the king's generosity, anticipating Kathryn's reaction when he told her the good news. She had been just as worried about the future, had insisted that they make plans together and face the future together. Her support and comfort as he'd worked through his anger and disappointment had been invaluable, helping him to sleep better at night despite his injuries and the constant pain. Of course, having her, soft, warm, and willing next to him wasn't so bad either.

"Have you heard any news about your brother?" the king asked as they settled back with a final cup of tea.

"No, Sire. I kicked him out of the house. I know he left, but to where I have no idea."

"I had a search done for him and he was found in a brothel in the city."

Once more, Rydul had a hard time keeping the surprise from his face. "Indeed?"

"He's currently in the dungeon, being well treated, I assure you, but there nonetheless. What would you like to do with him?"

A smile of mischief and glee passed over Rydul's face. "Draft him," he decided. "Put him in the army and give him the worst possible instructors and send him to the worst possible place for his first tour. Then reassign him and teach him discipline, respect and self-esteem."

Radine chuckled softly. "It will be done," he promised. He enjoyed it when he could part of devious plans, especially when they weren't his to conceive, only administer.

At the door to the bedroom, after a single hard rap, three people entered, led by the queen, followed by Purnia and another man dressed formally, curious as he looked around.

McKenna didn't hesitate, going directly to her husband, holding her hand up before Radine could speak, the thunderous look with which she'd entered softening at seeing the dishes in front of him.

"I'm not going to yell," she promised, "I read the note. And thank you by the way for sending it. Rydul, how are you feeling?" She pushed the table slightly to the side and settled on Radine's lap. One hand of the king's went around her waist, the other he placed on her rounded stomach, rubbing lovingly.

The warrior had to pull his attention away from the doorway, looking for Kathryn, expecting her to come in with the rest of the group, disappointed that she had not returned. "I am doing well, Your Majesty," he answered. "Where is Kathryn?"

McKenna reached for the piece of pastry that Radine had left on his plate, pinching off a piece and popping it into her mouth. "She's with my dressmaker. Bala was quite pleased to have someone who doesn't have a bowling ball for a stomach to make a dress for." At the two men's puzzled expressions, having no idea what a bowling ball was, she huffed and bit into another piece of pastry.

"Perhaps, if you wouldn't steal my pastry, you wouldn't have a bowling ball for a stomach," Radine chided softly with amusement.

As if his hand was something disgusting, McKenna lifted it from her stomach with two fingers and put it aside. "I lost three pounds worrying over you. I can afford some sweet." With deliberate satisfaction, she finished the treat. "Your Kathryn is quite beautiful," she complimented. "I love her hair color. Inoa is going to be very jealous. You two are going to have gorgeous babies."

Both men sputtered. "Aren't you being a little presumptuous, McKenna?" the king asked, first to recover.

"They obviously love each other. I would assume there's going to be a wedding. And if things go as they have in the past – meaning me and Joanna – she'll be pregnant in no time. If she isn't already?" she added coyly.

Rydul's furious blush set her to giggling, but he took a deep breath. "She is not," he assured firmly.

McKenna patted Rydul's uninjured knee sympathetically. "Well, I'm sure that'll change soon enough." She slid her glance to the two men who had entered with her and had waited patiently to the side of where the king and warrior sat. With a nod from her, Purnia brought the stranger forward.

"Sire, this is Haton. He has agreed to valet for Captain Rydul as long as he is needed. He also has some experience with caring for injured people."

The newcomer, a tall, somewhat older man, bowed to the trio. He had a strong build with thick shoulders and arms, long hands, and long hair that had been tied back with a piece of leather. He wore formal clothing, as a valet should, well-kept and pressed, his pants dark blue and his shirt off white. "Your Majesties, Captain," he greeted, his voice firm. "It would be an honor to valet for the Captain," he confirmed.

"Good," the king agreed. "I thank you for your service. Purnia, thank you for finding someone so quickly. And with that, we shall take our leave." He gave McKenna enough of a push to get her to stand, following. The queen wrapped a hand through his arm as Purnia gathered dishes to take to the tray.

"Don't forget to compliment her on the dress when she gets back," McKenna said. "She was feeling a bit Amazonian when I left."

"Amazonian?"

"Tall." She cupped her rounded belly. "I should have her problem," she sighed wistfully. "You know both Joanna and

I are short compared to you guys. I think she's perfect. But what I think doesn't really matter does it?" she asked as Radine turned her to lead her out. With a tray full of dishes, Purnia quickly followed. Rydul wondered if living with Kathryn was going to be as baffling and all-consuming as it appeared being the queen's husband was for Radine.

"How may I assist you, My Lord?" Haton inquired.

"First, it's not my lord. I am just a soldier, so Captain will do, or even Rydul."

"A valet should never call his employer by his name, sir."

"Then sir will work as well. And thank you."

"May I ask for what, sir?" He started to complete the job that Purnia had left, taking the empty tea cup to the side table to leave with the rest of the drink service.

"For taking me on. I will tell you I am not in the best of conditions right now and unhappy about being stuck here for a few weeks longer."

"But it is necessary for you in order to heal properly, if I understand correctly."

"I am used to being with my men, on my feet, in the practice yard."

Haton sighed. "We all have our burdens we must carry, Captain," he replied, a hint of rebuke in his tone.

With an eyebrow climbing into his hairline, Rydul chuckled at the put-upon tone. "All right, point taken. Can you help me get cleaned up? I've not had a shower since the accident, and I would like clean clothing."

"That will not be a problem, sir. Give me a moment to get some things in order to change your bandages."

He'd never had anyone to fuss over him as Haton did, gathering clean clothing, fresh bandaging, and finding where the clean sheets were stored. Helping him into the bathing room and undress, carefully taking the old bandages off and releasing the metal cast, there wasn't an inkling of embarrassment as he supervised Rydul's shower, making sure the warrior did not fall, then drying him with a very impersonal hand. After redressing the injuries and putting the cast back on, he helped him to dress and guided him back to the chair he'd been sitting in while the valet changed the sheets and made the bed. Sending Haton to fetch another pot of tea, Rydul was content sitting alone, his leg braced on the seat of the other chair, still in wonder about the turn of his fortunes.

He could marry Kathryn now. In fact, he was going to ask her today, since while before he'd mentioned that he wanted to get married, he'd never come right out and asked. He could start his breeding program as soon as the new crufas arrived. And the fragrance of blooming freemas would soon permeate the air around his estate as they blossomed. Life was good, and about to get much better.

After placing the tea near the warrior, Haton excused himself to consult with Dr. Tripp and Pologa as to Rydul's continued care, leaving him to daydream on his own. So it was with a start that he opened his eyes to see Kathryn standing in front of him.

She was an absolute vision, her eyes dancing with laughter and love. "You're out of bed," she exclaimed.

"Washed, dressed, and fed," he told her, eyeing her from head to toes.

She wore a pale green froth of a dress, the bust tight around her ample bosom, lifting and outlining her breasts. From there, it flared into a full skirt that touched the floor, but did not hide the matching color slippers on her feet. The slightest breeze would cause the skirt to dance and swirl about her legs, hugging her body in soft waves while allowing the viewer the slightest hint of the body that lay beneath. She smiled as his eyes roved over her with obvious desire then twirled. "Like?"

"You are stunning."

She stopped mid-twirl. "Really?"

"The most beautiful woman on the planet." Holding out his hand, he invited her to join him. She perched carefully on his lap, not wanting to cause him any pain. Embracing her brought her tight against his chest. "Honestly, Kathryn, I am the most fortunate man on Taburon." He kissed her lips. "Did the queen tell you what the king was going to do?"

With her arms around his neck, she reared back to look at him. "No. What happened?"

"He has sent his stable master to buy crufas for me, the best ones to be found. He has ordered the gardeners, even though he wants the Queen's Garden repaired, he has sent men to clear and replace the *freema* flowers. I may still be out what Khail took from my accounts, but I can start the breeding program, on time, and might make the next harvest for the flowers. I won't have to sell the estate after all."

"That's wonderful!" she squealed in delight and hugged him, his grunt of pain soft as she temporarily forgot his ribs, ignored by them both. "I'm so happy for you."

"For us, Kathryn, it's all for us," he corrected. "My brother has been found and will be joining the army soon, hopefully to finally grow up and become a man. There's only one thing that could make this day better than it's already become." She eyed him quizzically. "Marry me, Olana, become my wife and partner, share this with me, be the mother of my children and grow old with me."

Her whole body melted into his, a hand gently caressing the side of his face, winding along his strong jaw before tracing across the lips she loved to kiss. His eyes finally had that sparkle she so loved to see in them, filled with hope, promise, and desire. Her head tilted slightly to the side as she pursed her lips, contemplating the face she adored before raising her gaze to his. "Captain Rydul of the King's Guard, I can't think of anything I want more than to be your wife, to share your life with you and bear your children." She sealed her promise with a kiss, long, deep and passionate, her breasts swelling, nipples tightening, her heart beating madly in her chest, her pussy flooding with moisture. Beneath her buttocks, his reaction was more than obvious.

Laughing, he gave her a push. "I told you two days, and I lied. But I can wait no longer. We have some celebrating to do, and I feel as though I'm going to explode if I don't share nadryl with you now." His head tilted in contemplation. "It will not be pretty, with bits and pieces of me scattered all over the room, ruining your pretty dress," he teased. "Go lock the door and join me on the bed," ordered, laughter in his voice. "The sheets are fresh."

Laughing with him, she hurried to the door and flipped the lock, as well as slid the bolt while he heaved himself up and twisted to sit his arse on the edge of the bed. But instead of falling into his arms when she returned, she stood two feet out of his reach, a devilish smile on her lips.

"I have a surprise for you," she murmured and turned her back to him. "See that ribbon?" He'd seen it the first time she'd spun around for him, the dress an absolute dream with an open back, a ribbon criss-crossing over her delicate shoulder blades and tied into a bow just above the start of the slope of her arse cheeks. "Pull it." He tugged, loosening the bow. As it fell to the side, so did the dress, slipping from her shoulders, opening at her hips. Slowly, Kathryn turned, holding the material to her bosom until she fully faced him, then letting it drop altogether.

She was completely nude. And she was gorgeous. Her breasts were tipped with hardened nipples, drawn tight by the soft abrasion of the material of the dress. Her waist was pinched trim and small enough for his hands to easily span. And as his eyes traveled down her body, coming to rest at the junction of her thighs, he saw that she was nude there as well, not a single hair covered her mound to disappear between her legs and hide her treasures. He felt his cock grow larger, thickening down his leg, a drop of pre-cum wetting the tip and staining his clean trousers.

Her eyes danced with delight. "You can thank the queen later," she explained stepping into the space he made by separating his legs. She went to work on opening his shirt, her breath caught on a gasp as he closed his mouth around one nipple and sucked. "I suppose you have this all worked out," she said once she could finally breathe.

"Not one bit," he admitted, holding her nipple with his teeth as he moved his lips in speech. He gave the nub a final suck, then released it with a wet pop. "We'll play it by ear as we go along. It can only hurt so good." He now gave equal attention to her other nipple, latching on like a starving child.

She tried hard to keep her concentration, slipping buttons through button holes, but her fingers were slow. "Rydul," she pleaded with a groan, "This won't work if you won't stop for a moment."

"Nope. Missed this too much. You taste too good."

Determined to get him undressed at least enough, she backed out of reach, taking his shirt with her, allowing it to fall onto the pile of her dress. Rydul unfastened the placket of his trousers and opened it, pushing the garment down to his knees, his cock flipping up onto his lap, fully engorged and pulsing.

Dropping to her knees in front of him, she took his flesh in hand and brought it to her mouth, taking the drop of pre-cum with her tongue and pulling it into her mouth, moaning as if it was the best thing she'd ever tasted. She licked around the head several times to wet it, playing with that sweet spot below with the tip of her tongue, then wrapped her lips fully around the end of his shaft, sucking forcefully. If she tried to swallow him, he vowed he would lose it within seconds. But she'd not practiced enough yet to take him fully, so the part of him that she engulfed into the warm cavern of her mouth was all that received her learning experience. Someday, she would be able to give him the full pleasure of his teachings, but today was not going to be the day.

Life was grand once again. He was healing, he was in love, his future secured. He looked lower and watched as she licked his shaft, treating it like the most sweet treat she'd ever had, her low murmuring sounds of pleasure shooting right through his cock and thrumming low in his balls. He had no idea how they would indulge, but if it started out this way, it could only get better. Rydul relaxed, intending to enjoy the ride.

"I forgot to tell you," he murmured later, sated, laying with her to his side, her head on his shoulder, her hand tracing designs on the part of his chest not covered in bandage. They'd not disturbed the clean sheets, making love on top of them instead and now stretched out above them, naked, one of her legs draped over his uninjured one, her lush breasts pressed into his side.

"What?" she asked lazily.

"The king has given me, temporarily, a valet to help me get around."

"You could use the help. You're a heavy man, even for me." Circles and spirals crossed his chest with her fingers.

"You should know that he might come in on us at any time."

She sat up, all languor forgotten, her eyes wide. "What?" she cried in horror.

"Next time we share nadryl, we should either tell him to give us an hour or two, or make sure all cf the entrances into this room are locked."

Her eyes quickly scanned the room. No one besides the two of them occupied it – at the moment But her suspicions were aroused. "Did he?" she asked.

Rydul nodded. "Only very briefly. When he saw we were occupied, he retreated."

She flooded with color, from her hairline to her chest for a moment while she suffered embarrassment in silence. Rydul watched, more used to the somewhat more open practices of the palace life. Besides, Haton had already seen what he sported between his legs, and Kathryn had the most delicious arse…

She worked through whatever she had first felt and sighed, there was nothing she could do now that it had happened. Her look was quizzical. "What other doors are there, beside the balcony ones?"

"I forgot about the one by the bureau. There have always been secret entrances scattered throughout the palace. I'm sorry I didn't remember before we shared nadryl."

Reaching for the bedspread, she tugged it up and over their bodies. "I'll make sure that door is locked. I'm not comfortable with telling someone to give us time because we're going to have sex. Might as well shout it from the rooftops," she added in a mumble.

He laughed with delight. "If it lets everyone know I'm about to dip my cock in the sweetest pussy on the planet, I don't see any problem there."

He didn't think she could get any redder, but she did, her eyes darkening in threat. "Don't even think about it," she warned. "Or you'll be shouting that you're sleeping in another room, alone."

He laughed until his sides hurt, then gently cupped her cheek in his hand, turning her head his way. "I love you."

"I love you right back."

"I didn't wear a condom," he confessed.

"You plan on making an honest woman of me, don't you?" she asked.

"Of course. As soon as possible," he promised.

"Problem solved," she ended.

Sky Clad Rydul

CHAPTER TWENTY

They couldn't have picked a better or prettier spot for the wedding service – in the King's Garden surrounded by blossoming flowers whose fragrance filled the air and overrode the lingering scent from the explosion of three weeks ago. Rydul still used crutches to get around and nothing had kept him still these last few days.

Except Kathryn tempting him into bed for rest and a lot of relaxation.

He wore his best dress uniform, black trousers with one leg split to accommodate his cast, black boots, a white jacket with gold braid, buttons and a dozen medals. At his side was the sword she had given to him, its hilt polished and bright. He leaned on his crutches, occasionally straightening and arching his back to take his weight from his good leg. Kenlyn had suggested that he seat himself in one of the nearby chairs, which he'd done at least twice while he waited, but the royals were due any moment and he didn't want to be caught sitting when they arrived. Kenlyn had assured him that the royals wouldn't have minded in the least if their hero was being gentle to his body after the beating it had taken. Rydul waved him off with a hand and a snort.

But he was feeling nervous and anxious. Kathryn was going to become his wife soon. With his estate returned to a profitable enterprise, he knew that they would never have to worry about an income – it would take work but it was there for the effort. She could takeover keeping the books for the estate, since she'd become involved in learning the monetary system of Taburon through her work in the palace and the time she would spend at the royal treasury until his enlistment was over. They would move permanently to the estate then, raise crufas and with help from the gods, a family.

The only way life could be better would have been if none of the events of the past days had occurred, he was healthy and no one had died from a disease the people had never known existed nor experienced.

But that was in the past, and the future lay ahead, bright with promise and good things, laughter and love. Lots of love. Kisses too. He liked kisses. Especially those kisses he planted on certain parts of her body that drove her insane with pleasure.

Rydul sighed. Patience, he told himself. No one was going anywhere, the day was reserved for this. There were no crises, everyone was healing or healed, life was returning to normal on Taburon and in the city. He nodded to a couple from Earth, an older man and woman that Kathryn had befriended and invited to the wedding, a stand-in, he believed, for her missing parents. She had wished they could have been here, but was willing to wait until they could, as a couple, return to Earth so she could introduce her husband to her parents. Maybe by then, there would also be a grandchild. Nothing would make her mother happier than to have a grandchild, even one half Taburon.

Every eye turned to the back of the garden as two people entered, the king with his wife on his arm, both dressed in rich clothing as befitted the occasion, their faces flushed as if they had been running. The assembled participants began to look for and take their seats as the couple made their way to the front of the set area, stopping only once they'd come close to the groom.

Rydul bowed. "My apologies, Captain," the king said. "It would appear Jaima's new child has decided to make its arrival today. Joanna is in labor and we wanted to make sure there would be no problems with the delivery before we came down." He helped McKenna, herself big with child to a seat, making sure she was comfortable as he spoke.

"Your Majesty, if you wish to remain with the prince and princess, please do not feel you have to be here, though I appreciate you attending."

"Nonsense," Radine dismissed. "We'd only be in the way there anyway. They'll send word once the child arrives." He glanced around. "Are you ready? Do you feel all right?"

"I am more than ready, Your Majesty, believe me."

Radine chuckled with understanding. He'd been there, anxious to marry McKenna, especially after they had been tricked into separating temporarily the night before their scheduled wedding. Once he'd caught up to her on Earth, he'd not hesitated to make her undeniably his and crown her queen, marrying her while still on the ship returning to Taburon. "Then let's get this show going," the king ordered, taking his own seat. A magistrate moved into position as Rydul stepped to the side of the aisle to wait for Kathryn.

She was a vision. Dressed in a luminescent pearl piece of confection the women called a dress. The queen had gone all out for this event, a celebration after the horror of the last weeks, having the royal dressmaker search for the most elegant material she could find and designing a dress just for Kathryn. In a way, McKenna was reliving the wedding she never had, forsaken by a Taburon noble who didn't believe the king should marry an out-worlder. In a fit of rage at her 'desertion,' Radine had ripped McKenna's wedding dress to shreds, vowing to never trust another woman, that when he finally did take a wife, it wouldn't be for love. They had been fortunate in that the noble's duplicity had been discovered fairly quickly and the couple reunited.

Rydul fell more in love every day. Today would seal their lives together. Tonight he would make her his in every way possible, and he would become hers in turn. But for now, he had to remember to take a breath as he watched her approach, her hand around the arm of Dr. Tripp, who had volunteered to fill in for her father.

She was lead up to her groom, greeting him with a smile that encompassed all of the emotion of the day. He returned her smile with a nod, a split second of jealousy running through him as Tripp placed a light kiss on her temple before handing her off. Together they faced the magistrate.

"Thousands of years ago, our ancestors believed the Gods lived on our moons, Icide and Liva, and when the Gods came together once a year, the height of their passion cast down upon the people, granting them share in their good fortune. That day was called Sky Clad and it was then a man and woman became husband and wife.

"Today we honor Sky Clad as a tradition but reserve the right to marry as our hearts dictate. With this in mind, Rydul and Kathryn come before this assembly to exchange vows and join together as husband and wife." The magistrate's eyes shifted to the couple standing before him. He smiled and nodded to Rydul who twisted on his crutches to face Kathryn, taking one of her hands between both of his.

His eyes sparked with love and hope, his smile meant to ease her nervousness, his touch a connection that he would never forsake. "Kathryn, when I first met you I knew there was something between us that would have grown deeper with very little help. I so wanted to explore those possibilities but I knew I had little time. So I held back.

"The hardest thing I've ever had to do was when I boarded that ship and left you behind on Earth. Only after did I realize that I had left my heart there as well.

"Then seeing you again the day you arrived here was my greatest joy, made only more so today, for today I become your husband.

"You are my wife, my life. My heart, my body and my soul. All I own is yours in your trust and keeping. All I am today is because of you.

"As the years go by I will probably make mistakes. I am just a man. I may disappoint you and I would hope that you will let me know when I have done something to hurt you. But I will always cherish you and love you for as long as I live."

Kathryn took a deep breath, calming herself and bringing the overwhelming tide of emotion back to a slow simmer. She had felt herself shaking as she'd walked up to Rydul, but once he took her hand, all of the nervousness disappeared in the warmth of his touch and the absolute confidence in his eyes. She gave his hands a slight squeeze of thanks.

"Rydul," she began, "Until we met, I never believed a man such as you could have any interest in me. I was the little mouse that hid in the corner, afraid to come out. I was the butterfly content to remain in my cocoon. You have brought my life to fruition and proven me wrong time after time.

"I am so sorry I let you go that day and my heart nearly broke with the realization that the best thing to ever happen to me was leaving. I had an obligation I could not ignore. But loyalty is a part of your creed so I knew you understood.

"And though you were so far away, I heard you call to me across the stars every single day. To be able to come to you gave me such joy, but nowhere near as much as today, when I become your wife.

"I can't bring much to you in wealth or property, but I do give you everything I hold dear in my life – honesty, loyalty, and a love I know grows more every day. I cannot think of more I want from life than to spend it with you, to share your dreams and do all I can to help make them come true, and help raise any children we might create together.

"Like you, I am sure there will be mistakes and disappointments along the way. But we will learn from the one and overcome the other if we do it together side by side. And I will always love you until the day I die."

Tears glittered in Kathryn's eyes as she gave him her promises. Bending, Rydul leaned closer to give her a kiss to ally her emotions. The magistrate chuckled. "Not yet," he admonished sotto voice.

"Don't care," Rydul replied planting a kiss on her lips as the audience laughed softly.

With a shake of his head, the magistrate waited a moment for the couple to separate. "With the exchange of vows and promises made here today, let it be known throughout all time and in all places that Rydul and Kathryn are husband and wife. May they live together forever in love and peace." His smile for the couple was huge, indulgent "Now you may exchange a kiss."

Rydul wasted no time, scooping her close without losing his balance on his crutches to cover her lips with his own. Silencing with his mouth the soft squeal she'd uttered at his move, she fell into his embrace, her body going soft against his as he plundered her mouth.

"You might want to save it for later," Radine suggested from behind them, his voice full of amusement, his arm coming to lay on Rydul's back.

Both of them had the grace to redden in embarrassment as they separated, Rydul resetting his weight back on his crutches, though he held onto one of Kathryn's hands possessively. "Your pardon, Your Majesty."

Radine leaned closer to the couple so only they could hear, though his gaze slipped for a second to his own wife, watching as she dabbed at her eyes with a handkerchief. His memories were still so fresh in his own mind, though it had been over five years since he had exchanged vows with McKenna. He hadn't been able to help it, reaching for her hand while Rydul and Kathryn made their pledges. "Believe me, I understand completely. Been there myself," he confessed. "Come, greet your well-wishers, then let's eat. Quite frankly, I'm starved."

Kathryn slipped from the bed carefully so as to not wake Rydul. He'd been overtired yesterday after the ceremony and reception, so much so that as they'd prepared for bed, she'd made him take one of his pain pills so he could sleep in comfort. She'd had to swear that not sharing nadryl on their wedding night was fine with her before he would take the medication. Snuggling under the covers, they'd talked quietly, remembering the day, exchanging gentle touches and even gentler words until sleep had pulled them both under its spell.

Towards morning, an hour or so before sunrise was expected, he'd awakened her with kisses and caresses, promising that he felt fine. They consummated their marriage with tenderness. With long, slow touches and deep penetrating thrusts. With earth-shattering orgasms and sensual slides into soft sighs of bliss. Sated, Rydul had fallen back to sleep.

Kathryn, on the other hand, had lain awake, comforted by the sound of his steady breathing, listening to the early birds that rustled in the trees just outside the suite they shared. Watching as the light in the room steadily brightened with the rising sun. She knew Haton would be in soon to start the day, getting Rydul up and dressed. She was quite unused to and uncomfortable at having someone other than Rydul catching her naked, even if she were hiding under the covers. It had been enough that she had tolerated having the queen's personal servant Annatt fussing over her yesterday as she dressed for the ceremony, catching the young human woman as she emerged from her bath to wrap her in a towel and lead her to a chair to comb out and style her hair. When the dressmaker had entered carrying her gown, whipping the towel from Kathryn's body without so much as a by-your-leave, she had blushed sixteen shades of red and kept her eyes closed until she'd been covered halfway decently. Annatt had giggled. This would take some getting used to if it kept up.

Grabbing her robe, she tied it around her waist as she padded barefoot to the double doors that led to the balcony, stepping outside. The day was promising to be glorious, a perfect day to start a marriage. The temperature was brisk, the tiles under her feet cool. The sun was bright in a cloudless sky, the color quickening to a soft turquoise, something she was beginning to appreciate more and more. Filling her lungs with a breath of the cool, crisp air, she looked out over the grounds of the palace and beyond the walls to the town.

The people were already up and about. From this side of the palace she could hear the bustling noises of storekeepers as they prepared to open their shops. Workers called to one another, greeting friends, some hustling to make an early morning sale. Below, across the grounds, guards were heading to their posts while servants tended to their tasks, scurrying by with parcels in their arms.

Kathryn leaned on the railing. She could get used to this life – too easily – she decided. Being a part of palace life was exciting. Personally knowing the royals made her feel special, taking her back to the one time she'd attended the holiday party where Rydul had given her the necklace and told her he was soon leaving. That she'd been included in the invitation in the first place had come as a surprise. Now she dined in the midst of the king, queen, prince, and princess of Taburon several days a week and worked in the king's treasury alongside of the minister of finance. She had to remember she was just an ordinary woman married to an extraordinary man who, for the time being, had a direct line to the king. And while things would change once his enlistment was up and they moved permanently to the estate, there would still be that connection through his breeding program. She didn't think Rydul would ever forget that the king had thanked him for saving the royal family by saving his dreams. She too, would forever be in the king's debt for his generosity to the man she loved.

Knowing it wouldn't last too much longer, since Rydul was determined to find a place for them to live as soon as he could get around better, she decided to enjoy the time she had here and indulge herself where and when she could. Though she did refuse the help of a personal servant −very politely of course.

The job that had been given to her was exciting. Learning the Taburon monetary system challenged her mind and creativity, adapting what she knew to what they were teaching her. The hours she put into working with the minister would pay off when she became a full time worker, the money would help towards continuing in building his stable and improving the *freema* fields. As long as he was on the injured list, his needs were taken care of by the crown. He still received his pay, which he now banked as much as he could, so the little she made would go completely towards the estate expenses.

Though she knew he was chomping at the bit to get back onto the practice grounds and if nothing else, watch the men as they mock battled each other.

Yes, until they found a place to stay on their own with more privacy, she would simply enjoy having the time to learn a new job and spend the rest of her day taking care of her husband, sharing quiet meals and intimate nights. They would travel several times during the year to oversee the crufas and flowers. And if she had a baby….well, life was full of good things.

A gruff male voice caught her attention and she leaned further over the rail. Below, a pair of guards was escorting a single man, his hands shackled in front of him, each guard holding one arm. The guard on the left gave the man's arm a shake.

"Move along," he growled. "Stop lagging."

The man, easily identifiable as human because of his height and dark brown, almost reddish colored hair, tried with a shake of his own to dislodge the guard's hand. Swinging to the opposite side, he unsuccessfully only ended up stumbling. Both guards righted him viciously, tightening their grips. "Let me go," the man demanded.

The guards ignored the man, continuing to drag him across the yard. "You're lucky we let you walk on your own," the first guard responded. "I'm tempted to knock you out and carry you like a piece of meat." He punctuated the statement with a violent shake.

"Fucking prick," the man cursed, trying to shake off his captors, looking around, his glance inadvertently going up.

Kathryn felt her heart stop in her chest, her hands clenching on the rail, her vision narrowing down to the face of the man below. This was the man who'd tried to blow up the palace, who'd shot her husband and could have killed him – would have had he had the chance. This was the man who'd conspired with a woman to bring a deadly disease to

Taburon that had killed a hundred people – old people and innocent children.

This was the man who six years ago had disappeared from her life, breaking her mother's heart and sending her father into a month long depression. He was the reason she had thought the voice she'd heard at the dormitory several weeks ago had sounded so familiar. This was her brother, Sean.

He sneered at her when he saw her looking down at him. He was pale, his face drawn with lines of hatred and wretchedness for what he'd done and what he soon faced in justice. He looked haggard, his clothes unkempt and wrinkled and he appeared as though he'd lost a great deal of weight from the brother she'd once known. His hair was shaggy and uncombed, springing wild about his neck and head. Her eyes wide with surprise and the fright she showed at seeing him had no effect on him, his only concern for his own life. He'd called her a whore she'd been told, and he still believed it now. That she would sleep with one of these creatures, open her body to their perverted use, only made her less than a human in his mind. He had no respect for her and no care about how his family might have felt concerning his actions.

Kathryn already knew his fate. Her gasp as her breath caught got no response from him except for that sneer as the guards pushed him along, his attention now directed to the path before him. The three disappeared through a doorway further along the grounds.

Her legs gave out beneath her. Her brother was here on Taburon, accused of treachery beyond the pale and doomed to pay for it with his life. She'd loved him as a child, letting her tag along behind him and his friends even when he considered her a nuisance. He'd always found time to spend with her in her childish games and defended her as she grew up into a young woman attending high school and accosted by an upper classman. He'd been her hero for a while.

Then he'd gone to war. She'd fretted every day he was gone fighting, hoping he would come home safe, content to settle for simply alive if injured. She'd worried every night after he'd returned, a changed man, sullen and disenchanted, uncommunicative towards his family.

After he'd disappeared, she'd mourned his loss, but had always held out the hope that someday, when he'd buried his demons, that he would return to his family and the love they held for him.

Had he known she was on Taburon? Perhaps not the day she arrived, but somewhere along the line, he must have heard about the one woman who'd had a relationship with a Taburon soldier. She'd not kept it a secret from anyone, and he obviously knew of her before she'd recognized him. Was he aware that she was now the wife of that Taburon warrior? Could it have been just circumstance that he came here on the same ship as she? She didn't remember seeing him during the two and a half day journey, but then she hadn't met everyone on board. Of course, after landing, Rydul had occupied the greatest majority of her time and she hadn't spent much time with anyone from the ship from then on.

Her parents, once they found out the fate of their only son, would be devastated. Their son, lost, then found, then lost again forever. Executed on a planet far away from them, unable to speak with him one last time, though their daughter knew. Could she tell them? Or would she let them live with the peace they'd already found with his loss and keep silent? Could she hold that guilt in for the rest of her life? That she knew his fate and wouldn't let them know?

Her emotions overwhelmed her and she couldn't hold the pain in any longer, a wail of despair emerging from her, from deep inside her body with all of the force of a gale wind. Tears fell from her eyes in heavy drops as she started to sob.

She'd been so happy just moments ago. Now it was gone, destroyed in a single recognizing glance, her joy overwhelmed by grief, sadness and even anger. How could he do what he did, take everything he'd been taught as a child and toss it like so much garbage without consideration for the consequences? Had she known before the explosion exactly who was involved, she would have reported him if only to stop him and save him from the fate he now faced. He'd risked his life for the most inane reason. Her tears dropped unhindered.

"Kathryn?" Rydul questioned, dropping awkwardly down beside her, his crutches forgotten on the tile of the balcony. "Kathryn, what's wrong?" He'd awoken fully at her wail, hurriedly drawn on a pair of togs and followed the sound of her weeping.

Wrapping his arms around her he pulled her into his embrace, hugging her against his bare chest, smoothing his hand down her hair. "Shh," he soothed. "Olana, tell me. What's wrong?"

He rocked her gently. Yesterday had gone so well, had been so perfect. Kathryn had been beyond stunning in her gown, her face bright, her eyes happy. Her voice had trembled slightly when she'd said her vows, not from fright, but from excitement and anticipation. After, at the dinner held in their honor and in celebration, she'd kept a subtle eye on him, aware of his tension and if he seemed in pain but giving him his space and not hovering. He'd loved her for that.

They hadn't danced that first dance as was traditional, but he'd held her close while balancing on his crutches and they'd swayed back and forth to the music. As the night had progressed, she could see the increasing strain in his eyes and around his mouth. He was in pain from being on his feet too long, yet they remained with the group, anxious to hear the result of the impending birth. As soon as it came – the prince had a second son – she'd ushered him out through all of the jibes of hurrying him to the marriage bed. The king had been the last one for them to pass. The royal had taken Rydul's hand in friendship and placed a light kiss on

Kathryn's forehead before allowing them to pass. His own wife had already excused herself long ago.

He'd been willing to force himself beyond his present exhaustion to share nadryl on their wedding night, but she'd surprised him yet again by refusing his offer and tucking him into bed, making sure he took his medication. And she had not turned him down hours later when he turned to her and began to initiate nadryl, something he assured her he was more than capable of at the time. She was an enthusiastic lover and willing to learn, innovative in her own right much to his pleasure.

He'd been so satisfied that he'd fallen to sleep soon after.

On the verge of waking himself, aware somewhat of her slipping from the bed, he'd been content to lay there and wait for Haton to arrive before rising himself. Her cry of absolute despair had pulled him from the warmth of the bed in a state of shock, dragging on his pants and hurrying out to see what had upset her. She was crying as though her heart was broken and he was at a loss for what had changed her mood so dramatically so quickly.

Continuing to rock with her in his arms, he tried to soothe her. She had curled up tightly against him, burying her face into his chest, seeking his warmth and comfort as though she had none to find within herself.

"Olana, please, let me help. What is wrong?"

Her hands fisted open and closed on his arms, her breath coming in short gasps in between her sobs. His chest was wetted, the drops cooling quickly in the crisp air. "That man," she sobbed. "He's…he's…"

"What man?" Rydul asked, suddenly frightened. Had she been threatened as she stood on the balcony? "Has someone threatened you?"

Kathryn shook her head, catching her breath a moment, sniffling, choking on a sob. When she looked up at him, the concern in his eyes would have floored her had she not already been sitting safe in his embrace. She blinked, her eyelashes drenched in tears.

She loved him so much. She couldn't bear the thought that his life and dreams were maybe now in jeopardy because she was related to the man who tried to take down the kingdom. For the smallest of moments, she wished she'd never come to Taburon to endanger this man and his position in society here. The thought vanished as soon as it occurred. She couldn't give him up for anything, but she still worried about what the implications of her relationship to her brother might mean for him.

Would he still love her when he found out she was related to the man who'd nearly killed him? She cupped his cheek gently. "I love you, you know."

His hand covered hers. "I know that. And I love you."

She pet his cheek. "I didn't know, believe me. I had no idea."

"About what?"

She sniffed again. Her nose must have looked reddened and runny, she probably looked a sight. "That man, the one who tried to blow up the palace." She waited while he remembered, waited for his reaction, but only got a more curious look. "I saw him, this morning."

"Did he frighten you? Where were the guards?" He was truly frightened now. Did the prisoner somehow escape?

She shook her head. "No, the guards were with him, he was in shackles. But as he passed by the balcony, he looked up at me and I knew. God help me, I knew him." The tears that she managed to hold back filled her eyes again. "Rydul, that man was my brother, Sean."

He didn't believe her at first, his gaze straying out over the grounds, the trees that rose higher than the railing of the balcony, the bright sky overhead. She hadn't seen her brother in years. People change over time, memories fade and a person who looked like someone she'd known could pass for a long lost brother and still not be.

But were this based only on a suspicion, her reaction shouldn't be this strong. And she'd told him that there had been something about the voice she'd overheard at the dormitory that had brought a flare of memory, but she'd dismissed it a day or so later as a play on her imagination.

The intruder had known that he was involved with a human woman, threatening her with death if he'd not returned to his companion within a certain time, making him choose between his love and his duty.

"Are you sure?" he asked.

She nodded. "His voice sounded familiar, remember? When the light hit his hair, it was the same color as mine in places. He has my father's eyes. Rydul, I'm sure he's Sean."

Rydul pulled her even tighter to his chest. "I am so sorry, Kathryn." He rocked her, feeling her shiver bodily. "It's all right, love. It's all right."

"He's going to die, isn't he?" she whispered with faint hope, her breath warm next to his skin.

"That's why I said I'm sorry. His crime and the law are quite clear."

She started to sob again. "Why?" she asked of no one in particular. "Why would he do this? He had no quarrel with Taburons. He hasn't been hurt by any of your people. He's throwing his life away." She gave in to her crying for a few minutes, finding little comfort in his arms. "My parents," she wailed again. "It'll kill them to find out."

"Do they have to know?" he asked after a moment.

She took another moment to collect herself. "I don't know," she finally answered. "They accepted that he was dead years ago, or at least someplace where he'd found some peace. If I could be assured this wouldn't get out back on Earth…"

"I do not know how the king will handle this as far as Earth is concerned. We can no longer tolerate the animosity from humans, their constant attacks on our people when we've done nothing to provoke it except to exist." He placed a kiss on her head. "An example needs to be made."

She nodded. "I know. If his name could be kept secret, it would give me time to come up with a solution."

"Or none at all, if that is the answer."

"Or none at all," she agreed. "But a part me feels that they have a right to know the truth."

At the sound of a soft shuffling, Rydul released her enough to turn towards the doors to the balcony. Haton stood there, a puzzled expression on his face, but waiting patiently for his temporary master o explain if he so wished.

"Is everything alright, sir?"

"Haton, my wife has had a fright. Would you call for some hot tea and draw a warm bath for her, please?"

The servant bowed. "Of course, right away, sir." He turned and left the balcony doorway.

She cried out a final time and he wrapped himself around her. Rydul knew they couldn't stay out here too much longer.

The air was nippy and neither wore much in the way of clothing. The morning chill was becoming uncomfortable.

"I hope this doesn't affect you," she murmured.

"How would it?"

"I'm the sister of the man who tried to kill the king. I'm your wife. Who's going to trust me after that and by association, you?"

"That will never happen, Olana. You were the one who told me about the plan to blow up the palace. My loyalties have never been questioned – ever. You had nothing to do with his schemes. No one can blame you."

"They can question your loyalties now though. They could not buy the crufas."

He shook his head. "Never happen. I won't let it." He leaned back so she could see not only the determination in his eyes, but the truth. "And even if it does, so what? It won't change how I feel about you, about us. I love you, you are my life. We belong together, we always will." He swiped at her tears and wet cheeks. "Come on, a hot bath and warm cup of tea for you. Then we'll dress and go see that new prince. Maybe stop by the dungeon and talk to your brother." Reaching for the rail, he tried to pull himself up but failed, his legs cramping under him. Sheepishly, he gave her a distressed look and plea for help.

Her heart melted. Her distress of a moment ago was now forgotten as she offered her arm for him to grab, adding lift as he struggled to rise. Once he was on his feet, she grabbed the crutches and passed them over, waiting as he tucked them under his arms.

His expression changed as he glanced to her, his chest expanding on a lusty sigh. Reaching out, he took the sides of her robe and pulled them together. "Woman, you tempt me too much," he commented, tying the belt tight around her waist. "Come wife," he indicated, "I don't think you want what's running through my mind right now."

She slid a hand down his chest, stopping at one of his male nipples which she circled with her finger tip. The look she shot him was pure mischief though her eyes were still rimmed with moisture. "I always want what you have running through your mind right now, but you're cold, I'm cold, and I'm hungry- for food." She chuckled as he took her wandering hand in his, his expression desperate with building lust. "I so love you."

CHAPTER TWENTY-ONE

King Radine sat on his throne in the throne room, his eyes, though appearing uninterested, seeing all that was going on around him. His skin was pale, the result of weeks of being ill, cooped up indoors, and more weeks of having to play catch up with what had happened during his illness. He longed to get outside, to join the men in training and get over this languid feeling he'd been stuck in for the last weeks. He longed to spend the day with the sun on his face, to go riding, to take his son with him on the back of his crufa and just feel free.

The boy was nearly vibrating with pent-up energy, anxious to get out with his father and ride or sword fight. Since he was feeling flabby himself, a little time in the practice yard wasn't out of the question. Once this unpleasant business was taken care of, he would take time to spend it with his men, including Prince Jaima, who was also feeling soft, but had been seen huffing his way through a practice just yesterday, mock fighting, determined to whip himself back into shape.

Of course, with McKenna so close to delivering, any time away from the palace would be limited. He wouldn't miss the arrival of his next child – his final child if McKenna had her way – for all the days in the sun in forever.

Queen McKenna was on the floor talking with several lords, her hand in constant motion swiping across her expanded belly. She was gorgeous in pregnancy – he'd keep her that way forever if it had been up to him. Not to keep her under control, but when her body swelled with child, and her breasts became larger, and she responded with greater emotion every time they shred nadryl, he felt so virile and so very much in love with her. He sighed. He knew if he even expressed such an idea anywhere in her presence, he'd be sleeping in the nursery with the children for a long period of time. A very long period of time.

She was the love of his life. He'd known it the minute he'd met her, and he believed it every hour of every day. Had he lost her to that madman bomber, he would have been but a shell of a man, useless and defeated for all time. She had proven herself over and over during his illness, taking charge of both the kingdom with help from Queen mother Inoa as well as overseeing his care, even from a distance. He couldn't have been more proud of her. Now if she'd only slow down since he'd recovered....

With another sigh, Radine listed to the side of his chair, propping his chin on his hand. His crown slid slightly to the side and he reached up to straighten it, bored beyond knowing, impatient. This was one of his least favorite things to do – pronounce sentence on a person who had injured the realm in some way.

He was a strict king though when it came to the safety of his people, nothing was too harsh to assure justice. This treachery had gone way too far, threatening his life, his family, his rule and his people. In reality, he had no choice, the law was clear. It only required of him to make the pronouncement.

But for the sake of propriety, of having to have everything appear above board since he intended for this to send a message to Earth and humans, the two criminals would have been put to death days ago. This time it all had to be without prejudice, without question about favoritism, without racism – or speciesism - in the judgement.

So it had taken weeks for the investigation to be conducted, all of the evidence examined and everyone questioned thoroughly. The Council had made their recommendations and the king had agreed to their decision. All that remained was to make it official.

Rydul and Kathryn entered the room, arm in arm. The warrior still used crutches. His wife of one week kept a close eye on her husband, ready to lend a hand if he needed. But the warrior wouldn't show such weakness, at least not if he could help it. Radine understood, he'd felt the same way since his illness. Give someone interested in taking over your throne any idea that you're incapable of defending it, and it will fall.

The marriage of the two had been a second highlight in the tragedy that had surrounded the last weeks. The first, of course, had been the birth of his nephew, Prince Tylene. McKenna had gone all out for the young woman, getting the best dressmaker in the city to create and sew the dress, harassing the cooks to make the best meal they could, making sure the garden was pruned and beautiful for the ceremony. She'd bullied several of the Council members to attend, blackmailing them he heard later with favors if they attended, though the favors she promised amounted to unimportant things. She'd checked with him before making the promises, to his delight. She was devious woman when she wanted to be.

At the opposite end of the room the doors opened enough to allow a guard to peek through. Radine nodded to the man, he was ready to get this done and over with.

He straightened, pulling all of his kingly manner about him as he caught McKenna's eye. She bowed to the lords and strode up to take her place next to him, reaching out to slip her had into his in unity. Rydul and Kathryn sat in the front row to the right of the thrones. A strained hush fell over the observers.

"If the prisoners are ready, bring them forward," Radine ordered.

With the doors fully opened, two guardsmen stepped through, their hands on their weapons, at the ready should there be any signs of treachery. Behind them came two more guards with a woman between them, a second set of guards flanking a single man, and finally a fourth row of two guards, their hands also on their weapons. The first set of guards marched smartly to the king, bowed and separated to allow the woman to face the monarch.

Hostility filled the atmosphere. These two people were responsible for the deaths of over one hundred people and the horror brought to Taburon in the form of a virus that was now a part of their lives forever, hidden and sleeping until time for it to return and wreak havoc among the people again. Had the mob had their way, there would be no need for these proceedings. The two wouldn't have made it this far without the protection of the crown. They were safe – for now.

"Nadine Visio, you have been found guilty of crimes against the people of Taburon, bringing disease and death to the planet for no reason save that of sheer malice. Before I pronounce sentence, do you have anything to say for yourself?"

The woman's face twisted in a scowl. She was a pretty woman, young, about twenty eight years of age, her whole life ahead of her. It was unfortunate that hate had scarred her features. Prison hadn't been kind to her either, her hair scraggy and oily, her clothing wrinkled beyond any ironing possible. She'd lost weight while incarcerated, refusing to eat the food provided except for the basic bread and water. From all that she'd heard while in the dungeon, she wasn't going to survive for much longer anyway. What was the point in keeping alive a body that was already pledged to death?

She twisted in her bondage then realized the futility of trying to fight these stronger, heavier men who held her tightly in their grip. "I'd do it again if I could," she snarled. "You have no authority over me. I am a citizen of Earth and I demand you return me there. You have no right to pass judgement on me."

Radine drew in a breath to reply, but McKenna's hand on his arm stayed him. Glancing her way, she gave him a slight nod, confidence in her eyes as she rose.

"Why did you come to Taburon?" she asked, her voice calm and steady. "If you hate us so much, why not just stay on Earth where you need never have any contact with us?"

"Us?" she replied with astonishment. "You're human, not one of them!"

"I am as much a Taburon as my husband, as my children, as the child I carry. Answer my question, why did you come to Taburon?"

"To stop these – things – from coming to Earth. To let them, and all others like them know that we don't need their kind, that we humans don't want them."

McKenna smiled knowingly. "You have it all wrong. Taburons don't need humans, not in the slightest, but you should be grateful for their interests in Earth.

"You have no idea what – or who – exists beyond Earth. Who or what eyes that little blue defenseless planet every single hour of every single day and makes plans for how they could use it, its resources, its people. The Taburons are one of a consortium of planets that keeps those others in check, their mere presence deters those others from advancing on Earth to rape and pillage the planet. The Taburons save the asses of every man, woman and child on Earth and you should bow down and thank them for it

"And don't be fooled," she continued. "You may think Taburon backward with their swords and crufas, no big scale technology like Earth, but they could lay waste to Earth with the lift of a finger and not break a sweat.

"You should thank these people for their benevolent interest. All they want is peace, to become comrades, maybe share a great source of energy that would solve a lot of Earth's energy problems.

"But instead, you come here to maim and kill innocent people, old people, and children. Babies. Those could have been my children," she said vehemently, rubbing at her unborn child. "They were my children, my Taburon children. The loss of even one was one too many.

"So, yes, we have the right to judge you, to consider giving mercy to someone who showed none and therefore will receive none.

"I do not trust that your punishment on Earth by humans will equal the severity of your crimes. Throughout history, each race has reserved the right to mete out justice as they saw fit according to their beliefs and laws.

"And just so it cannot be said that you were mistreated by a non-human and to prove to all Earth these attempts against Taburons will no longer be tolerated, I will pronounce sentence.

"In memory of those you caused to die with consideration of the families who mourn them, the sentence is death by execution." She turned and went back up to her throne, sitting heavily, facing the crowd. Not a sound was heard, not a peep, not a sneeze, not a single throat being cleared. She looked out over the assembled people, giving each one a single quick glance. She was truly a queen now. Raising her hand, she waved to the guards. "Guards, see to it immediately," she ordered.

The guards surrounding Nadine bowed, each taking an arm in hand, turning the young woman and escorting her away. As the other prisoner was moved forward, Radine leaned closer to his wife. "I love you, little one," he whispered.

"I know," she whispered back before turning her attention forward.

With a nod, the next prisoner was hustled to face the king. This time, Radine stood, moving to the top of the steps to look down on the prisoner.

His face was defiant, there was no fear there, nor any attempt to appear remorseful for what he had done. Radine felt himself anger, his body tightening, taking a deep breath to calm for he had to also condemn this man without any outward show of hostility.

"John Taker, you have been found guilty of crimes against the people of Taburon, endangering the lives of the royal families and attempting to overturn the rightful rule of this planet without any reason except that of sheer malice. Before I pronounce sentence, do you have anything to say for yourself?"

With a sudden jerk, the man twisted free, but made no other sign of aggression, even though the guards pulled their laser weapons free to point at him. They would protect the king and his wife at all costs. His back straightened, stiffening. "My name isn't Taker," he said.

"Then what is it?" the king asked. "The sentence still stands."

Raising his hand, the man pointed towards Kathryn and Rydul. "Ask her," he ordered.

Radine frowned, turning his head towards the couple, stepping down to face them directly. Kathryn's head was bowed, her face tucked out of sight. Rydul had draped an arm across her shoulders, pulling her tightly to his body, his own face impassive as the king glanced to him.

But it was obvious that she was terribly upset, her shoulders hunched. While he had at first wanted to demand an answer from the woman, Radine's stance softened. "Kathryn?" he queried.

Her face was wet, tears in her eyes as she looked up at the king, her body was visibly shaking, so Rydul tightened is embrace, his only concern for his wife. "It's all right love," he whispered soothingly, his lips buried in her hair. The king repeated his query with a raised eyebrow.

She took a deep breath, wiping across her face with her sleeve. When she finally spoke, it was with regret and sorrow. "His name is Tehyr, Your Majesty, he's my brother Sean."

Abruptly, the king swiveled, his glance going from the prisoner to Rydul, and back to Kathryn. Dropping to his haunches, he took one of her hands into his, a gentle touch but from the king nonetheless. "You knew?" he asked.

She nodded. "Yes, Sire."

"For how long?"

"The morning after our marriage. I saw him from our balcony as he was lead across the courtyard."

"Why did you not say anything?"

She shook her head. "Your Majesty, when I was young, I had a brother I followed everywhere, annoying him to no end. I idolized him and he tolerated me as a good brother will. His friends teased me, but he defended me from their bullying. He was my knight in shining armor. I knew that boy would grow into a fine man one day.

"But then he went to war, and he changed, became cold and unfeeling, barely acknowledging me or our parents until one day he disappeared. I cannot express the pain my parents felt, every single day until years later they resolved to accept that their son was dead to them.

"As did I." Tears ran down her cheeks, dripped onto her lap, her voice wavered. "My brother, the one I knew as a child, would never have done what this man has done. I will always love my brother, I cannot help myself in that regard. But I cannot defend what his man has done to you, your people, to Taburon, to my husband. Nor will I beg for mercy on his behalf. I have given my vows to my husband, and through them, to Taburon. Do what you will with him." Finished with her speech, she tucked her head back into Rydul's shoulder, gently pulling her hand away from the king's grip. He released her, remaining on his haunches for a moment longer, checking with Rydul. The warrior nodded his head once and slid his attention back to his wife. Radine rose and went back to where he had stood before this secret had been revealed.

McKenna's face showed horror and sympathy for the woman. She'd not had any idea of this news, and was in a state of shock, as were many of the people in the audience, their voices raised in a hushed whisper as the king glanced over them.

But this was a brave woman, her words proving where her heart truly lay, with her husband and the people she was coming to accept as her family, a loyal and fierce citizen.

On the other hand, Sean Tehyr's face had fallen. For a heartbeat, he had thought that perhaps his sister would make a plea for him, to spare his life. Then she had given her little speech and his hopes had fallen as his resolve rose. He had known the chances he took, that there was a high probability that he would be caught and the punishment severe. Yet he had decided to take the opportunity to end the incursion of aliens onto Earth, to set an example for all alien races to keep away from his planet. They had enough problems without the added one of people from another planet bringing their different ideas and culture to set new ideas into people's minds. Earth needed to build their own arsenal of weapons capable of keeping these creatures away from entertaining any idea of ingratiating themselves into human society.

Instead, he would become an example of what happened to any who tried to interfere with a peaceful association between aliens and humans. For the time being. There were others who believed as he did and the 'war' was not over, not yet.

His expression hardened as the king came to stand over him on the steps. He had to at least acknowledge that this man was a picture of power, his emotions under tight harness, except for his eyes. There was a hardness in his eyes that brooked no defiance and gave no quarter. He ruled with an iron, but gentle fist and would protect his people to the death.

"Satisfied?" Radine asked.

"She is no sister of mine, and a traitor to her people."

"No. She is Taburon, and the wife of a Taburon warrior. And she is welcomed among us," Radine added so that all in the room would understand that he would tolerate no disrespect or retribution made against the couple, especially the woman.

"The sentence is death by execution. Guards." The man was lead out without a fight, he accepting his fate like a man. The only sound in the room was Kathryn, softly crying.

Once the doors had closed behind the procession, Rydul struggled to his feet. "Your Majesty, I would ask a boon of you."

Wearied by the whole proceedings, Radine sat heavily in his chair. "What, Rydul?"

"That after the…after it is done, that the body be cremated and given to me."

"For what purpose?" An attendant entered the throne room from a side door and handed off a scroll to the king. Popping the seal, Radine unrolled the parchment and began to peruse the contents while still listening to his guardsman.

"No parent should be left in the dark as to what happened to their child. The day may come when we might return to Earth. I would like to take his ashes home to his mother and father."

McKenna responded to the questioning glance Radine sent her with a slight nod of her own. She would want to know, no matter how terrible her child may have acted. He loved her so much – she was his life. They had built a life together that he would defend with his life if necessary. "Very well," he replied. He looked to one of the other guards that had entered with the prisoners. "See to it," he ordered. The guard bowed and hurried from the room. Radine went back to reading the scroll as the audience waited. They couldn't leave until the king dismissed them.

After a moment, Radine raised his gaze, allowing the scroll to roll back on itself. "Captain Rydul, present yourself please," he commanded. "Bring your wife with you."

Equally startled and puzzled, Rydul reached back to grab one of Kathryn's hands, waiting as she wiped her face again. Together they went the few feet to stand before the royal couple. The king's face was impassive, the queen had a contented expression on her face. Kathryn, on the other hand, nearly vibrated with fear. The hammer was about to come down on them because of her brother. Her fears for Rydul were about to come true.

"It'll be okay," Rydul whispered to her in her ear. "No matter what, I love you."

"Can you kneel?" the king asked.

Rydul frowned, but then nodded. "With help, yes, Sire." Immediately, people from the side rows of chairs stepped forward and with Kathryn's help, the warrior sank to the floor, his crutches laid flat beside him. Kathryn then knelt, trepidation in her expression, one hand held tightly in her husband's grip, the other buried in the folds of her dress.

"Captain Rydul, over the past week, I have had the historians researching our records and they have found a very interesting item that concerns you and your wife directly.

"When my father granted you your estate and all of its lands, he failed to give you everything. I would like to think that he was unaware of this information. As you know, the original owner many generations ago had fallen out of favor with the crown, very far out of favor, and the estate became just another property owned and all but forgotten by the crown until it came into your hands.

"What the researchers found was that not only was the estate and land confiscated, but also the title and income. You have provided an invaluable service to this crown, risking life and limb to preserve us. And while you may think you've been compensated more than enough, *I* do not believe so, though I may change my mind after this.

"Anyway, I am reinstating that title. From this day forward, what was once a Ridom is now a Ridom again. You shall be known from now on as Rydul, Lord Raden, with your wife as Kathryn, Lady Raden, with all of the rights and privileges, and income, those titles entail." He passed the scroll to the kneeling warrior who, flabbergasted, took it with a shaking hand. Drawing his sword from its sheath, the king stood in front of newly made lord, tapping the flat of the blade to Rydul's right shoulder. "Give your oath to your king, Lord Raden, and rise."

Rydul was at a loss for words for a moment, but he finally took the end of the sword in hand and brought it to his lips where he placed a kiss on its point. "I, Rydul, give my pledge and loyalty to Radine, King of Taburon, for now and forever, to honor him and his progeny as my liege lord and to obey his rightful commands."

The king transferred the sword point to Kathryn. "My lady?"

Kathryn took the point as well, but at a loss for words, gave the king a smile as she also pressed a kiss to the point. "Your Majesty, I don't know the right words to say, but you have my undying pledge to be loyal to you for as long as I live."

Radine grinned. "That will do, madam. Rise, Lady Raden. And both of you take your rightful place in my kingdom and our history."

Again, with help, Rydul was brought to his feet, the crutches set under his arms, no time for reading the scroll more thoroughly as well – wishers gathered around the couple. A brief glimpse at the scroll had shown that he was now a rich man – very rich – but just how much and where all of the monies lay were buried deeper in the paper. He would have to spend more time going over it in detail. For now, his life couldn't be more perfect, his reward for being who he was more grand, his future with a woman he loved beyond all care at his side with joy in her eyes and love in her heart.

CHAPTER TWENTY-TWO

It was misty this year on Lanzess Mountain, the path shrouded in a fine brume, the ground moist under the feet of those climbing the trail to the top. But it did little to discourage them, Sky Clad only coming once a year. At least one hundred couples had already picked their spots and set up tents for the night.

Kathryn pulled her cloak tighter around her body, a shiver going through her, watching as Rydul finished securing the tent they would use for the night.

The skies had promised to clear before the moons' rising, otherwise this year's Sky Clad would be a pleasant few days of camping out. That didn't mean couples couldn't be content. After all, Sky Clad was a tradition these days, observed out of respect and honor for the ancient Taburon ancestors who believed the gods actually lived on Icide and Liva.

One could only hope for good weather tonight.

Or make the best of whatever came.

Replacing the hammer in the saddlebag, Rydul eased the small ache in his back from being bent over for so long and faced his wife. She offered a smile that she hoped didn't convey too much how uncomfortable she felt.

He fell to his haunches in front of her, his hands on her knees. "I'm sorry, Olana. Just a few more minutes, then you can warm up. All right?"

She should have known, not much got by her husband. That wane smile she plastered on her face became one of unbridled trust. "I'm all right."

His hand slid along her legs until they met over her abdomen and the moderate swell there. "And the little one?" he asked.

"He's fine too," she promised. "Though he's a little hungry."

Rydul's grin was full of mischief. "He, huh?"

She nodded. "When I have this overwhelming desire for food, yes."

"And when you don't?"

"Then she's being a good girl."

He laughed, rising up far enough to plant a kiss. "Five more minutes, promise." He stood, grabbed a second saddlebag and disappeared into the tent.

Six months since they'd married. Six months of the best time of her life with a husband madly in love with her and now a baby on the way. Six wonderful months with no concerns except what to wear to work at the palace every day to accommodate her now ever expanding waistline.

Only four months along and already she felt like she looked like a two legged whale. His constant reassurance that she was beautiful, no matter what – helped – a little. Both Queen McKenna and Princess Joanna has assured her that she was progressing normally – that Taburon babies grew faster and larger than human infants – and by making her part of their small circle of 'hens.'

She loved her work in the royal finance office and was well-liked by her co-workers. She was often invited to attend meetings with the king concerning the planet's financial situation and plans for the future. The Taburons genuinely were interested in her ideas, making her feel more a part of Taburon life every day.

She loved her husband dearly. He'd recovered from his injuries, though at times if he overdid things on the training field he would spend the better part of the evening with a mild but deep ache throughout his right leg. A warm bath and deep massage usually set things to right.

And she remembered fondly the first time she'd been invited to watch the men training, standing at a private balcony with the queen and princess above the balcony on which stood several ladies of the court. All three husbands had been giving the soldiers a good workout, their bodies sweating and glistening in the sunlight, muscles rippling as they thrust and parried and swung around, pivoting on their feet. Kathryn later found out that the men knew their wives had been watching and had put a little more show-off in their efforts just for them.

Kathryn couldn't help the bolt of lust that ran through her watching Rydul. And the rush of indignation that raced right behind it listening to the comments of the ladies from below, their giggling and highly inappropriate suggestions making her blush at times. McKenna and Joanna giggled quietly at her reaction, having endured it themselves in the beginning of their marriages. When Kathryn had been anxious to go down and tell those women to watch their language as well as their roving eyes, she'd been held back by the two other women. McKenna had taken care of the problem with a well-placed, and loud comment, the women below scrambling to exit before incurring the ire of the queen. The three women had collapsed in gales of laughter, causing the men to stop and glance their way. Radine merely shook his head then grinned full heartedly. He knew McKenna could be quite devilish and possessive when it came to him and was not above reminding certain females in the most provocative way just who slept in the king's bed.

Not having money worries any more eased Rydul's mind a great deal. The estate was back up to par, the crufas installed in a brand new stable with two of the mares pregnant. It would be a contest to see who delivered first – the crufas or Kathryn.

They'd made the freema harvest after intense labor and constant oversight. The fields were now in the process of being tilled, fertilized and readied for next year.

Purchasing a house in Duguid kept them close to the palace yet gave them their privacy. Kathryn got to know his comrades well. Their home had a constant flux of visitors from his unit, especially his best friend Kenlyn. The title he'd been given of Raden had not influenced their behavior towards him in the least, except for the teasing he suffered. In the beginning they'd bowed continuously every time he entered a room, calling him 'mi lord,' until he'd erupted in a fit of temper and told them to stop it or else. The men had fallen all over themselves in laughter and ceased, but it had all been in good fun and companionship. Kathryn was glad he had such friends and by proxy, she as well.

Haton had stayed with the couple after they'd left the palace, becoming valet for Rydul and friend to Kathryn, helping her to interview possible young women to become members of the household, as was expected of a titled individual. And to help her as she expanded in her pregnancy, suffering through bouts of morning sickness that on occasion lasted an entire day, making her miserable and despondent.

Of course, being titled meant that Rydul also now had a seat on the Taburon Council. So, in addition to his Guardsman duties, he was now required to regularly endure the sniping and political maneuvering that occurred among that group. He did his best to remain apart from it and stay out of their way.

He'd run into Khail twice since the explosion at the palace. The first time he'd visited him while the younger was at training camp. The 'boy' had looked wearied and worn-down, but he'd lost the excess useless weight and was putting on some muscle.

Khail was genuinely contrite, apologizing for what he'd done, asking how he might make restitution. Without telling him about his sudden good fortune – except that he'd gotten married – Rydul forgave him and said they'd speak again once the younger had finished training. Rydul wasn't ready yet to completely forgive Khail, the blow had been too great at the time. Nor was he prepared to offer his own apology for what he exacted in return.

The second time they'd met, Khail had been on his way to his assignment on board a ship patrolling the solar system that Taburon called home. A boring assignment but one that would force Khail to keep himself amused without getting into trouble. Any discrepancies would result in harsh military punishment which the boy would not find pleasant.

And Khail had seemed excited to discover that he was going to become an uncle, promising to clean-up his life to be a good influence on the child. Rydul had been very pleased with his brother. The 'boy' was becoming a man. One Rydul could be proud of.

And he could now feel comfortable in offering his complete forgiveness as well as ask for his own pardon in his actions against Khail, if the other could forgive him his outburst of anger. The two spent several hours reminiscing, finding those common times when they had been closest, reforging a familial bond that both men hoped to carry them for the rest of their lives.

So it was with a new understanding and brotherly love that they parted in joy and a small bit of sadness, for it would be months before they would see each other again.

Folding the flap back on the tent, Kathryn could see that he'd made the inside a comfortable nest for the two of them. He'd laid out a single double-wide bedroll, complete with stuffed pillows. A warm glow from a portable heater lighted the interior with a soft umber. Above the bedroll was a low table replete with food and drink, including a carafe of warmed tea.

"Come, Olana," Rydul invited, holding his hands out to her. "Come, come, come to me love. Our bower's made ready, all soft and warm."

She smiled as she took his hands to allow him to help her to stand and remembered. "Here, here, here I am love, beside you forever, safe in your arms."

Once inside, he took her cloak from her, his own tightening as her body was revealed to his gaze. She might as well have been naked. Her breasts were covered with the thinnest strip of material that covered from the top of her areolas to just under the curve of her breast and hold her fleshy mounds contained. They'd grown since her pregnancy, becoming fuller and more round and were more sensitive to stimulation.

Around her hips was a similarly thin strip of material, tucked under her tummy and wide enough to just barely cover her pussy. He could see that despite the chill, she was already moist. And he was instantly hard as a rock.

Holding onto one of her hands, he guided her as he settled onto the bedroll, crossing her legs Indian style, tempting him further with the open display of her feminine secrets.

"We'll be too busy for Sky Clad if you insist on sitting that way," he admonished softly.

"And you've been too busy the last week to share nadryl with me," she complained prettily.

"I'm not busy now."

She cupped her hand around the length of his cock against his thigh. "So," she asked, "what are you waiting for?"

"We are supposed to wait for the moons to rise."

"And I've been told that if we wait, things will be over and done before they have a real chance to get started."

An eyebrow quirked. "And from whom did you hear that?"

She squeezed his cock. "Don't you know the palace is a hotbed of gossip? As soon as it got out that we were coming here, I got all kinds of advice whispered in my ears."

He chuckled and dropped to his knees in front of her, sitting back on his heels. Reaching behind her back, he unbuttoned her breast band, pulling the material free. Her breasts fell with a slight bounce, the nipples tight and pointed. He palmed one full mound, hefting it, weighing it in his hand. "I love your breasts."

Her eyelids fell as he played, giving the breast in his hand a squeeze. Pregnancy hormones rushing through her, it didn't take much to get her revved. "I know. You always have."

He cupped her other breast. "Our baby will be very fortunate."

"How so?"

"He'll get to suck on those nipples several times a day every day for a long time." With thumb and middle finger, he pinched the hardened nubs in question. Kathryn groaned softly.

"Jealous are you?"

"Extremely," he confessed. "My son will get to play with his mother's breasts more than I have."

"He won't be playing with them," she pointed out. "He'll be nursing."

"He'll have his mouth around these delightful nipples, tasting their sweetness, sucking them into his mouth, nibbling once he gets some teeth…" His pinch was tighter, rolling the tips between his fingers.

Kathryn giggled. "We have a saying on Earth – 'the difference between men and boys is the form of their toys.'"

Leaning forward, he placed a kiss on each nipple. "There's only one toy better than these." Releasing her breasts, his hands slipped between her thighs. "This toy is mine," he claimed, parting her folds and exploring her pussy.

"No sharing allowed." She was already wet, his fingers soaked as he delved through her flesh.

Intending to wrap her hands around his cock and balls, Kathryn set her forearms on his thighs and found herself distracted by the healed pucker of the gunshot wound there. Tracing it with a delicate fingertip, she placed a kiss in the center of the scar. The nightmare of his injuries and the cause of them had yet to completely release her from its grip. Those times when she was particularly tired brought dreams in the night of the incident, her near loss and the guilt of her brother. She sometimes believed that had she known, she might have been able to prevent it all, to save Sean and Rydul and guilt weighed heavily upon her when those thoughts intruded in the happiness she had found with this Taburon warrior.

Following her gaze, Rydul touched her hand gently. "Kathryn, leave off," he said softly. "It is done, I survived, and am content with you by my side as my wife."

"I know, but sometimes…"

"There are no sometimes," he argued. "You need to forget the pain and anguish, let it go, and remember the love and joy we share now." He caressed her cheek. "Can you do that, if not for yourself, then for me? For our child?"

In response, she slid her hand up to glide along his length. His cock had hardened and expanded, a rod of steel encased in what she knew was a velvety covering of flesh. "I can try to do anything for you," she countered, "as long as you want me." Taking her hand from him, she reached for the opening to his trousers. "Sit up," she ordered. Lifting his arse from his heels, she pulled his trousers down far enough to expose his rigid shaft, the long pole falling into her waiting hands, his balls hanging free.

Without hesitation, she leaned forward to enclose the head of his cock in her mouth, licking at the drop of pre-cum that glistened at the tip. She'd become a first rate, accomplished cock sucker over the last six months, nearly able to take him completely into her throat, considering the length of his organ. But she always managed to bring him either over the brink of orgasm or very close to it, saving the ultimate goal for actual intercourse. She knew him like the back of her hand, and he knew that she knew this, appreciative of her skills.

They had a satisfying sex life, sharing nadryl at least four times a week, even after she'd become pregnant, except for those days when morning sickness caught her and stayed with her throughout the day. Then he'd been comforting and attentive, wiping her brow with a cool damp cloth, bringing her broth that would settle easily on her stomach, making sure she had plenty of *billa* tea. At times he suspected she faked the morning sickness just to get his attention, keep him home, and spend the day together. He really didn't mind all that much.

Settling onto all fours, Kathryn licked his shaft like a lollipop, up one end and down the other, spending an inordinate amount of time at the head where she suckled hard enough to draw a hiss of pleasure from him.

Rydul leaned slightly forward to smooth his hands down her back, ending at the split between her buttocks then sliding back to her neck and hairline. Following the curve of her shoulders he let his fingers wander until they brushed against the sides of her breasts. Cupping the hanging mounds of flesh, he squeezed them tenderly, milking them, the blood pooling in the tightened nipples that dangled so temptingly below, pointing to the ground.

When his hips started to rise in to thrust himself into her mouth, Kathryn sat back, releasing his cock form her lips with a wet pop, licking her lips with the tip of her tongue. Rydul groaned deep in his chest.

From outside the tent, a cheer rose, muffled by the material of the tent. Standing, Rydul peered through the split in the opening. The skies had cleared enough that the rising of the moons was visible, Icide was near halfway above the horizon. All over the mountain top, couples were emerging from their tents, nude for the most part, though some were cloaked against the chill, taking a place before the rising moons, waiting anxiously.

About to turn to reach back for her hand, Rydul jumped instead when her hand slipped between his legs from behind to cup his testicles, hefting the heavy sac, causing his cock to bob, standing straight out from the plane of his belly. He growled playfully, moving away from her mischievous fingers, facing her with lewd expression on his face.

"You are in so much trouble," he promised.

She chuckled. "Promises, promises," she teased.

"Icide comes," he informed her. "Soon, Liva will follow and then the light will shine down. Grab your cloak if you do not wish to freeze those pretty nipples, but it will not be on for long. We can use it as a blanket when the time comes."

Her look at his shaft was explicit. "The chill will not affect you?"

H glanced down at his engorged, pulsing cock. "It'll take more than a slight chill to discourage this fiend," he confirmed. "Especially with you naked, aroused and your nipples like hard points as now."

She chucked once. "You are such an arse," she huffed lovingly. "All you men ever think about; sex, sex, sex," she murmured as she reached for her cloak, standing and swinging it over her shoulders.

Taking her chin in hand, he kissed her. "You love it and you know it," he reminded her. Her hand in his, he pulled her from the tent.

EPILOGUE

Rydul raced Ferrin through the streets of Duguid, steering the animal with his right hand as he waved his left arm and yelled at pedestrians to look out and move. Nothing was going to keep him from getting home, not the people on the street, not the other riders on the road, not the rude gestures and even ruder comments tossed his way as he passed. All he knew was he needed to get home and now!

It was the rider behind him following close on Ferrin's hooves who apologized to those who seemed the most put out by the racing riders as the two hurried along. Not giving much pause in their flight to offer a more complete apology, the second rider continued on the heels of the first, jacket flapping in the wind.

The animal hadn't come to a complete stop in front of his in-town house before Rydul jumped from the saddle, raced up the front steps and burst through the door. He didn't stop, taking the stairs two at a time until he came to the top landing.

Kathryn's cry of pain halted him in his tracks with a sudden jerk. His heart pounded in his chest and he couldn't seem to breathe, his knuckles turning white from the death grip he held on the railing at the top of the stairs. She cried out again, a long, drawn out wail, which got his feet to move, carrying him to the doorway of their bedroom. And there he halted once more, taking in the scene before him with undisguised surprise, unprepared for what was happening even though they'd gone through a number of trial runs over the last weeks.

Kathryn was seated on a birthing chair to the right of the doorway, a short shirt covering her chest, her body from the waist down naked. Her legs were spread to the sides, her hands gripped the arms of the chair and she scrunched her face as she labored to expel their baby from her body. Behind her was a midwife apprentice wiping her brow with a cool cloth, to the side was the midwife, handing equipment to the doctor who sat in front of his wife between her legs. Both Haton and Frita, the servants, stood nearby, clean and warmed blankets and towels in their hands. And totally unconcerned about the commotion, the afilene, named Pib the Second because he also had white feet and socks, slept on the bed, ignoring the people who had made him a part of their lives. This birthing uproar was boring.

Seeing that Rydul had entered the room, the apprentice whispered to the doctor. Without looking up, Dr. Tripp, carefully monitoring the process, invited the soon to be father to come further inside. "You're just in time," he commented. "The baby should be here any minute now." He accepted the clean cloth the midwife passed to him. "You can come closer," he continued. "Kathryn, one more really good push now."

Cautiously, Rydul approached, his eyes never straying from Kathryn's face after a quick glance to the activity below. His throat worked with a deep gulp, keeping whatever considered coming up out of his stomach from doing just that. "Kathryn?" he queried anxiously.

They'd watched the videos of women giving birth just weeks ago, the process bloody and messy and almost making him want to vomit and swear off having more children. She'd giggled at his comment, as if he had to go through the process of expelling a child out of his body and not her. The pain the mothers went through tore at his heart and frightened him at the same time, for he knew childbirth wasn't always a safe, easy undertaking. He feared for Kathryn, since she was human and he Taburon, for even though she was all over a larger woman than either McKenna or Joanna, she was still small compared to most Taburon females.

Her pregnancy had gone very well with the usual bumps along the way with the exception that she seemed to have gained a lot more weight than either of the two other human females. Both Dr. Tripp and Pologa showed concern that she might not be able to deliver normally, that they – whichever attended – would have to resort to surgery in order to safely deliver the child. It was a decision that would be made when the time came. And it was here now.

He'd taken a small unit of lower ranking Guardsmen on a bivouac to the botanical park where the king and queen had spent the night all those years ago just before Espis had kidnapped the queen to be. Since Kathryn was ten or so days from her due date, they – Rydul, Kathryn and the physicians – had felt it was safe enough for him to be gone for the five days he needed for the exercise. Only two days had passed when Taryn had ridden up to the camp to inform them that Kathryn had gone into labor and he needed to get home. He'd made the normal two hour ride back in just under an hour and a half, Taryn hot on his heels the whole way. No one seemed to notice the female soldier as she took a quiet place just inside the doorway, having taken the time to make sure the crufas were properly cared for before entering the house.

"I'm okay," Kathryn grated out, her face clenching, her eyes shutting closed, taking a deep breath.

"Good," Tripp encouraged, "Now push, hard. The head's already crowning, just need to get a little more out and the rest will follow. Push. Push!" he instructed.

With a groan that nearly ripped him in two, yanked his guts from his belly and stomped them into the ground Kathryn exerted as much pressure as she could, falling forward slightly to add weight to the effort. "Good," Tripp complimented, bringing the cloth close and wrapping it around the baby as it emerged, turning the infant slightly to encourage first one shoulder then the other to slip from the birth canal with little effort. The midwife accepted a warm towel from Frita, standing ready.

In the space of an instant, the entire child fell into the hands of the physician, the cord still connecting the mother and baby together. Tripp wiped the face of the infant with a corner of the cloth. Reaching for a suction bulb, the doctor cleared the baby's mouth and nose, then flipped it onto its stomach. Rubbing vigorously, the bluish color of the child's skin tone turned almost immediately pink as it wailed in indignation from the rude way its life was now forever changed.

Turning the baby face up, Tripp reached for a small tube of medication which he opened one handed, squeezing a bit of the contents into the baby's eyes. Taking two clamps, he attached one close to the baby's stomach and the other several inches above that. Scissors in hand, he twisted slightly to look up at Rydul. "Here, papa, cut the cord," he offered, handing the scissors to Rydul.

Shaking off the 'deer caught in the headlights' expression on his face, Rydul took the scissors gingerly and placed them where the doctor indicated, squeezing the handles gently. The flesh cut easily, permanently separating the child from its mother. The baby had stopped its wailing, settling into a soft snuffling.

"Is it okay?" Rydul asked, not having looked to see if the child was a boy or girl, too stunned still to take it all in completely.

"Your daughter is beautiful," Tripp confirmed, lifting the baby to hand her over to the midwife who would continue to tend to the newborn. He turned his own attention back to the new mother. "Congratulations."

Kathryn lifted her head from the back of the chair where she had laid it after the baby had been born. "A girl?" she asked.

Tripp nodded, tossing used equipment to the side on a towel placed on the floor just for that purpose. She had torn slightly from the birth and he would need to put in a stitch or two. He reached for the sterile sutures, opening the package and setting it to the side without touching anything with his hands. He would need to clean her skin slightly before he could stitch. "Looks like her daddy, full head of golden hair."

Following the midwife as she crossed the room with the newborn, Rydul watched with excitement as the child was bathed. She was a small thing, no bigger than his two hands and he wondered how such a little thing had made her mother looked so huge. He wanted to hold her but was afraid of hurting her, or even, gods' forbid, dropping her if she squirmed even the slightest. Her head was pointed, he'd expected that from the birthing lessons he and Kathryn had taken, but it would round out in a few short days. The coating that had covered her at birth washed away to reveal a fine peach tone skin color, the same as her mother's. She had dimples in her cheeks and her lips pursed with some infantile thought that he would never know.

And he fell head over heels in love with her. She was his future, his very own to cherish, and teach, and watch over as she grew. His to protect, to make sure she learned all she wanted to learn, and to keep the boys away from when she came into her young womanhood.

He covered her head with his palm, his impossibly large palm, and filled with contentment.

Until he heard Kathryn cry out again in pain. Turning, he watched as Dr. Tripp suddenly came alive, sitting back on the stool he had seemingly just vacated, his gaze intent on Kathryn and the area between her legs. "Uh, oh," he murmured. "I'm going to need some help here," he called, wanting the midwife to come to his aid. "Simio, switch places with Altha here, would you?" Handing the newborn off to the apprentice, Simio took her place next to the doctor, her body tense. Altha placed the baby on the changing table that Kathryn had set up in their bedroom, continuing to clean the child and finish with the birth record before dressing her.

His voice trembled with fear. Rydul didn't know how he would live if he lost Kathryn. Even the child wouldn't ease the ache in his heart if she died. Taryn's hand came to rest on his shoulder, but it did little to stop the shaking of his body. "What is it?" he asked hesitantly. He almost didn't want to know if Kathryn's life was in jeopardy. "Is she all right?"

Tripp didn't bother to look at the soldier. "Well, now we know why she looked so big. There's another one coming."

"Two?" he whispered in disbelief. Behind him, Taryn laughed with delight as she thumped him on the shoulder in congratulations. She couldn't wait until she could get back to the rest of the Guards and tell them the news. Rydul was in for some heavy duty teasing about the potency of his seed.

"Twins. And this one's not needing any help," Tripp added as the second baby neatly dropped into his waiting hands. Repeating the earlier process, he wiped the newborn's face, cleared its mouth and flipped it to rub until it squalled loud and clear. The drops were placed in its eyes, the cord was cut - which Rydul shook his head no to this time, immobilized with shock - and a new blanket was wrapped around its body before Tripp handed the child off to the midwife. "Another girl," he pronounced. "Good job, Mom. Don't know how that got by any of us during the pregnancy."

Kathryn took a deep breath, then started to laugh, pointing a finger towards the brave Guardsman who just a year ago saved the palace from being destroyed. It was true then throughout the galaxy, childbirth was not for even the brave. "If you could only see your face," she told her husband. That 'caught in the headlights' look was back in full force and she would never let him forget it, once she got over the shock herself. She was exhausted, her hair rimmed with sweat, her body aching from head to toes. But she was overjoyed as well. Not just one, but two babies to fill their lives, to make them a family, and she wanted to hold one of them.

Now!

Altha brought the first child to her, placing a now clean, dry, and blanket wrapped infant in her arms. The baby gazed at its mother with golden eyes and yawned and Kathryn broke into tears.

Which got her husband finally moving. Enclosing her in an embrace with one arm, he looked down at the babe she cradled against her chest. He frowned as he heard her sniff. "Kathryn? You all right?"

"Happy," she sobbed softly, "very, very happy." With the back of her finger, she gently caressed the cheek of her new daughter.

Rydul placed a gentle kiss on her temple. "Thank you, Olana, for giving me two wonderful children." He kissed her again. "I love you."

"I love you, too. And I already know what to name at least one of them. I want to call her Myrysca, after your sister."

"Are you sure?" he asked, though the thought moved him more than he could say. He'd loved his little sister and had been devastated when she'd died, especially so young.

"Yes. We'll give her all of the chances your sister never had."

"Thank you, Olana, it' a wonderful gift, and I am honored."

Simio brought over the second child and after showing Rydul the proper way to hold her, placed her in his arms. Kathryn tensed as the afterbirth began its journey out of her body, but she wasn't about to give up her baby just yet. "What do we name this one?" he asked in an effort to take her mind off of the rest of the birthing process. This child responded to its father the same way its sibling had to the mother - with a puzzled expression, a yawn, and a sigh before settling down to some well-earned sleep. She had had a rough day.

She also sported a full head of golden hair, curly and bright, and there had been the barest hint of golden eyes before her lids had fallen to cover them.

"How about after your mother?"

He looked thoughtful for several moments. "I loved my mother very much, but you just lost a brother. What about after him?"

"There's no female equivalent name for Sean that I know of. But Sean can also be used for Evan, so we could call her Shiobhan."

"Myrysca and Shiobhan," Rydul repeated, then said it again several times until it flowed easily. "I like it. They look so similar, but the names should give them their own identities. And Siobhan sounds Taburon."

"That's important to you, isn't it?" Kathryn asked.

"I am Taburon, as are you now. It is only right that our children be Taburon, even down to their names," he explained. Then he remembered that she wasn't completely Taburon, but human by blood and her heritage might have been just as important to her as his was to him. "We can change it if you wish."

"After what happened nearly a year ago? No, it's fine as it is."

"How will you tell them apart?" Taryn asked, moving closer now that the actual birth was over. "Congratulations, by the way, Captain, Madam."

"I have no idea," Kathryn replied.

"Some parents paint the fingernails of one twin until they've learned to tell them apart," Tripp suggested, collecting all of the used materials, including the afterbirth now, and placing them into a bucket nearby. Had this happened on Earth, the blood from the umbilicals would have been tested and perhaps stored for the future, since it had been discovered umbilical cells could be used for treating some illnesses. But here on Taburon, he had no idea what these people did, so he would turn it – them - over to Simio to do with as she practiced. Before he stood, he opened a clean drape and placed it over Kathryn's lower body. No need for everyone to see her all and sundry. "It's up to you," he added, standing and stretching. The midwife would continue Kathryn's care, helping her to clean up, showing her how to keep the bleeding contained, instructing her on breast feeding.

"We have two children," Rydul wondered.

"Yes, and not enough of everything for them." Altha came forward to take little Myrysca from her mother so Kathryn could finish cleaning up and get settled on the bed. She would need her rest now for a while before the full force of becoming a mother of not only one but two babies hit her. There were going to be some very long days and nights ahead of the couple and they would need a lot of support and help until they got a system worked out to get through the coming times.

"I can see if there is some sort of color you can use on newborns," Taryn offered. "Stay here and take care of them. I'll get the things you need, just tell me what they are." She squatted in front of the two and listened as Kathryn rattled off a bunch of things they had not prepared or purchased now that they had two babies to care for.

Tripp glanced at the young woman, the first woman accepted into the army, he understood. She was as tall as he, her eyes at his eye level. Her hair, when loose, had hung down her back to her buttocks, but she now had it pinned back and rolled into a tight bun at the nape of her neck. Even though she wore a uniform, her curves and softness showed through, her long fingers clenching on the hilt of her sword. There was a brightness in her expression, her eyes glittering in undisguised emotion, pleasure for the couple in their good fortune and arrival of their newborns.

Tripp gave the woman a second look, for the first time in a long time an emotion moving through him that hadn't existed for a number of years. He perused her from her head to her feet and wondered. It had been a long time for him since he'd been with a woman, his wife sickly the last five years of their marriage until her death. He hadn't been of a mind to seek gratification while she lived, believing it to be a violation of their vows, even though she'd encourage him to find release if he needed without guilt. Once she'd passed away, he'd been too uninterested to seek out female companionship, burying himself in his work until he'd come to Taburon and made the decision to remain. It hadn't been out of grief. While he'd loved his wife, he'd realized after that she hadn't been the love of his life and her death saddened him, but hadn't broken him. Plus, he'd found he was anxious to explore this new planet and learn more about these people, now that he'd met several of them, and to see if there was more he could learn about himself. Having never had any adventuring in his life, he suddenly found a wanderlust that had been hidden and was screaming out to be explored.

He'd met Taryn on the ship that had brought him and the medicines to Taburon during the influenza outbreak. She'd been friendly, but only as friendly as one would be to a stranger who was about to help save the people of their planet. Occasionally since then she'd crossed his path during the course of the day, on her way to some post or on some normal, nominal mission. They'd stopped and spoken casually then moved on to their individual tasks. Tripp had taken on the care of the humans who'd emigrated while he learned about Taburon methods of health care. Once Kathryn had become pregnant, he'd become her primary care doctor with Pologa watching over him. And he'd begun making lists of things he would request be brought to Taburon to help improve their health care. He was here to stay, he might as well do what he could to become a viable part of their society.

And that's when the fact that he was alone set in. All around him couples were pairing off, the human women married to the Taburons were having children, and he felt empty despite having a place where he was needed and wanted.

He was still young, only forty-two. He was healthy and active. He had a long life ahead of him. And this new world was full of possibilities.

So he gave Taryn a good look the way a man looks at a woman, the way a man who is interested in a woman would look, and wondered.

AUTHOR BIOGRAPHY

Karen L. Milstein has always wanted to write, penning her first story while a teenager in middle school. Her varied interests include listening to music; reading voraciously, mostly Romance, Sci-Fi fantasy and comedy; wildlife and animals; and playing Dungeons and Dragons where she roles as a dragonborn sorcerer and high elf warlock, among others. She loves dragons and hopes to someday own one –or at least a fire lizard if possible.

She lives in West Palm Beach, Florida with her husband, son and a small pride of furballs. The star of her first book, Fergus, a purple emo dragon, sits above her desktop to keep her inspired as she writes. She loves hearing from her readers at rmimzadi@hotmail.com.

SKY CLAD MARTIN - Book Four in the Sky Clad Series

Dr. Martin Tripp went to Taburon to help during the influenza outbreak, bringing with him medicine to help fight the infection.

Recently widowed, heartsick, and dissatisfied with his life on Earth, he decides to make Taburon his permanent home, becoming the primary care physician for emigrating humans.

When a request comes for the rescue of two human females living on another planet, Dr. Tripp volunteers to accompany the rescue ship. On board is Taryn, one of the few Taburon women allowed to join the army. Betrothed to a noble while still a child, and discovering she'd rather be a soldier than wife, she hides out in the army to delay a wedding she doesn't want.

Until she meets a human physician with dark hair, intense brown eyes and a voice a girl could get lost in.

Thrown together on a mission to rescue humans, the two find a budding relationship. But how much can love grow between a man with a broken heart and a woman pledged to another?

Coming late 2016.

OTHER BOOKS BY   Karen L. Milstein

Fergus and the Princess – When Princess Ciara is kidnapped by a dragon, she finds herself in the cave of Fergus, a purple dragon who prefers making flower wreaths to being the cliché everyone believes of dragons. Together, they gain insights into their lives and the truth about what it means to be a princess and a dragon. A Young Adult fantasy for tweens and teens.

Sky Clad – The Series

Sky Clad Radine – King Radine of Taburon has found his life mate in the human woman McKenna Primm. But not everything goes according to plan - not even for a king. Adult Romantica.

Sky Clad Jaima – Lord Jaima, after being severely wounded, falls for his pretty human nurse, Joanna Sims. Can he convince her to return to Taburon with him, then find a way to keep his sanity when she turns him down? Adult Romantica.

All books are currently available through barnesandnoble.com, Amazon.com, or on Amazon kindle.